CHAFFS

CHAFFS

A Novel by
DOUGLAS P. LATHROP

MaxM LTD

CHAFFS
A novel by Douglas P. Lathrop

Book designed by David Maxine.
Cover art by V-X awesomedome.com
Author photo: Carleton Starr

ISBN 978-0-9825132-3-1

MaxM LTD

You've got to know the truth
Before you say that you've got pride
— THE DESCENDENTS

Part One
FAITH

THE bus hits a pothole, and rattles like a garbage truck. Up front, the two Wide Awakes shift in their seats, but keep watching us, switching their joltsticks on and off. Two more guard us from the back row. Four Wide Awakes for about four dozen prisoners.

I turn away before they catch me looking at them. Outside, through the steel mesh on the windows, the Joshua trees glide past, their limbs twisted skyward like they're waving goodbye.

Taunting us as we go to be Reoriented.

"Thanks for letting me sit here," says the wispy fourteen-year-old next to me—Steven, I think that's his name.

I frown at him. "I told you, keep your voice down." Seriously, does he *want* to get joltsticked again? It's already happened twice. And I wish he'd stop thanking me every five minutes. It's not like I had a choice of seating companions.

I stretch my legs, slowly. It's no use trying to get comfortable. The bus swelters from lack of AC, the suspension is nonexistent, and underneath me, the cracked and peeling Naugahyde seat upholstery feels like a bed of nails. I'm still sore from all the beatings.

Suddenly we both tense up. One of the Wide Awakes is coming up the aisle. Steven cringes and scoots toward me, pulling his head into the V-neck of his prison scrubs like a pink-shelled turtle. We're all wearing pink. It's our color. The holding tank back in Los Angeles had the whole rainbow—gray for politicals, orange for criminals, brown for Mexicans, yellow for Jews, and so on. But not here. On this bus, it's nothing but pink, pink, pink. Except for the Wide Awakes in blue, of course.

The guard reaches our row. I brace myself, waiting to hear his joltstick's frying-bacon sizzle.

Nothing. He keeps going, this time.

"So how did they get you, Tyler?" Steven whispers.

I hesitate to answer. Steven doesn't seem like an informer—I figure he's simply glommed onto me because I'm one of the more athletic guys here, and because he thinks I'll protect him, or at least won't abuse him—but the worst snitches are always the ones who don't appear to be.

I ought to know.

Still, if he is a snitch, clamming up altogether would only alert him that I've got something to hide.

"They didn't get me. I volunteered."

"Really?" Steven's eyes widen. Then he backtracks, like he's afraid he just insulted me. "That's good. No, really, that's a good thing, right? They go easier on volunteers—that's what I heard. You don't have to go through the whole program."

The guard reappears. Steven and I fall silent until he sits back down.

"And how did they get you?" I ask.

Steven goes deeper into his pink shell. "Under my mattress I had some pictures I tore out of the Sears catalogue. Of guys in their underwear. My little sister found them."

"She turned you in?"

"She got a Morning Glory merit badge for it." He passes a hand over his eyes. "I never actually *did* anything, you know? I just liked looking at the pictures. I never . . . defiled myself. Do you think that'll matter?"

I sure hope not. If hoarding underwear pictures was enough to get Steven sent to a Reorientation Center, I don't want to know what the things *I've* done will get me.

He sniffs. "I just want to go home."

"I know."

It's a lie. I *don't* know—I *can't*.

I lean back, gaze out the window, and let the monotonous landscape hypnotize me, take me back.

Back to when I still had a home to go to.

WE *are the Dawn Patrol. We are the sons and daughters of America's Fourth Great Awakening. We stand ready to fight for Our Nation against foreign invaders from without, and immorality and corruption from within. Our selves, our lives, our blood—these we pledge to the survival of our race and the future for our children.*

"*FAITH!*

"*FAMILY!*

"*FREEDOM!*"

The lunch bell rang just as we finished the pledge. As the meeting adjourned and the auditorium emptied out, I hung back, looking for Kevin. I thought he might have snuck in late, but there was no sign of him.

"Tyler! Neighbor Treppenhouse!"

I jerked to attention as Billy Hanna marched up. He looked mad, though it was hard to tell with him. Our Troop Leader always looked like he had a pool cue up his butt, even when he was happy.

Billy snapped off a salute. "Where's Kevin Sanders? He didn't check in."

"I haven't seen Neighbor Sanders since homeroom, sir."

"It's not like him to miss a meeting."

"No, sir. Maybe he forgot. His eighteenth birthday is tomorrow. That means—"

"Don't make excuses for him. That Reclaimee ought to know better than to goof off, with his Evaluation tomorrow." Billy took out a black-covered booklet and scribbled some notes in it. "Tell him to report to me before the next meeting on Friday—*if* he makes it to Friday. Is that clear?"

"Yes, Troop Leader."

Another salute. "Nation First!"

"Nation F—"

Before I could finish, Billy pivoted on his heel and stomped off the way he came.

Instead of following the rest of the troop to the cafeteria, I took a detour to my locker, next to Kevin's in Building C. It was pouring rain, so I took the long way around the quad to stay dry. Given Billy's mood at the meeting, he'd put me on report for sure if I got my uniform soaked.

Sure enough, Kevin was there. Shelly Dobbs was with him—the two had been dating for almost a year. She coaxed a kiss out of him, then spun around as I walked up.

"Hey, Tyler. I'll see you at lunch. Could you please tell your friend here that if he doesn't climb out of this hole he's in, in time for his birthday, he's not getting his special present? I've been waiting a *long* time to give it to him."

The lustful edge in her voice made me blush. She was so . . . forward. Shelly was overdue for another visit with the Morality Officer. My own girlfriend was much more reserved, thank the Lord.

Shelly skipped off. Kevin remained slumped against his locker. People were always saying we looked alike. I didn't see the resemblance—yeah, we were the same height and our hair was the same brownish blond, like dry brush during fire season, but beyond that? Kevin's slim physique looked nowhere near as good in uniform as my own muscular frame, though

12

his intense blue eyes outshone my dull green, no question.

Right now, those eyes looked haunted, and he was all curled in on himself. He seemed a whole foot shorter, like he was twelve all over again.

"What's with you, Kev?" I opened my locker and grabbed my books for the next three periods. "You missed Dawn Patrol."

"I know, OK?" Kevin's gaze stayed glued to the floor. "Shelly's already given me grief for it."

"Well, where were you? Billy Hanna's on the warpath. You want to get put on report?"

"Fuck Billy Hanna."

I almost dropped my books. Dawn Patrol members weren't supposed to swear. At least not out loud.

"Maybe I'll fail tomorrow and I'll never have to kiss up to that little dweeb again," Kevin said.

"Fail the Evaluation? You?"

"Just be glad you don't have to go through it."

He finally raised his eyes. His posture was still like a little kid's, but his face—he looked worn out, like an old man.

"Wait. Kev, you're not really worried, are you?" I slammed my locker door shut. "Dude, you're going to ace that thing. You're not some dirty Chaff—you're the star of this school."

"I'm still a Reclaimee."

"A Reclaimee with the best grades in the whole senior class. Not to mention the best shortstop North Topanga High has ever had." I clapped a hand on his shoulder. "Nobody cares about what your real parents did—you've *proven* your worth to the Nation, and everybody knows it. You're practically indispensable."

He scraped the floor a couple of times with the sole of one shoe, then straightened up. His lips fluttered into a smile. "My batting average is higher than yours, too."

"That was last season. We'll see who ends up on top this year, Sandman."

By the time Kevin was done laughing, he was his old self again. He tossed his books in his locker and gave me a light slug on the arm. "Thanks, T. You always know what to say." A pause. "You're a really good friend, you know?"

For a second I was worried Kevin might try to hug me or something. But he just gave me a friendly shove toward the exit. "Let's go before Brad eats all the Tater Tots."

Normally, during lunch, the students spread out all over campus, but today the rain had forced everyone into the dim and moldy-smelling cafeteria. Even so, there was very little pushing. The enormous mural of Our Commander-in-Chief, President Harold Muldoon—with his toothy smile and emerald-green eyes that followed you around—kept us all in line.

Kevin and I gave the C-in-C a respectful nod as we walked by. You were supposed to salute, but that was hard to do while carrying a food tray.

"Hey, TNT! Sandman! Over here!"

It was Brad Nemechuk. He, some of the other players— Danny Magruder, Rick Nagy, Deke O'Beirne, nearly half this year's Varsity starting lineup—and a couple of female hangers-on were shooing some ninth-graders off one of the prime tables. Shelly had already sat down. Kevin slid onto the bench next to her while I took an empty spot on the other side of the table.

As I opened my carton of milk, Brad flung down his bulk beside me. He straddled the bench, stretching one leg across the aisle so people had to step over him to get by.

"Man, I hate this monkey suit—it's choking me to death." He tugged on the collar of his Dawn Patrol uniform, then pulled his lunch toward him—a plate piled high with Tater Tots, and nothing else. "You guys gonna watch the executions tonight?"

I paused with my milk carton raised halfway to my lips. "They're showing them on TV again? My dad said they'd been canceled. The ratings were too low."

"This one's a big deal. Some beaners in Texas—tried to blow up the Alamo, or something."

At least *I* wouldn't have to watch them. Dad had given up trying to make me. My little brother Eric ate up every second—the trials, the executions, even the commentary afterward—but when I was his age they just made me ill. Dad used to tell me I was too squeamish and needed toughening up. Like I couldn't hate terrorists and criminals enough until I enjoyed watching them die.

I snuck a quick glance at the ceiling. There was a Hawkeye right above the table—a shiny black sphere, staring down at us. Staring *and* listening. Not that I was about to do or say anything *wrong*, of course.

"I'm not going to see the executions." I took a gulp of milk. "Unity's coming over tonight. To study."

"To study, huh?" Brad popped a Tater Tot in his mouth and then leered. He turned the leer on some passing girls, who pulled in their elbows and hastened away from him. "Geez, TNT, when are you gonna start around the bases with her? Have you even stepped up to the plate yet?"

I felt a dryness in my mouth. I clucked my tongue to conceal it. "Why don't you mind your own business, dude?"

"Seriously, you've got me worried. You and Unity have been going out for how long? Six months, nine months, and you haven't gotten any yet? People are gonna start thinking you're queer."

The dryness was spreading down my throat. I swallowed.

Shelly rolled her eyes. "Oh, lay off him, Brad. He's just being a gentlemen. Some girls like that."

"Do you?"

I thought Shelly was going to rip Brad's face off. But she just smiled and hooked her arm around Kevin's. "What do you think?"

She and Kevin made lovey-dovey eyes at each other. Brad responded with gagging noises. I just kept on squirming. I hated it when Kevin and Shelly got all kissy-face like that, though at least it had gotten Brad off my back.

"I won't be watching the executions either." Kevin looked away from Shelly and let his gaze drop to the tray in front of him. "I need to try and get some sleep tonight. Tomorrow I've got my, um . . . "

"Oh yeah. Your Evaluation." Brad picked up another Tater Tot and held it between his thumb and forefinger, aiming it at Kevin like a bullet. "You'd better pass, Sandman.

Coach'll take it out on the rest of our butts if he has to find a new shortstop."

Kevin snorted. "Gee, thanks for your support."

"I'm just saying, we've got a shot at the championship this year. But you can't expect me and TNT here to carry the whole load."

Brad raised the Tater Tot to his mouth, but then froze. His eyes zeroed in on the next table. His upper lip curled with hostility. I looked over to see what—or who—had incurred his wrath.

Oh, God. It was Casey Monahan.

Casey didn't move. He just crouched there on the table-top, tall and gangly, staring at Brad down that beak nose of his. Strands of oily black hair dribbled down his forehead and over his pale, sharp-angled face.

Brad threw the Tater Tot to the ground and clenched his fists. "Something I can do for you, Chaff?"

"Nah." Casey smirked at him, eyes unblinking. "Just thinking about my last trip to the zoo, that's all."

For a second, Brad went still. Then he erupted off the bench and leaped at Casey, who just barely dodged him— Brad might look like a lummox, but he was fast and agile when his anger was up. Casey scrambled across the table and rocketed through the cafeteria amid a ruckus of shouts and flying food trays. Brad charged right behind him.

Kevin stood up. "Come on, T. We'd better go stop Brad from killing the punk."

"Stick our necks out for some Chaff? What for?"

"Coach has already benched Nemechuk once for fighting, remember?" Kevin was already moving so fast I could hardly keep up with him. "Besides, Monahan's a Reclaimee like me. I ought to do one more good deed before tomorrow."

A Reclaimee like him? Technically, maybe—he and Casey might both be orphans from all the arrests years ago, but there were a lot of those. Kevin Sanders was one of the Reclamation program's success stories. Casey Monahan was just a waste of oxygen.

We caught up with them in the boys' bathroom. Brad had Casey's arm twisted behind his back and his face shoved into one of the toilets. The bowl was overflowing—the toilets at this school were always backing up—and the water was murky, with lumps in it and greasy-looking air bubbles rising to the surface.

"Brad, come on." I reached down and tugged on his shirt. "Knock it off. He's not worth it."

No use—Brad just ignored me. As I watched, the clawing of Casey's free hand at Brad's merciless grip on the back of his neck grew more and more frantic.

"Brad!" Kevin thumped his fist against the side of the toilet stall. "Neighbor Nemechuk!"

The voice cut right through Brad's bloodlust. He let go of Casey, jerked upright, and stood at attention. As Casey's head surfaced, he sucked in a gasp and slid to the floor, panting and coughing. He came to rest with his head against the base of the toilet, his long limbs sprawled across the grimy tile.

Kevin shot Casey a look and then paid no more attention to him. "You've soiled your uniform, Neighbor Nemechuk. Go clean up. Before Troop Leader Hanna sees you."

They both left the bathroom—Brad shuffling his feet, Kevin marching like a drill sergeant.

I didn't leave with them. For some reason, I couldn't make my own feet move. I jammed my hands in my pockets and glanced around the bathroom, looking for something to focus on.

Anything but Casey.

By now he'd gotten his breath back and was pulling himself up off the floor. His shoulders were heaving, like he was crying. But once he was on his feet, and I could see his face, he had a huge grin splitting it.

The Chaff was *laughing*.

Crap. Now I *really* wished I wasn't there.

He looked at me. His eyes were this golden brown color, like honey. As I met them there was a jolt, like a connection snapping into place, and then what felt like a million spears of clear ice shooting through every nerve in my body. Those eyes . . . they were laying me out, peering into me, finding out things . . .

Finding out everything.

Get out of there. It was a command, booming over and over along with my heartbeat. But I stayed put. I wasn't about to let this Chaff see me run. I felt my tongue moistening my lips.

"Uh, are you OK?" I asked.

This just made him laugh again. When he was done he raised an eyebrow at me, still grinning.

"Yeah, I'm OK. Are you?"

I COULDN'T concentrate for the rest of the day. Whenever I blinked, I saw Casey's eyes, turning me inside out.

I tried to talk myself down. *You're reading too much into two seconds of eye contact. And nobody cares what some Chaff thinks.*

But as soon as my own voice paused, I'd hear Brad's. *People are gonna start thinking you're queer.*

I wasn't queer. I wasn't.

Yeah, I had . . . thoughts . . . about other guys. I played baseball—I'd seen my teammates in the shower a million times. I'd have to go around blindfolded not to notice who looked good with his clothes off, who was carrying a lot of wood.

But I'd never *acted* on those thoughts, and I wasn't about to. I was a Son of the Fourth Great Awakening, disciplined, moral. *"Swifter than an eagle, tougher than leather, harder than steel,"* like Our Commander-in-Chief said.

The exact opposite of queer.

Back in middle school, we were shown a video. The whole seventh-grade class had looked forward to it for months, the Queer Video.

We filled the AV room, hooting and hollering and throwing garbage at the screen—at the old footage from before the Awakening, of those parades the homosexuals used to have. Ugly, buzz-cut women on motorcycles, wearing filthy leather jackets that hung open to show off their sagging and wrinkled boobs. Goblinlike man-creatures in feathers and glitter and make-up, humping and tongue-kissing in the middle of the street.

Pride parades, they were called. Pride in what? Being freaks of nature?

Later on, in Race Hygiene class and at Rooster and Dawn Patrol meetings, there were more videos, lectures—more horror stories from the old days. About the smut shops, the man-boy sex clubs, the perverts hunting kids in public parks, the bars with torture chambers in the basement, the drugs, the diseases—and then, at last, the quarantines, the lockdowns that Our Commander-in-Chief ordered on whole cities when he took power fifteen years ago, shutting down the bars, cleaning up whole neighborhoods, shipping the homosexuals where they could no longer infect us.

Nowadays we caught them much earlier. If we got to them while they were still young, some of them could even be cured, welcomed back into the embrace of the Nation. That was what the Reorientation Centers were for.

Still, not all of them could be Reoriented. And then there were those who slipped the net, who went underground. Them, we dealt with ruthlessly. Because sometimes an infection grew so severe that you couldn't just treat it—you had to cut it out.

Brad was full of it. Unity and I were making plenty of progress around the bases. To first base, anyway. Maybe even second.

She and I had spread out on the living-room couch. Unity had a biology test to study for, but she already had the material covered—this was really just an excuse for us to make out. We had the house to ourselves—Dad had a late meeting at Paramount Studios, Mom was already in bed, and my brother

Eric had gone to a friend's house to watch the executions over pizza.

Unity drew back, rested her head on my shoulder, and let out a sigh. Her breath felt like a feather tickling the skin on my neck.

"Ty? Am I doing something wrong?"

"Wrong? No, of course not. What makes you think that?"

"You just seem like you're not really *here* tonight."

I didn't answer. Anything I said would only hurt her feelings. I couldn't even explain it to myself.

Unity was a keeper, as Dad would say. I'd never had much skill with girls. There were a dozen at school who would have jumped at the chance for a date with the Mighty TNT—the name everybody called me by, because of my explosive home runs, and because Tyler Treppenhouse was such a tongue-twister—but I always choked when it came to asking them out. So, when Unity started going to our church, and our fathers introduced us, I was grateful for the assist.

That was nine months ago.

Sure, our dads had practically shoved us together—an arranged match, like a couple of Arabs or something—but Unity was sweet and pretty, and she adored me. With her around, I started feeling more confident—more male, in a way. The fact that we went to different schools was a blessing, too—it kept the gossip under control. We were both headed for USC—me in the fall on an athletics scholarship, Unity next year on a home economics track—and I was planning to propose to her at Prom.

Unity was perfect.

Except that lately, when I kissed her, there was something in the way. Like I was trying to kiss her with a mask on.

I fingered a lock of Unity's hair. "I'm just worried about Kevin, that's all."

"Oh, Kevin will do fine."

"Yeah, I told him the same thing. Still, what if something goes wrong with the Evaluation? What if somebody makes a mistake?"

Unity looked at me, her eyes hooded. "They don't *make* mistakes, Tyler."

Her tone stopped me cold. Unity's dad was in the DDS, the Department of Domestic Security. That didn't automatically make *her* a Dentist, but she still got peeved at anything that sounded even slightly subversive.

In the corner, our antique grandfather clock chimed the hour. The tone made me think of those executions in Texas. It was eight o'clock—the nooses were tightening right now. No, that was wrong—the hangings had already happened three hours ago. Executions were always tape-delayed for the West Coast.

"Kevin doesn't have anything dirty in his racial history, does he?" Unity asked.

"Nah. He's as white as we are." As far as I knew, anyway.

"He hasn't broken any laws? Done anything to dishonor the Nation?"

I laughed. "Kevin Sanders? He's so clean, he squeaks when he walks."

"See? We need all the uncorrupted blood we have—we're not going to throw someone like Kevin away." She smiled and kissed me on the cheek. "There was this Reclaimee girl at my old school up in Portland. She was like Kevin, a real star—second cheerleader, Future Homemakers of America, Dawn Patrol, everything. She was *so* nervous the week before her Evaluation—she spent lunch every day crying in the girls' bathroom. But then she passed, and that was that—she was laughing about it afterwards."

She straightened up and laid open her biology textbook on the coffee table. I rubbed her neck with one hand while I read over her shoulder. She was on the section about pheromones—oh, man, I remember that! Pheromones were these chemicals that animals, including humans, secreted to attract mates. It had taken my bio class forever to get through that lesson because Brad Nemechuk kept making jokes. For weeks afterward he went around pushing his sweaty gym clothes in everybody's face—*Hey, get a whiff of my pheromones! You getting horny yet?*

The book also said different races put out different pheromones. The ones from the nonwhite races were especially powerful. That was why they were threatening to out-

breed us, and one reason Our Commander-in-Chief sep-
arated the races—sending the blacks to Africa and to the
Homelands, confining the Hispanics to the Protection
Zones—to keep the Nation from becoming polluted.

Maybe that was the problem with me and Unity. Our
pheromones weren't strong enough.

During the night I had one of those dreams—the messy
kind. I knew it as soon as I woke up. The maid was coming
today, so I stripped the sheets off the bed and stuffed them
in the hamper so Mom wouldn't see them.

Always it was the same dream. We were in a dark, confined space—a closet, or a jail cell—just me and whoever
I was with. We were on the brink of some disaster—on
board the *Titanic,* or at the top of the Empire State Building
in the last moments before Nuke York. The awareness of
our approaching doom only made things more intense. But
no matter how many times I had this same dream, I could
never remember *who* I was dreaming about. I'd get flashes—a pressing of skin against skin, a brush of fingertips, a
warm mouth—but nothing I could attach his name or his
face to.

His. Yeah. I did know that much.

In the shower, I tried fantasizing about Unity. Nothing
happened—it was too soon after popping, probably.
Sometimes, if I held it in for a day and then focused hard
enough, I could do it imagining I was with her. But it took
work, and it was never as hot as in these dreams I couldn't
even remember. I needed to practice more.

I got dressed, threw on my letter jacket, and hurried
down to the kitchen. Dad and Eric were already at the breakfast table, Dad in his suit with the badge of the OCPM—the
Office of Communications and Public Morale—Eric in his
Rooster uniform, eating cereal. Dad had one eye on the news-
paper and the other one on the TV. On the screen there were
tanks rolling across . . . I couldn't tell where. Either Texas or
the Middle East. Someplace with oil wells.

Dad glanced at his wristwatch, then at me. "You're five minutes late."

"It's not a problem. I don't have to pick up Kevin—he's going for his Evaluation this morning."

Shoo-in or not, Kevin had to be a basket case right now. The whole process sounded nerve-wracking—getting up before dawn, taking the train downtown, and then spending hours in a room with a bunch of other eighteen-year-olds waiting for their fates to be decided. Pass or fail. If you passed, you went home and celebrated. If you failed . . . nobody knew what happened if you failed.

I adjusted the cap on my brother's head. "You see the hangings last night?"

"Yeah." Eric shrugged. "I thought there'd be a lot more kicking."

Dad chuckled. "That's what you get for watching so much *Zero Hour*. Reality is never as dramatic as TV."

He beamed at Eric, then aimed a cooler look at me. I kept my own face deadpan. *No, Dad, I didn't watch—and yeah, you think I'm a wimp. I get it.*

"You still bringing your mother her coffee?" Dad asked me.

"Yes, sir." I was already taking Mom's cup off the hook next to the coffee machine. I filled it, added the usual four spoonfuls of sugar, and headed back upstairs.

Mom was still asleep. I moved the empty pitcher and martini glass on the nightstand to make room for the coffee cup, then leaned over and touched my lips to her forehead. Her eyelids twitched against the light for a few seconds before they opened.

"Tyler. There's my sweet boy."

"Morning, Mom."

Her face was puffy around the eyes, her skin blotchy, her hair disheveled, but to me, she looked more beautiful now than she would later in the day. This was our time, mine and Mom's—the only part of the day I got to spend with her before the cocktails kicked in.

"Did your father come home last night? From his *meeting*?" The word *meeting* had an odd spin when Mom said it.

"He's downstairs. I don't know when he got in."

She fell silent, and then grimaced. I couldn't tell if she was grimacing from last night's martinis, or from the thought of dealing with Dad.

"I've got to get to school. I'll be home after practice." I took her hand and kissed the back of it. "I love you, Mom."

I gathered up the cocktail paraphernalia and carried them down to the kitchen for the maid to wash. Eric had left to catch his ride, but Dad was still there reading the paper.

I grabbed a banana out of the fruit bowl and waved good-bye as I made my way out, but then Dad's voice stopped me. "Tyler, hold on a minute."

I turned around, swallowing. Did I do something wrong? At least I was too old for the belt now.

"Uh, sure, Dad. What's up?"

He pulled out an envelope and handed it to me. My jaw dropped when I saw the Los Angeles Dodgers logo.

"Opening Day?"

Dad was smiling. "Take a closer look."

I examined the tickets, and my mouth fell open even wider. "The *Muldoon Box*? How did you—?"

"A little thank-you from the people at Paramount. They were having political issues with one of their summer releas-es—the director was . . . problematic. I made a few phone calls—problem solved." He pushed back from the table and stood up, buttoning his coat. "There are four tickets, a pair for you and a pair for Kevin. You can take Unity, Kevin can take . . . what's his girl's name?"

"Shelly. Dad, this is awesome. Thank you." I stashed the tickets in my pocket. "So are you going to make it to *our* opener? It's coming up in two weeks."

"Well . . ." Dad suddenly became fascinated with the tips of his shoes. "I'll do my best, but you know how unpredict-able my schedule is. These Hollywood types that I have to deal with—no discipline."

Ah. So the tickets were to cushion my disappointment that my own father would, once again, not be coming to watch me play. Still, things were getting better—Dad actually seemed to regard me as a real athlete now, and not just some pansy who couldn't hack it in football.

I was humming "Take Me Out to the Ballgame" as I got into my two-door Fenris coupe and drove off to school. Opening Day wasn't until April, two months away, but tickets were already sold out. And . . . the Muldoon Box at Dodger Stadium! It was great having a father with connections. Kevin was going to be stoked, too—I'd make sure to tell him when I saw him tonight.

How dumb, worrying about him. Unity was right. The Nation wasn't about to treat Kevin Sanders like some worthless Chaff.

Kids like Kevin were why Our Commander-in-Chief had created the Reclamation program in the first place—to give them an opportunity to make amends for whatever their parents might have done. Kevin didn't know a thing about his parents—he was only a toddler when they were arrested. But he knew a chance for a better life when he saw one, and he took it and ran with it.

If Chaffs like Casey Monahan—the Reclaimees who didn't even try—wanted to throw their own chances away, that was *their* problem.

Brad came out of his crouch, took the ball out of his catcher's mitt, and threw it toward the pitcher's mound. "So I talked to that recruiter today."

"For the Wide Awakes?" I stepped away from the plate, hooking my bat behind my neck, holding it at both ends, and swiveling my upper body to loosen up. "What did he tell you?"

"As soon as I graduate, I'm in." Brad was grinning through the grill of his mask. "OK, I have to go through training first. But once I'm done I can put on the blue uniform and start cracking skulls. Woo-hoo!"

"Sounds like fun. I guess."

"Oh, don't get all holy with me, Mr. On-the-Fast-Track-to-the-Major-Leagues. Not all of us can go to the Show, or even to college. For the rest of us, it's the Wide Awakes or the Army—and I'll take staying in the U.S. of A. and waling on beaners over getting shot at by ragheads in some sandpit any day."

I couldn't argue with Brad's logic. And becoming a member of President Muldoon's private militia was nothing to scoff at.

I raised my bat and dug my cleats into the rain-dampened clay in the batter's box, waiting for Danny Magruder to quit pacing around the pitcher's mound. Danny had a killer arm, but he was easily agitated and he took forever to settle down and pitch. When he finally did, this time, his windup was pitiful, and the ball came in below my kneecaps. I swung for it anyway—this was just a scrimmage game, but I thought I could still get a piece of it—and hit a pop fly that went into foul territory and behind the dugout despite Rick Nagy's attempt at a jumping catch.

"Come on, Treppenhouse!" Coach bellowed. "Don't swing at every piece of crap. That's why you strike out so often. And you, Magruder—this isn't Powder Puff League. *Throw. The ball.*"

That got Danny's blood pumping. The next pitch thumped into Brad's mitt before I was halfway through my swing.

While Danny paced some more, Brad sidled up to me and nodded toward the bleachers on the first-base side. "Check out your girlfriend."

Huh? What was Unity doing here? She hated baseball. She came to our home games, of course, to support me, but practices bored her.

I glanced at the bleachers, and my guts clenched.

It was Casey.

Him again?

He was perched on the top row, his knees apart, a skateboard propped up on end between them. A *skateboard*—God, what a delinquent. A lit cigarette dangled between two fingers, completing the image. He took one long drag on it, ground it out underfoot, then hunched forward and rested his chin on his clasped hands, gazing down at the field.

"I bet he's picturing you naked," Brad said.

"That's gross. He's not even looking at me."

"He is when *you're* not looking. You ought to try batting from the other side, show him your butt."

"Dude! Geez!"

"Ah, I'm just screwing with you, TNT." Brad laughed, but then he looked up at Casey again, and his eyes narrowed. "What say we take care of that freak for real, after practice? You, me, Danny, Rick, Deke, we can—"

"No." The idea that this creepy Chaff might be shadowing me—it made me want to pound him myself. But . . . "You know how Coach feels about that sort of thing. Besides, I'm heading straight home from here. Kevin should be back by then."

"Whatever." Brad crouched down again behind the plate. "You and Sandman should have let me deal with him yesterday. That's all I'm saying."

I retook my position and choked up on the bat, pretending it was Casey's neck.

Another fastball. Even before the ball left Danny's hand, I knew it was going over the fence. My swing was flawless, the bat connected in just the right spot, and the smack of cowhide against wood resonated like a dynamite blast. Every head on the field turned to watch the ball sailing up . . . up . . . up . . . shrinking into a black dot against the sky and then falling to earth, dropping behind the huge face of Our Commander-in-Chief above the left field scoreboard and landing somewhere out on Lemarsh Street.

"Yeah-hah!" Brad leaped up and did a fist-pump, his voice booming. "You see that, Neighbors? *That* is why we call him the Mighty TNT!"

As I rounded the bases, I snuck another glance at the bleachers. Casey was gone.

Mom was yelling at the maid again. Her voice was thick and slurred. I winced and stuck my fingers in my ears as I walked in the front door. The maid—Lupita? No, that was the last one, I hadn't learned this one's name yet—stood and took the abuse, uncomplaining, probably praying she wouldn't get fired and dumped back in the Protection Zone. Mom went through the help faster than the Freedom to Work Program could replace them.

"Mom? Mom!" I sharpened my tone to cut through her tirade. "Did Kevin call?"

She stopped ranting. Her hair was in place, her makeup perfect, her eyes unfocused and watery. "I dunno, honey. Check th'answerin' machine."

I did. Nothing.

Come on, Kev, what's the deal?

"I'll be on the phone upstairs," I said.

Mom had already gone back to berating the maid. As I headed up, the words *stupid spic bitch* trailed behind me.

I grabbed the phone out of my parents' room. It was the only line on the second floor, and the cord stretched across the hall. I sometimes wished I had one of those wireless phones small enough to fit in your palm, like they were rumored to have in Canada or Europe. I knew they didn't really exist, that the rumors were just propaganda designed to make us look ignorant and backward—like those stories about supercomputers the size of a school notebook—but it was still fun to daydream about.

The maid had already cleaned my room. My dirty clothes had been picked up off the floor, my Little League and JV trophies dusted off, my schoolbooks stacked neatly and pencils lined up parallel on the desk.

I sprawled on the freshly made bed, and dialed.

Maybe I'd be lucky and Mr. or Mrs. Willhoyt would answer, rather than one of Kevin's foster-siblings. That foster home was like Union Station, with twelve kids of different ages crammed under one roof. If any of the other eleven picked up, I'd have to listen to five minutes of giggling and obnoxious comments while Kevin ran the gauntlet to get to the phone.

"Hello?"

"Hi, Mrs. Willhoyt. It's Tyler Treppenhouse. May I speak with Kevin?"

Silence. Just a second's worth, but it seemed to last forever. The air in my lungs went stale as I held it in.

"I'm sorry. There's no one here by that name."

MRS. Willhoyt hung up. The clicking sound was like a slap. I shot to a sitting position and hovered on the edge of the bed, my hand still clutching the phone.

Wrong number? I could have sworn that was Mrs. Willhoyt's voice. But . . . Yeah. I must have dialed the wrong number.

I tried again, counting off each digit.

"Mrs. Willhoyt? It's Tyler. Is Kevin—?"

She hung up again. This time it made me recoil, as if I'd just been punched.

The receiver slipped from my fingers and thumped on the carpet. I couldn't move to pick it up—I had to fight just to keep breathing. There was this cold pressure on my chest, like a truckload of wet cement pouring down on top of it.

My eyes darted around at the baseball trophies and Dawn Patrol banners. They finally landed on the *Zero Hour* poster over the bed—the poster Dad got me a few years ago, autographed by the show's entire regular cast. As always, DDS Special Agent Dirk Brennan was defending the Nation, one muscular arm embracing the blonde babe he'd just rescued while the other one blew away apelike Red-Mex terrorists with an automatic rifle . . .

An act. A joke. Kevin was playing a joke on me. He was probably on the other end of the line just now, listening, laughing his butt off.

Call Shelly. Kevin wouldn't dare pull a stunt like this without letting her in on it.

I picked up the receiver. I swore, the next time I saw Kevin, I was going to punch him in the face and then give him a huge hug . . .

"Dobbs residence."

"Hi, Mrs. Dobbs. Is Shelly there?"

Another too-long silence.

"She . . . Shelly can't come to the phone right now."

"I just need to talk to her for a minute. Please?"

A few seconds of muffled arguing.

"Tyler?"

"Shelly! Have you talked to Kevin today? Is he over there?"

"No." Her voice was tiny. "Tyler, I . . . No."

The cement started pouring down on my chest again.

"Shelly, come on, this isn't funny. Where's Kevin?"

"He's . . . I'm sorry. Tyler, I'm . . . I can't . . ."

A clunk as Shelly set down the phone. Then, footsteps, running away. I sat there, hyperventilating. My hand gripped the receiver—I didn't dare drop it again. If I did, I'd lose it—my whole world would shatter.

Mrs. Dobbs came back on. "Tyler, Shelly's very upset. Can she talk to you at school tomo—?"

This time I was the one who hung up.

I bolted down the stairs and tore out of the house, ignoring the maid's looks and Mom's slurred questions. I had to do something, be somewhere. Anywhere but here.

This wasn't real. This was *not* happening.

God damn it, Kev . . .

Chaffs

I jumped into my car and pulled screeching out of the driveway. It was rush hour, the streets choked. I made turns at random, leaned on the horn, zipped into the opposing lane to get around slow-moving traffic. At one point I ran a red light and didn't even notice until I heard shrieking tires and saw in the rear-view mirror that I'd come within inches of getting T-boned by a bus.

Eventually I found myself at the North Topanga Reservoir. We called it that even though it was long dry, drained after an earthquake to keep the dam from failing, years before I was born. Around the rim ran an old bike path, unmaintained, the pavement crumbling away. Kevin and I often went jogging here.

I got out of the car and started around the path.

The puddles from yesterday's rain splashed around my feet. Above me, the sky was bluer than I'd ever seen it, washed clean of the usual smog. Small, puffy clouds danced across it, like animated marshmallows. Everything was heartbreakingly bright and colorful. Part of me expected Kevin to appear around the next turn and give me grief for being late.

My legs pumped faster. Faster. I was no longer just jogging—I was running for my life.

I made one full circuit, and another, and then I stopped. I couldn't run any farther—my heart and lungs were about to explode. My sweat-drenched clothes clung to my skin and turned icy in the early evening breeze, making my teeth chatter.

High overhead, I spotted a bird—a hawk or a falcon. It traced lazy circles in the air, searching for prey. There was plenty of it down in the dry basin of the reservoir—field mice, squirrels, possums, minding their own business amid the oaks and willows and waist-high grass, ignorant of the danger.

Any second, one of those innocent creatures could wander into the open, and that bird would go into a dive, snatch it up, and carry it away to its doom . . .

My eyes were boiling over. The tears splashed down my cheeks, my legs buckled, and I slumped to my hands and knees. I remained there, sobbing quietly, as the sun dropped behind the hills.

I drove around for a few more hours, until I wound up at Unity's. She lived in a ritzy area south of the freeway, in a house with a deep, white-pillared front porch, like on one of those sitcoms set in the Old South. You half-expected to see black guys—or actors made up to look black—singing and tapdancing on the porch.

It was almost nine, and the lights were off, except for one in Unity's bedroom window and another one down in her dad's study.

I'd stopped crying a while ago. Now I just felt numb and dead, every nerve shorted out. I leaned against the doorframe for support as I rang the bell.

The porch light came on, and the door opened. Unity's dad stared down at me with his Dentist's gaze—cool and smooth, as polite as a bank teller and as unyielding as death. Pure DDS.

"Tyler. What are you doing here?"

"I know it's late, Mr. Ludlow—I'm sorry. May I talk to Unity?"

"She's getting ready for bed. This can't wait until tomorrow?"

"No, sir, it can't. Please?"

He pursed his lips, took off his round, wire-rimmed glasses, and interrogated me with his naked eyes.

"Wait here," he said.

Oh, crap—I just remembered, I was supposed to call Unity tonight! I'd totally forgotten. She was going to be furious.

She did look peeved when she came to the door, but the look melted into worry as soon as she saw me.

"Ty? You look terrible. Are you OK?" She took my hand, and the worry deepened. "Sweetie, you're shaking. What's wrong?"

"It's . . ." My throat spasmed shut. I didn't want to say it.

If I said it out loud, it would become real. But I had to. "It's Kevin. He . . . he failed."

What a weak word for it. *Failed.* Like he'd just flunked a trig test.

Unity blinked at me, then drew me into her arms. "Oh, Ty, sweetie, I'm so sorry . . ."

I wanted to cry some more. But it was like my eyes had been sandblasted dry. I settled for letting Unity hold me. It was the first time in months that I'd been this close to her, and actually *felt* her.

"It's OK," she whispered. "Don't blame yourself. You couldn't have known. None of us could have known."

Huh? I flinched and broke off the embrace. What was she talking about? Couldn't have known *what?*

"I'm not blaming myself. I'm not." Even if I did, there was no cure for it. "I'm just . . . how could this happen? I've known Kev since kindergarten—he did everything right, *everything.* He got straight A's, he lettered in a million sports, he could have been Dawn Patrol Troop Leader if Billy Hanna hadn't beat him out. He couldn't possibly have failed. There must have—"

Unity looked at me, and I bit back the rest of that sentence. *There must have been a mistake.*

"There's more to it than that." She spoke slowly, like she was humoring me. "It isn't just about grades or sports or Dawn Patrol. The Evaluators look at other things too—psychological things. They must have seen something in Kevin that the rest of us didn't. Something he was hiding from us."

I took a step back. "What are you saying? That Kev *deserved* this?"

"No, sweetie, no. I'm not saying it was his *fault*—he couldn't help being what he was. But Reclaimees aren't like us—they just aren't. We can save some of them, but the rest . . . Well, it's best that we get to them early. Best for them, too."

That closeness to her I'd been feeling—it evaporated. Suddenly she seemed millions of miles away.

"I'd better go." I already had one foot on the edge of the porch. "It's late. I'm keeping you up."

"Ty, please. Come in and sit for a while. I hate seeing you so upset. You can talk to Daddy—he explains these things much better than I do."

Listen to a Dentist tell me why my best friend deserved to disappear off the face of the earth? Jesus God, no.

"I can't. It's almost curfew. I'll call you tomorrow."

"OK." She reached for me again, stood on tiptoe, and laid a gentle kiss on my lips. "I love you."

She watched me from the porch as I shambled to my car. I climbed in, turned the key, and looked over—she was still there. Only after I put the car in reverse and backed out of the driveway did she go inside and close the door.

Once she was gone, I finally gave in to the urge to wipe her kiss off my mouth.

SOME ninth-grader was breaking into Kevin's locker—some pipsqueak in a cardigan, with a bookbag so heavy it made him lean to one side.

I bolted down the hall, zigzagging through the pre-homeroom obstacle course of students.

"Hey! *Hey!*"

I body-slammed the kid and sent him flying. As he hit the floor, the bookbag flew open, spewing its contents halfway down the hall. Around me there were gasps of surprise, giggles, applause.

"What are you doing?" I advanced, fists clenched. "That's my friend's locker, you punk!"

"I-I'm sorry, Neighbor!" The kid crab-crawled away from me. "I'm new here. This is the locker they gave me. I swear!"

He dug out some papers and handed them over. The first one was a transfer slip. The second was a locker assignment card, with the locker number and combination. The combo was different than Kevin's, but . . . yes, the number was the same.

The locker door was ajar. I eased it open the rest of the way . . .

Empty. Kevin's belongings—his books, his baseball glove, the pictures of Shelly taped to the door—all gone. Even the Dawn Patrol decals had been scraped off. I took a sniff and caught a hint of acrylic, touched the inside and felt the slight tackiness of a fresh paint job.

I let the papers fall to the floor. The kid scurried after them. From out of nowhere Gwen Smith, this girl in my homeroom, materialized to help him pick up his books.

Around us, a crowd was gathering. I pressed my hands over my eyes to blot out their faces, but I could still feel them, like they were stoning me to death with their thoughts. My pulse roared in my ears . . .

Then I was pounding my fist against the locker door. The crowd jumped and shrank back—one step at the noise, another as I spun around, my fist still clenched, the knuckles throbbing.

I saw a crack open up in the wall of people. In a blur, I shoved my way through it and ran full speed down the hall.

Homeroom was another kick in the teeth. In the middle of the room, Kevin's chair sat unoccupied. Gwen and a few other kids gave it furtive glances, but nobody dared say anything.

Then Mrs. Ridderhoff did the roll call. I listened to the names, in alphabetical order. *Sacchetti . . . Sallinger . . . Samuels . . .*

Selby . . . Smith . . .

No more Sanders. Already, Kevin's name had been deleted from the rolls. I looked again at his former seat. By homeroom tomorrow the seating chart would be redone, the empty space filled. No sign would remain that Kevin Sanders had ever existed here.

I spent the day in a fog—thick and opaque, but lit up now and then with blinding flashes. Between classes I plodded around like a sleepwalker, veering off if anyone I knew came too close. I couldn't deal with their questions, listen to their stupid theories—or worse, watch them go on like this was just another Friday.

It would have been easier if Kevin had died in a car wreck, or gotten blown up in a terrorist bombing. People would be mourning him. Girls would say how much they loved his blue eyes. His teachers would remark on how smart he was. His teammates would reminisce about how he saved that game against Thousand Oaks High last year, leaping for that line drive in the last inning with the bases loaded. Even Billy Hanna, who hated Kevin, would honor his service to the Nation, declaring him a true Son of the Fourth Great Awakening.

Kevin Sanders' name would be on everybody's lips. Not scrubbed from their memories.

I thought about going home after sixth period, but I rousted myself to go to practice. At least here, in the locker room, I wasn't the only one affected. Even Brad seemed to have had the swagger knocked out of him.

When Coach Ferguson came in, we all scrambled to our feet and gathered around him, without needing to be told. He clasped his hands behind his back and drew his heavyset and powerful form up to its full height.

"We have . . . an unexpected opening in the roster. Whoever wants to try out for shortstop, raise your hand." No one did, so Coach pointed at Rick Nagy. "Nagy, you've been angling for a change in position—now's your chance. You're at shortstop today. Devereaux, you take Nagy's place at first. Are we clear?"

Nods all around.

"OK. Now let's bow our heads."

Coach never made us pray—not out loud. He said prayers were meant to be private. Still, today's moment of silence was twice as long, and a hundred times as silent.

Practice itself was an embarrassment. I'd hoped that playing some ball would take my mind off Kevin, but every time

I looked over at Rick, in Kev's old spot at shortstop, my mind went blank. Eventually Coach got tired of watching me whiff at every pitch, so he put me on fielding practice, where one ground ball after another rolled right past me.

After an hour, it was over. I blew out a deep breath and followed the rest of the team to the showers, slamming my fist into my glove.

"Neighbor Treppenhouse." Coach was standing at the entrance to the locker room, his arms folded across his chest. He jerked his chin in the direction of his office. "A moment of your time, please."

Instantly, I felt a knot in my stomach. Coach almost never called any of his players *Neighbor*.

Walking into his office was intimidating even when you weren't getting chewed out. Dale Ferguson had been at this school forever, and the walls testified to it. There were pictures from his own Varsity days, in that garish old orange and gold uniform—as part of the legendary team that won North Topanga the first in its long string of championships—awards and commendations from the school district, the Party, even Our Commander-in-Chief himself. One picture, the biggest and most prominent, showed Coach shaking the C-in-C's hand at that Dawn Patrol Athletics Summit in D.C. last year.

"Look, Coach, I know I was off my game today." I was babbling. He wasn't going to cut me from the team after just one bad practice, was he? "I'm sorry. I'll do better on Monday, I—"

Coach cut me off with a gesture. "Have a seat."

He closed the door. The high-backed chair behind his desk creaked as he sat down. He leaned forward, his elbows on the desk, his voice so low that I had to concentrate to hear him.

"I know why you're . . . off your game." Those weird pauses Coach took between words—like he had to assemble them before letting them out of his mouth—were even longer than usual. "You've suffered a loss. It's perfectly normal to feel pain and grief. But you need to be much more cautious about how you . . . express that grief. You're being observed."

That knot in my belly was corkscrewing up into my lungs. Observed?

"Coach? A-am I in some kind of trouble?"

"You had a close friendship with a failed Reclaimee. Some people might suspect he had a corrupting influence on you. Or . . . that you corrupted him." His eyes made these quick but shifty movements from left to right, and then he reached across his desk to adjust a photo of a very blonde, very athletic-looking woman—his wife. I'd seen her at our games. "Don't fuel their suspicions. Keep your . . . game face on, and when you grieve, do it quietly, and in private. Do you understand?"

Why was he telling me this? I looked again at the memorabilia on the walls. Why hadn't Dale Ferguson followed his teammates to the major leagues? We'd all wondered about that, why Coach never made it to the Show. He claimed he blew out his knee in college, but nobody believed that. What if it was a political thing? Coach said politics and baseball didn't mix—but the Party mixed *everything* with politics, and Coach knew it. He'd have to know it, just to stay out of prison, let alone keep his job.

"Yes, Coach. I understand."

He got up and went to open the door. "You're a good kid, and a talented ballplayer. I don't want to lose you."

As Coach showed me out of his office, he clapped one hand on my shoulder. He meant it to be all Neighborly and reassuring, no doubt, but it did just the opposite.

Lose me? To what?

By the time I showered and got dressed, it was after five, and my car sat alone in the parking lot. The afternoon shadows were long and stretched out, and the breeze had a bite to it.

You're being observed.

I turned up the collar of my jacket and tucked my chin into my chest, for protection—and not just against the chill.

As I pulled out my keys, I heard something. I tensed up and turned around in a circle. The wind made it hard to tell where the sound was coming from. But it was getting loud-er—a rolling and clattering of wheels.

A skateboard.

Casey was coming right toward me. He was trying to look casual, meandering with the board around the bumps and rough patches in the asphalt, but I somehow knew he'd been here for a while, waiting for me to come out.

My keys jingled in my hand. Part of me was screaming to get out of there, to get in the car and just drive away—but I'd gotten caught up in watching Casey. The way he moved, sway-ing like a dancer, steering that board like it was as much a part of his body as his arms and legs—I was mesmerized. Even my heartbeat was speeding up to sync with his movements.

He flowed into a 360, then stopped. As he got off the board he stepped hard on one end and snatched it with one hand as it jumped into the air. The maneuver made me flinch—it was beautiful. Athletic, like a perfect home-run swing.

"Hey," he said.

My heart was still racing. I shouldn't even be talking to him. My head swiveled, scanning the parking lot—no other humans around, but lots of Hawkeyes.

Keep your game face on.

"What do you want, Chaff?"

Casey took out a stainless steel flask, unscrewed the top, and offered it to me. I wrinkled my nose and shook my head. With a shrug, Casey brought the flask to his lips and took two big swallows. He was way taller than me—I'd never noticed that about him. I wasn't a runt like Rick Nagy, but still, my eye level barely reached Casey's chin. His Adam's apple was point-ed and prominent, and it bobbed energetically as he drank.

He lowered the flask and looked at me. "You're friends with that guy Kevin, aren't you?"

My throat tightened at the sound of Kevin's name. The first time anyone had spoken it all day, and it had to be Casey Monahan, of all people?

I managed a nod.

"I heard he had his Evaluation today. Did he—?"

"He failed."

Chaffs

Talk about game faces. Casey's was pretty good. But it still cracked for just an instant. His pupils dilated, and his Adam's apple jumped again. He took another swallow from the flask—a huge gulp that made him cough.

"Fuck." His voice was hoarse, from fear, or from the burn of whatever was in that flask. "I'm sorry to hear that. We weren't best buds or anything, but he did stop Neanderthal Man from killing me the other day. Not that it means dick, in the end."

He's looking his own fate in the eye. How much time did he have left until *his* Evaluation? Chaffs always acted so nonchalant about it—nothing to lose, eat drink and be merry, blah blah blah—but even the most hardened ones had to hear the clock ticking now and then.

"Well, it's over." I put the key in the lock and opened the car door. "I guess I didn't know him as well as I thought. He was just fooling us all."

Casey tilted his head. His longish black hair fell over his eyes, and he brushed it aside to stare down at me. It was another turn-you-inside-out look, though different from before—just as penetrating, but not harsh or mocking, just very knowing.

"Yeah. I'm sure you really think so." A faint smile. "I swear, it's impossible to tell who's bullshitting who around here."

Before I could think of a comeback to that, he'd gotten back on his skateboard and was gliding away.

I shivered and pulled my jacket closed, then got in the car. As I did so, I watched Casey in the side mirror . . . until he reached the gate, and I looked away, so I wouldn't see which way he went.

Because I found myself wanting to follow him.

I N *those days came John the Baptist, preaching in the wilderness, saying, 'Repent ye, for the Kingdom of Heaven is at hand!'"*

The pastor of our church, the Reverend Nicholas Blanchard, used to be a pro wrestler. He definitely looked the part. He sounded it, too.

Under the church's domed ceiling, his voice boomed like a cannon. His meaty hands throttled the pulpit. His face—in person, and blown up two stories high on the JumboVision— was so red, you'd have sworn he was sweating blood.

"'I baptize you with water, but after me cometh one mightier than I, whose sandals I am not worthy to bear. He shall baptize you with the Holy Spirit, and with fire. His winnowing fork is in his hand, and he will purge his threshing floor and gather the wheat into the granary, but the chaff he will burn with unquenchable fire.'"

Behind him, fanned out along the back of the stage, Unity and the rest of the choir waited to sing the next hymn, garbed in blinding white robes with blood-red trim and emblazoned with the red and gold cross of the Nation's Covenant Church. The same symbol towered over them on the wall, thirty, forty feet high. Where the lines of the cross intersected there was a gold circle, with rays shining out from it like the sun's. That circle was supposed to represent the Fourth Great Awakening, but it looked more like the cross-hairs of a rifle.

"Are *we* worthy of bearing Our Lord's sandals, Neighbors?" A blast of laughter. "NO! But that is not the role He has pre-scribed for us. We—men and women of the Party, of the Armed Forces, of the DDS, of the Wide Awakes—young people of the Roosters, of the Morning Glories, of the Dawn Patrol—we are not the cringing slaves tending our Master's footwear. We are the winnowing forks! It is through us that He purges the floor, gathers up the wheat, burns off the chaff . . ."

I blocked out the rest of the sermon and bowed my head. I'd heard it all before, and I needed to pray for Kevin. Somebody ought to.

Why Kevin? I wanted to scream. He was no Chaff. He loved the Nation—he loved *you*. And now he was just . . . burned off? Because of a stray mark on somebody's clip-board?

When I looked up, I saw Unity smiling at me. I squeezed out a return smile and then hid my face again—from her, from Reverend Blanchard, from my family seated on either side of me, from everyone except God. You couldn't hide your true face from God.

After the service I hung around the refreshment table in the Fellowship Hall, building a strawberry and cheese cube pyramid on my plate and sending out please-don't-talk-to-me signals. Some people did anyway, to ask how I was doing— in this weird roundabout way that avoided ever mentioning Kevin, who'd gone to this church too and been well liked— but I fended each one off with a few grunts and gestures. And I smiled a lot. *Nothing wrong here, Neighbors.*

I was just waiting for Unity. As soon as she changed out of her choir robes, we were out of here.

At one end of the hall, Reverend Blanchard was holding court with Mom and a handful of other women. Mom was animated and laughing—a nice change from usual. Dad ought to let her out of the house more often—she was so bored, with nothing to do at home but drink and yell at the help. At least she had Sundays to look forward to.

Dad was in the opposite corner, schmoozing with a cluster of guys in suits. Hollywood types, obviously—people in the Industry all had that same pat-you-on-the-back-stab-you-in-the-gut fakeness about them. As I watched, Mr. Ludlow—Unity's dad—walked up. The suits stiffened at the sight of his DDS badge, but he stopped just long enough to say hello and then moved on.

Then someone else joined them, a young woman with sculpted hair and a low-cut dress that looked way too glamorous for Sunday worship . . .

"Hey, Ty." Unity came up beside me, slipped an arm around my waist, and kissed me on the cheek. "You ready to go?"

I returned the kiss, then pointed at the woman. "Who's that? She looks familiar."

"Oh, that's Charissa Dunbar."

"The actress? She goes to our church?"

"She just started. You didn't recognize her? I thought every guy in creation had that *Massacre at Eagle Pass* poster in his room."

"My brother does." I stammered a bit before going on. "I . . . I mean, she just looks different when she's not onscreen getting ravaged by Red-Mex soldiers, you know?"

Unity laughed. "I guess. Want to go to the park today?"

"Sure. Let's tell our folks we're leaving."

Dad's schmooze cluster was breaking up. By the time we started toward them, Dad and Charissa Dunbar were the only ones left. Dad leaned over and said something to her—she laughed, touched him lightly on the arm, and swanned off. Dad's eyes stayed focused on her as Unity and I stopped to say our goodbyes.

Chaffs

While we were making out in the park, something happened. It had been happening since Friday, whenever I closed my eyes. I was still kissing Unity, but in my head I was watching Casey—his tall and lean form bobbing and weaving on that skateboard like it was a part of him, those honey-colored eyes staring straight at me. I couldn't make the image go away, and after a few heartbeats I no longer wanted to—I wanted to make it more vivid, not just see him, but feel him . . .

"Mmmm, that's nice, Ty." Unity brushed a eucalyptus leaf out of her hair. Her gaze drifted downward, and she giggled. "Well, *you're* sure in a good mood today."

"Huh? Oh, geez!" I sat up fast and pulled my legs in to hide the tent pole in my uniform. My heel caught on the blanket we were lying on, bunching it up under my foot. "Unity . . . I'm sorry . . ."

"You don't have to *apologize*. I'm flattered." She squeezed my hand, and her smile widened. "And I love how you blush when you're embarrassed."

I straightened out the blanket, using the motion to stall for time. If Unity knew who had been giving me wood just now, she would not be smiling.

Eventually I settled back and put my game face on. "What can I say? You just have that effect on me."

"I'm glad. And I'm *really* glad you've cheered up. I was so worried about you the other night."

"What's done is done—there's no point fretting over it." Some lines from the Dawn Patrol Handbook popped into my head. *"We Sons and Daughters of the Fourth Great Awakening do not indulge liberal sentimentality. We not only accept brutal necessities, we welcome them, and grow stronger from them."*

Unity nodded and reached for me again. This time, as we kissed, I kept my eyes open so Casey's face wouldn't superimpose itself on hers.

"Ty, can I talk to you about something?"

"Yeah, of course."

She fixed her hair, smoothed out her skirt, and turned to face me squarely, tucking her legs underneath her.

"We've been going out for nine months now." Her words sounded rehearsed, though her tone was bright and sincere.

"I've been thinking a lot about us. We're such a good match. Our bloodlines are pure—I mean, I know *mine* is, and I'm sure yours is too. What we have—it's *right*, I can feel it." A sigh. "We're meant to be together, Ty. It's time we took the next step, don't you think?"

The next step? Was she asking me to marry her? I thought I was supposed to be the one making proposals.

"Ty, I want to be with you."

I blinked at her, then glanced around at the patch of grass we were sprawled on. "Uh, you *are* with me."

Unity laughed. "Don't play dumb. You know what I mean."

I did. But I wasn't *playing* dumb—my brain really was sputtering. My arms and legs were twitching like a trapped animal's.

"You're nervous, sweetie, I know. I am too. Everybody is, their first time."

"It's not that. It's not." *Nervous* didn't even come close. *Terrified* was more like it. "What brought this on? We always said we were going to wait."

"Well . . . I've been thinking about that." She took my hands in hers, her eyes wide and earnest. "We need to start doing our duty to the Nation."

More sputtering. "Our . . . Doing what?"

"We're being outbred. Our numbers are dwindling, and theirs are increasing." She waved one hand, as though at some teeming horde just beyond the eucalyptus trees. "We've been talking about it in class. Europe has already been lost—the white people there have been totally overrun, by Negroes and Arabs and Hindus and God knows what else. It'll happen here too, if we don't do something."

She made it sound like saving the race from extinction rested solely on our shoulders. "So . . . you want me to impregnate you?"

"Well, you don't have to make it sound so *clinical.*"

"I'm sorry. I . . ." I stared hard into the tree branches, hunting for an escape route from this conversation. "Aren't you thinking about this backwards? Having babies? We aren't even out of high school yet."

"You're graduating in June. And I can handle going to school while I'm pregnant. What are we waiting for?"

"Oh, gee, I don't know. To get *married* first?"

Easy, TNT. Unity didn't get sarcasm.

"We can get married later—when you're done with college and playing baseball professionally. The Nation needs us *now*, Tyler."

"And is the Nation going to help us *raise* this baby?" I was on dangerous ground, saying that, but this was nuts. "Forget about baseball—if we had a kid I'd have to drop out of school and get a job." Pumping gas or flipping burgers or something, probably. Either that or join the Army. Or the Wide Awakes. "You can't just have a baby and then walk away. How are we going to support it?"

Unity's eyes brightened. Looking into them, I knew I was going to regret asking that question.

She grabbed her purse from where it was lying on the blanket, and took something out—a pamphlet or brochure of some kind. "This is how."

She opened up the brochure and handed it to me. It was four full pages, printed on glossy paper, bursting with color photos—chubby-faced newborns, toddlers, preschool kids, cooing at the camera, running through fields of flowers, hanging from brightly painted jungle gyms. The text covered half of the front page, in a bold and easy-to-read typeface:

THE VIRGINIA DARE INSTITUTE

Named for the first White child born in the New World, the Virginia Dare Institute offers a safe, comfortable environment where your baby can grow to adulthood—free of corrupting influences and steeped in the virtues and ideals of America's Fourth Great Awakening! With first-class education and morals training, and medical care unmatched by any in the world, your child will come to embody the Nation at its finest! Secure your child's welfare! Ensure your race's future!

I kept reading. *Prenatal genetic screening . . . state-of-the-art birthing centers and postnatal care . . . schools and care facilities staffed from among the Nation's most racially fit . . .*

Unity was still smiling. My eyes felt like they were about to fall out of my skull. "So . . . you want to have our babies and then just give them up?"

"Not give them up—donate them. Lots of other couples are doing it. And the Party supports it. For every child we donate, the Institute will gift us up to one hundred thousand dollars, to use however we want. We can put it away for college, use it to help buy a house after we get married, start a trust fund for our own children . . ." A puzzled frown. "I swear, I don't get you sometimes. Your girlfriend just told you she wants to sleep with you. Most guys would be jumping for joy."

Clearly, I wasn't like most guys.

"It's just . . ." I fumbled around for a nonincriminating way to respond. "I'm happy, I really am. But . . . have you really thought this through? You're going to carry a baby around, for nine whole months, and then just hand it over to this Dare Institute? Why haven't I heard about this place before?"

"I guess it's pretty new—I just found out about it myself. Isn't it a great idea?"

She was practically bubbling. The only part of me bubbling was my stomach.

I took another look at the brochure, at the rosy-cheeked children, the blonde pigtailed young mothers . . . at the official seals of the Party and the U.S. Department of Race Relations on the cover. This outfit had official approval? Seriously? I could see unwed mothers going there, to redeem themselves—but to have babies out of wedlock, on purpose, and get *paid* for them? Did Unity have any idea what people would say about us? At school? At church? In the Dawn Patrol?

Heck, what would the *Dentists* think?

The Dentists . . .

"Have you asked your dad about all this?"

Unity rolled her eyes, smiling again, and gave me a playful jab in the upper arm. "Well, sure! Daddy's the one who *told* me about it."

THIS Virginia Dare Institute had a higher profile than I thought. That night, after Eric left the dinner table, I asked Dad about it.

"Are you and Unity thinking of applying?" Dad took a sip of brandy and held the snifter in one hand, gazing at the swirling amber liquid inside. "Good for you."

"Well, Unity wants to." I took my fork and batted a shriveled-up pea around my otherwise clean plate. "I told her I had to think about it."

I had a decent enough excuse to put it off, with our opening game coming up—I needed to stay focused. But that was just delaying the inevitable. Saying no wasn't an option—not with Unity's dad, the Dentist, behind her. And besides, what kind of pitiful waste of manhood would turn down sex with his own girlfriend?

Dad was picking up on my lack of enthusiasm. "If you're worrying about your pedigree, don't. We filed the records for you and your brother with the Department of Race Relations years ago—pure Nordic and Anglo-Celtic ancestry, going back at least four generations. You'll be a shoo-in." Another sip of brandy. "You should seriously consider this, Tyler. It's a great opportunity to serve the Nation."

From the other end of the table, Mom gave Dad a cool look over the rim of her own glass. "You *would* think that."

Dad ignored her. "Anyway, you're almost eighteen, so it's your own decision. Unity will still need her father's consent, of course."

I coughed out a feeble little laugh. "Oh, that's . . . not a problem."

"You're not concerned about what your friends will say, are you?"

"Not really. But what about Unity's? I've heard what people say about girls who have babies out of wedlock."

"This girl's father is with the DDS. *People* won't say anything."

I excused myself and carried my dishes into the kitchen. I could have left them for the maid to deal with, but I needed a reason to get up from the table. That queasiness from earlier was returning. This interest that our dads, mine and Unity's, were taking in their kids' procreation—what were they getting out of it? It was like they were breeding us. Like show dogs.

By the time I came back, Dad had gone to his den to have a cigar. Mom was at the liquor cabinet, making a gin and tonic instead of her usual martini. We were out of vermouth—she'd had a fit about it today after getting home from church.

I headed for the stairs, but then Mom stopped me. "Come here for a minute."

She took her drink into the living room. I followed. It was quiet, broken only by the ticking of the grandfather clock and the clinking of ice cubes in Mom's glass.

Mom started to sit down, but then changed her mind and drifted over to the dark corner, next to the clock, with the shelf holding her books—the ones she'd written. *The New Chastity: The Second Sexual Revolution. Homosexuality and Its Victims. A Helpmate Fit for Him: Women and Traditional Marriage.* Several more, all bestsellers, all published before I was born, before Mom had even met Dad. I'd never actually read any of them. There were videos, too, recordings of

Mom on old talk shows, or what they called talk shows back then—verbal gladiatorial combat was more like it. I'd tried watching one of those videos, once, but all the yelling just gave me a headache.

"Tyler, I want you to be honest." She kept her back to me, holding her drink in one hand, caressing the spines of her books with the fingertips of the other. "Do you care about this girl?"

"Of course I do."

"I won't ask if you're in love with her, because I know that's not true." Her fingers stopped on the book about homosexuality. I froze. In my head, the tinkling of the ice cubes in her drink sounded like boulders tumbling down a mountain. But then she went on. "Boys your age don't know what love is. Some boys never learn."

She turned away from the bookshelf. As she did, my limbs thawed out and I could move again.

"So, do you think Unity and I should go through with this? With this Dare Institute?"

Mom paused with the glass halfway to her lips, brows arched. "I think what your father thinks, of course. That's how it was meant to be."

The way she held her glass, it looked like she was spitting her words into it.

Shelly was leaving. On the way to Wednesday's Dawn Patrol meeting, I ran into her. She was coming out of Building A, where she'd been collecting the paperwork to change schools.

"I'm going to live with my aunt and uncle in San Diego." She pulled out a handkerchief and dabbed at her eyes. "My uncle's a local Party chairman down there."

"Shelly, why?" My voice spiked in volume. There were Hawkeyes all around us, but suddenly I didn't care what they might overhear. "You don't have to go—"

"I need a fresh start. I need to forget." She looked crumpled, like a shoebox that had been trampled on and then thrown in the trash. "And I need a more wholesome environment. Mom and Dad say I've been corrupted, and they're right."

She walked away, leaving me alone in the hall. The Dawn Patrol assembly was starting, and I was late. But that was the last place I wanted to be right now.

I need to forget. I seemed to be the only one who couldn't. Less than a week since Kevin disappeared, and for everyone else it was already, *Kevin who?*

And I'd better play along. Otherwise I could disappear just as fast.

It still happened sometimes, and not just to Reclaimees. People heard a knock on the door in the dead of night, and then they vanished. In the first few years of the Fourth Great Awakening, hundreds of thousands disappeared—maybe millions. That was why so many Reclaimees were around my age—a lot of orphans were created back then.

Nowadays it didn't happen nearly as often—once or twice a year at the most. Just often enough to keep everyone aware that it *could* happen.

I'd always believed what I'd been told—that many of those who disappeared were traitors fleeing the country, while others had been taken into protective custody to keep vigilantes from killing them. And the rest? Those were dangerous times, requiring drastic measures—*brutal necessities,* just like the Dawn Patrol Handbook said—to keep us safe. And I did feel safe—at least I used to.

But now? It felt like I was walking down a dark tunnel lined with spinning knives that would slice me up like bologna if I made a single misstep. Or maybe even if I didn't.

I dragged myself to the assembly a full twenty minutes late. Billy Hanna lit into me for being tardy, but I didn't miss much—the whole agenda involved preparations for this Saturday's paintball war in Malibu Canyon. Next to me, Brad spent the whole meeting grousing about how we should be using real rifles.

Chaffs

The next two days were a blur. Excitement had begun to build for our season opener. Let other schools gush about football—our baseball program was one of the best in the country, and during the season that meant a quick trip to the apex of the school's social pyramid for the Mighty TNT. Girls flirted with me, guys slapped me on the back, and when I, Brad, Danny Magruder, and the rest of the team strode into the cafeteria, the crowds parted like the Red Sea before Moses.

I was looking forward to the game as much as anyone else. Once the season started, I could channel all this churning rage into playing the sport I loved—in the meantime, during practice, I could vent some of it and pass it off as pregame aggression. I swung the bat like a home-run machine, and my fielding at third base was so flawless you'd have sworn my glove was magnetized.

At night, I wouldn't even make it to bed—I'd sit down to do homework and then fall asleep at my desk. Holding myself together during the day was taking everything I had. And when I couldn't stay awake any longer, I'd have dreams.

About Casey.

I could see him now—he was the one in that dark room with me. There was still this sense of doom, this desperate need for us to devour each other before disaster struck—but in the midst of that, I also felt a calm. In these dreams I opened myself, became who I really was, and it was OK . . .

Until I woke up, with a giant sequoia in my pants and whole mountain ranges of shame and fear crushing me beneath them.

I almost made it to Friday free and clear. But then, during sixth period, I got a summons.

From Neighbor Lenskold. The Morality Officer.

My heart was ricocheting off my rib cage as I walked to Building A. What was this about? I must have done something wrong. Neighbor Lenskold didn't call you to her office just for the heck of it.

I handed the summons to the receptionist. Above Neighbor Lenskold's office door, you could still see the word COUNSELING, under a thin coat of whitewash.

I didn't have long to wait. The door opened, and Neighbor Lenskold—a big woman with a soft and greasy appearance, like someone who ate nothing but butter—loomed over me. "Neighbor Treppenhouse. Thank you for coming."

Thank you for coming. Like I had a choice?

The friendlier she acted, the more on-edge it put me. This was worse than getting paddled by a teacher, or even by the principal. Neighbor Lenskold didn't need a paddle. She could destroy my life in so many ways, I'd need a computer—like the one in her office, one of those new computers small enough to fit on a desk—in order to count them all. A single word from her, a declaration that I wasn't morally fit, and major-league scouts would stop showing up at my games, USC would revoke my scholarship, every other college in the country would slam its door in my face. I'd be lucky to get a job cleaning toilets.

She could even have me arrested. Rumor had it that Neighbor Lenskold reported to the Dentists.

She paused to close another door—to a coat closet, it looked like—and directed me to an armchair. The office was better furnished than any other room at this school—lots of pastels and earthy browns instead of institutional green. A faint but gagworthy smell pricked at my nostrils—a cheap perfume of some kind.

"You can relax—you're not in any trouble." Her voice was pleasant—velvety, and almost as deep as a man's—a contrast with her beyond-gruesome appearance. "I just thought we should talk, see how you're doing."

She squatted in a chair at right angles to me. On her lapel she had a pin with the Party emblem, and around her neck a silver cross, the chain of which had been swallowed up by the folds of skin.

"So, Tyler. How *are* you doing?"

I shrugged. "OK."

An unreadable, lopsided smile. "Seriously, you can talk to me. By all accounts you've always had a very strong moral character—I just want to make sure it hasn't been damaged. I know you've been quite shaken by recent events."

So that was what Kevin had been reduced to—a Recent Event. Not even Neighbor Lenskold would say his name.

"Yeah, I guess so." I stared at the floor, kicking with the toe of one shoe at a seam in the linoleum. Single-word answers weren't going to get me through this. "I lost my best friend. It hurts."

"It sounds like the two of you were very close."

The words had no spin on them at all. Was this sympathy, or disapproval?

"Tell me, Tyler—what was he like, just before the Evaluation? Did he say or do anything out of the ordinary?"

"He was a little nervous, that's all. But he thought he was going to pass." I lifted my gaze from the floor. "Everybody thought so."

"I see. Are you concerned the Evaluators may have made a mistake?"

"No, ma'am. They don't make mistakes."

The answer was too automatic. Neighbor Lenskold peered at me, and her eyebrows twitched. She knew—she knew I was only telling her what I thought she wanted to hear.

She reached back, grabbed a piece of paper, and handed it to me. Every time she moved, that disgusting scent hit my nose anew. "Take a look at the names on this list. Did your friend ever mention any of them?"

There were about thirty, all told—individuals, groups, and what sounded like code names. None of them rang any bells. Who in the world was the Junk Man? And the Secret Six—that sounded like something straight out of *Zero Hour*. I kept reading, until I reached the bottom . . .

Casey Monahan.

I flinched. Neighbor Lenskold saw it.

"Tyler?"

My tongue glued itself to the roof of my mouth. Was Casey in trouble? Other than in my dreams, I hadn't seen him all week. Chaffs like him only came to school when they felt like it. But now an insane worry possessed me. Had he been arrested, just for speaking Kevin's name on Friday?

Neighbor Lenskold had a knowing look. What should I tell her? I had no doubt she'd heard about my run-in with Casey at lunch last Wednesday—the whole cafeteria had witnessed the first part of it—and chances were good she already knew about Friday as well. If I tried lying, she'd nail me on it.

"This last one." I pointed to Casey's name on the list. "Me and Kevin saw him last week. He and Brad Nemechuk got in a fight. We stopped it."

"Yes. And?"

I swallowed. "He . . . also came up to me in the parking lot on Friday, after baseball practice. He just asked me about Kevin. I told him what happened, and he left."

"And you've had no other interactions with him since then?"

I shook my head.

"What about before?" Neighbor Lenskold asked. "Any recent contact with him before last week?"

"No. I don't hang out with Chaffs, ma'am."

"You shouldn't use that word, Neighbor Treppenhouse. It's vulgar."

She heaved herself to her feet. Another blast of perfume punched me in the face. "That will be all for now. You seem to be coping very well." She took the paper back from me as I stood up. "Now, do you have anything that you'd like to ask me?"

Huh? Ask *her*? It threw me. Before I could recover, the question just slipped out of my mouth.

"What happens to the Reclaimees who don't pass?"

I stood there, frozen. Stupid, stupid! There were certain questions you didn't ask, ever. I was practically *begging* to get dragged off in the middle of the night.

Neighbor Lenskold just gave me another off-center smile. "I assure you, they're all well taken care of. Even the most incorrigible ones end up thanking us, for saving them. Is that all you wanted to ask?"

"Yes, ma'am." I covered my misstep as best I could, with a snap to attention and a salute. "Nation First."

Her smile went even more crooked. "Nation First, Neighbor Treppenhouse."

Chaffs

I sucked in lungfuls of perfume-free air as I left. Sixth period was almost over, so I decided to head straight to practice and suit up early. I needed to hit and throw things.

About halfway there, I started thinking—about the weirdness of Neighbor Lenskold's smile, the tone of her voice, the smoothness with which she'd answered my question. And I knew. Not just suspected—knew. Until a week ago, I never would have dared even to suspect it of anyone wearing a Party badge.

She's lying.

I STILL wish they'd given us real ammo," Brad was saying. "I would have fragged Hanna by now."

"Shut up." I cradled my gun against my chest and watched my step, picking my way around the rocks and tree roots breaking up the trail. "He'll hear you."

"Yeah, so? Let him put me on report. I can't wait to join the Wide Awakes—I'm sick of this faggot playacting." He glowered at the kid staring at us over his shoulder. "What are you looking at, Nelson? Eyes front."

Nelson, an asthmatic ninth-grader with eyes so pale that even the whites looked grayish-blue, cringed and turned back around, hunching over—probably taking another puff off that inhaler he thought nobody knew he was carrying. A decent kid, but really, he should have washed out of the Dawn Patrol by now.

Then again, Billy Hanna should have, too. At the very least, he had no business being Troop Leader.

This should have been a no-brainer, a simple elimination battle—two troops hunting each other until only one had anybody left standing. We'd won the last paintball war easily last fall—but back then, Troop Leader Hanna had commanded us in name only. The real mastermind behind our victory—the one who'd made all the brilliant tactical decisions Billy took credit for—had been Kevin. Now, with Kevin gone, Billy's incompetence was out there for everyone to see.

The day was less than half over, and our troop had already lost two thirds of its members—picked off by snipers one at a time, or ordered by Billy into obvious ambushes and massacred in bunches.

We were heading into the canyon. At least it was cooler here than up near the crest of the hills. But the way down was steep and treacherous, slippery with mud and sliced up with deep ruts as the trail dropped toward the gurgling creek below. I divided my attention between the ground underneath me and the bluffs rising on both sides—taking a step, making sure my footing was steady, and then scanning above for signs of the Troop 407 shooters who were probably already in position, just waiting for us to emerge from under the scrawny willow trees that were our only cover.

This was the perfect spot for another ambush. Any idiot could see that. But our fearless leader?

He was at the front of the column, strutting around and barking orders like General Patton. Only cowards led from the rear, he said.

Ahead of me, Nelson stepped on a rock. It slipped out from under him, taking a chunk of wet ground with it. Nelson scrambled, fell, and started to slide. I grabbed for him but managed only to bring myself down too. I quickly recovered, clutching at tree branches and bracing my legs to halt my descent, but it was too late for Nelson—he was in free fall. He careened down the muddy slope, faster and faster, until he hit the creek bed with a splash, a twig-snapping sound, and a scream.

"Nelson!" I scooted down to where the kid had fallen. "You OK?"

He lay half-submerged, his face twisted with agony, the rest of his body shivering from the cold water. His foot was wedged between two large rocks, his lower leg bent in the middle like a used toothpick. On the back of his skull a huge goose egg was rising, red and angry under his blond crewcut.

I tried to free Nelson's leg, but the rocks were too heavy and algae-slickened to move. Between his knee and the top of his boot, the swelling had reached melon size.

"Nemechuk!" I turned and waved at Brad, who was already making his way down the slope. "Give me a hand!"

Brad came to help, grumbling under his breath. Between the two of us, the smaller of the rocks moved. Nelson jerked his leg free, then screamed again and went into what looked like a full-body spasm. His breath was whistling through his windpipe. He clawed in his pocket for his inhaler, shook out the water, and began sucking on it.

Just as we were dragging Nelson's gasping, pain-wracked form onto dry land, Billy Hanna came storming up. "What's going on here?"

"His leg, Troop Leader." I snapped to attention and saluted. "It's broken. I think he has a concussion, too. We need to—"

"Leave him."

"*What?*"

"You heard me. Leave him. We have a *mission* to complete."

Billy's voice rose to a screech on the word *mission*.

I goggled at him. Even Brad looked stunned. Mission? This was a game—a game we'd already lost, thanks to Billy. Even in real combat, mission or no mission, you did *not* leave a fallen man behind—that was *gospel*.

"Neighbor Nelson is injured, *sir*," I said through gritted teeth. "I can radio for help and wait here while the rest of you go—"

"Are you deaf, Treppenhouse? *Leave him.* That's an order."

He spotted the inhaler in Nelson's hand. With a curse he lunged forward and snatched it away. "Jesus Christ! Are you a freaking *wheezer*, Nelson? That's it. I'm putting you *and* Treppenhouse on report." With a casual flick of the wrist, he tossed the inhaler sideways into the creek, where it sank into the water and vanished.

Chaffs

Watching him throw away Nelson's inhaler made the whole world go blood red. I stepped in front of Billy and gave him a hard shove in the chest, sending him stumbling into the men behind him.

"Fine!" Billy was white around the lips and shaking all over. "Stay here with the gimp if you want! You're out, Treppenhouse! You want to get lovey-dovey with cripples and Chaffs, be my guest!"

My fists clenched, and I moved toward him. But then part of me remembered the paintball gun.

The rest of the troop dove for cover. They needn't have bothered. I was focused totally on Billy—on his face, and the way it went all *You wouldn't dare* and then shifted to *Ow! That hurts! Stop it!* within seconds . . . and on the glowing pink paint blotches that blossomed first on his chest and stomach, and then on his back and his butt as he flopped to the ground, rolled, and tried to get away—distracted only by the *poppop-poppop* of the gun emptying and by the roar of all my grief and anger from the last ten days pouring into my hands, through the trigger, and out the muzzle.

At last I ran out of paint pellets. I stood still, my eyes glassy and out of focus, my head millions of miles away.

Gradually, I came back to awareness—of Billy spitting threats, and of Brad laughing his butt off.

"I take it back, dude," Brad said once he caught his breath. "This is *way* better than live ammo!"

Before passing sentence, the Patrolmaster asked if I had anything to say in my defense. I rose, looked him in the eye, and said no. I had no defense. No excuses.

I was determined to take my punishment like a man.

If this were the army, and we'd been using real bullets like Brad had wanted, I would have faced a firing squad. As it was, the Patrolmaster sentenced me to twelve strokes of the paddle, to be administered publicly at the next meeting.

Billy was furious. Only twelve? He'd no doubt hoped for thirty-nine lashes, or crucifixion, or something else Biblical.

63

But then he found out that, as Troop Leader, *he* would be carrying out the sentence. Once he heard that he flashed me a smug little grin.

When the day came, the auditorium was packed—not just with members of the troop, but with civilians as well, kids who'd skipped third period just to watch me get paddled. Normally Dawn Patrol meetings were members-only, but Billy had thrown the doors wide open. He wanted the whole school to witness this.

The crowd went silent as I walked in. Their eyes turned toward me, all at once, and then panned over to the stage, where Billy was waiting.

The paddling bench had been brought over from Building A. It was like a sawhorse, but padded, with a pair of hand grips on a crosspiece at one end. It sat on the stage with the crosspiece end toward the audience, so I'd have to look them in the face.

Billy had the paddle in his hands. It wasn't one of the small wooden paddles the teachers used to give out licks in class, nor was it the bigger one the school kept for more severe punishments. This one was huge, at least two feet long, made from something hard but still flexible—thick leather, or maybe vulcanized rubber. There were holes punched in it to cut down wind resistance, and carved into the surface, the emblem of the Dawn Patrol and FAITH, FAMILY, FREEDOM in sharp-edged, welt-raising capital letters. Just one look at the thing made my butt clench.

"Tyler Treppenhouse." Billy was gazing at the paddle like it was a work of art. "Step forward."

I took the stairs onto the stage one at a time. At least we were getting this over with early.

Slowly, Billy raised his eyes to meet mine. "Explain your crime, Treppenhouse."

"I . . . I disobeyed a direct order from my Troop Leader, and . . . and assaulted him physically." Crap. I'd been rehearsing these lines for two days—I'd resolved I wasn't going to stammer. "I am deeply sorry. I take full responsibility for my actions and gratefully accept the discipline of the troop."

"Pull down your pants and take your position."

I couldn't help flinching. Pull down my pants? That wasn't procedure. Billy was trembling with excitement—he'd obviously been given leeway to make this as humiliating as possible. Out in the audience, there was tittering.

I unbuckled my belt and let my pants slide to the floor. I paused, waiting to see if Billy would make me pull down my briefs as well. Thankfully, he didn't.

With a deep breath, I hobbled up to the bench and leaned over, wrapping my hands around the grips. The snickering had stopped—now the whole room was dead quiet, broken only by the *whoosh* of the paddle slicing through the air as Billy practiced his swing.

Then, nothing—nothing but my own heartbeat. I was right underneath an AC vent, and the cold air raised goose-bumps on my bare legs. I tightened my hold on the grips and got ready to chant the required words . . .

Whoosh . . . whack!

"FAITH!"

The first one wasn't too bad—just a little sting —

Whack!

"FAMILY!"

That one stung harder . . .

Whack!

"FREEDOM!"

Now it was starting to burn . . .

Whack!

"FAITH!"

Whack!

"FAMILY!"

Whack!

"FREEDOM!"

By the halfway point, the pain was pouring down to my feet and spurting up to my kidneys, like liquid fire. I throttled the grips and pressed my face against the padding, fighting to keep my voice from cracking.

Whack!

"FAITH!"

Whack!

"FAMILY!"

Whack!

"FREEDOM!"

Billy was slowing down, stretching out the time between strokes—ten or fifteen seconds at least, long enough for me to feel the full effect of the last lick and get gnawed at by anticipation of the next one. I could have sworn the letters on that paddle were ripping off patches of skin.

Whack!

"FAITH!"

Whack!

"FAMILY!"

Whack!

"FREEDOM!"

"Stand up," Billy said.

I couldn't, not yet. If I tried, I'd just topple over and lose what little dignity I had left. I slumped against the bench, drenched with sweat, breathing hard.

Then, I felt a tapping—the paddle again. Not hard, but enough to make me jump and shudder. Gingerly, I reached down, grabbed the waistband of my pants, and struggled upright, pulling my pants back up as I did so.

"That'll be all, Neighbor Treppenhouse." The satisfaction in Billy's voice dripped like syrup. "Take your seat."

On the way back down the steps, I slipped and almost fell. Nobody in the audience came forward to help—they just watched. Their faces were just a blur, but I could feel their eyes, each taking a piece of me, picking apart everything that the paddle had left untouched.

After the assembly I went to the school nurse, who sent me off with two aspirin and a donut-shaped foam cushion to sit on for the next few days. The thing was pale blue, looked like a toilet seat, and wouldn't fit in my bookbag or under my jacket—I had to carry it around openly, a big puffy reminder to the whole school that I'd just gotten my butt tenderized.

Lunch period was almost over, thank God. I couldn't show my face in that cafeteria today. It would be open season on me—the Mighty TNT, paddled like a preschooler who'd wet his pants. Billy Hanna would be there too, gloating.

I did have an off-campus pass, though—I could blow off the rest of my classes, stop at Sambo's for a burger and a shake, and then come back for practice. But I'd still have to run the gauntlet on the way to my car until lunch was over.

I decided to wait in the library. Nobody hung out there, not even Chaffs. People only went to the library when they needed to hide.

Sure enough, I had the place to myself, except for the librarian. As I walked in, she glared at me like I'd just broken into her house, but then immediately went back to the cross-word puzzle she was working on.

I didn't expect to find anything worth reading—not that I was much of a bookworm, anyway. I came in here maybe twice a year, and each time the shelves looked emptier than before. I bypassed the shelves loaded with copies of *Rise and Shine*, Our Commander-in-Chief's manifesto, and ran one finger along the ratty and sad-looking books beyond them—Race Hygiene and history texts, paperback novels, and a set of the *Encyclopedia Americana* with lots of pages missing and whole passages blacked out—leaving a trail through the dust and stirring up a musty smell of decaying paper and ancient binding paste. The novels had lurid covers that told you the stories without having to read them—cowboys and Indians, broad-shouldered spacemen firing ray guns at big-lipped and swarthy-skinned aliens, couples kissing on the verandas of Southern plantations, big-bosomed white maidens menaced by Red-Mex soldiers.

I drifted into the stacks. As I moved away from the windows, the sputtering fluorescent lights crowded out the sun and gave everything a strobing bluish tint.

Near the floor, a splash of color caught my eye. I crouched down for a closer look. On the bottom shelf sat a row of skinny, album-sized hardcover volumes—four or five dozen of them, in different colors, from washed-out pastels to once-bright Day-Glo hues now dull and grimy with age. I reached for the first one in the row and worked it loose—the books were packed so tightly that they were stuck together.

Clearly, no one had looked at these for quite a while . . .

The Topangan.

Holy crap—this was North Topanga High's yearbook! All of them, from when the school first opened—the one in my hands—all the way to last year.

I blew the dust off and opened it, careful not to crack the binding. The pages were yellowed, but still glossy, with a faint chemical smell. The handwritten messages inside were almost unreadable, but I could still make out a few. *Have a great summer,* stuff like that. The sort of message you wrote when you had nothing else to say.

I laid that stupid blue cushion on the floor, sat down crosslegged—behind the stacks, where neither the librarian nor the Hawkeye in the ceiling could see me—and began flipping through the pages. My butt protested, but I hardly noticed. You almost never saw images from the old days, before the Fourth Great Awakening—photos in textbooks, and heavily edited news footage, but nothing real, nothing like this.

I went through the others, in order. At first I was struck the most by what *hadn't* changed. The clothes had, sure—wearing stuff like they wore in the nineteen-sixties would get you *arrested* today—but if you dressed the kids in uniforms instead, they'd look just like the crowd at a Dawn Patrol rally.

Or . . . at least the *white* kids would.

As I skimmed through the years, the sight boggled my mind—all these black and brown faces, in growing numbers, laughing and horsing around with the white kids and, oh my God, even *kissing* their white girlfriends and boyfriends like it was normal, not sick or unnatural at all. I didn't know how to react. I knew how I was *supposed* to, of course—with revulsion and rage—but mostly, I was just surprised these books hadn't been destroyed, or at least had the offending pages removed. Nobody thought high school yearbooks were important enough to censor, maybe.

A noise startled me—somewhere in the stacks, a tapping of shoes against the floor. My heartbeat fluttered, and the yearbook dropped into my lap, suddenly too heavy to hold. This was a mistake, this was *dangerous*—I was looking at things

I wasn't meant to see. And yet I couldn't put the book back on the shelf. I didn't even want to.

The tapping ceased. I picked up the book again, and it was like a hand simply lunged out of the pages and pulled me in, towing me through the past. I was looking now at pictures of school clubs—lots of them, way more than we had today, when every club required Party sponsorship. Some of them . . . jeez, this wasn't just a different time, this was a whole different *country*. The Black Student Union? A group of Hispanic kids who called themselves MEChA, whatever that meant? The . . .

The Gay and Lesbian Students Alliance?

Every tiny hair on my body sprang up—on my arms, up my spine, across the back of my neck. I looked up to make sure no one was watching, then hunched over the yearbook and examined the picture, every detail.

It was a small group—two boys and a girl. The girl wore her hair short and spiky, and one of the boys had . . . Good God, was that an *earring?* . . . but they were smiling at the camera, totally at ease, happy. They looked . . .

They didn't *look* like freaks of nature.

What year was this? I closed the book and looked at the cover. It was gray, somber, a stark contrast from the bright and playful colors of the volumes leading up to it. Across the front ran a black silhouette—the shadows of buildings, long gone but still instantly recognizable, seared into all our memories as if by the heat from a nuclear blast.

The old Manhattan skyline.

This was the year of Nuke York. Just a year after I was born. And the year before Muldoon—Our Commander-in-Chief—became President.

A shiver rolled through me. I returned to the page I'd been on. The kids in the picture were still smiling, but there was something tragic about them now. I couldn't look anymore. I had to close my eyes—I felt shrunken, helpless. Those were no longer smiles of joy—they were grins of defiance in the face of imminent doom.

When I opened my eyes again, I was on the verge of tears. It took so much effort to fight them off, so much con-

centration, that I didn't hear him walking up. I didn't even see
him until he was standing right in front of me.

Casey again.

That confirmed it. First at practice the day Kevin disappeared, then the next day in the parking lot, and now here.
He *was* shadowing me.

He had that skateboard tucked under one arm. He hadn't
spotted me yet, or at least he was pretending he hadn't. He
took a book off the shelf and skimmed a few pages, but then
rolled his eyes and replaced it with a tongue-cluck of contempt. Finally he glanced over and gave me an upward jerk
of the chin.

"Hey, Treppenhouse."

His gaze fell to the yearbook in my lap. I slammed it shut,
but it was too late—he'd already seen what I was looking at.
His eyes zeroed in on me.

I puffed out my chest. "What are you doing here,
Monahan?"

"Just looking for something to read. You should try it
some time, reading. That's what those squiggles next to the
pictures are for."

"Very funny. You want your head shoved down the toilet
again?"

"I'm faster than you. You've got a killer bat, but you can't
run for shit."

He leaned against the stacks. He didn't skulk around like
other Chaffs—he acted like he had just as much right to be
here as I did. With my eyes I traced his form under the khaki
pants and light blue shirt—his limbs were long and loose,
but full of energy, like coiled springs. No question, he could
outrun me—outjump me, too. He should have gone out for
basketball, or track.

"See you around." Casey straightened up and turned to
leave.

"Hey. Hang on a second."

He gave me a sidelong look. I just sat there. What on
earth was I doing?

"Have you eaten?" I asked. "I haven't had lunch yet.
Want to come with?"

Casey inched away. He probably thought I was setting him up to get pummeled by Brad and the others. "Why?"

"I don't know. I've just had a really bad day." I put the yearbook back on the shelf. "I was thinking of going to Sambo's."

"Sambo's? That place is full of Hawkeyes. And since when do you hang out with Chaffs, anyway?"

Since today?

"How about the Munch Box instead?" I stood up, hooking that foam cushion under my arm. "We can sit outside. No Hawkeyes."

Casey pursed his lips, thinking.

This was crazy. Billy Hanna had just made me his whipping boy—being seen having lunch with this Chaff would wreck my reputation even further. But I couldn't stand the thought of being alone right now, and suddenly, Casey was the only person I wanted around.

He shrugged and hefted his skateboard. "So are you buying? I'm broke."

The Munch Box was exactly what its name said—an orange-painted cinderblock hut next to the railroad tracks, selling the best burgers and hot dogs in the whole West Valley. Cheap, too—only thirty bucks for a double cheese with extra chili.

We went there separately. Casey came gliding up on his skateboard just as I was claiming one of the concrete tables with fiberglass umbrellas in the eating area. The lunch rush had come and gone, so there weren't many other customers, just a couple of guys who looked like hobos waiting to hop the next passing train.

Casey took a long, slow bite out of his chili dog and swallowed luxuriously, staring at me the whole time. "I've got to ask. Did you really unload on Billy Hanna with a paintball gun?"

I nodded, squirming in my seat. Casey's face split into a wicked grin.

"Nice. I wish I'd gotten to see that. I hate that little choad."

"He's my Troop Leader." I picked at the waxed paper my burger had come wrapped in. "I shouldn't have done it. It got me in a heap of trouble."

"Yeah, you got paddled. I heard."

"You weren't there? The rest of the school was."

"I've got better things to do." He took another bite of his hot dog. "So how many licks did you get? Twenty? Thirty?"

I could feel myself blushing. "Twelve."

"Ah, you got off easy. One of the perks of being the Mighty TNT, I suppose."

Was he making fun of me? Probably, but I couldn't blame him. Twelve licks had been bad enough—the thought of twenty or thirty was nauseating. Yet Casey threw those numbers around like they were part of his daily routine.

He seemed to know what I was thinking. "Look, don't be so hard on yourself. Your ass will stop hurting in a day or two. A week, and nobody will even remember. You'll still be the Big Man on Campus, and Billy Hanna will still be a waste of oxygen. You win."

That made me smile. Next to us, a train rumbled by. I used the noise as an excuse to sit, drink my soda, and not talk for a few minutes.

Once the train had passed, Casey grinned again. "So do you think it got him hard, paddling you?"

"What?" I nearly choked on my soda.

"He just seems like the type—a total perv. The Dawn Patrol is crawling with them." At my shocked look, he added, "Hey, I'm not saying *you're* one. But come on—Hanna? I bet he couldn't wait to go home and whack the piñata."

"Holy crap! Shut up!" I twisted around to see if anyone was eavesdropping. We were still alone, except for the hobos—or at least that was what they looked like. You never knew for sure who might be DDS. "Are you trying to get arrested?"

"Settle down, slugger. I'm just some Chaff. The Dentists don't give two shits what I say."

I remembered that list. What was Casey doing on it? And

why had Neighbor Lenskold shown it to me? As a warning, or just to rattle me?

"I don't want to get arrested either," I said.

"You should have thought of that before asking me to have lunch with you." Casey raised the hot dog to his mouth again, but then paused. His head tilted. "Why *did* you ask me to lunch, anyway?"

I stared down at my burger. I'd barely touched it. The layer of chili on it had gone cold and was coagulating.

"I guess I just need somebody to talk to." I took a sip of soda to counteract the dryness in my mouth. "For the last couple weeks . . . ever since Kevin . . . it's like I've been locked in this dark room."

"Like a closet?" Casey raised an eyebrow.

"Kind of, yeah. Everyone's on the outside, going on like Kevin never existed, and . . . it's like I'm cut off from them, like *I'm* the one who doesn't exist." I heaved a sigh. "I thought maybe you'd understand."

"Actually, I think I do."

Was that the *only* reason I'd asked him to lunch? He was right—I should have thought this through. But even with his bad language and worse attitude, it felt weirdly soothing, being around him. Even my butt was hurting less.

He polished off his hot dog, then took a pack of ciga- rettes and a lighter out of his pocket. "Do you mind?"

I turned up my nose. "Those things will give you cancer, you know."

"Not in the next three months, they won't."

It took me a second for his words to sink in.

"Oh. Oh, God. You mean—"

"I turn eighteen in May." He put a cigarette between his lips and lit up. The exhaled smoke draped his face like a shroud. "They probably won't give me a formal Evaluation. The last kid at my foster home, a couple of Wide Awakes just showed up that night and took her. Happy fucking birthday."

His Adam's apple was bouncing like a Mexican jumping bean. He was scared—way more scared than he wanted to let on.

"So is there . . . ?" I fumbled for words. "Is there, you know, a way out of it?"

Casey just chuckled. "A way out?"

"I mean, something you can say, something you can do—"

"What, sign up for the Dawn Patrol? Turn my life around? Become a good little Muldoonie?" He drew in and blew out a huge blast of smoke. "Do me a favor. Don't try to save my soul, OK? I like you, Treppenhouse. You're pretty cool, for a jock, and you're one of the few guys at school who isn't a dick. Don't start being one now."

"I'm not. I'm just . . ." I looked down at my cold chili burger, and with a pang of disgust I pushed it away. "It just doesn't seem fair."

"Fair? What world do *you* live in?"

He stared at the lit end of his cigarette. "You're upset about your friend—I get that, and I'm sorry. But it happens all the time where I come from—people just disappear. So if you're shopping around for sympathy, you're in the wrong part of the mall." He gave me another turn-me-inside-out look, and then frowned. "You've been wondering what happens, haven't you? What happens to the ones who don't pass?"

"Well, sure."

"Don't. Dude, I'm serious. You do *not* want to go there."

"So you *do* know."

"I know it's nothing good."

Under the table, Casey was rolling the skateboard back and forth. The wheels clattered.

I leaned toward him, spreading my hands.

"Look, I know I need to get over this. I know." I lowered my voice to where even I could barely hear it. "But there's this feeling I can't shake—something went *wrong* here. The other day I asked the Morality Officer what I just asked you, and she flat-out *lied* to me."

"Wow. What a shock."

He was looking at me like I was the biggest idiot he'd ever met.

"So what do you want from me?" he asked. "To join you on some grand-ass quest for the truth?"

"Honestly, I have no clue *what* I want. Except . . . to get out of that dark place I was talking about. Knowing what really happened to Kevin—it could be the key I need, to let myself out."

"And you think I can help you find this key."

"Maybe. You said so yourself—you live in a different world than I do. You know different people, hear different things."

"And if someone's going to put his neck on the line digging into things that he shouldn't, let's get the dirty Chaff to do it."

"That's not what I meant."

"If you say so."

How did I wind up *here?* Begging with some guy I hardly knew, for help with something that could get us both in deep trouble, something I hadn't even thought about doing until that very moment? He was going to say no—by all rights he *should* say no . . .

But he just sat there. The tip of his tongue prodded at one cheek, slid over his teeth to the other side of his mouth, poked at the other one. He flicked the ashes off the end of the still-glowing cigarette, then flung it down and trapped it under his shoe.

"Ah, what the fuck." He ground the cigarette against the concrete until there was nothing left but dust and tiny scraps of paper. "I've still got three months left—I might as well make them exciting."

WE'D better stop talking about this in public." Casey crumpled up his hot-dog wrapper and dropkicked it under the table. "Can I come over to your house?"

"Um, my house?" My mouth had gone dry again. I took another sip of my soda but got nothing but a cupful of ice. "Today?"

"Nah, someone might have seen us leaving school just now. Let's wait a week or so." He looked at me, and rolled his eyes. "What? Can't have some Chaff stinking up your nice house? I promise, I'll shower first."

"Oh, come on. It isn't that." He smelled pretty good, actually—kind of spicy. Or maybe that was just the chili on my burger. "I just never have people over. Except for my girlfriend."

"Yeah, we'd better come up with a cover story." His face brightened. "How are you at math?"

"Math?" I laughed. "I suck at it. I'll be lucky if I get a B this year."

"I'm pretty good, believe it or not. Want a math tutor? Nobody will bat an eye—they'll just think I'm getting desperate about my Evaluation and trying to score some last-minute kissy points. How about it?"

Good grief, this is really happening. It had already cracked open—the door to that cell I was trapped in. The light was leaking in—so beautiful, so dazzling—and I was dying just to kick down the door and storm through . . . but what then? What if the way out simply led to *another* cell? A real one?

"OK." I took my soda cup, then my uneaten burger, and landed them with two clean tosses in the nearest trash can. "Sure. I could use some help. With math."

Casey swung around and sprang up, one foot already resting on the deck of his skateboard. "Cool."

I must have looked scared to death, because before skating off, he said, "You need to unclench, you know? Trust me, we'll be fine if we play things straight. And I can tell you're a world champion at that."

Before the season opener against Canoga Park High, Coach Ferguson gave a short locker-room speech. "Men, you're no longer just a team—you're an army. You are the North Topanga Conquerors, and you are at war—it's you versus every other team in the division. That field is your country, your home, and you're the only ones standing against those who would plunder and rape it. Tonight I want each of you to give ten times what you've got. I want you to strike so much fear into the enemy that they spend the rest of the season wetting themselves. Are we clear?"

"YES, SIR!" we barked in unison.

Coach nodded. "Game on. Now go own that diamond."

And we did. We strode onto the field like blooded warriors, and as we took our positions and glared into the opposing team's dugout, the enemy's faces crumpled and went pale as death. On the pitcher's mound, Danny Magruder paced like a hungry mountain lion while, behind the plate, Brad Nemechuk crouched and, through his mask, fixed each batter with a look that shrank him three uniform sizes.

At third base—holding down the hot corner—we had me. The Mighty TNT. Not the loser who'd just been paddled in front of the whole school. News of that had reached Canoga's ears, of course, and they tried to rattle me with it—*"Hey, Treppenhouse! How's your ass?"*—*"Look out, Neighbors, he's got a paintball gun!"*—but they were wasting their breath. The guy they were taunting wasn't on the field. He was forbidden to set foot on this hallowed ground.

The game started off slow. Canoga had some good bats in their lineup, but our defense was more than a match for them. Likewise, their pitcher kept our own hitters quiet for the first three innings.

That changed at the bottom of the fourth. Rick Nagy hit a single, and then stole second. The next two outs came fast—Brad went down swinging, and Deke O'Beirne popped up to shallow right field. It was up to me, batting cleanup, to bring Rick home.

The chanting rose from the bleachers before I was halfway to the plate.

"T-N-T . . . T-N-T . . . T-N-T . . . T-N-T . . ."

I scanned the crowd for familiar faces as I stepped up. No sign of Dad, but Mom was here, sitting next to Unity behind the dugout. Unity looked bored—she didn't go in for sports, really, hard as she tried to like them for my sake—but when our eyes met, she smiled and blew me a kiss. I did the same.

Going back a few rows, I spotted Casey. He must have shown up late—I hadn't seen him during my last at-bat. He was with a girl—this chubby girl named Freya, who I'd been sort-of-friends with back in elementary school, but had drifted away from when she started hanging out with Chaffs.

Seeing her with Casey bothered me. *Is she his girlfriend? He didn't tell me he had a girlfriend.* Then Casey and I locked eyes, he jerked his chin, and I felt a rush of energy. I raised my bat, planted my feet in the batter's box, and went into my stance.

"T-N-T . . . T-N-T . . . T-N-T . . . T-N-T . . ."

Canoga's outfield was playing deep—they were expecting me to go for the fences. In my head, I heard Coach's words—

Don't swing at every piece of crap. I needed only to get us on the scoreboard, not blow the cover off the ball.

I took the first two strikes, then fouled off the next couple of pitches. *Patience, TNT. Wait for one that you like.*

The next set of pitches were all over the place. Canoga's pitcher was getting rattled—his control was slipping. I let the bad pitches go by and kept on fouling the good ones until I'd maxed out the count—three balls, two strikes. Then, a curveball, headed right down the middle and then dropping at the last moment . . .

I saw it coming, and I adjusted my swing. The ball met my bat with a weak-sounding *thunk*, not the dynamite blast that was my trademark—still, its trajectory was perfect. The left fielder made a valiant try for it, but he was just too far back, and the ball dropped into the dead zone between him and the shortstop. By the time he scooped it up, all he could do was hold me to a double—Rick Nagy had already crossed home plate.

Our first run of the new season. And my first RBI.

The crowd went nuts. Once the volcanic roar subsided, the chanting started anew.

"*T-N-T . . . T-N-T . . . T-N-T . . . T-N-T . . .*"

I didn't acknowledge them openly. Coach was watching—he hated it when we got cocky. But the look of approval on his face, and the war-whoops and thumbs-up signs from my teammates, were all I needed. I felt a hundred feet tall, like one of the gods in those Wagnerian operas Dad took me to when I was a kid.

The rest of the game was a seesaw. Canoga scored twice, putting them briefly in the lead, but then a two-run homer by Brad put us back on top. Finally, in the last inning, with one out and runners at first and second, Canoga's best hitter swatted a grounder right at the five-hole between me and Rick. I lunged for the ball, scooped it into my glove, and lobbed it to Deke at second, who tagged the base and then fired the ball to Jay Devereaux at first. A double play, and a game-ender—3-2 North Topanga.

I left the field feeling higher than I had in weeks. Yes—this *was* my country, my home. One day, I would take off that

Dawn Patrol outfit for good and step into a major-league uniform. I lived for this game, and I always would. A million paddlings would never take that away from me.

Monday was bright and sunny, so at lunch we commandeered a corner of the quad. To one side of me and Brad, Deke was locking lips with Andrea Hilgendorf while, farther away, Rick and Jay were having a contest to see who could toss ketchup-soaked Tater Tots into the air the highest and still catch them in his mouth. From the red splotches all over Rick's face, he was losing.

"So did you hear about Nelson?" Brad asked.

Geez. Why did Brad have to dredge that up? I was still coasting along on Friday's victory—the last thing I wanted was to rehash the paintball disaster.

"I heard he's out of the troop," I said. "I can't say I'm surprised."

"It gets worse. When he was at the emergency room getting his leg fixed, they did some tests. Turns out he's got some disease—some genetic thing that makes his bones brittle. The little feeb didn't even know he had it."

"Oh, no." Having a birth defect would have gotten Nelson barred from the Dawn Patrol anyway, but . . . "He's not going to get put away, is he?"

"Beats me. Either way, I bet you a million bucks he'll have to get his . . . " Brad held up two fingers and made a scissors-snipping motion—once, twice.

"Ugh." I had a sudden, intense urge to press my knees together. "God, Brad. Why do you have to *say* stuff like that?"

"I'm just stating facts, dude. You don't want that garbage polluting the race, do you?"

What I really wanted was to get up and leave. It wasn't just Brad, and it wasn't just that my girlfriend had become possessed by the idea of us repopulating the white race all by ourselves. I kept thinking about those old yearbooks—all those kids of different races, mingling like it was no big deal. They looked so happy, so alive—it was beautiful. Then I looked around at the ones I knew, and it seemed as if the more unpolluted *we* tried to be, the uglier we became.

The bell rang. Brad and I got up and headed for our Current History class. But then, ahead of us, there was a commotion. The students filling the breezeway around the quad clammed up and froze in place.

Amid the silence, I heard them coming from Building A, growing louder.

Boots. Lots of them.

As the crowd parted, the first thing I saw was a flash of grayish blue.

"Wide Awakes," Brad said. There was an awed, worshipful note in his voice. "I wonder who they're coming for."

Not me! I haven't done anything! The thought blasted through me, riding on top of a bolt of panic that nailed my feet to the ground and kept me from running. There was no place *to* run. Not from the Wide Awakes.

The Shock Troops of Liberty—that was what President Muldoon called his private militia. They operated by their own rules—nobody could touch them, not the police, not the courts, not even the regular military. They answered only to Our Commander-in-Chief himself.

They stormed past, amid a reek of boot polish and gun oil. On TV, or seen from a distance at Party rallies, they always had this heroic glow around them. But not up close. Their movements were thuggish, deliberately menacing—if they wanted to, they could stomp anyone in their path into a bloody gelatinous mess without breaking stride. Their jolt-sticks swung from their belts, the metal prongs at the business ends glittering. Under the visors of their caps—hardened ballcaps, just like batting helmets—their faces were blunt and unlined, like clay masks, with deep-set eyes that missed nothing and yet had no human feeling behind them.

Brad snapped to attention and saluted. The look on his face was almost dreamy. I copied the salute and forced my features into an expression I hoped was similar to his.

The Wide Awakes kept going, and I started to breathe again. Then I saw the man at the rear of the pack—a tall man, older than the others, wearing a charcoal gray suit with a DDS badge on the lapel. His head turned toward me, and I nearly fainted.

Mr. Ludlow. Unity's dad.

He glanced at me, then blew right by, obviously not here to socialize. I stood blinking, unable to move, until he and the Wide Awakes turned a corner and disappeared.

Around me, the silence of the crowd gave away to a low murmur of anxiety, and I heard Brad's voice. "Come on, TNT. Let's get to class."

I ambled in that direction, following Brad . . . and then someone bumped into me, hard. I wheeled around just in time to see who it was.

Freya, that chubby girl I'd seen with Casey at the game. She ducked into the crowd, without stopping.

I checked my pockets to make sure she hadn't picked them. Freya had a reputation as a klepto. But no—everything was still there. My wallet, my keys . . .

And, in my jacket, a tightly folded piece of paper that hadn't been there before.

I FINGERED the piece of paper in my pocket. A message from Casey, using Freya as a go-between? It had to be. But I didn't dare read it here, and there was no time before class to go anyplace private.

Brad was waving his hand in front of my face. "Come on, TNT, we'll be late."

I took my seat just as the tardy bell rang and Mr. Scudder's bald, artillery-shell-shaped form claimed his spot at the front of the room. The class snapped to attention and turned as a unit to face him.

"Nation First, Neighbors."

"NATION FIRST, MR. SCUDDER!"

A few students gave him questioning looks, as if hoping he'd tell them why the Wide Awakes were on campus, but he was all business.

"Take your seats. You will now open your books to Chapter Twenty-Seven, 'Brown Power, Brown Peril' . . ."

I hadn't done the reading, but I didn't have to. I'd been hearing this stuff since I was a kid—how America had won the war with Mexico in the 1840s and taken half its territory, but had been too softhearted to expel the . . . *racial degenerates,* the Party called them . . . living there, and instead let them multiply and take root, with their mongrelized genes and decadent culture. And how, soon, we'd have to do what our ancestors couldn't and solve the race problem once and for all.

I could recite this material in my sleep.

Eventually the class ended, and I made for the bathroom. I was in such a hurry that I almost ran into Gwen Smith coming out of the girl's bathroom next door. She muttered an excuse-me, tucked in her chin, and gave me a wide berth as I kept going.

I closed the stall door, unzipped, and did my business, unfolding the piece of paper with my free hand. The writing on it was all capitals, compact, and neater than I'd expected.

YOUR HOUSE, FRI NIGHT, 7 O'CLOCK. I GOT THE ADDRESS.
— YOUR MATH TUTOR

I scanned it twice, then a third time, as though rereading might squeeze more information out of it. Like, *How did Casey get my address?* We weren't listed in the phone book.

Finally, I tore up the note and dropped the pieces into the toilet. I had to flush twice—some of the pieces wouldn't go down the first time.

My hands were sweating. Before leaving the bathroom I ran them under the faucet, without soap—the dispenser was empty, as usual—and kept drying them until I'd destroyed a half-dozen paper towels and rubbed my palms raw.

Friday. That gave me four whole days to build up a full-blown panic. Awesome.

Later that day, I found out who the Wide Awakes had come for. Danny Magruder had seen them hauling off Forrest Van Zell—another Chaff, this big guy who looked like Frankenstein. He'd been flunking most of his classes but got A's in art, and spent every lunch period by himself, just him and a sketch pad, never talking to anyone.

Rumors flew fast and heavy. Some said Forrest had been molesting a boy in his neighborhood, and that the kid's mom had found out and called the Dentists. Others had heard that his sketchbooks contained blueprints for a bomb, and that he was planning to blow himself up along with the whole school, like those Muslim fanatics in the old days.

The whole episode put me even more on edge about Friday. When the day came, I embarrassed myself yet again at practice—I thought Coach was going to blow a blood vessel watching me. Afterwards, the rest of the guys went out for pizza, but I told them I'd promised to call Unity, and I headed home.

The grandfather clock in the living room was chiming seven when the doorbell rang. I was on the couch, playing Border Warrior on the video console. I put down the controller and bounded toward the door.

Casey was standing on the porch, his head swiveling, like he was unsure if he had the right house.

"Hey."

He had his bookbag, but no skateboard—he must have taken the bus so as not to attract attention. He'd neatened up a bit as well—combed his hair, tucked in his shirt.

"Let's go upstairs." I waved him inside. "My mom is—"

"Who's that?" Mom materialized in the doorway from the dining room, frowning.

"This is Casey. I told you about him. He's helping me with math, remember?"

"Oh, yeah. Sorry, Tyler. I thought it might be your father. Foolish me." With a snort she returned, swaying, to the dining room.

Casey raised an eyebrow at me. I just shrugged. *Yeah, my mom's drunk. Welcome to my life.*

On the way up, I stopped at Eric's room and peeked inside. The little snoop was supposed to be on a Rooster campout this weekend, but I wanted to be sure. No sign of him. Good.

I ushered Casey into my own room and shut the door. "OK, how did you get my address?"

"Through my criminal connections. How else?" He paused long enough for my heartbeat to speed up, and then he laughed. "Dude, seriously—we go to the same school. It doesn't take a detective to find out where the Mighty TNT lives."

He set his bookbag on the bed and flopped down sideways on the mattress, stretching out his long arms and legs as far as they'd go. "Whoa. Your bedroom is huge."

I stood in the middle of the room, glancing at the four walls. "It is?"

"It's twice the size of my room at the Reclamation Home. Plus, you get it all to yourself—I have to share mine with five other guys."

"That sounds . . . crowded."

"Ah, it's not that bad. I'm hardly ever there, anyway. The people who run the place are assholes—I'd just as soon not deal with them."

"Don't they check up on you?"

Casey made a face. "Yeah, right. That check they get from the government every month for my room and board—that's all they care about. Fuck them."

That didn't sound like Kevin's Reclamation Home at all. His was spacious and well kept, from what I'd seen of it, and the Willhoyts had always insisted on knowing his whereabouts. Though of course, after Kevin disappeared, they'd acted like he'd never existed, the same as everyone else.

Casey brushed the hair out of his eyes and propped himself up on his elbows. I swallowed. *What am I doing, what am I doing?* I'd never had anyone up here before, not even Unity—much less someone I'd been having intense dreams about for weeks. Seeing the star of those dreams sprawled on my bed was making me nervous and sweaty. And excited, if the wood sprouting below my belt was a clue . . .

I turned around and fumbled in the dresser for a clean shirt—the one I had on was feeling damp and clingy. I'd just taken a white T-shirt out of the drawer when Casey said, "Put on something dark. Something that'll make it hard to see you at night."

I gave him a sharp look in the mirror over the dresser. "What for?"

"I thought we'd go on kind of a field trip later. You game?"

"A field trip? Where? Does this have anything to do with K——?"

"Yeah." Casey did one of those side-to-side, the-walls-have-ears glances. "I'll tell you about it in the car."

I looked down. While I wasn't paying attention, my hand had put the white T-shirt back in the drawer and was fingering a midnight blue one instead. I pulled the old shirt off over my head and tossed it in the laundry hamper. As I did, Casey blinked, grabbed his bookbag, and set it in his lap.

I put on the blue shirt, squaring my shoulders as I smoothed out the creases. "I don't know . . . Something's up. The Wide Awakes showed up at school a few days ago. Did you hear?"

A grim nod. "They got Forrest."

"Did you know him?"

"Not really. We didn't hang out—he was kind of a head case. His Evaluation was coming up—they must have thought he was about to do something stupid." He unzipped the bag and took out a copy of the same book I used in math class. Then he got up, crossed over to the desk, and flashed me a grin. "Relax, slugger. I'm not stupid."

For an hour or so, we did exactly what I'd told Mom we'd be doing—my math homework. Casey really was a wiz at it. Normally it took me half a day of scribbling and hair-pulling just to finish one assignment—this time, thanks to Casey, I got through a whole week's worth in less than an hour. And that included copying it in my own handwriting to make it look like I'd done all the work myself.

I pushed back from the desk and frowned down at the paper. "I've never cheated on my schoolwork before."

"Everybody cheats at something. They make it impossible not to." Casey was crouched down beside me, one elbow resting on the back of my chair. "And this isn't really cheating, anyway. It's not like I did all the work for you, is it?"

"I guess not."

A drawn-out silence followed. From down the hall came the murmur of the TV in my parents' room—by now, Mom would be passed out in front of it. With Eric gone, and Dad off at some meeting or other, the rest of the house was like a tomb.

Casey made some stretching motions and stood up. As he did, he laid a hand on my shoulder for support. His touch was quick and casual, but it hit me like an electrical shock and sucked the breath out of me. His hands were slender, but powerful. Even through my shirt, I could feel every ridge and whorl on his fingertips.

He put his book back in the bag and zipped it up. "Ready to go?"

"It's almost curfew. There'll be checkpoints all over the place."

"I'll steer us around them. I've done it a million times." He cocked his head and smiled again. "Trust me."

And I did—I did trust him. As he looked at me, the spot on my shoulder where he'd laid his hand grew warmer. It was a comforting warmth, calming.

I got up from the desk and reached for my jacket.

"Just be cool." Casey straightened up and put on his seat-belt as the spinning lights of the police checkpoint came into view. "Remember our cover story."

I rolled to a stop and lowered the Fenris' side window, keeping my hands in plain view until the approaching police officer asked for my driver's license. It was a chilly night, but the sweat was beading on my forehead.

"Treppenhouse . . ." The officer studied my license. "You related to James Treppenhouse? With the OCPM?"

"Yes, sir. He's my dad."

"He know you're out past curfew?"

"That's my fault, officer," Casey said. "We were studying for a test, lost track of time. Neighbor Treppenhouse is just taking me home."

He gave me his ID card, which I passed along to the

policeman. It was too dim to see the man's expression, but I noticed his posture get tense.

"Monahan. You're a Reclaimee?"

"Yes, Neighbor. Just trying to do my best for the Nation."

The officer took both our cards and went to talk to his partner. I felt like I was dissolving into the seat upholstery. Next to me, Casey sat gazing out the windshield. His profile was serene—angelic, almost.

The policeman returned and handed our cards back. "Go straight home after you drop him off." He stepped back and waved us through. "Nation First."

I'd gone several blocks and turned a corner before I dared say anything. "Geez, that was close."

"Not really. They're just cops, not Wide Awakes. You think some LAPD dipshit's going to risk his job hassling a Party official's kid? You could get away with murder if you wanted to." Casey was staring into the side mirror. "Turn left at the next signal."

I followed his directions. We wound along side streets, avoiding intersections where there might be more check-points. Eventually we swung into a cul-de-sac, looped around so we were facing outward, and stopped.

"Wait a minute." My intestines were tying themselves in knots again. "I know where we are. No."

Up ahead, the street ended in a T-intersection facing an apartment complex. I recognized it. In a flash, I realized what Casey had in mind. Go to the intersection and look right, and I'd see it a couple of blocks down—the brilliantly lit sign saying NORTH TOPANGA HIGH SCHOOL.

"No." I was shaking my head so fast, I could have snapped my own neck. "We aren't. We are *not* breaking into the school."

"Not the school-school. Just Lenskold's office."

"The *Morality Officer?*" My voice shot up a full octave. "Are you *crazy?*"

"She keeps files on all the Reclaimees. If anyone knows what happens to them, she does."

"We'll get caught. We'll get *arrested*. We'll get sent off to the *Dentists*." Still shaking my head, I gripped the steering wheel with both hands. "Forget it. This is nuts. It's too dangerous."

Casey turned toward me. In the stark, razor-shadowed light cast by the streetlamps outside, his mouth twitched into a half-smile.

I took one hand off the wheel and ran it over my scalp. "You're trying to make a point, aren't you?"

"Yeah. Trying to find out shit that the Muldoonies don't want you to know? You're right—it's dangerous. Guys like you have no idea. You want to find out? I'll help you, but you'd better be ready. If you're not, you should just go home, stay safe, and forget the whole thing."

Was I ready? If I went home now, Casey would peg me as a chicken. Besides . . . stay safe? I'd done that my entire life, and in return, I'd been lied to—about Kevin, about everything. If I turned back now, the lies would never stop.

"I'm ready." I took a deep breath. When I exhaled, it came out sounding like a whimper. "Oh, *fuck*."

Casey's eyebrows arched. "Dude! Language! Do you say the Dawn Patrol Oath with that mouth?"

Before getting in the car, Casey had put on a dark blue hoodie. As we got out, he pulled the hood up over his head. "Take your jacket off."

"What? Why?"

"Those letter jackets are personalized, aren't they? That's a dead giveaway—you might as well just write your name on a piece of paper and hold it up to the nearest Hawkeye. Put a cap on, too, if you've got one—it'll help hide your face."

I shucked off my jacket and donned a Los Angeles Dodgers cap that had been lying under the back seat. The nighttime chill hit my bare arms, the goosebumps rose, and I shivered.

Casey had taken out that flask of his. He raised it to his lips, swallowed, and offered it to me. "Liquid courage. Go for it. Just one shot."

I took two. The stuff went down like molten lava, and the fumes singed the hair out of my nostrils. But once I stopped coughing, the chill was gone, and I felt less jittery.

We took off jogging toward the school. Casey led the way down the middle of the street, tracing a path through the shadows cast by the streetlights. There was no traffic, and all the houses were dark. Dead silence hung over the neighborhood.

Climbing the security fence around the school grounds was no big deal. Kids did it all the time, to escape the cafeteria and forage for real food at lunchtime. I'd never needed to, having an off-campus lunch pass, but I knew it could be done. Casey, no doubt, had done it a million times.

He headed straight for what I assumed was a blind spot between two of the Hawkeyes mounted on top of the fence. As we reached it, he dropped to one knee and laced his hands together, palms up, forming a stirrup. "You first."

I planted one foot in his linked hands and let him give me a boost. Even with the assist, scaling the fence was a struggle—the posts had some sort of slippery coating, and the thin crossbars gave me almost no footing. But with some flailing I made it to the top, got my legs over, and slid halfway down the other side before flopping onto the grass like a bag of oranges.

Now it was Casey's turn.

He sprang, uncoiled his arms, and grabbed hold of the fence just a few inches shy of the top. A few swift, graceful movements, and he was up and over. He landed on his feet like a cat, coming to rest in another crouch with his fingertips just touching the ground, letting his legs absorb the impact.

I slumped back, gaping at him

Holy crap, that was hot.

Casey was already halfway to Building A. He leaped up the front steps and then halted, waiting.

"Take this." He pulled a bandana out of his pocket and handed it to me. "Anything you touch in there, wipe off your fingerprints."

The door lock had both a card swipe and a numeric keypad. Casey produced a keycard and another bandana, which he draped over the fingers of one hand before punching the keypad, slowly, like he was trying to remember the code. When he finished he tensed up, but then relaxed when the light on the keypad flashed green. He slashed the card through the swipe, and opened the door.

I pointed at the card. "Where did you——?"

Casey shot me a look. *Later.*

We crept past the display case with all the school trophies, past the team pennants and Dawn Patrol banners. At night, with no one else around, our footsteps resonated in my ears like bomb blasts no matter how quiet we tried to be. Even the rustling of our clothes seemed to echo up and down the hall. Above us, in the ceiling, the Hawkeyes glittered, black and shiny and all-seeing. I pulled the visor of my cap down over my eyes and kept my face angled toward the floor.

We reached the center of the building, where the two main corridors intersected, and started past the mural of Our Commander-in-Chief on the steps of the U.S. Capitol, giving his inaugural address fifteen years ago. Here, Casey halted. He swung around to face the mural, struck a pose mimicking the C-in-C's—eyes aimed skyward, one grasping hand held high as if pulling lightning straight down from Heaven—clicked his heels, saluted, and kept going. The mockery made me cringe. I half-expected lightning to strike for real.

Neighbor Lenskold's office was around the corner. Another keycard swipe, and we were inside.

"Jesus," Casey whispered, wrinkling his nose. "It smells like a perfume grenade exploded in here."

I stood there, waiting for my eyes to adjust to the dark. Part of me was screaming inside. *Get out of there! You'll get caught!* But another part was just as pumped as during our opening game. *T-N-T . . . T-N-T . . .*

Casey sat down at Neighbor Lenskold's desk and switched on the computer. "I've got this. Go check her paper files."

I crept over to the filing cabinet and switched on the gooseneck lamp on top of it. The first two drawers were labeled RECLAIMEES, alphabetized by last name. I opened the N-Z drawer and combed through the folders, using the bandana to wipe down any spot where I touched them. Behind me, I could hear Casey's fingers clicking on the keyboard.

I made two passes through the S's. Nothing. If a file existed on Kevin Sanders, it wasn't here anymore.

Chaffs

With a groan of disappointment, I closed the drawer. But then an impulse hit me. I pulled open the other drawer and started going through the M's.

There it was—MONAHAN, C. The folder was huge, almost four fingers thick.

"Hey, Casey—I found your file. Want to see it?"

The keystrokes stopped. "Fuck, no."

"Really? I'd want to see it if I were you."

"I said no."

His voice had taken on a brittle edge.

I stared down at the file, tempted to look through it myself, but then went over it with the bandana instead, put it back, and closed the drawer. There wasn't enough time, and we weren't here to see what Neighbor Lenskold had on Casey, anyway.

I finished wiping down the cabinet, then turned back toward the desk. "Anything on the computer?"

Casey didn't answer. His fingers sat frozen on the keyboard. In the phosphorescent glow from the screen, his face was colorless, his eyes wide, his mouth hanging open in . . . shock? Fear? Anger? Whatever it was, Casey was freaked.

"Casey? What's wrong?"

"Huh? Oh, nothing." With one tap on the keyboard, he made the screen go blank. Then he reached over and switched off the computer. "I really thought Lenskold might have something. Sorry about the wild goose chase."

"No worries. But what were you looking at just now? It looked impor—"

Somewhere in the building a door slammed. Casey and I both froze. I listened, hoping it had just been the wind or something . . . but no. I heard voices, what sounded like the squawking of a radio . . . and footsteps, coming up the hall toward us.

Not just footsteps. Boots. In my head I could practically see the men in blue uniforms wearing them.

Wide Awakes!

Casey's gaze darted over to the coat closet, and he made a beeline for it. I started to follow, but then doubled back to switch off the lamp on the filing cabinet before joining him.

The knob on the closet door had one of those old-fashioned mechanical locks on the inside. Casey twisted it as he shut the door.

There was barely enough room for the two of us. My body was pressed up against Casey's, trapping him between me and the door. Behind me, empty coathangers tickled the back of my skull. I didn't dare move for fear of making them rattle. I couldn't see a thing in the blackness, but I could feel Casey's hot breath on my forehead and smell the harsh tang of our mingled fear sweat.

Someone switched on a light. Shadows flickered around and under the door Muffled voices came through it. Two, four, a dozen? I couldn't tell how many.

The doorknob jiggled. I squeezed my eyes shut and held my breath. More voices. Debating whether to open the closet, maybe? I couldn't make the words out. My pulse battered my eardrums. *This is it. We're dead. We are so fucking dead . . .*

The radio squawked again. Whatever it said, it sounded urgent. There was an explosion of movement on the other side of the door. The light went off, the boots stampeded away, and the voices faded.

Casey inhaled deeply, then blew it out. His breath rippled in sync with the shudder I felt go through him.

"I think they're gone," he whispered.

Every muscle in my body had gone slack and was quivering. It was an adrenaline rebound, like I'd just dodged a fastball aimed right at my head, only a million times more intense. I slumped against Casey. I had to grab his shoulders just to keep standing.

Even in the dark I could sense the amber gleam of his eyes, looking at me. Looking into me.

I tilted my head up to meet them.

And then we were kissing.

C ASEY'S mouth had a faint taste of cigarettes, but with something underneath, like honey spiked with red pepper. I couldn't get enough of it. The more I consumed, the more I needed. I felt like I was going to die if I didn't devour it all . . .

I gripped his waist and pulled him to me with all my strength. His hands engulfed my head. His fingers seared the rims of my ears. Our heartbeats were falling into sync. Casey's thigh was rubbing the wood between mine. He made a low, throaty sound through our locked lips, his hips pressed against me, he was . . .

He was just as hard as I was.

There was a screeching in my head, a slamming of brakes. I catapulted away from Casey, against the back of the closet. The coathangers clanged like alarm bells.

Get out of here.

I almost knocked Casey over lunging for the doorknob. "Tyler—wait—"

Get out of here. Now.

I stumbled into Neighbor Lenskold's office, and bolted. Into the corridor. Around the corner, past the mural, toward the door—toward my escape. My escape from . . .

Across the lawn, the fence loomed. I went for it.

Something—someone—*Casey!*—grabbed my arm, yanking me sideways. I staggered under the eaves of the building, into the shadows.

I whirled around, fists up. *If that faggot touches me again —*

He didn't. He reared away, both hands in the air. His head jerked toward the fence, once, twice . . .

At the van parked on the other side. Around it, a half-dozen Wide Awakes stood on alert. If Casey hadn't stopped me, I would have run right into their arms.

Another head-jerk. *This way.*

We stuck close to the building until we'd crept around the corner. On this side the fence was only a few feet away. I flew over it, panic blasting through me like rocket fuel. My legs started pumping the instant I landed. Once I cleared the school grounds I looped around the apartment complex across the street, turned onto the next block, and exploded into a full-tilt run back to my car.

I tried to get there ahead of Casey, but he outran me. By the time I reached the car he was already grabbing his book-bag out of the back seat.

I collapsed against the driver's side. I couldn't catch my breath. This was like reliving every scare I'd ever had, all at once. I was defenseless, exposed, naked.

Casey was holding the bag in front of him. Like a shield—or a weapon. "OK, *that* was close. In more ways than one."

"Are you . . . ?" Between gasps, I tried to speak. But I kept running out of air before I could get the last word out. "Are you . . . Are you . . . ?"

"Am I gay? Yeah."

How could he say it so matter-of-factly? And . . . *gay?* What an old-fashioned word. Nobody said *gay* anymore.

"And what about you?" he asked.

"A-am I queer?" *I don't know.* My chest felt like it was being crushed in a vise. "No. I'm not queer. I'm not."

Casey shrugged. "That's cool. A lot of straight guys like to fool around now and then." His voice had a smile in it. "You're a better kisser than most."

"A better . . . ?" My breath had come back. Now it was hissing through my teeth. "You kissed *me*."

"OK. I kissed you."

Even in the dark, I could picture him rolling his eyes.

"I'm not queer. I have a girlfriend. I'm going to marry her."

"Congratulations."

I leaned on both hands against the car—it was either that or wrap them around Casey's neck. Except . . . who was I kidding? Even if I had been close enough to throttle him, I probably would have just kissed him again.

He was scratching his head behind one ear. "Look, I won't cause you any trouble, OK? You've got way more to lose than I do. If you want to pretend nothing happened—"

"Nothing *did* happen."

"No worries. Nothing happened."

With his usual athletic grace, he slung his bag over one shoulder, then the other.

"I need to walk this off." He made a quick gesture in front of his crotch. "Be careful going home—there may be more Wide Awakes around."

"Casey—"

But he was already gone, leaving me alone on the dark, dead-end street.

I'm not queer. I can't be queer. I can't be.

I backtracked home, following the same route Casey had navigated, as much of it as I could remember. No checkpoints, no Wide Awakes. By the time I pulled into the driveway, the house was dark.

I went into the bathroom and ran a hand through my hair. I'd forgotten something—I could feel it. But my brains were too scrambled to figure out what.

I splashed some water on my face and tried to look in the mirror. I couldn't. My own reflection made me want to curl into a ball on the floor. I saw my face superimposed on one of those glittery freaks in the videos. Or one of the depraved souls that Reverend Blanchard fire-and-brimstoned about on Sundays.

"If a man lie with a man, as he lieth with a woman, it is an abomination. Both of them shall surely be put to death."

Going to bed didn't help. Casey had been lounging on it, and now he was on the bedspread, the pillow, even the sheets. His scent was overpowering, like the taste of his mouth—and it was all over me, *in* me. Lying on this bed was like . . . lying with him.

My hands were thinking the same thing. I pulled up the covers and clutched the blanket in a death grip. I had to quit giving in to these urges.

"If a man lie with a man . . . "

Casey wasn't even that good-looking. He was too tall and gawky, and he had that weird nose, and his hair was black and shiny like a Mexican's.

Yeah. That hair, which practically begged me to grab handfuls of it. That nose, which when angled a certain way gave him a profile like a Greek statue. And that frame, which contained more self-confidence in a single movement than I would ever possess in my life, and which transformed into a picture of ultimate grace and athleticism as soon he stepped onto that skateboard . . .

"Homosexuality is not a 'preference' or an 'orientation.' It is a key tactic in the psychological castration of the White American Male."

That one came from the Dawn Patrol Handbook. It was a quote from Our Commander-in-Chief himself.

Well, I for one had not been castrated, psychologically or otherwise. I was the Mighty TNT. I wasn't some sissy-boy. I wasn't . . .

I wasn't a traitor to the Nation. We *executed* traitors. On TV.

Preference? What did *that* mean? Did a homosexual simply wake up one morning and say to himself, "I *prefer* guys"? That was insane. Who would do that? Not me.

But I still thought about guys, still dreamed about them. Fighting those thoughts and dreams only made them stronger.

And when I tried not to think about Casey, I simply wound up wanting him more.

It wasn't fair.

The next day, I called Unity.

"Sweetie! Hi!" she chirped. "Are we still going to the movies tonight?"

"Actually . . ."

Casey had said it himself. Lots of guys had thoughts about other guys. Some even acted on them. That didn't make *them* queer.

"I've been thinking. About what we talked about a couple weeks ago?" I took a breath and composed myself. "You're right. It's time."

Her squeal made me wince and hold the phone away from my ear.

"Oh, Ty! I'm so happy! Thank you!" She took a moment to settle down. "Why don't you come over around six? Daddy got called into work this weekend—some big investigation. We'll have the whole house to ourselves."

To ourselves. Perfect.

"Six it is."

"Don't be late."

Unity was all smiles. As she let me in, her arms coiled around me. I made a point of kissing her more deeply than usual.

"Ooh, Ty." She fanned herself with one hand. "That was . . . nice. I got a bottle of wine—come open it for me, would you?"

She detached herself from me and skipped off toward the kitchen. "Are you hungry? I can heat up some spaghetti."

"Nah, I just ate." Or poked around my plate with a fork, anyway—I had zero interest in food.

Unity handed me the bottle and a corkscrew, then took a pair of wine glasses out of the cupboard. She was almost bouncing off the walls—from happiness, I hoped, rather than anxiety. I was anxious enough for both of us.

I'd been opening bottles for Mom since I was a kid—the cork came out of this one with no trouble at all. Unity beamed at me—her face had this you're-so-strong-and-masculine look.

The label on the bottle made my jaw drop. "From France? Where'd you get this?"

"Oh, Daddy can get anything. Those Europeans—they're so self-righteous. Like they're going to hurt us with some stupid trade embargo."

"But this stuff is expensive, isn't it?"

"This is a special occasion." She filled the glasses, handed me one, and raised the other one by the stem. "To the Nation."

"To the Nation."

We clinked glasses, and sipped like we were taking Communion. Except we used grape juice when we did it in church.

"Sweetie, it's OK." Unity saw the glass wobbling in my hand, and laid her own hand on my forearm. "This is my first time too, you know. Let's go watch TV for a while, and relax."

We migrated into the living room. It felt like a bunker, with thick, sound-swallowing carpet and heavy furniture that could double as shelter during an earthquake or a terrorist attack. On the mantelpiece, flanked by two candles, there was a portrait of Unity's mom. I didn't know exactly how she died—in a traffic accident, or maybe a plane crash, before the Ludlows moved to L.A. It made Unity sad to talk about her, so we hardly ever did.

The overstuffed couch was super-comfortable. Unity and I sank into it.

There wasn't much on TV—just the news. Victories in the Middle East, anti-insurgent campaigns in Texas, excerpts from Our Commander-in-Chief's daily address, arrests in the

Chaffs

Christmas Eve bombing of that church in Oklahoma—the usual. Although the price of gas had dropped to sixteen dollars a gallon. That was worth hearing.

After a few minutes, Unity reached for the remote, switched off the TV, and tuned the radio to the oldies station.

I settled back and slipped my arm around her. The wine was doing its job. This was nice—warm and safe, like it was supposed to be. Unity was bringing out the male in me, just like she used to when we first started dating.

She tilted her head up, her lips close to mine. I bent down to meet them. Kissing her didn't give me the same rush I got from kissing Casey, but it didn't matter—I pushed through and kept going, into uncharted territory. I pulled her closer and slid my free hand under her skirt, up the baby-smooth skin on the inside of her thigh, farther. She was soaking wet up there. I explored gingerly with my fingertips. Her breath caught and then sped up. So did mine.

Between whispers she laid a chain of light kisses down my neck and chest. "I'm going to go change. Wait five minutes and then come upstairs."

As soon as she left, the anxiety returned. *What if I can't do this?* I had wood right now, but for how long? If I couldn't do this, she'd know—*I'd* know. It would prove beyond a doubt that I was —

I grabbed the wine bottle, filled my glass, and emptied it in three gulps. I sat back, closed my eyes, and listened to the song on the radio—some slow doo-wop ballad. The singers sounded black, which surprised me. But then, I never listened to the oldies station—maybe songs with black musicians were OK if they were from fifty years ago.

The harmonizing voices poured over me. Then the song ended, and I opened my eyes. Five minutes had gone by.

Time to do My Duty to the Nation.

At the top of the stairs, an amber glow wafted from the half-open door to Unity's room. I entered, and found myself surrounded by lit candles—a dozen at least, all over the room. Unity lay on the bed, wide-eyed, expectant, vulnerable. I could tell she'd been building this moment up in her head for a long time.

She was wearing a white silk robe, with lace around the neckline and a sash tied around her waist. It clung to her, sheer and translucent, revealing the bare skin underneath.

I ran my dry tongue over my even dryer lips. "Um, wow."

"I'm glad you like it." Her smile went crooked and devious. "Aren't you a little overdressed?"

"Huh? Oh, yeah."

I fumbled out of my clothes—shirt, shoes and socks, pants. I hesitated for a second, then took off my briefs as well and joined Unity on the bed, kneeling above her. As she gazed up at me, her eyes went wider, and her cheeks and the V of her neckline started to redden. I was blushing too, though more out of embarrassment than lust. Hopefully Unity wouldn't know the difference.

I blinked at her, wondering what to do next. Smiling again, she took one end of the sash and flicked it at me. I got the hint, and with a nervous laugh I loosened the sash, opened the robe, and peeled the delicate fabric off her shoulders.

Her body looked different than I expected. I'd seen pictures of naked girls before—Brad's dad headed the local chapter of the Vice Prevention League, and for research he had a big stack of illegal magazines, which Brad busted out whenever the guys came over—but Unity was less . . . airbrushed. With shaking hands, I reached for her. Her skin was creamy and smooth, her breasts pleasantly soft. But what I was feeling, down below . . . I *admired* her body, sure, but I wasn't *wanting* it, like I ought to be. . .

I laid down on top of her and kissed her again. With concentration, I got myself stiff enough to proceed. My attempts at entry kept missing—after the third failed try, Unity reached down and guided me into her. She tensed up, then relaxed, raising her knees. Her gaze drifted to one side, to the picture of President Muldoon on the wall. In the candlelight it looked like Our Commander-in-Chief was smiling right at us, blessing this sacred ceremony.

"Unity? Is this OK?"

"Yes . . . oh, yes. Make love to me, Ty."

How?

Chaffs

Damn . . . I was losing my wood! I pressed down to keep from falling out of her, and she winced.

"I'm sorry, Unity. I'm just . . . I'm just nervous."

Focus, TNT. I didn't need to hit a grand slam—all I had to do was get around the bases. I kissed her again, closed my eyes . . .

And I felt him—Casey. It was his lips I was kissing, not Unity's. He pulled me back into that closet, the door closed, and suddenly I was at full attention. I didn't resist him—I let it happen. This was all in my head, after all—Unity didn't have to know . . .

Move.

I started carefully. Unity felt so fragile—I didn't want to hurt her. But soon her leg muscles tightened and she was moving with me. I opened my eyes and looked at her. Her jaw was clenched, one set of fingers digging into my back, the other clutching the sheet beside her. I increased the rhythm. This wouldn't take much longer—I was already close. As I felt the pressure building I screwed my eyes shut again and went back . . . back to the closet . . .

Finally, I popped. Underneath me, Unity tensed up, then went still.

I rolled onto my back, panting. On the ceiling, shadows from the candles were dancing like living things. I stared up at them, searching for patterns, for signs that anything had changed. I felt caved-in, hollow.

By the time I caught my breath, Unity had turned onto her side to face me, her head propped on her arm.

I returned her gaze. "Was that OK?"

"That was wonderful."

She kissed me, nestled into the crook of my shoulder, took my hand, and laid it against her stomach. "We're going to make such a beautiful baby. We're going to make the Nation so proud." She let go of my hand and wiped away a tear. "I love you, Ty."

We lay quietly. After a while we had sex again. The second time was easier, physically. But I was still only going through the motions, and at the end of it, that hollow feeling was even more painful.

By then it was eight-thirty. Unity got up and blew out the candles while I picked up my clothes and got dressed, in a rush to get home before curfew.

I DREADED seeing Unity at church the next day. Despite what she'd said, I was convinced the whole thing had been a letdown for her. But when I saw her in the choir, my worries disappeared. Her face was glowing.

Her dad was still pulling a weekender at the DDS, so after church we went back to her house. This time she asked me to sleep over. Sex with her still left me feeling hollowed-out, but maybe guys were *supposed* to feel that way—how was I to know? I did enjoy making Unity feel good, and judging from her . . . reactions . . . I was getting better at that, with practice.

Maybe I'd eventually grow to like it myself. Or at least get used to it.

I left Unity's house before dawn and ran two laps around the reservoir. By the time I'd gone home, showered, and gotten dressed, I was late for school. I arrived to find a jam-up of cars at the entrance to the parking lot . . .

And a pair of Wide Awakes at the gate.

More Wide Awakes roamed the campus, checking IDs and doing random searches. The students were all doing their best to ignore them. Nobody was succeeding.

At my locker, it took a full minute of deep breathing just to steady my hands enough to work the combination. Based on what I'd overheard in the halls about what was going on, there were already three or four distinct rumors, ranging from plausible to ridiculous—but I knew the truth.

This was about Friday night. It had to be.

Then I remembered—*my Dodgers cap!* I'd been wearing it in Neighbor Lenskold's office, but when Casey and I got back to my car, it was gone. It must have fallen off in the closet while we were —

I slumped against the lockers. My insides couldn't decide which direction to spew out of me.

My cap—they'd found it, no question. And it wouldn't take long to trace it to me. The DDS had labs that could do it, that could read my DNA. A single hair caught in the headband, a speck of dried sweat—that was all they needed . . .

A hand clamped down on my shoulder. I spun around, and almost screamed like a girl. But it was only Brad.

"Geez, TNT, you're awfully jumpy. Know what this is all about?"

I shook my head, a little too fast. "Sorry. Not a clue."

"I hate this—the suspense is killing me. I'd ask Hanna, but he's going to be in meetings with people all morning."

He straightened up and saluted. Some Wide Awakes were muscling their way down the hall. There was nowhere to run, so I just stood there, petrified. But the Wide Awakes stomped by without stopping.

"Dude, are you OK? You look like you're about to blorf."

"Yeah . . . I'm fine. I guess the suspense is getting to me, too."

Brad put his hands on his hips and sighed. "I guess we'll find out soon enough."

During homeroom the principal made an announcement over the PA system. "Students, there will be an assembly today at second period. Attendance is mandatory. Teachers and staff, at that time report to the faculty lounge. Thank you. Nation First."

The auditorium was already filling when I got there. As I walked in, I spotted Freya in the back row, looking fantastically unimpressed with everyone and everything. There was no sign of Casey.

Those of us in the Dawn Patrol were sitting together in the first several rows—except for Billy, who had a seat on the stage and was in full uniform, as Troop Leader. Next to him sat Neighbor Lenskold, looking like she'd just bitten into something gross. Occupying the last two seats were a granite block of a man in Wide Awakes blue . . .

And Mr. Ludlow, in his dark suit with the DDS badge. So. This was why Unity's dad had been at work all weekend.

The principal—a thin and weaselly creature who'd been here only since the start of the semester, and whose name I didn't even know yet—walked up to the podium and tapped on the microphone. "Good morning, students. Thank you for your punctuality. You all know Neighbor Lenskold, of course, and Troop Leader Hanna of the Dawn Patrol. Also joining us are Squad Commander McClintock of the Wide Awakes, and Investigator Ludlow of the Department of Domestic Security."

Silence fell.

"You've been hearing rumors, no doubt, so I won't waste time. On Friday night, there was a break-in here at North Topanga High. Nothing was stolen, but some sensitive files were compromised—including campus security and emergency procedures."

Compromised? Casey and I didn't compromise anything . . .

The principal raised his voice to be heard above the anxious murmurs of the crowd. "*At this time,* we have no reason to believe an attack on the school is imminent. However, your safety is our primary concern, so as we work to identify and punish the culprits, we have introduced some enhanced security measures. Effective immediately . . ."

He ran through the measures. No leaving campus during school hours, no exceptions—all off-campus lunch passes revoked until further notice. No wandering the halls or other public areas during classes unless accompanied by a faculty or staff member. No loitering in bathrooms, on stairs, or at building entrances. Daily locker inspections. Random spot-checks of purses and backpacks. And so on.

"In addition, the North Topanga High School Dawn Patrol will be in full uniform and assisting with campus security for the duration. Troop Leader Hanna will be meeting with them immediately following this assembly. On behalf of the school, I have promised him, Neighbor Ludlow, and Neighbor McClintock our full cooperation as we see our way through this crisis. Does anyone have questions?"

No one did, of course. They wouldn't have asked them, anyway, not with a Dentist sitting right there. This whole time, Mr. Ludlow had been scanning the crowd, scrutinizing faces—mine included. God only knew what he was learning from our expressions.

"Thank you all for your time. Hopefully things will be back to normal very soon. Nation First!"

"NATION FIRST!"

While the crowd filtered out, Billy came down and rejoined the rest of the Dawn Patrol. He had even more of a look-how-important-I-am spring in his step than usual. He was holding something behind his back, out of view. If it was my cap, I swore, I was going to have a heart attack right there in the auditorium.

Brad was the first to speak. "Aw geez, do we really have to wear our uniforms every freaking day? What's up with that?"

Billy's voice was arctic. "Most of us are proud to put on the uniform, Neighbor Nemechuk."

"Hey, I'm plenty proud. It's just uncomfortable, that's all."

"Get used to it. That goes for all of you." Billy puffed out his scrawny chest. "At the briefing this morning I received some additional information. Some evidence that hasn't been made public."

He showed us what he was holding. No, thank God, it wasn't my cap. It was a single sheet of paper, sealed in a clear plastic bag with an official-looking yellow label. Both sides of the paper were covered with typewritten, single-spaced text. I couldn't read it—the print was too small, and Billy kept waving the paper around—but on what I assumed was the front, I made out a color rendering of an upside-down American flag and a stark black headline saying WE ARE THE SECRET SIX.

"During their search, the Wide Awakes found these flyers stuffed into some of the lockers in Building H," Billy said. "It appears that the spreaders of this filth were interrupted and fled, otherwise they might have hit every locker in the school."

The Secret Six—I recognized that name from the list Neighbor Lenskold had shown me. So that was why the Wide Awakes had double-timed it out of her office before discovering me and Casey. Our lives might well have been saved by whoever had been distributing that flyer.

"What's it say?" The question came from behind me.

"Seditious lies, what else?" Billy held up the flyer for us all to see, though again waving it around so that none of the poisonous words on it could be read. "If you see a copy, confiscate it and bring it to me or Investigator Ludlow immediately.

"And one more thing." He fixed each of us with his gaze, one by one. "I received another piece of news that is even more disturbing. The DDS believes this break-in was an inside job. A teacher, or a student. Maybe even one of us."

Suddenly every head in the troop was swiveling, regarding everyone else with suspicion. I joined in. I wished I had a mirror in front of me so I could see my own face. Was I incriminating myself already, just sitting here?

"We've been tasked with helping the DDS identify the traitor," Billy said. "I want you all on high alert. Report anything unusual you see—keep an eye on everyone around you. And on each other—*especially* each other."

"When we find him, can I break his legs?" Brad asked.

"You'll have to get in line." A grin slithered across Billy's face. "But yes. Once we ferret out this . . . this *stain*. . . I'll make sure we get the payback we deserve—*before* the Dentists take him in. You have my word, Neighbors."

"So how was your date, TNT?"

I pretended not to hear Brad. It wasn't difficult—I was so distracted by the Wide Awakes stationed around the cafeteria. Every time they moved, another knot twisted in my stomach.

"Dude. Hello? Your date. You told me you and Unity were going out Saturday night. What did you guys do?"

"Oh . . . nothing. We stayed in."

"Stayed in, huh?" Brad's eyebrows shot up. "OK, spill. How far did you get? Second base? Third?"

I squirmed in my seat, blushing.

"Well, I'll be damned. The Mighty TNT hit one out of the park!" He did a fist-pump and then swung around to face the rest of the table. "Check it out! Treppenhouse here lost his cherry!"

The whole table erupted in applause.

I glowered at Brad from under the hand shading my eyes. "I swear, I'm going to kill you."

"So how was she?" Brad leaned toward me, eager for a full report.

"What, like I'm going to tell *you* anything?"

"Aw, come on. If it was the other way around, I'd tell *you* all the gory details."

Chuckling, he glanced past me . . . and went dead still. The color fled from his face. He cleared his throat and sat up at attention. I twisted around to see what he was looking at, and —

"M-Mr. Ludlow."

"Tyler." Unity's dad—*Oh God, he didn't overhear Brad shooting his mouth off just now, did he?*—peered down at me through his glasses. "I thought I should stop by and say hello. Would you like to introduce me to your teammates?"

The whole table had fallen into poleaxed silence. I went around it, stammering out names. Mr. Ludlow acknowledged each one with a smile and a polite nod.

"It's a pleasure meeting you all, Neighbors." He gave me the same inscrutable smile. "Tyler, may I have a moment?"

He directed me to the edge of the eating area, near the big portrait of Our Commander-in-Chief. My mind was gibbering. This had to be about me and Unity—if this were about the break-in, he'd have summoned me to the office he'd taken over in Building A, or ordered that I be brought there, bodily—but that knowledge reassured me not at all.

There were a pair of Wide Awakes propping up the nearest wall. One glance from Mr. Ludlow, and they saluted and left.

"So." He steepled his fingers. "My daughter tells me that the two of you spent quite a length of time together this past weekend."

"Um, yeah—I mean, yes, sir." I couldn't decide what to focus on—Mr. Ludlow, or the face of the C-in-C staring down at me. "Unity . . . we . . . she said you—"

"You misunderstand me. I'm not chastizing you—I'm thanking you."

As Mr. Ludlow moved, his glasses caught the glare from the fluorescent lights, shooting white discs into my eyes. "Unity loves you very much. You do realize that."

"Yes, sir. I do."

"After her mother died, I honestly feared I'd never see her smile again. But now . . . " For a second, his own smile became more genuine. "You make her very happy, and I'm grateful."

I didn't know what to say. *You're welcome?* That sounded tacky.

Mr. Ludlow went on. "This . . . proposition, regarding the Virginia Dare Institute—I gather you have reservations about it. Would you care to share them with me?"

Not really, no.

"Sir, it's just . . . we were going to wait till we got married. Faith, Family, Freedom, right? Having a baby now, out of wedlock, just to give it up—it just seems, I don't know . . . "

"Hypocritical?"

"Well . . . yeah."

"There's a fine line between hypocrisy and pragmatism. When you're older, that line will be easier to discern." He angled himself toward the larger-than-life face of Our Commander-in-Chief. "The Nation needs to increase its numbers—that is a fact. We mustn't allow our Puritan moralism to become a means of racial suicide, don't you agree?"

He nodded at the C-in-C, then turned back to face me. "Of course, it's what Unity thinks that matters here. This isn't simply about duty to the Nation, for her. She wants to bear *your* children, not some anonymous donor's. However much it may run counter to your . . . inclinations, I'm glad to see you putting her desires—and the Nation's—ahead of your own. That shows a great deal of maturity."

Inclinations?

"Thank you, sir," I managed to say. "I just want to make her happy. And serve the Nation."

"As do I." The glare from the lights hit the lenses of his glasses again, blanking out his eyes. "We do what Our Nation requires. You, me, Unity—all of us."

I need to see Casey.

Concentrating in class was impossible—though, thanks to the Wide Awakes swarming the campus, and the presence of a Dentist in our midst, none of my classmates were paying attention either.

They ought to count their blessings. They weren't on a first-name basis with that Dentist. They weren't dating his daughter.

Just what, exactly, did Mr. Ludlow already know about my . . . inclinations? He hadn't picked that word at random. Dentists were masters of double meaning, of making even a compliment sound like a warning, or a threat.

I need to see Casey.

But how? I didn't even know where he lived. And I couldn't just walk up to one of the other Chaffs and ask him. Or her.

Freya. She would know.

As soon as the final bell sounded, I sprang up and broke into a run, slowing down whenever I spotted Wide Awakes on patrol. I staked out a position near the gym, halfway between the main gate and the entrance to the baseball field. From here I had a clear view of the only escape route off campus—Freya would have to go right past me.

Chaffs

I tried my best to become invisible. I couldn't stay here long, what with the new anti-loitering decree. I checked my watch—only ten minutes until practice. The other guys would start showing up before then, and any minute Coach could appear and bark at me to go inside and suit up . . .

There.

She was on the edge of the crowd, in her own bubble of space. People tended to give her a wide berth, worried that she might pick their pockets.

"Freya!"

I pushed off from the wall of the gym and jogged toward her. She halted and turned, looking at me coolly.

"I need to talk to Casey," I said. "Have you seen him today?"

"No."

Silence. I waited for more, but got nothing.

"Do you know where he is?" I asked.

"And I should tell you, why?"

"Look, don't play games, OK? It's important. He might be in trouble."

"Casey's always in trouble. He can handle it."

Not this kind of trouble, he can't.

The procession off campus had slowed to a crawl. At the gate, a couple of Wide Awakes were doing searches.

Freya folded her arms across her chest. "How much cash have you got?"

"You want me to *pay* you to tell me where he is?"

"Information costs money."

I glanced back in the direction of the gym. Brad, Deke, Danny, and Rick were walking toward it. None of them had seen me, but they were closing in, and it was only a matter of time until . . .

With a glare, I dug out my wallet and handed Freya a fifty-dollar bill. She held the bill up to the sunlight, scrutinizing the engraving of Our Commander-in-Chief on the front like she was a counterfeiting expert, before pocketing it.

"He's at the Peach Pit." Freya rolled her eyes at the blank look I gave her. "That apartment building that was wrecked in the earthquake?"

Which building? There were lots of them in the Valley, buildings damaged and left to decay because no one had the money to repair or demolish them. "Could you narrow it down a little?"

"Off Reseda Boulevard. Big and pink, like a peach. Hence the name."

Clearly, an address wasn't forthcoming, so I returned my wallet to my pocket and hurried back to the gym to catch up with my teammates.

It took some driving around, but I eventually found the place, on a palm tree-lined residential street with several other complexes. From a distance it simply looked run-down—with sagging eaves, and with bare patches and surface cracks lacing the peach-colored stucco, but no worse than any other two-story apartment building in a sketchy neighborhood.

Then I got closer, and I saw that the building used to be *three* stories.

I climbed through a hole in the fence surrounding the property, past a gauntlet of fading CONDEMNED and NO TRESPASSING signs barely hanging on to the rusty chain link. The front entrance had collapsed and was impassable, so I snuck around to the side alley to find the way in. The complex was huge, deeper than it looked from the street. Most of the debris from the former ground floor had been eroded, gnawed away by rats, or carted off by scavengers in the years since the quake, but here and there in the alley, the crumpled ends of cars still poked out from where the building had pancaked onto them.

With a shudder, I kept going down the alley. Eventually the building became three stories again. In this intact section there was a passageway between two garages, leading down a few steps to a gate with a busted lock. As I opened the gate and hacked my way through the thicket of overgrown oleander bushes on the other side, I heard sounds—voices, clattering skateboard wheels, and an ear-torturing noise that I gathered was someone's idea of music. The air reeked of urine and mold and rotting garbage, along with something else, a musky herbal smell.

I emerged into a paved courtyard. The wrecked front half of the building leaned sickeningly over one end of it. A twinge of panic seized me, and I came within a heartbeat of turning around and running full-speed back to my car—but it was already too late. They'd spotted me.

The voices went quiet. The Chaffs' eyes took in my letter jacket and way-too-short haircut. I counted about two dozen, boys and girls, from grade-schoolers to my own age, scattered around an empty kidney-shaped swimming pool. The skateboard sounds came from the bottom of the pool, the so-called music from a portable cassette player sitting on the deck.

Closer to me, a small group was passing around some kind of hand-rolled cigarette under the skeletal remains of a wooden gazebo. I walked up to them.

"Uh, hi. I'm looking for Casey?"

No answer.

I tried again. "Casey Monahan. Is he here?"

One of the group—a reedy-faced girl, lying on a plastic chaise lounge, with straight blonde hair that looked like it hadn't been washed in months—offered me the cigarette. "Want some pot?"

"Pot? You mean marijuana?"

The girl laughed. "*You're* a dumb one."

She took a long draw off the cigarette and made a gesture toward the pool. Her voice was tight from holding the smoke in her lungs. "Casey's skating. Who are you?"

"A friend of his."

She exhaled in my direction and gave me a once-over. "A friend of his. Uh-huh. I bet you are."

I excused myself and inched over to the pool. There were three kids—no, four—swirling around the bottom like marbles in a bowl and yet managing not to collide with each other. I picked out Casey right away. He was the tallest.

Damn. He looked like sex on wheels, riding that thing.

He was wearing shorts. I caught myself watching the workings of his calves. His legs were hairy and well-muscled, but sleek, and the way they propelled him into the air defied the laws of physics. I blinked and forced myself to stop ogling.

Casey spotted me. He did a sharp turn and swooped up the side of the pool. Once clear of the edge, he angled the skateboard so it was parallel with the ground, then drew in his legs, striking sideways with one foot as he did so and making the board spin lengthwise in midair. It leveled out, Casey set his feet on it again and descended smoothly to the deck . . .

But then he landed wrong. The board slipped out from under him and went rolling across the concrete. He scrambled to recover, but then stumbled and fell.

I rushed forward. "Are you OK?"

Casey was laughing. "Yeah. I just got distracted. Serves me right for being a show-off."

Without thinking, I held out my hand to help him up. He grabbed it, and again his touch was like a jolt of electricity. We locked eyes, and I saw . . . something—happiness, or maybe just relief—but Casey quickly erased it.

He dusted himself off and walked over to the blonde girl.

"You gonna introduce me to your playmate?" she asked him. "You're getting careless, EML, telling your boyfriends where we hang out."

"Fuck you, Bec. I didn't tell him." Casey laughed again, took the cigarette, and shot me a sidelong look. "It was Freya, wasn't it? How much did she make you pay her?"

I jammed my hands in my jacket pockets and mumbled into my shirt, staring at the ground. "Fifty bucks."

"Wow, she gave you a discount. She must like you." Casey took a hit off the cigarette. "Tyler, this is Rebecca. Bec, Tyler."

He held the cigarette between his thumb and forefinger and offered it to me. I was tempted—maybe the marijuana would settle my nerves—but no. I'd just start coughing, and then I'd have to listen to all these Chaffs making fun of me.

I shook my head. "No, thanks. Casey, can I talk to you? In private?"

"You guys going to the show?" Bec asked.

"I am," Casey said. "How about it, slugger? This band we like is playing a show downtown tonight."

Did the band sound anything like the screeching from that cassette player? I'd rather keep my eardrums intact.

"I'd better not. It's a school night." I shuffled my feet and shot Casey a pleading glance. "Look, I really need to talk to you."

"Yeah, I heard you the first time. This way."

"Have fun, boys," Bec sing-songed after us.

Casey led me across the courtyard and into a one-room apartment in the uncollapsed part of the complex. The walls were covered with layer upon layer of graffiti, but the room itself contained only a bare mattress on the floor, a battery-powered camping lantern beside it, and two garbage bags in the corner, one filled with beer bottles and the other with aluminum cans.

"Is this where you live?"

"Nah." Casey switched on the lantern and closed the grimy vertical blinds across the front window. "I just crash here sometimes."

His bookbag was sitting on the floor. He crouched down, took something out, and flung it at me. "Think fast, TNT."

My hand made the catch—no thinking, just pure third-baseman's reflex. Then I looked at what I'd caught. It was my cap. My knees wobbled, and I nearly fainted.

"Oh, my God . . . Casey, thank you! How—?"

"I went back for it. Getting past the Wide Awakes was a chore, I've got to say."

His gaze seemed to be searching mine. His hands rose, like they were about to reach for me, but then he looked away, his shoulders slumped, and he stepped back.

My relief over the cap didn't last long. I started pacing like a caged animal, my fists clenching and unclenching. "Casey, we're in trouble."

"I know. That's why I'm here. I figured I'd stay away for a week or two, wait for things to blow over."

"But what am *I* going to do? I've got baseball, classes, Dawn Patrol—I can't just disappear."

"Well, what do you want from me?" Casey threw himself down on the mattress. He snorted. "Want to run away together? Hop a freighter, find some deserted island, spend the rest of our lives lying naked on the beach, feeding each other bananas?"

"Damn it, Casey, this isn't funny!" I spun around and slammed my fist into the nearest wall. "This is my *life!*"

From the ceiling, some flakes of old paint, shaken loose by my fist, fell on my face like snow. I reached up to brush them off . . . and felt my tear ducts swelling. I sank down onto the edge of the mattress, next to Casey, and hunched over, my head between my knees, my hands clasped behind my neck. It felt like the last remnants of this decrepit and devastated old building were about to cave in right on top of me.

Casey didn't react at all. What was he waiting for? Had I frightened him with my outburst just now? What *did* I want from him, anyway? Besides . . .

Besides the obvious?

I raised my head. I'd kept myself from crying, but just barely.

"So does anybody else know . . . about you?"

Casey shrugged. "Guys I've been with, sure."

"What about your friends?"

"Freya knows. Bec knows—she's figured it out, anyway. She's not happy about it." A pause. "She's been wanting to get with me since forever—I'm just not interested. I'd do it, though, if she was the EML and not me. A going-away present."

"EML?"

"End of the Motherfucking Line. A Chaff whose number is coming up soon."

The tears threatened to start flowing again. I kept forgetting how little time Casey had left. How could he talk about it so calmly?

"Have you ever done it?" I asked. "I mean, with a girl?"

"Yeah. It was OK—I didn't hate it or anything. But it just felt forced. Like I had to *work* too hard. Unnatural."

He tilted his head and hooded his eyes, scrutinizing me through long, delicate lashes. "And what about you? Have you done it with your girlfriend yet?"

I choked down the lump in my throat, and nodded.

"How'd it feel?"

"Uh . . . unnatural."

There. I said it.

I braced myself, waiting for Casey to . . . to kiss me, or to push me away in disgust and give me a few kicks in the nuts for good measure. But he did none of those things. He simply positioned himself behind me and, without saying a word, coaxed me out of my jacket and began rubbing my neck and shoulders. I sighed deeply and leaned into it. The mere touch of his fingers drew all my fear and anguish and frustration straight up and out of my body, like fluid out of a blister.

After a while, Casey slipped his arms around me, and I laid back, resting against him. I couldn't move—wouldn't have moved even if I could. The door was wide open, the cell was unlocked, I was free to leave it whenever I chose. But I didn't want to, not yet. I just wanted to take in the bright, magnificent view beyond it, to fill my lungs with the freshest air I'd ever breathed in my life.

And so Casey and I lay there, absolutely still, lost in the light of our own world while the real one went dark.

S OME time later, there was a knock at the door, and I rocketed to my feet. *The Dentists! They found us! Already!*

Back on the mattress, Casey sat up and yawned. "Come in."

The door opened, and the blonde girl, Bec, appeared. Freya was with her, along with one of the Chaffs who'd been smoking marijuana earlier—a short guy with a wispy beard and hair the same dirty blond color as Bec's.

"Up and at 'em, boys." Bec marched into the room, clapping her hands. "Jason's here with the van. Time to go." Another chilly up-and-down look, like the one she'd given me earlier. "Is Mr. Clean coming with?"

Casey's eyes were glaring as he stood up. He and Bec seemed to be having some kind of silent argument. Then he broke it off and tilted his head at me. "If you want to get home before curfew, you'd better—"

"No. I'm coming." Screw curfew. I wanted to hang out with Casey.

"You sure? What about your parents?"

"I've been out late before—they'll just think I went out with the guys after practice, or over to Unity's. If they even notice."

Casey's brows rose. One corner of his mouth twitched. I could tell I'd just surprised him. Pleasantly.

"Can you drive?" He took off his shorts, then stooped and grabbed a pair of jeans off the floor. "You don't want to ride in Jason's van. It smells like a toilet. So does Jason."

We piled into the Fenris. Freya and the short, bearded guy climbed into the back. Casey and Bec both went for the front seat, and at the door their eye-fight flared up again until Bec retreated and joined the others.

Casey slid in next to me and gave me another shoulder-squeeze. This time, before drawing back, he let his hand trail down my arm. Even through my jacket, the touch made my skin tingle.

"Buckle up, slugger."

Again, he steered me down side streets to avoid the checkpoints. A car filled with Chaffs was asking for trouble. But soon enough, we reached the 101 and were zooming along at freeway speed.

The bearded guy glanced at me in the rearview mirror. "So, Muldoonie. How many black babies have you killed?"

"Shut the fuck up, Randall," Casey snapped, before I could answer. "Ignore him, Tyler. He's too political for his own good—ours, too. He's probably working for the Dentists, trying to get us to do something stupid so they can arrest us."

"I am not!"

"Then prove it. Keep your fucking mouth shut. Don't make me shut it for you."

I avoided Randall's eyes and kept mine on the road. "I never killed anybody."

We took an offramp just past the downtown skyscrapers, and headed south. On the right, the tower of the Los Angeles City Hall gleamed ivory white, just like on the million TV shows I'd seen it in. Near the top, the JumboVisions— four of them, one on each side—were showing one of the

Commander-in-Chief's speeches. No one was watching it this late at night. The streets around us were deserted.

Thank God Casey was navigating—I'd have been totally lost otherwise. I almost never ventured over the hill, into L.A. proper—for Dodger games a couple of times each season, and for the annual Awakening Day rally at the Coliseum, but that was it. The Valley might as well be an island, for how often I left it.

"Start looking for a place to park," Casey said. "Not too close—we want to be outside the perimeter, if there's a raid."

We'd left the wide streets and high-rises far behind. The streets here were almost too narrow to drive down. Half-dead streetlights dribbled a sickly yellow illumination onto blocks crammed with warehouses and scrapyards surrounded by razor-wire fences. Most of the warehouses looked old—hulking brick buildings, their windows opaque with grime, their arched doorways frowning. Others, much newer, were nothing more than gray slabs laid against each other, like concrete houses of cards.

To the east, there were lights in the sky, circling and hovering. Helicopters.

"What's over there?" I asked Casey.

"Oh, that's the Barrio."

"The Protection Zone?" I tensed up. "We're not going over there, are we?"

"Nah, not tonight. Maybe another night."

"You're joking, I hope."

Except for Wide Awakes, white people weren't allowed there, not even Chaffs. And those inside weren't allowed out, unless they had permits from the Freedom to Work Program, like the maids Mom kept hiring and firing.

Behind me, Randall sneered, "Don't worry, Muldoonie. We won't let the mud people get you."

I found an empty space, parked, and followed the Chaffs for a dozen or more blocks to one of the bigger, more ancient warehouses. I left my jacket behind—I could already tell that jocks would not be welcome here.

At the door, a man shaped like a refrigerator—if a refrigerator had arms covered with tattoos—was letting people in one at a time. He took one look at Casey, apparently recognized him, and waved him through.

"Not so fast, *Neighbor.*" The refrigerator man blocked my way. "What's the password?"

"He's with me," Casey said.

The man sized me up, with a curled lip and a side glance at Casey, but then gave me an unpleasant shark-smile and moved aside. "Have fun, cutie pie."

The door swung open. I went in—and instantly jammed my fingers into my ears. I'd never heard anything so loud in my life. It was agony. It was like I'd just gone to Hell and was getting my first listen to the lamentations of the damned.

I was jostled, slammed into, shoved. I couldn't see. I was deaf to everything but this horrific noise. When I tried to breathe I gagged on a fog of stale beer, BO, smoke, and ozone. No, this wasn't *like* going to Hell, this *was* Hell . . .

Someone took my arm. It was Casey—I recognized his grip. I let him tug me to one side and out of harm's way.

I touched a wall. I turned so my back was to it, then opened my eyes.

On one side of the dank, cement-floored room, some wooden pallets had been stacked and pushed together to form a stage. The band thrashing around on it—a beefy drummer in a ripped T-shirt, and two skinny guitarists, one of whom was dividing his time between playing his instrument and shouting into a microphone—was dwarfed by the towers of speakers and amplifiers on either side, and half-hidden by the crowd in front of it . . . *dancing?* That wasn't the right word for what the crowd was doing. Flailing? Brawling? Ramming each other like deranged gorillas?

Casey was whipping his head and shoulders up and down to the music. When it stopped, he cupped his hands around his mouth and screamed his lungs out.

The band blasted into another song. Casey looked at me, pointed to the other side of the room, made a drinking gesture with the other hand, and plunged into the crowd.

No! Casey, don't leave me here —

He was already gone. I'd lost sight of the others, too. No, wait—Freya was up near the stage, throwing elbows. Bec was in the corner, next to a poster—an ugly caricature of Our Commander-in-Chief, with a black smudge of a mustache on his lip and human skulls piled around his shoulders—staring at where Casey had been standing, then shooting poisoned eye-darts at me. There was no sign of Randall.

I pressed up against the wall. This was an illegal gathering, performing illegal music—I could get in serious trouble for being here. Anybody could tell I didn't belong, even without the jacket. I needed a bunch of tattoos, like the guy at the door . . . or some purple dye in my hair, like that girl who had just jumped onstage and was throwing punches at the singer . . . or at least I should have rolled around in the dirt before coming. . .

But the music was sounding better. Now that I'd gotten used to the volume, I found myself starting to like it. By the time Casey came back with a beer bottle in each hand, I was stomping my foot on the floor and punching the air with my fist.

Casey handed me one beer and raised the other one in a toast. We clinked bottles . . . and then Casey, with a lecherous grin, slowly rubbed the neck of his against the neck of mine. I returned the grin and rubbed back.

The beer was warm and sour-tasting. It went down much easier after Casey spiked it with a few shots from his flask.

Yeah, I was *definitely* enjoying this music now. None of the songs lasted longer than a minute or two, but that didn't matter—the inhumanly fast drumbeat was getting under my skin, agitating my blood. This was raw, unfiltered emotion. Naked, tribal, erotically violent—*decadent*, that was the Party's word for it.

And the crowd! This swirling, sweat-spewing throng of guys—mostly guys, though the girls in their midst gave as good as they got—was as much a part of the show as the band. And it wasn't enough just to stand on the sidelines and watch—if you had the guts, if you thought you could survive, you had to join in.

The band came to a break between songs, and Casey put his mouth to my ear. The vibrations of his voice stirred the hairs on my neck.

Chaffs

"You're thinking about it, aren't you?"

"About what?"

"Going in the pit. You think you're ready for that?"

It was a dare. There was no way I could leave it unanswered.

Watch me.

Keeping my gaze fixed on Casey, I sucked down the last drops of my beer. The music roared, and again the pit began to churn. I threw down the beer bottle. It shattered on the floor. And I jumped.

Casey was right behind me.

It was like leaping into a flesh tornado. Arms and legs and other body parts pelted me from all sides. Right away, some bull-necked creature slammed into me. A pair of hands behind me broke my fall. I got my footing back, and I gave Bull Neck a return shove into a gangly kid with shaved eyebrows who almost fell down, but then spun around and kept dancing.

I lunged into the vortex. I slammed, slugged, dodged. My reflexes were knife-sharp, my nerves on high alert. There was a system to this, an etiquette—it didn't take long to see that. If someone fell down near you, you helped him up. If anyone hit you for real, you and your buddies had the right to hit him back ten times harder. But hardly anyone went that far. Just once, some lunatic jumped in with a bike chain, swinging it in circles and almost taking off Freya's jaw with it—and instantly, a squad of guys, Casey among them, piled on the guy with the chain and drove him out of the pit. This wasn't about the strong beating up the weak, this wasn't kill-or-be-killed—it only looked that way to the uninitiated. This was chaos, but with order at its core, solid, true. No decrees, no directives, no marching orders, no rules except the ones you made and enforced on your own. Total freedom.

And Casey was right there with me. He watched my back, I watched his. We were together in the center of the storm. At some point Casey's shirt came off. Trickles of sweat gleamed like liquid moonlight against his skin. His eyes blazed at mine, taking in all my lust and joyous rage and sending it back to me, magnified . . .

A new noise. An alarm. The lights went out, then turned red. The music stopped, the pit went still, and then it became a stampede. The door smashed open. From outside came harsh yelling voices, helmeted forms, swinging joltsticks.

I felt Casey's hand take mine, heard his voice in my ear. "It's a raid. Follow me."

I gripped his hand tighter and let him lead the way.

Our escape from the warehouse was a blur. My sole focus was on not letting Casey out of my sight. I didn't look around to see if we were being pursued—I just followed. Into the basement, through a tunnel into another building, up a fire escape onto the roof. Spotlights shone down from above—we swerved and zigzagged to avoid them. The wind from the helicopters blasted through our hair. Sirens scoured ears that were still ringing from the music. We went down another fire escape, into an alley, onto a side street, then a sharp turn and a hurtling run down another alley, and another . . .

I was terrified. I was elated. If the Wide Awakes caught me now, I would have laughed in their faces.

I was already laughing when Casey and I reached the car.

I caressed the hood. This was like being reborn, with every texture new and fascinating. Then I rolled over and looked back at the helicopters still circling the warehouse a half-mile away. The sirens and harsh voices had faded to a safe distance. Here, it was quiet. I sat up and broke the silence with a long, lung-emptying howl.

Casey had just finished catching his breath. His mussed-up hair crowned him like a black demonic halo. On his torso, more hairs dotted his chest and thickened into a trail that lured the eye down his abdomen and then vanished under his belt. I couldn't look away. Even the fitful glow from the streetlights made his skin glisten and outlined muscles I'd never noticed before.

With a smirk, he came up and planted one hand on either side of me, trapping me against the car, easing his legs between mine.

"Damn. You're a wild man. I was only joking about you getting in the pit—I didn't think you'd really do it." He leaned closer. His scent filled my nostrils. His voice dropped in pitch, and there was a growl in it. "You looked *so* fucking hot in there."

"So did you."

I grabbed him and pulled him down to me. This time it was full speed ahead, no panic, no screeching brakes. So *this* was how it was supposed to feel, that physical *want* for somebody, for every part of him, with every part of me . . .

Casey was panting when we drew apart. "Let's get out of here. Or do you want to do it in the car?"

"What about the others?"

"They'll find their own way back. Let's go."

The drive back into the Valley was blissful torture. Casey couldn't keep his hands—or his lips, or his tongue—off me. The car swerved and drifted across the freeway, back and forth—I couldn't keep it in one lane, could barely keep my eyes on the road and my own hands on the steering wheel. I had to turn on the defroster to keep the windshield from fogging up.

We made it to the Peach Pit, leaped over the fence, and ran back to the apartment. Our mouths were colliding again before the door had even closed.

Casey grabbed my shirt, pulled it off over my head, and then backed up until he was standing on the mattress. I joined him there. In the dark, I heard him taking off his shoes, unbuckling his belt, and stepping out of his jeans. In my haste to do the same, I forgot to start with the shoes—my feet got tangled and I fell forward, laughing, onto my knees. With an answering laugh, Casey turned on the light and came to my aid, peeling off shoes, pants, briefs, brushing lips and fingers across every naked square inch of me. With my nerves stripped bare by the violence of the pit, the lightness of his touch made me groan out loud. I was trembling, feverish, every cell on fire.

He got the last of my clothes off, kissed and caressed his way from the soles of my feet to the back of my neck, and then swung around so we were kneeling face-to-face.

"This body of yours. God *damn*." His eyes were dripping honeycombs of pure lust. "The other night, when I was up in your room and you took your shirt off? I thought I was going to pass out."

His wood was pulsating against my thigh. Gently, he took me by the wrist and guided my hand onto it. He was already leaking.

"Um, I've never touched . . . anyone else's . . ."

"Don't worry, you won't break it. You haven't broken yours, have you?"

He took hold of mine, without warning, and squeezed. I gasped.

"Oh, *fuck*."

Casey chuckled in my ear. "See what I mean?"

We matched each other's movements, stroke for stroke, faster and faster, harder and harder. With my free hand I grabbed Casey's hair and pulled his head back, sucking on his neck, feeling his pulse galloping beneath my lips. His own fingertips hooked into my shoulder, like he was dangling from a cliff, about to fall . . .

He tensed up and thrust against me. He let out a moan . . . a louder one . . . louder . . . and gushed all over my stomach.

"I'm sorry." I looked at him, suddenly anxious. "I didn't mean to make you pop so soon . . . "

Casey laughed. "So soon? I've been holding that in for days." He folded me into his arms and laid his sweaty head against me, sighing over and over. Then he straightened up and gave me a playful shove. "Your turn now. Give me your dick."

His words almost made me pop all by themselves.

He nudged me back until I was lying underneath him. A few more kisses, and then he headed south. He stroked and licked, zeroing in and attacking every hot spot I had, teasing me until I was biting my lower lip and gripping the edge of the mattress overhead with both hands. When he finally took me into his mouth, a soul-deep cry tore loose from my lungs and my whole body launched itself into the air.

I hung there, right on the edge. Casey was holding me there, playing with me—I saw the wicked glee in his eyes when he looked up. Then, with just a slight change in his movements, he pushed me over . . .

And it took forever to come down to earth.

I lay covered with sweat, as weak and helpless as a baby. My limbs were twitching. My skull felt like a bowl of pudding. This was like no dream I'd ever had, no quick jerk in the shower. I didn't feel fake and hollow like I did with Unity. I'd been opened up, my soul laid bare and then ignited, lighting up the sky.

Next to my ear, I heard Casey—laughing, but also sounding a little worried. "Dude? Are you alive?"

I flopped my head to one side and smiled at him. "I am now."

"Casey? Can I ask you something? It's kind of personal."

Well, *that* sure sounded stupid. Kind of personal? I'd just had my penis in his mouth—you didn't get much more personal than that.

He rolled toward me and raised an eyebrow. "We're playing True Confessions already? That didn't take long."

"Nothing like that. I was just wondering—when did you figure out . . . I mean, how long have you known that you're . . . that you're, um . . . "

"Gay. Practice saying it a few times."

"OK. Gay. Gay gay gay gay gay." It sounded so old-fashioned, like saying *groovy* or something. "But seriously. When did you know?"

"I've known my whole life. I didn't always know what it *meant*, but I always knew I was different. Didn't you?"

"Not until now." The glow from tonight was fading, and a cold regret was creeping in—not about what I'd done tonight, but about what I *hadn't* done before tonight, about all the time that I'd wasted. "Or maybe I did know, but just never *knew* that I knew. That sounds crazy, doesn't it?"

"Nah."

A quick burst of movement, and Casey was on top of me, pressing down with his body, his face hovering inches from mine. "Do you remember those videos they made us watch in middle school?"

"The ones with the parades?"

"Yeah. Get a load of all those disgusting perverts prancing down the street—that's what they wanted us to think. But me, I was like, *Give me a time machine—I want to join them.*"

"You, in high heels and feathers? I can't picture that."

"Me neither." His smile faded into a thoughtful look. "But who knows? Can you even *imagine* being able to live like that, without being ashamed or afraid? Not having to *hide* all the time? That must have been so awesome."

"I guess." Those parades still seemed like freak shows to me. Sure, Casey was gay . . . *I* was gay . . . but neither of us would ever be mistaken for the guys in those videos. If only they'd acted more like us, more *normal*, the Muldoonies wouldn't have cracked down so hard and things today would be different. Maybe.

"So how did you know about me?" I asked.

Casey shrugged. "I just had a feeling. I get them sometimes. I'll pick up these . . . I don't know, signals. Like some sort of homo alarm system."

"I was putting out *signals?* You could have *told* me."

"And if I was wrong? You and your jock buddies would have taken me apart. Or you'd have gone to the Dawn Patrol, and *they* would have taken me apart—then put me back together and shipped me off to the Dentists. I may be an EML, but I'm not suicidal."

"Are you wrong very often?"

He answered with a kiss, hard and deep. True Confessions time was coming to an end. Fine with me.

I pushed up, and rolled—a maneuver I learned back in ninth grade, when I tried out for the wrestling team—flipping Casey onto his back and pinning him underneath me. He let out a small woof of surprise, but managed not to break lip contact.

When we finally came up for air, Casey's smile was sheepish.

"Am I often wrong? Actually, no. Hardly ever."

Part Two
FAMILY

ONE of the pink-clad prisoners has peed himself. The acrid stink fills the bus, making my eyes water. One of the Wide Awakes is stomping up and down the aisle, looking for the pants-wetter.

Next to me, Steven's narrow shoulders are convulsing.

"Don't throw up," I whisper to him. "You'll catch hell for it."

"I know." Steven gets the heaves under control and sits up, hugging himself. "I know. I'm OK."

His body language says otherwise, but at least he's learning. Don't show weakness, don't show fear. Our tormentors eat that stuff up.

It's dark out—we've been on the road for hours. We must be in Nevada or Arizona by now, or one of the next states over. Or maybe we're still just outside of L.A. and they've been driving us around in circles, to confuse us. I wouldn't put it past them.

Survive. Resist. Escape. Evade.

Those words keep tumbling through my head. They're from the Dawn Patrol Handbook, from the section on how to behave as a prisoner of war. It makes sense. There aren't any bombs falling, or soldiers shooting at me, but I'm at war, no question.

I'm not really a prisoner, though—I volunteered for this. That changes everything. Resistance, escape, and evasion are off the table.

That leaves me with survival.

Part of me wants to believe I've already made it through the worst. It's bad, where I'm going, but not like the cells of the DDS—maybe even a little better. Then another part tells me to stop lying to myself. It never gets better.

I turn my face toward the window so no one will see how scared I am. I can't do this—I'm not brave enough. But I have to be. I *have* to survive.

The bus slows down, pulls over, stops.

"What's going on?" Steven asks. "Are we there? Is it over?"

I shake my head at him. "Don't bet on it."

It's just a bathroom break—we're being herded out to relieve ourselves in the bushes. As I step off the bus and into the parched desert night, one of the Wide Awakes shines a flashlight on my crotch, to see if I'm already wet. Then he gives me a shove toward the side of the road.

I untie the drawstring of my scrubs and do my business. The others line up on either side, and I choke back an urge to laugh. Casey would have something so smart-alecky and hilarious to say about this—about this chorus line of homos in bubblegum-colored outfits, whipping their dicks out and peeing in sync.

We could overpower the guards if we wanted to. We out-number them. But of course no one makes a move—I doubt the thought even occurs to anyone besides me. And I'm the one who supposedly *wants* to be here.

Behind me, there's a scuffle. The Wide Awakes have found the pants-wetter. Their joltsticks come crackling to life. I keep my eyes forward, fixed on the black void of the desert at night. It's so quiet. The buzzing of the joltsticks, and the screaming that follows, must be audible for miles, but no one except us is around to hear.

It never gets better.

C ASEY ventured into the predawn dimness and glanced around the courtyard of the Peach Pit. It was empty— the other Chaffs either were still asleep, or hadn't made it back from the show last night.

"So . . ." He was shuffling his feet. "Want to do this again?"

I started to laugh, but the strangely brittle look on Casey's face made me throttle it back. "Heck yeah. What makes you think I wouldn't?"

A shrug. "Some guys freak out and run away."

"I'm not running anywhere."

If it hadn't been a school day, I wouldn't be leaving at all. I felt full of energy and yet totally relaxed, both at the same time—I never knew it was even possible to feel this way. Right now, this condemned apartment building, reeking of garbage and marijuana smoke and haunted by the ghosts of earthquake victims, was the most beautiful place in the world.

"Other guys do the opposite," Casey said. "They get reckless. It's like they *want* to get caught."

"Well, I don't want to get caught either."

That made him smile. "OK. Just checking."

We leaned in for another kiss, but then the oleanders in front of the gate stirred, and a couple of Chaffs appeared. Casey and I stepped away from each other, keeping a discreet distance. But it was only Bec and Randall, who, I'd just learned, were sister and brother. Randall was another EML—his number was coming up even sooner than Casey's.

Bec was seething. "Thanks for waiting around last night, asshole."

"Come on, Bec, you know the score—when the cops come, it's every Chaff for himself." Casey looked past her, and his eyes narrowed. "Where's Freya?"

"She got picked up. Don't worry—I'm sure Mommy and Daddy have sprung her by now." A withering look at me. "Must be nice, having parents."

Freya's dad was a regional Party chairman, with even more connections than my family. That was probably what had kept Freya out of jail after she got caught shoplifting in seventh grade and was kicked out of the Morning Glories.

I didn't want Bec's hostility to ruin my mood, and I had to go home and shower off the beer and sex before school, so this seemed like a good time to get going. As I did, I locked eyes with Casey and held them. I was dying to kiss him one more time, but not here, not under Bec's glare of disapproval.

It took us over a week to arrange another meeting. I wasn't reckless—I knew we had to be careful. Though I could also see why Casey might worry, why some guys might take crazy risks—not just for the sex, but for this rush of excitement. It was like a drug, some potent cocktail of hormones and adrenaline.

I had a math test coming up—a perfect excuse to have my tutor come over. Mom was in bed with her last martini by seven-thirty, and she wouldn't bother us so long as we kept the noise down. Still, Casey and I controlled ourselves—just a lot of kissing and groping. Plus a little grinding.

"So what do you think?" Casey leaned back on the bed, flashing me this come-and-get-it grin. "Are you a pitcher or a catcher?"

"Huh?" I pushed back from the desk and stood up. "I'm the third baseman. You know that."

Casey blinked at me, then began snorting with laughter. He rolled onto his side, his face turning red.

"Oh, dude." He sat back up and wiped tears from his eyes while he caught his breath. "You are *such* a noob. I love it."

"Noob?"

"Rookie. Virgin."

He then explained what he meant by *pitcher* and *catcher*— and I became the one turning red. I flopped forward onto the bed, face down so I wouldn't accidentally look in the mirror and see how hard I was blushing.

"So what . . . position . . . do *you* play?" I asked.

"Depends on my mood. You might say I'm a utility player."

"But being the . . . catcher . . . doesn't that hurt?"

"A little, at first. But then it feels great—you just need someone who knows what he's doing." A wicked look, sweeping from my face to my butt to my face again. "I know what I'm doing."

I laughed. "You're kind of conceited, you know that?"

He just shrugged. Like it mattered, anyway. Whatever it was Casey had—conceit or confidence—it simply made me want him even more.

In a heartbeat, I was all over him. A rookie, huh? *This* rookie wanted to learn the whole game—pitching, catching, the squeeze play, the hidden ball trick . . .

Casey was breathing hard, and as I nibbled on his neck I heard a barely audible *ohfuckyeah*, but then he pushed me back and nodded at the door. "Slow down, slugger. Not here. Besides, we need condoms for that, and I'm all out. Do you have any?"

"I don't have a prescription." Or Party approval, which was granted pretty much never, for condoms, pills, any kind of birth control.

His eyes widened. "So you and your girlfriend have been doing it . . . unsheathed? What if you get her knocked up?"

"Well . . . "

I didn't want to lie. So I told him—about the Virginia Dare Institute, about Unity's plan for the two of us to repopulate the white race all by ourselves.

"Jesus," Casey said. "That's fucked up."

"I'm sorry. I wish I didn't have to do it."

"No worries. You have to keep playing the game—I get that. Still . . . " He clasped his hands behind his head, staring up at the ceiling. "That's fucked up. This whole country is fucked up."

From the portrait above my bed, the eyes of President Muldoon tugged on my own. I had a sudden, intense urge to fling the picture out the window.

"Wait." I rolled off him. "What do *we* need condoms for? It's not like *we're* going to get pregnant."

"You're shitting me, right? You know. Those diseases?"

"We wiped them out. Like, five or six years ago. Our Commander-in-Chief gave a big speech about it."

"I don't believe a word that guy says. Do you?" A snort. "It's just like all the other garbage they feed us at school—that crap about Abe Lincoln sending all the slaves back to Africa and whatnot—though at least *those* lies can't kill you."

Before I could say anything, I heard footsteps coming up the stairs. They didn't sound like Mom's or Dad's.

They had to be Eric's.

The footsteps grew louder. Past his bedroom, heading toward mine.

I sprang up from the bed and landed back behind the desk. I shot a panicked look at Casey, but he was already sitting up, his own math textbook open in his lap.

The door opened. Eric was in his Rooster uniform. He swept the room with his gaze, and frowned. When he saw Casey, the frown deepened.

I conjured up my best irritated-big-brother voice. "Geez, Eric. Haven't you heard of *knocking*?"

"Your door was closed. What's going on?"

"I'm studying for a test. Like it's any of your business." My fingers were playing with the cover of my textbook, as if getting ready to present the book as evidence. "What are *you* doing here? Don't you have a Rooster meeting?"

"It got out early." He aimed his gaze at Casey again. "Who's this?"

"A friend. Now get out. Go do your own homework."

Eric looked at me, at Casey, at the books and papers on the desk. Then, without another word, he turned and left, shutting the door behind him.

I gave Casey a half-smile-half-grimace. "My brother."

"When do we kill him?"

Casey sounded like he was only half-joking.

I crept over to the door and opened it a crack, just to make sure Eric wasn't still out in the hall, listening. I'd gone through this phase too, when I was a Rooster—eavesdropping, searching under beds, imagining Mom and Dad engaged in dark conspiracies under our own roof. Both the Roosters and the Morning Glories gave out merit badges for surveillance and intelligence gathering, though I'd never earned one. Eric was way more enthusiastic about that stuff.

Once I determined we were safe, I rejoined Casey on the bed. I really wanted to jump his bones again, but Eric's snooping had knocked the self-control back into me. We could always sneak off to the Peach Pit later, after everyone else was asleep.

"Anyway, condoms." Casey closed his book and took it off his lap. "I'll score some before the next time we meet up. They won't be cheap on the black market, but I can do it." A quick glance at the door. "Better safe than sorry, you know?"

A few days later, Rick Nagy and I were roaming the halls in our Dawn Patrol uniforms, doing spot-checks. Normally I was paired with Brad, but Troop Leader Hanna had tapped him for some special project, and Brad had jumped at it. He was going out of his way to look good for the Wide Awakes recruiters these days.

"There's a rule against bags over a certain size, Neighbor. Give it to me." Rick and I were bracing a puny tenth-grader.

He didn't obey fast enough, so Rick—who was small, and constantly getting too physical with kids who were even smaller—gave him a shove that sent him tumbling and the glasses spinning off his face. "What are you, retarded? Give me the bag!"

The other students in the hall walked by without stopping, averting their eyes to lessen the chances that we'd go after them next.

Except for one. Freya.

She was heading straight toward me. I let my hand drop to the side. She brushed past, and my fingers closed around the note she slipped me.

After fifth period, I ducked into the bathroom. I opened the note, and almost choked forcing myself not to laugh.

It was a crude drawing of a penis with a condom on it. And five words that gave me wood just reading them.

I GOT THEM. BATTER UP.

T Y, sweetie, could you *please* quit fidgeting?" Unity laid a hand on my knee to stop it from bouncing up and down. "You're starting to give *me* the jitters."

"OK." I slumped back, put down the three-year-old issue of *Sports Nation* that I'd been skimming—the lone guy reading amid the waiting room's rack of baby magazines and race hygiene pamphlets—and put my arm around Unity instead. "Sorry."

She settled closer. "It's a good thing you look so cute when you're nervous."

The cushy, softly lit waiting room was about half full of girls in their teens and twenties, most[RTF bookmark start: }_GoBack[RTF bookmark end: }_GoBack of them already visibly pregnant. Unity and I were the only couple.

Above the reception desk, there was an old-style engraving of a little girl, with a bonnet on her head like the one the Pilgrims wore. This, if I had to take a guess, was Virginia Dare.

Somehow, that little girl's gaze was even more unnerving than President Muldoon's from the portrait next to hers.

Eventually a man came out to meet us. He was pleas-ant-demeanored and good-looking, but with a mustache that looked like a piece of dryer lint stuck to his face.

"I'm Dr. Fleming." The man shook my hand. "Welcome to the Dare Institute. Did you have any trouble finding our campus?"

"Not at all," I said. The place was just north of L.A., on the site of the old Magic Mountain amusement park—from the freeway you could still see a couple of the roller coasters that hadn't been dismantled yet.

"This way, please." Dr. Fleming led me and Unity to an office, showed us over to a couch, and perched himself on the edge of the desk in front of it.

"You've both watched the orientation video?" He went on before we had a chance to nod yes. "I have excellent news. We've completed our preliminary review, and I'm happy to report that, based on the questionnaires you and your parents sent us, your medical histories, and your ancestral records on file with the Department of Race Relations, your pairing falls well within the acceptable compatibility range." He took in our blank stares, and added, "In plain English, you two are a fine match—your offspring will be worthy additions to the Nation. Have you conceived yet?"

"Not yet." Unity smiled and squeezed my arm. "But soon."

And not for lack of trying. Between her and Casey, I was afraid I might end up sexed to death.

"I must say, it makes me proud to see young people so eager to do their duty to the Nation. If only we all had the same initiative." With a placid smile, Dr. Fleming picked up a file folder and opened it. "OK . . . Neighbor Ludlow, I see your father has mailed us the parental consent form. Good. Neighbor Treppenhouse, since you will be eighteen by the time any of your children are born, you of course will not require your parents' consent. Everything else seems to be in order." He pressed a buzzer on the desk, and a nurse came in. "Now all we have to do is collect your sample, Tyler—may I call you Tyler?—and then we can begin our tour of the campus."

He meant a sperm sample. I'd been dreading this part. The video hadn't gone into any detail on how the sample was to be collected—only that the Institute wanted to make sure that my boys were healthy, and that I had enough of them. Were they going to hook me up to some sort of machine, like a cow being milked? Or was it this nurse's job to do the . . . collecting . . . herself?

"Follow Nurse Swanson," Dr. Fleming said. He gestured for Unity to remain seated. "Just wait here a moment, please, Neighbor Ludlow."

As we walked down the hall behind Nurse Swanson, Dr. Fleming patted me on the back and spoke to me in a quiet, man-to-man voice. "Just relax, Tyler. Believe me, there's nothing to be self-conscious about." We halted at a door, and Dr. Fleming reached for the knob as the nurse handed me a clear plastic cup with a lid on it. "This room is soundproof, and can be locked from the inside. You won't be disturbed."

I blinked at the cup. They wanted me to . . . do it myself? Into *this*?

"Some of our male clients prefer to have their partners in the room with them. Shall I bring over Neighbor Ludlow?"

Oh, God . . .

"No, that's OK, thanks."

Another smile. "Well, there's an ample supply of visual aids, if you need them. Take your time—there's no rush."

He closed the door, leaving me alone. The room was tiny, with a vinyl-covered couch, a TV set, a NO SMOKING sign on the wall, and on a shelf, a pile of pornographic magazines and videos. No Hawkeyes here, thank the Lord.

I didn't even look at the pornos—I just closed my eyes and thought about Casey. It was safe here, it would get the job done fast, and it would crack Casey up when I told him about it later. I got the whole chore over with in three minutes, tops.

When I opened the door, Dr. Fleming and Nurse Swanson were waiting for me, along with Unity this time. Dr. Fleming took the sample cup and eyeballed it, like some snooty wine connoisseur checking the color of a glass he'd just poured. He then passed it to the nurse, who wrote my name, the date, and the time on the lid before whisking it off down the hall.

"Well, now," Dr. Fleming said. "That wasn't so painful, was it?"

Unity was clasping my hand between both of hers, smiling, murmuring thank-yous and I-love-yous. Her attempts to make me feel less embarrassed weren't working, but she was trying so hard, I had to smile back.

Dr. Fleming nudged us down the hall. "Time to see the rest of the campus."

The birthing center was actually kind of interesting. Unity lit up, peppering the obstetricians and neonatal care specialists with questions that flew way over my head—she'd been reading up on the science and technology lately. I myself spent a lot of time studying the ultrasound machine. If I used it on my head, could I see my own brain? I was dying to know, but it seemed stupid to ask.

Then, we moved on to where they kept the older kids. At the entrance to this section, FAITH, FAMILY, FREEDOM beckoned from an archway above a larger-than-life statue of President Muldoon with his arms around two adoring youngsters. Beyond swarmed dozens of real live kids, from toddlers to grade-schoolers, in matching outfits—blue for boys and pink for girls—playing on the grass or walking along landscaped paths that meandered between homey, single-story buildings with adobe shingles. The place looked like a boarding school for rich orphans—there were dorms, a Nation's Covenant Church chapel, a gym, a baseball diamond. Some of the old Magic Mountain rides were here, too—I spotted the merry-go-round, the Ferris wheel, the barrel roll, a few others.

"Anthony." Dr. Fleming waved to a fair-haired boy playing tetherball. "Would you come here for a moment, please?"

The boy came over and stood at attention. He looked about eight or nine, with smooth skin, weirdly broad shoulders, and very pale blue eyes that were as cold, harsh, and unmoving as glaciers.

"Anthony, this is Neighbor Treppenhouse and Neighbor Ludlow," Dr. Fleming said. "They're going to be donating new members to our family."

Chaffs

"Thank you, Neighbors," Anthony said.

Unity smiled at him. Her smile could melt the polar ice caps, but it did nothing to warm up this kid.

"What's your last name?" she asked.

"Fremont."

"All of the children here have the same last name," Dr. Fleming said. "Each of our campuses, in every state, gives its children a different surname, to honor an important figure in the state's history."

"So what's your real name, Anthony?" I asked. "You know, from your mother and father?"

The pale eyes looked straight through me. "The Nation is my mother. Our Commander-in-Chief is my father."

For a second I wondered if he'd had meant that last part literally. But before I could ask, Dr. Fleming flashed another smile. "Thank you, Anthony. You may go now."

Anthony saluted. "Nation First."

Dr. Fleming's gaze followed him back to the tetherball court. "As you can see, our children are devoted to the future of the Nation. No corrupting, sentimental attachments to the past. You know what Our Commander-in-Chief says, about today's youth? *Swifter than an eagle—*"

"Tougher than leather," Unity said.

"Harder than steel," I added automatically.

Dr. Fleming smiled. "Well, we're perfecting that youth, right here. With help from you, and others like you."

I was fidgeting again. This place was giving me the creeps.

"So were all these kids born here?" I asked.

"About half," Dr. Fleming said. "Most of the rest were adopted by the Institute shortly after birth. We're also fostering a small number under the Reclamation Program."

"Reclaimees?" My head whipped around to face Dr. Fleming. "You've got Reclaimees here?"

"Until they pass their Evaluations at age eighteen, yes." His voice took on a soothing tone. "It's a *very* small number— only the most promising ones, with absolutely spotless racial histories. You needn't worry about contamination."

I had to fight to keep from busting up. *Oh, if you only knew, Doc. If you only knew how badly I'd been . . . contaminated . . . already.*

145

I was so busy controlling the urge to laugh, I didn't think to stop the next thing out of my mouth. "What happens to the ones who don't pass their Evaluations?"

Dead silence. On my arm I felt Unity's grip, tightening. "Tyler . . . "

Dr. Fleming furrowed his brow. "Why do you ask, Neighbor Treppenhouse?"

Shit. Think fast.

"Um . . . no reason. I have a fr—I know someone whose Evaluation is coming up soon. I'm just curious."

It wasn't a *total* lie. I was simply being vague. Unity would assume I was talking about Kevin, and was just using the present tense as cover for having screwed up. Dr. Fleming, though . . . God only knew what he was thinking.

"Well, I'm certain that *our* Reclaimees will pass with flying colors," he said.

Unity didn't speak again until we were halfway home. The silence hung so heavy and thick, I thought I might choke on it—I had to roll down the car window to get some fresh air.

"I'm not mad at you, Ty."

"OK."

It wasn't true—Unity was steamed. But who was I to give her grief for lying? I'd been lying to her nonstop—about Casey, about her and me, about everything. The fact that I *had* to lie—that I could end up in a cell, or with a noose around my neck, if the truth ever became known—didn't make the guilt weigh any less.

"Look, Unity . . . it just came out." I glanced sidelong at her, trying to make eye contact while still paying attention to my driving. "I wasn't thinking."

"I told you, I'm not mad." She sighed, gazing out the passenger-side window. "I just thought you'd gotten over that Reclaimee stuff."

"*Over* it?"

The words shot out of me like bullets. Behind them came this volcanic rage—the same rage I'd spewed at Billy Hanna that day in Malibu Canyon. Only this time I didn't have a paintball gun. All I had were my words.

"*Over* it? I've *tried* getting over it—over having my best friend get *ripped out of the fucking universe!*" I could hear my own voice climbing in volume. "I *can't do it*. I can't just shut my brain off—I'm not some fucking zombie, like that kid Anthony back there. Is that what you *want* me to be, Unity? Is that what you want our *kids* to be?"

I'd never raised my voice at her before, much less cursed at her. From her reaction, I might as well have punched her in the face. She was trembling, pressed up against the side of the car, as far away from me as possible, one hand covering her mouth. The tears had already started flowing.

"Oh, God. Unity, I'm sorry." My anger was gone, as quickly as it had erupted. Suddenly, all I could think about was placating her. "I didn't mean it. I've just been under so much pressure—I feel like my life is being turned upside down. Please don't cry."

Gradually, Unity got hold of herself. The sobbing diminished to an occasional sniffle.

"Ty . . . " Her voice was small and fragile. "I thought we . . . the baby . . . I thought it was what we *both* wanted."

"I do want it. I do."

No reply. I didn't think for an instant that Unity believed me, but I also knew there was no way she'd ever accuse me of lying.

She wouldn't stay upset at me, either. She never did. She'd probably be halfway to forgiving me by the time we reached her house. Because, for all the Muldoonie crap stuffed into her head, for all that her dad could order me sliced into bite-sized morsels and fed to the guard dogs at the nearest DDS detention center, Unity was still a good person—forgiving, kind, just plain good. Way better than me.

And a part of me hated her for that. If only she were just a little more of a bitch—maybe then, deceiving her wouldn't hurt so much.

A S expected, when I told Casey about the visit to the Dare Institute, the sperm sample story cracked him up.

"In a *cup?*" By the time he'd finished laughing, his face was beet red. "Did they at least give you some *gay* pornos to rub off to?"

"Didn't need them." I waggled my eyebrows.

"Huh? Oh . . . wow. Thanks, dude. I'm flattered."

Heck, the story *was* funny. This was insanely dangerous, what Casey and I were doing, and that danger hung over us like that sword in Greek mythology I'd read about in lit class—but if I couldn't laugh, I'd go crazy. And I could count on Casey to find the humor in anything.

"So is your girlfriend still pissed off at you?"

"She says she isn't, but she's been jumpy ever since I blew up at her. I feel really bad about it."

"You're not the one who wants to manufacture babies for the Master Race—she is. That shit's twisted. "

"Yeah. But it's not her fault. None of this is."

Maybe she and I just needed some time apart. Easter Break was starting next Monday. At church, Unity would have seven solid nights of choir rehearsals and performances—I was relieved of My Duty to the Nation from Palm Sunday on. I had a few Dawn Patrol activities that week, baseball practice in the afternoons—and of course, I still had Casey.

"I don't want to talk about Unity, OK?"

"OK with me. How many condoms have we got left?"

I rolled over and picked up the strip of foil-wrapped packages lying on the floor. "Just two."

"Damn. I'll have to get more—you've been going through them like potato chips, you animal."

He sat up and leaned toward me. Suddenly he looked like a man who hadn't eaten in days, eyeballing a juicy medium-rare steak. "OK, so we know you can pitch. How about catching?"

I froze. "Uh . . ."

"C'mon, slugger. First time for everything."

My apprehension was no match for the lust in his eyes. I laughed, tore off a condom, tossed it to Casey, and did what might have been the worst-ever impression of Coach Ferguson's voice.

"Suit up, Monahan."

We had a big game coming up on Saturday—against Bakersfield, one of the toughest teams in the division—so for the week leading up to it, Coach had mandated early morning practices on top of our usual after-school sessions. Around six a.m. on Wednesday, just as I was heading out, the phone rang. It was Brad.

"Hey, TNT. Glad I caught you. Can you give me a ride? My car's in the shop."

"Why didn't you call me about this last night?"

"Had a meeting—got home late. Come on. I'll be out front when you get here."

Brad lived less than a mile away, in the next neighborhood over. He was waiting at the curb when I pulled up at his house.

"Thanks for doing this, TNT. I hate riding that stinky bus to school."

"Where's your Dawn Patrol uniform?" I reached up with two fingers and clawed at the collar of my own. It was feeling tight today. "Billy Hanna's going to have a cow if he sees you out of it."

"It's in here." Brad hefted the garment bag he was carrying. As he got in the car, he laid the bag in the back seat and threw his catcher's mitt on top of it. "I'll put the monkey suit on after practice—Hanna won't see me till then, anyway."

Traffic was light this early in the morning. Along the way, I spotted a few clusters of police cars—the curfew checkpoints from the night before were just now being lifted.

"So it sounds like they're closing in on those guys who broke into the school," Brad said.

"Really?" I concentrated on my driving and pretended I didn't feel icy needles jabbing me in the spine. "Where'd you hear that?"

"That's what the meeting was about—that project Hanna put me on. He really should have brought you in on it too."

"I'm not surprised he didn't. Billy hates me."

"Ah, he's just still bent about the paintball thing. He'll get over it." His gaze wandered around the inside of the car. "Anyway, the Hawkeyes got footage of the guys, I guess. It's really dark, and you can't see their faces, but the DDS is running it through some fancy computer in Washington, to sharpen the image."

"Cool."

I craned my neck to see myself in the rearview mirror. Was I sweating? I squeezed the steering wheel, resisting the urge to tug on my collar again. It wasn't really strangling me. It only felt like it was.

"Man, I can't wait to take those faggots apart," Brad said.

We reached the school, showed our IDs to the Wide Awakes at the gate, and parked near the gym. It looked like Brad and I were the first ones here.

Just inside the entrance to the locker room, Brad halted. "Crap, I forgot my mitt. Give me your keys—I'll go back and get it."

"I can come with, if you want."

"Nah, it'll only take a minute. Go on in—just put my uniform over by my locker, would you?"

"Yeah, sure."

I tossed Brad the keys. He snatched them out of the air. "Be back in a flash."

My locker and Brad's were on opposite sides of the room—mine was near the showers, his was around the corner from Coach's office. I hung up the garment bag, then went to see if Coach was here yet.

He was.

And there was someone with him.

The office door was closed, but I saw them through the window. I saw Coach, anyway. All I could see of the other one was the back of a head, and one hand, which was gesturing wildly.

I slinked away, peering around the corner. I had a sudden sense that it would be a bad idea to let Coach know I was watching.

He was sitting behind his desk, listening while the other one spoke, listening with . . . I couldn't make out his expression. I'd never seen anything like it on Coach's face before. Was it anger? No, I'd seen Coach angry plenty of times—anger turned his face into a slab of granite. It looked nothing like this. Right now his jaw was tight, his lips white at the corners. His brow was furrowed, but his eyes looked like they were about to shoot out of their sockets, and his hands gripped the edge of the desk like it was the only thing keeping the spin of the earth from flinging him into space.

He said something to his visitor, and then they both stood up. I scrambled back, retreating behind the first set of lockers just as I heard the door open. From my hiding place, I heard footsteps, then saw the visitor turn the corner and walk, furtively but in an obvious hurry, toward the rear exit and out. It was . . .

Gwen Smith.

What the . . . ?

I'd known Gwen since kindergarten. Or, I knew her name—we'd never really been friends. She was absolutely unremarkable—not too pretty, not too homely, not too smart, not too dumb—one of those kids who existed outside of the school pecking order by being totally average in every way. She just faded into the background, like a ghost.

So why was she haunting Coach's office?

Heck, why was she even in the boys' part of the gym? She had no business in this sanctum of maleness.

"Treppenhouse? What the hell are you doing?"

Coach was standing there, scowling at me. There was no trace of the freaked expression he'd had just a minute ago.

"Nothing. I-I just got here."

"Well, you're not getting on the field dressed like that. Put your gear on."

"Yes, sir."

Just as I started toward my locker, Brad came back in. He had his mitt in one hand, my keys in the other. He made as if to throw them back to me, but then faked me out and underhanded them instead. I bobbled the catch, and it took both hands to keep the keys from hitting the floor.

"Geez, TNT, you really do need practice." Brad laughed. "So, I miss anything?"

The next time I saw Casey, he had a bruise around one eye and down one cheek. That wasn't unusual in itself—he always had scrapes and contusions here and there—but I could tell this wasn't just another skateboarding injury.

"Casey, what happened?"

"Not now. Let's just fuck, OK?"

His voice had an uncharacteristic tension. So did the sex. Casey's trademark self-confidence was missing—he kissed me like he was floundering in deep water and he needed my breath to stay alive.

But then, afterwards, he was back to normal. He stretched out on the mattress, naked and at ease, taking deep draws off one of those hand-rolled cigarettes.

"So what happened to you?" I asked again.

"You mean this?" He waved a hand over the bruise on

his face. "No big. I was skating in the park and a couple of Dawn Patrol dickheads jumped me."

"Who were they?"

"I didn't recognize them—they weren't from your troop. It was stupid, going there by myself—we usually skate in groups. Strength in numbers, all that shit." He looked at me and did a combined smile and eyeroll. "Dude, I'm fine—they just roughed me up a little. I've taken worse."

He offered me the cigarette, and I took it. This was only the second time I'd smoked marijuana—I'd practically coughed up both lungs the first time. But the stuff went down easier now. Coach would blow his top if he found out, but I figured an occasional hit wouldn't hurt me.

"I wish I'd been there with you," I said. "I would have kicked their butts."

"No. Don't say shit like that." Casey's tone sharpened. "I don't want you sticking your neck out for me."

"But—"

"No." He sat up, swung around, and straddled me, his hands pinning my shoulders. "Look, Tyler . . . I'm on borrowed time. You aren't. Don't fuck things up for yourself. Promise me."

I blinked at him a few times, then nodded. "I promise."

Inside, though, I was thinking, *bullshit*.

If only I had Casey's fearlessness, his street-savvy. He was right about me—I was a total noob.

But I knew one thing. When the day came to risk everything for Casey—and with barely a month and a half left until his Evaluation, that day was coming soon—I'd do it.

Whether he wanted me to, or not.

W E needed to find a new meeting place. According to Casey, it was unwise to use the same spot more than two or three times in a row. And going to the Peach Pit too often was asking for trouble—too many other Chaffs hung out there, only a few of them knew Casey was gay, and not even they could be trusted to keep their mouths shut about me.

"You mean, Chaffs hate us too?"

"Everybody hates us." Casey was picking at his finger-nails. "A lot of Chaffs were molested in the Reclamation Homes, so they think all queers are perverts who rape kids."

I didn't know what to say to that. I wanted to ask if that had ever happened to him, but I was also afraid of how he'd answer.

We still hadn't set up our next rendezvous yet, so . . . "How about Monday night? You can come to my house."

Casey's brows shot up. "Are you serious? I do know other places we can go. I mean, fucking around in your own room, with your folks downstairs? Not to mention that creepoid brother of yours."

"Eric won't be there. He's spending Easter Break in Yosemite at that big Rooster gathering. And my parents will be out for the evening—some movie-industry schmooze. Dad's getting an award." The latest in a long string of them. It was one of the things people did in Hollywood when they needed to kiss up to the Party—they gave Dad another brass plaque or chunk of Lucite. "They won't be home till late— we'll have the house to ourselves till midnight at least."

I was feeling cocky and adventurous going into Easter Break. The team had beaten Bakersfield—*slaughtered* them, 6-0, putting us squarely on target for the division playoffs. Danny Magruder had ruled the mound, pitching a shutout that was only a sixth-inning single away from a no-hitter. At the plate, the Mighty TNT had made his bat sing, hitting not just one, but two home runs, including a three-run blast that accounted for half the final score.

"You've been on fire lately, Treppenhouse," Coach had told me after the game. "I don't know what you're doing special, but keep it up."

"Yes, sir. I definitely will, sir."

When Monday evening arrived, I made a point of showing Casey around the house. The other times he'd come over, I'd rushed him upstairs so fast, I'd never given him the tour.

He smirked and shook his head as he looked through Mom's old books and videos. "You know, you're the first guy I've ever been with who wanted to do it in his own place."

"Where do you find these guys?" I asked. "At those bars?"

"Hell, no. Most of those bars were shut down. And the ones that weren't are full of Dentists. The DDS just keeps them open to trap people."

"So where *do* you find them?"

"Here and there. A lot of them pick *me* up—that homo detection thing works both ways." He chuckled. "I sound like a total slut, don't I?"

"Yeah. But it's hot." Thinking about all the guys Casey had been with just made me hornier for him. "Right now I want to do you in every room of this house."

"Maybe I'll do you first."

"Want to wrestle for it?"

"You're on."

The contest went back and forth until we both were about to explode. It was an even match, with my superior strength and training against Casey's height, agility, and longer reach—though of course, there were no real winners or losers when *we* wrestled. Inevitably, one of us just gave in to the other.

Tonight, I did.

Casey had me pinned and was unbuttoning my shirt when the phone rang. I let it ring—Unity was at rehearsal, I wasn't expecting anyone else to call, and Casey was doing that thing to my ear with his tongue that drove me crazy—but then I heard the answering machine.

"Tyler, pick up the phone."

It was Dad.

"Shit! Let me up!"

Casey rolled off me, and I ran hurtling for the phone in the kitchen.

"Sorry, Dad. I was in the garage. What's up?"

Either Dad didn't notice me panting like I'd just run ten laps around the reservoir, or he didn't care. "I need you to come and get your mother. Right now."

"Mom? Oh, no." I already knew what this was about. "How bad is she?"

"Just come and get her." His voice was buzzing with barely controlled anger. "We're at the Beverly Hills Hotel. Do you know where that is?"

"I'll look it up. I'll be there as soon as I—"

Dad hung up before I could finish. As I put back the receiver, a cold nausea hit my stomach. This was going to be ugly. Just like the other times.

Casey was behind me, rubbing my shoulders. I took a deep breath before turning around. "I have to go. I'm sorry. I have to go pick up my mom. She's—" I had to shut my eyes. I'd caught myself looking around for something to throw. "Damn it."

"Do you want me to come with?" Casey asked.

God, I wished. But Casey's presence would be too hard

to explain. And besides . . . "Thanks, but no. You don't want to see this, believe me."

A knowing nod. "No worries."

He bent down, kissed me, and then laid his hands on my shoulders again. "I'll be at the Peach Pit. Come by later, if you can. You want to try again tomorrow?"

"Definitely."

From my house it took about forty-five minutes to get to Beverly Hills. I spotted the hotel—a sprawling, garishly painted structure, glowing against the night sky like fluorescent bubblegum—and pulled up, tires screeching, in front of the entrance. I leaped out of the car, waved off the parking valet, and jogged up the red carpet into the lobby.

As I walked in, a man in a burgundy-colored blazer came around from behind the concierge desk. "Tyler Treppenhouse?"

I nodded. With a grimace, the concierge directed me over to a cluster of overstuffed armchairs, across one of which my mother was draped.

She had a martini in her hand. Or, she had the *glass* in her hand—the contents had all dribbled down her dress and onto the chair's velvet upholstery. At the bottom of the glass, a single olive lay dried-up and shriveled, like a tiny dead frog.

Another burgundy-blazered man was trying to take the glass from her.

"Mrs. Treppenhouse . . . Neighbor . . . I'm afraid I must insist that you—"

"Don't you *Neighbor* me, you spit-shined piece of white trash! I was having people like you lined up and shot while you were still in diapers!"

Quickly, I stepped between the two of them. "Sir, please. I'm her son. Let me handle this."

Mom's head lolled, she looked up at me, and a gashlike grin split her face. "Tyler! Honey! Are you taking me home? Is your father too Jewish now to pay for a cab?"

"Where is Dad?"

"Off having everyone in Hollywood tell him what a great man he is, of course. Gonna be a lot of lips in this town smelling like Party ass tomorrow."

She cackled like she'd just told the funniest joke in the world. I saw the Hawkeye in the ceiling, and cringed.

"Come on, Mom." While she was still laughing, I took the opportunity to ease the martini glass out of her hand and pass it off to the man in the blazer before shooing him away. "Let's go."

I hadn't lost my touch—I could still get Mom to obey me in this condition, even when no one else could. I helped her to her feet, gave her my shoulder to lean on, and wrangled her out of the lobby.

"I'm really sorry," I murmured to the concierge on the way out.

He raised his eyebrows in what might have been sympathy. "Have a good evening. Nation First."

I buckled Mom's seatbelt extra tight to keep her from sliding under the dashboard. As I drove away from the hotel, I rolled down the passenger window to give her some fresh air—and a place to puke if she had to before we got home.

"You look nice tonight, Mom."

Mom made a raspberry. "Don't lie. I look like a twenty-dollar whore. Just the way your father likes it."

She was playing with the string of pearls around her neck. Before I could stop her, she tore them off and flung them out the window.

"Mom! Those were Grandma's!"

"For God's sake, Tyler, are you really that stupid? They're fake, like everything else about your father. They probably came from some spic's junk drawer."

I was hyperventilating, and my head was throbbing. Shouldn't I be going back and looking for the necklace? Yeah, right—on a busy street, at night. There was no way I'd ever find them. Those pearls had belonged to Dad's mother, and *her* mother, and *her* mother—God only knew how many generations back they went. And now they were scattered all over Sunset Boulevard. Dad was going to kill both of us.

I kept quiet the rest of the way home. The long drive settled Mom down, and I got her in the house without protest. I laid her on the living room couch, her head elevated—I didn't dare put her to bed until I'd gotten some water into her, to dilute the alcohol and keep her from choking on her own vomit as she slept.

"It wasn't supposed to be this way." Her voice was heavy and groggy. "I knew my place—*a helpmate fit for him.* But I worked *hard* for the Nation. I did."

I took the glass of water I was holding and touched it to her lips. "Just drink this, OK? You'll feel better."

"For our race, for our values—I *fought.* I fought just as hard as he did." She snorted. "Your father, the Man Who Cleaned Up Hollywood—ha! He'd be nothing but an office rat or a detention camp guard without the connections *I* gave him."

She drained the glass, then tilted her head back and closed her eyes. When she opened them again, they zeroed right in on me, like they were seeing me for the very first time. "You were an accident, you know."

"What?" I jerked away, like she'd just slapped me. The water glass slipped out of my hand and thumped on the carpet.

"He wanted me to abort you. I said no—I wasn't about to throw our values out the window. *I* wanted you. He never did."

"Mom, stop it!"

"Be glad, Tyler. At least *one* of your parents isn't a god-damn hypocrite. That's the only reason you're alive today."

"Mommy, *please!"*

I grabbed the glass off the floor and fled into the kitchen with it. I stuck it under the faucet, turned the water on, and let it run. There was a cracking sensation behind my eyes, like a dam about to break. I turned up the water, letting it spill over the rim of the glass and onto my hand. Part of me just wanted to fill up the sink and shove my head in to drown.

By the time I pulled myself together and went back into the living room, Mom was crying. That was actually a good sign—it meant she was sobering up.

"I'm so sorry, baby. You're my sweet boy, you always have been. I didn't mean it, what I just said."

"I know, Mom." I held the water glass and made her drink some more. "It's OK."

"You're not like your brother. Eric's his father's son— you're mine." She looked up at me, her eyes moist and puffy. "You're all I've got. I love you."

"I love you too."

I got her to finish the glass, and another. Then I just sat with her. I curled up at the foot of the couch, let her stroke my hair, and told her again and again that I loved her.

This would be over soon. Mom would drift off to sleep, and then I'd carry her upstairs and put her to bed. Once she was safely tucked in, I'd get out of here and go see Casey. I probably shouldn't, I should stay here in case Mom needed anything . . . but I needed Casey. I needed him more than ever . . .

I heard the roaring of the engine from blocks away. I shot to my feet. Then tires screeching in the driveway, and a car door slamming.

Dad.

I was halfway to the door when it burst open.

"Dad?" I stepped in front of him, holding my hands palms-out at my sides. "Dad, just calm down—"

He blew past me, knocking me out of the way like I wasn't even there. His face was red verging on purple, the veins bulging across it. He barreled into the living room, straight at Mom, who, like me, had jumped up the instant she'd heard his car coming.

"How *dare* you?" Dad stabbed a finger at her. "You alkie bitch. How dare you humiliate me like that?"

"Ha!" Mom's laugh sprayed contempt all over the walls. "Hurts, doesn't it? Now you know how it feels."

"Are you *insane?* I *work* with those people! I see them every day!"

"Not to mention every night."

They started yelling at and over each other. Their voices rose to pain-inflicting volumes. I pressed my hands against my ears, trying and failing to block them out. They hadn't had one of these screaming matches since I was a kid—nowadays it was all sullen, bitter silences and razor-tongued carping at each other from opposite ends of the dinner table. That long ceasefire only made things worse now.

Chaffs

"I ought to never let you out of the house again!" Dad was roaring. "Jesus. There were *Party officials* there! People after my job! And you gave them the perfect opening to stick a knife in me, you know that?"

Mom just laughed again. "Serves you right, what with all *your* sticking things where they don't belong. Oh, they'd *love* to hear about that, wouldn't they? They'd be happy as hell to find out where you enjoy sticking your—"

I'd never seen Dad hit Mom before. The scene sputtered, like I was watching a video and the pause button kept getting stuck. The back of Dad's hand slammed into Mom's face . . . *pause* . . . her head whipped around . . . *pause* . . . she spun and tumbled back onto the couch . . . *pause* . . . Dad advanced on her . . .

And I jumped in.

My fist traced a perfect arc through the air to my father's jaw. There was no pain, no sound, just a shock wave rolling up my arm and breaking against my shoulder. Dad stumbled back, one hand shielding the side of his face.

His voice came to me muffled by the rushing of blood through my head. "So. My pussy of a son thinks he has balls now."

"I'll kill you." I wasn't yelling. My voice was quiet, and as flat and cold as the surface of a frozen lake. "You hit her again, ever, I swear to God, I will fucking kill you."

I stood absolutely still, feet apart, both fists clenched. I braced for him to throw a punch himself . . . but then he took a step back, and I saw it—his fear. Fear of me. I was bigger than him now, stronger, more lethal. What I'd said—I meant every word. And Dad knew it.

"Fuck this shit," he muttered.

Without looking again at me or Mom, he turned and fled the scene.

The door at the Peach Pit was unlocked. I opened it and shambled into the apartment. Casey rushed forward and caught me just in time as my legs gave out, and I collapsed.

"Tyler! Are you OK? Are you hurt?"

I shook my head, slowly and carefully. Too fast and I'd throw up. I was shaking like an epileptic. I didn't say anything—I didn't want to speak. All I wanted was for Casey to hold onto me until the tremors stopped.

T HE next morning, Casey and I cleared out of the Peach Pit and went over the hill to Santa Monica.

It was warm, so we took our shirts off. There were Wide Awakes on the pier and at the lifeguard stations, plus Dawn Patrol squads on the beach stopping girls who showed too much skin and making them cover up. Guys usually escaped harassment unless their swimsuits were too tight, but still, we had to be careful—no touching, no standing too close, no lingering gazes.

All around us, boy-girl couples strolled hand in hand, giggling, trading whispers, feeding each other bits of cotton candy. They made me fume with envy.

"OK, slugger, what's on your mind?"

We were near the end of the pier, past the shabby souvenir shops and boarded-up carnival rides, with no one nearby except a few fishermen on the level below us, none of them within earshot. Farther away, a troop of Morning Glories was practicing some sort of drill. Good—the girls' chanting voices would be all that the Hawkeyes picked up, if we kept our own voices down.

"I'm thinking about the photo I saw in that old year-book," I said. "The one of the gay student club? I wonder what happened to those kids."

"Dead, I'm guessing, or Reoriented. They'd be, what, in their thirties now?"

"Something like that." I leaned against the railing and breathed in the salty air, staring across the bay at the mountains above Malibu shimmering blue in the mist. "Can you imagine what it must have been like for them, to be so . . . open? What would they think of us, of all this cloak-and-dagger crap we have to go through?"

Casey laughed. "It'd probably make them hard."

"Come on, dude. I'm serious."

"So am I. There have always been guys who get off on the danger." A sly look. "You get off on it. Admit it."

He had me there.

I still had a few hours before I needed to head back to the Valley for practice, and with me and Casey both walking around shirtless, it wouldn't be long before one of us—probably me—jumped the other. So that was it for the beach.

We made for one of Casey's other meeting places, an empty office suite twenty-odd floors up in a skyscraper near the La Brea Tar Pits. Apparently half the office space in L.A. was vacant these days.

Casey was only partly right—it wasn't just the danger that I got off on. When I was with him, I felt *real*. Even in this abandoned office, which reeked of mold and copier fluid and looked like the Red-Mex army had ransacked it—busted chairs and shreds of paper everywhere, cables poking out of the drywall and snaking across the floor, holes in the ceiling where the Hawkeyes had been torn out. Other than on the baseball field, these stolen, secret hours with Casey were the only times I felt like my true self.

We lay quiet for a while, slick with sweat, our limbs tangled, and then I got up, stretched, and walked over to the window. No one outside could see me—the glass was tinted, and we were hundreds of feet above street level—but still, I felt like I was putting my nakedness on display.

"Last night, my mom said I was an accident."

"You mean, a whoops-the-condom-broke type of accident?"

"Yeah. The funny thing is, I think I've always known. My whole life, I've been trying to prove myself—to my parents, to the Nation, to Muldoon. To prove that I'm . . . worth having been born, that I'm not some—"

"Some dirty Chaff?" With a snort, Casey got up and stood beside me. "That's the game they make us play—prove you're not worthless, or else you get flushed. People like me aren't the only ones being Evaluated."

"You could play the game too, if you wanted. Why don't you?"

"I do play it. Just not by their rules. The only one I'm playing against is myself."

"Do you ever win?"

"Sometimes."

Again, those kids in the yearbook came to mind—and those guys in the videos. Who did *they* have to fight against?

"Things didn't use to be this way," I said. "They don't *have* to be this way."

"Heh. You're starting to sound like Randall. He's always going on about the Revolution, like he's Che Guevara or something."

"Who?"

"Nobody. Never mind." He turned to face me and leaned against the window. "Things are what they are. Sure, if I had a time machine I'd go back—but I don't have a time machine. That world from before—it's gone forever."

"And our world? You don't think it could ever get better?"

"My parents thought it could. Look at how that worked out." Casey shrugged. "Anyway, we're all accidents, when you get right down to it. Some accidents are just luckier than others."

The noise hit my ears as I left the gym after practice. Shouting and scuffling, over by my car. One of the voices was Brad's.

I took two steps toward the noise, and then broke into a run.

Brad had Casey on the ground, one knee pressing down on his stomach and both ham-sized hands wrapped around his neck. Casey's face was turning purple, his eyes blood-shot and as big as baseballs, his struggles reduced to useless kicking and clawing. Around them, a few others—Danny Magruder, Rick Nagy, a few random passersby drawn by the promise of bloodshed—were cheering on the violence.

I pushed my way past the onlookers, and jumped.

Brad didn't see me until I was on top of him. Startled, he let go of Casey. Normally, grappling with Brad Nemechuk would have been like an ant wrestling an elephant, but rage and adrenaline had taken hold and I had him in a full nelson before he could even think of a countermove. Through my red-stained vision, I saw Casey scoot away and against the front wheel of my car, wheezing and rubbing his throat.

Brad wrenched free and spun around, fists raised. I disengaged and backed up before he could throw a punch.

"Brad! What the heck are you doing?"

He flinched as he recognized me, and then stabbed a thick finger at Casey. "I caught this Chaff trying to break into your car! I'll kill him!"

I could see him about to charge Casey again. I stepped between them and gave him a shove.

"Neighbor Nemechuk! Stand down!" I tried to use the same tone Kevin had used to rein Brad in the last time. In my mind, the cover story for me and Casey rose to the surface. "Monahan's helping me with math. You know how these Chaffs are—they'll do anything for extra points when their Evaluations are coming up. He was just leaving me some notes—weren't you, Monahan?"

Casey tried to speak, started coughing, and nodded instead.

"You see, Brad? Now go cool off before Coach comes out. You've already gotten benched once—you want to be off the team for the rest of the season?"

That got through to him. He took a deep breath and passed a hand over his face. "I'm sorry, TNT. You're right. I saw that garbage hanging around your car, and I just—"

"Look, thank you for keeping an eye out. But I've got this. Just go."

Brad nodded. Then he glanced at Casey, and his temper flared again. "You'd better watch your backside, Chaff."

I braced myself for Casey to say something smart, and set Brad off anew. But he didn't. Without another word, Brad stomped away across the parking lot.

I glared at the bystanders. "What are you people looking at? Get out of here."

I waited until Casey and I were alone, then rushed over to him and crouched down. "Are you OK?"

He sure didn't look OK. He was swallowing over and over, wincing. The bruises on his neck were already an angry red—they'd be fully black and blue by tomorrow.

Just one look at his perfect flesh, so brutally marred—it made my own anger surge back. How *dare* Brad lay a hand on —

"Ty!"

My head shot up. Unity was right there, on the other side of the car. I didn't know how long she'd been there—I hadn't seen her walk up. Instantly, the volcanic rage in my veins froze into hard, black terror.

"Wh-what are you doing here?"

"Looking for you, sweetie." She came around to my side, smiling. "Aren't you glad to see me?"

It was just her normal smile, I told myself—those were *not* the bared teeth of a mountain lion pouncing on a deer.

"Of course I am." I smiled back, reached for her, and planted a quick kiss on her lips. As I did so, I turned my head so I wouldn't have to see the look on Casey's face. "I just thought you had choir rehearsal today."

"Reverend Blanchard let me go early—I'm not feeling well. I had Daddy drop me off here."

Another bolt of panic. "Your dad's here?"

"No, he went back to work. I just needed to see you. I miss you, Ty."

She did look a little peaked. But otherwise, she was her usual cheerful self—no sign of suspicion. Thank God Mr. Ludlow wasn't here with her. One look at this scene, with his Dentist's eyes, and he'd know everything.

Unity smiled down at Casey, who was starting to get his feet underneath him. "Hello. I don't think we've met. *Someone* here forgot his manners."

"Oh. Sorry. Unity, this is Casey." I bent and grabbed his arm to help him up. "He's been tutoring me in math."

Casey cleared his throat, croaked out a faint, "Hi," and then raised one hand in a nervous wave.

"I saw what happened, Ty. You are *such* a great guy, sticking up for your friends like that." She gave me another kiss, on the cheek this time. "Anyway, can we go? I really am not feeling well. Casey, can we give you a ride home?"

Casey was getting his skateboard, which had rolled under a nearby pickup truck during the melee. He shook his head and cleared his throat again. "No. Thanks. I'm OK."

"Are you sure? You look hurt. Maybe you should go see a doctor."

"He'll be fine." I glanced at Casey just long enough to see the relief in his eyes, then went over to the car and opened the door for Unity. "I should get you home. Casey, I'll see you later, OK?"

Casey nodded. "Yeah. Later."

I risked one more look at him before joining Unity in the car. Casey gave me a faint smile—*don't worry about it*—then hooked his skateboard under his arm and walked off, still a bit unsteady. After that, in the parking lot, it was just the two of us.

The three of us. Me, Unity, and my churning guts.

Casey zigzagged down the old bike path at the reservoir, then tipped the skateboard onto its rear wheels and executed a tight 180-degree turn to face me. "You shouldn't have done that, you know. Pull Nemechuk off me."

"Like I'm going to stand there and watch him strangle you?"

Casey was recovering. His voice was still hoarse, and his neck still looked chewed on. But even if he seemed none the worse, I was still shaken up. I had no doubt Brad would have killed him—and been applauded for it—if I hadn't intervened.

"I'm just saying, you've got to be more careful," Casey said.

"Look who's talking. What were you doing there, anyway?"

"I was leaving you a note, about where to meet me after practice. I wasn't expecting the Missing Link to show up." Another turn on the skateboard, a 360 this time. "I worry about you. I'm not going to be around much longer—you have to start thinking about this shit on your own."

It was the second time in three days that he'd alluded to his impending Evaluation. In spite of his Oscar-winning performance as the Stoic Tough Guy, I knew it was weighing on him.

But I didn't want to think about it any more than he did—not right now, anyway. It was too early—even the birds were just getting up.

I should have thought of this a long time ago—meeting Casey first thing in the morning. As far as anyone else knew, I was simply doing my laps around the reservoir, like always. Casey had complained at first about having to get up before dawn, but I made it . . . worthwhile . . . and the complaints stopped.

"Do one of those jumps again," I told him. "The one where you make the board spin around before you land."

"A kickflip—that's what it's called."

Casey obeyed, pushing along the ground with one foot to build up some momentum and then springing into the air. I tried to track his footwork, but it happened too fast for my eyes to follow—the board spun completely around and then just seemed to level out on its own. He landed, glided into a wide semicircle from one edge of the path to the other, and came to a halt in front of me.

"I swear, I'm never going to get tired of watching that," I said.

"Want to learn how to do it?"

"Uh . . . " For a second my tongue stuck to the roof of my mouth. "Seriously?"

"Sure. Why not? I mean, you won't get it right away. First you have to learn how to ollie, and then . . . " He grinned at the blank look on my face. "Never mind. Here, try standing on the board first."

He stepped down and gave the board a nudge. It rolled to a stop at my feet. I stared at it, petrified.

"Come on, slugger. Give it your best swing."

I felt like I was sticking my foot in a bear trap. I placed it on the surface of the board, but then yanked it away. My head was swiveling. Part of me expected to see a police helicopter overhead, or a squad of Wide Awakes jumping out of the bushes.

Nothing. I was being stupid—it was just me and Casey here. I'd had sex with a guy, I'd smoked marijuana, I'd listened to banned music—and I was scared of what might happen if I put my foot on a skateboard?

My first attempt sent the board skittering down the path and me stumbling the other way. My second try was no more successful. Nor was the third. I was getting frustrated. Where had my coordination disappeared to? I was an *athlete*, for chrissake.

After my fourth failed try, Casey came to my aid. Grinning, he put one foot in front of the board to keep it from escaping, then leaned down and kissed me, for encouragement. The kiss was an instant confidence booster—for a moment, the rest of the world fell away and I no longer felt watched and judged. A single firm step, and I was standing on the board.

"OK, now what?"

"Just relax. Focus on keeping your balance."

The wheels had some kind of suspension system—I could feel the springs giving under my weight. It seemed like this was going to be the shortest skateboarding lesson in recorded history—there was no solid ground, nothing to grab onto . . .

Then I looked at Casey. Standing on the board had put me close to eye level with him. As I gazed at him, everything stabilized. *I can do this. I can do anything.*

I tried moving forward. I came close to falling on my butt

twice before I got twenty feet . . . but I made it. I couldn't do any of those turns or other maneuvers that Casey made look so easy, but I still managed to get back on the board unassisted and return to the starting point.

"Fun." I stepped off and nudged the board back to him. "But still, I'll never be as good as you."

"You'll have a lot more chances to practice." He gazed down at the board, rolling it back and forth with the toe of one shoe. "I'm giving it to you."

"Excuse me?"

"After I'm gone. I want you to have it."

"You want me . . . " My brain was sputtering again. "I . . . Casey, thank you, but . . . what am I going to do with it?"

"Learn to skate. Or just keep it. This is my one and only possession. I want it to go to a good home."

I knew it the instant he looked at me. This wasn't just a possession he was offering me. It was a piece of himself.

"Of course I'll take it. Casey, I—" I clenched my jaw to keep from saying the rest, but the words pried at my teeth until I had to let them out. "I love you."

Casey didn't answer—he didn't have to. Blinking away tears, he grabbed me and crushed me against his chest, and I realized that I was the first person in his life who'd ever said those three words to him.

And that I was also going to be the last.

APRIL was going by way too fast. As we drew closer to the End of the Motherfucking Line, as Casey called it, the vibe of our meetings grew more and more frantic. We'd show up, tear our clothes off, and maul each other until neither of us had any energy left. Then, maybe, we'd talk—a lot of the time, though, we'd just lie spooning, not daring to speak. Sometimes, amid that silence, I'd feel Casey's body trembling. That was the only way I could tell how scared he really was.

I kept thinking about that incident with Brad. I could have lost Casey there and then. We had such precious little time left already, and yet even those dwindling hours could have been robbed from us. The thought made me desperate to save him, no matter what it took.

Except Casey didn't want to be saved. Every time I raised the possibility—running away together, changing our identities and disappearing, bribing the Evaluators to pass him, anything—he shot me down.

"I told you—don't stick your neck out for me." He raised his flask to his lips and took two huge gulps—whatever he kept in there, he'd been downing it like lemonade. "This is how I chose to live—and I've always known when the bill would come due. I just want to have a big smile and a busted nut when I pay it. Are you going to help me with that, or not?"

Maybe I was just being selfish. Was I really afraid for Casey, or simply afraid of facing the future without him? My life was all laid out—baseball games to win, tests to pass, babies to father for the Nation . . . and after that, college, marriage, more babies, more games, a spot on a major-league farm club and a ticket to the Show if things went well, or a job landed using Dad's Party connections if they didn't.

But when I imagined going on without Casey around to keep me level, I thought, *I can't do it.*

On the Tuesday following Easter, I went over to Unity's house. I stayed until about a half-hour before curfew. By then Unity had fallen asleep, so I got dressed, made my way downstairs, and tiptoed across the foyer . . .

"Neighbor Treppenhouse."

Mr. Ludlow was standing at the entrance to his den. One hand was on the doorknob, the other one holding a briefcase. From under the flap of his unbuttoned suit jacket peeked the strap of a shoulder holster.

He opened the door, directing me inside. "I need to speak with you."

My heartbeat was practically rattling the windows. Something was wrong—I could feel it. I made a point of looking at my watch, hoping the nearness of curfew would let me off the hook. "Right now?"

"Right now."

The furnishings in the den were even more like a bunker's than in the rest of the house—a military-looking desk of green-hued metal, a credenza in the corner, harsh overhead lighting, filing cabinets, computer, portrait of President Muldoon on the wall. The only cheerful thing, on the desk, was a framed photo of Unity and her mom, taken when Unity was a baby. Both of them were smiling.

Unity's dad wasn't.

I sat down in a chair beside the desk. I couldn't get comfortable in it—the seat was too narrow, the back was too straight, and one of the legs was shorter than the others, making it wobble. It was almost like the chair had been designed that way on purpose.

Mr. Ludlow set the briefcase on the desk and, with his back turned, opened it with a clicking of the combination lock and two jarring pops as the catches released. When he swung around again he was holding a thin manila folder, which he thrust at me.

There were photos inside—eight-by-ten glossies, black and white, surveillance photos from the graininess of them—taken in that vacant office, the one Casey and I had used for one of our trysts last week. They'd been shot from above, probably from one of those holes where the Hawkeyes had been torn out. Or where we *thought* they'd been torn out.

They showed me and Casey.

They showed . . . everything.

"Sir." I could hardly talk. I could hardly breathe. "Sir, I—"

"Think very carefully about the next thing you say." His voice sounded like it came from the bottom of an open grave. "You know who I am, you know what I do. You aren't planning to insult my intelligence any further than you already have, are you?"

I swallowed hard. "No, sir."

Mr. Ludlow removed his jacket and hung it on a coat rack by the door, then unsnapped his holster and took out the gun. I shrank away. The chair wobbled. Its feet scraped against the floor.

He cradled the gun in his hands. His gaze focused on it, floated up toward Unity's bedroom, descended onto me. I could feel the tears welling up, feel the pleas taking shape on my quivering lips . . .

Then Mr. Ludlow checked the gun's safety, removed the clip and the chambered bullet, and put it all in the briefcase.

"So." He took the folder out of my hands, closed the briefcase, and laid the folder on top of it. "Tell me. Have you been using protection with this boy?"

Protection? Maybe I was too dumb with relief at still being alive, but I didn't get what he meant by —

"Condoms, Tyler. Have you been using them?"

"Yes! Yes, of course."

His shoulders relaxed a little. "So you haven't been completely irresponsible—thank you for that. You've heard about the diseases. It would be *deeply* unfortunate for you if your perversions resulted in my daughter becoming ill. Am I clear?"

"Does Unity . . . Are you going to tell her?"

"No. And neither are you. It would break her heart."

Mr. Ludlow kept me squirming with his gaze, then sighed and looked away, taking off his glasses and wiping the lenses with a handkerchief he pulled from his shirt pocket. Resetting his glasses on his nose, he rolled his office chair around from behind his desk and sat down close to me.

"Tyler, I've always been very fond of you." He leaned in, his voice low and intimate. "And you know how Unity feels. Frankly, she and I are all that's standing between you and a detention center."

I hung on his every word. Even when he was being complimentary, it was like listening to the eulogy at my own funeral.

"You see my dilemma, don't you? I have a conflict of interest here. Professionally speaking, I ought to step aside and hand your case off to someone else. But personally, I find that idea . . . distressing, and not just because of the grief it would cause my daughter. Are you aware of what happens to homosexuals in detention? I'll spare you the details."

He paused, obviously waiting for my mind to fill in the details for him.

"You have so much potential. To waste it over some youthful . . . experimentation serves no useful purpose. I know you. You're a decent young man. You want to serve the Nation."

I managed a nod.

"That Reclaimee boy, Monahan—he has some, you might say, questionable associates. The DDS has been watching them for a while now."

"You have?"

The Dentist's eyes were hooded. "Please, Tyler. Those Chaffs, as you call them—do you really think there's anything about those hooligans that we *don't* know? The drugs, the petty crime, that cacophonous howling they call music? For now we're content simply to monitor them, so long as they pose no threat. In a way, they actually benefit the social order, by providing an outlet for deviant impulses." An open-palm gesture in my direction. "Case in point."

He was studying me, analyzing. I hadn't broken down pleading yet. But still, I had to bargain. And not just for my own life . . .

"Casey's not a threat," I blurted. "He's not."

"Do you sincerely believe that, or is this simply a feeble effort to protect him?" He tilted his head back, staring at me under the rims of his glasses. "I've read Monahan's file—his Evaluation is next month. His prospects are not good. They could easily become even worse."

I choked back a sob.

Mr. Ludlow reached out and patted me on the forearm. "But perhaps we can help him, you and I. The DDS carries significant influence with the Reclamation Program. Perhaps we can tip the scales in your friend's favor."

"You'd do that?"

"With your assistance. And assuming that Monahan is, in fact, as harmless as you claim." A thin, tight-lipped smile. "As it turns out, you're in just the right position to help us make that determination."

He lifted his eyebrows. That, and his smile, said it all—he had me, the trap had been sprung.

"You'll be doing your Nation and your Commander-in-Chief a great service, Neighbor Treppenhouse. You might well help prevent another Nuke York. And to bring things closer to home, by assisting us, you'll be making that"—he waved at the folder with the photos in it—"go away."

"You want me to be an informer." A spy, a snitch, one of the millions the DDS employed, everywhere . . .

"Be our eyes and ears, that's all. You'll check in with me regularly—just a friendly chat, like we're having right now.

And—as a bonus I'm sure you'll appreciate—you and Monahan can continue seeing each other. As a matter of fact, I insist on it."

"But Unity—"

"It will be our secret. Handling other people's secrets is my job. You think you're the only man in the world leading a double life?" He let out a small snort of contempt. "You'd be surprised."

He stood up and loomed over me, his demeanor once again ice cold. He tipped his head toward the folder on the desk. "Actions have consequences, Tyler. I'm making you a very reasonable offer. Ask yourself, what would be the consequences of not accepting it? Would that save your friend? Would it save *you?*"

I DIDN'T believe Mr. Ludlow for one second. He might work the system to keep *me* out of a cell, but Casey? The Chaff screwing his daughter's boyfriend? Unity's dad would be dumping him into the pit like so much garbage, the first chance he got.

Still, I had to hope. So long as even a remote chance existed that Mr. Ludlow would keep his word, I had to play along. He had me by the nuts and we both knew it.

With all the recent craziness, I'd totally forgotten about the tickets Dad had given me to Opening Day at Dodger Stadium. It was going to be a double date, once—me and Unity and Kevin and Shelly. But Kevin had disappeared, Shelly had moved away, and Unity only sat through my own games out of duty as my girlfriend—she didn't care for baseball.

Casey, meanwhile, had never seen the Dodgers play in person. I nearly hit the ceiling when he told me. Never? That simply would not stand. Casey was not going to reach the End of the Motherfucking Line without seeing at least one game.

At the stadium, I traded my tickets for a pair of seats on the reserve level. It killed me, giving up a chance to sit in the Muldoon Box, with its plush seats and air conditioning and hors d'oeuvres brought to you by smartly dressed waiters, but the box would be full of Party bigwigs, any number of whom might know Dad. Bad enough that Mr. Ludlow knew about me and Casey—I didn't want my family finding out, too.

Casey was wearing a brand-new Dodgers jersey, along with an expensive-looking and probably-stolen pair of designer sunglasses. "An early birthday present from Freya. Do I look like a total L.A. nightmare, or what?"

He looked hot, like always. But I didn't dare say it. The Dodger uniforms weren't the only shade of blue here—the ballpark was seething with Wide Awakes. No surprise, what with the bombing at Wrigley Field last year, but they still made me jumpy.

The Opening Day ceremonies dragged on forever. A combined Rooster-Morning Glory color guard marched onto the field carrying the Stars and Stripes, the banner of the Party, the Bear Flag of California, and the blue and white flag with the Dodgers' team logo. Jet fighters streaked overhead in formation. And on the JumboVision above the bleachers, President Muldoon gave his prerecorded address—lots of recycled phrases about the Fourth Great Awakening and the renewal of the Nation and the inherent Americanness of baseball and so on. The same canned speech he gave every year.

About halfway through the C-in-C's speech, I stole a glance at Casey, worrying that he might be fidgeting or rolling his eyes or doing something else that might attract attention. But no, his posture was straight, his facial expression perfect—just the right mix of worship and gratitude a good Son of the Fourth Great Awakening was supposed to have when his leader was speaking. It surprised me. Casey could do a pretty decent impression of a patriotic citizen, when he had to.

Then some Party official I'd never heard of threw out the first pitch, we sang—first the National Anthem, then *The Battle Hymn of the Republic*—the umpire shouted "PLAY BALL!" and we settled in.

My disappointment over missing out on the Muldoon Box soon faded. It was a beautiful day, the stadium was packed, and it was baseball! We were playing our archrivals, the San Francisco Giants—who on earth would want to be cooped up in some climate-controlled luxury box for an epic showdown like that? Roasting in the sun on plastic seats, scarfing down hot dogs—that was how God meant this game to be enjoyed.

Two innings in, and the game was already a seesaw. The Giants took an early 1-0 lead, but then, in the bottom of the second, Sikorski hit a single, Jenkinson walked, and Nystrom drove them both in with a double—2-1 Dodgers.

Casey went for a food-and-soda run. After a full inning—just long enough for me to start worrying—he reappeared, carrying a cardboard tray with two hot dogs and a pair of cups filled . . . with a foamy substance that looked and smelled nothing like soda.

"Jesus, you should have seen that line." Casey balanced the tray on his knees and handed me one of the cups. "You'd think the beer ration was running out."

"OK, how did you get beer?" I'd seen Casey buy alcohol before, but at Dodger Stadium? They were ruthless about the drinking age here. Even Brad got carded at Dodger games, and he was the oldest-looking guy on our team.

"That's what fake IDs are for." Casey raised his own cup in a toast and then took a sip. "I can fix you up with one, if you want—I know a dude who does them, cheap. I'll get hold of him before . . . "

Before his number comes up? I shook it off. We still had a whole month together, and today was special. I wasn't about to ruin it.

By the top of the seventh it was a 3-3 tie. My eyes tracked every pitch, every swing. For all that it was only the season opener, I might as well have been watching the final game of the World Series. Beating our upstate rivals was that crucial.

Chaffs

Could this day be any more perfect?

The sun was hot, the beer was cold, the game was intense. I was young and alive, watching the best players of the game I loved more than anything in the world, with the guy I loved more than anyone in the world. The only way to make this day better would be to put me down on the field—at the plate, batting clean-up, with fifty thousand delirious voices roaring in my ears. *T-N-T . . . T-N-T . . . T-N-T . . . T-N-T . . .*

I looked over at Casey. He was leaning forward, his knees brushing the seat in front of him, his hands clasped like he was praying. He was as into the game as I was.

We reached the seventh-inning stretch. The crowd rose to its feet, the stadium organ swirled to life, and fifty thousand baseball fans launched into song.

"Take me out to the baaallgaaame . . . "

In the middle of the song, five lines in—surrounded by that mass of voices root-root-rooting for the home team—I took Casey's hand. Casey tensed up and shot me a startled look, but then tightened his grip and went back to singing.

And why not? Nothing could touch us now. Our impending doom seemed infinitely far away. This moment, right now, was all that mattered. I could have even kissed Casey if I wanted to—but that would have been tacky, like I was trying too hard to prove something to the people around us. Casey and I had nothing to prove.

"For it's one, two, three strikes you're ou . . . "

Casey's voice died. His jaw dropped open. His eyes were on the JumboVision. I was afraid to look. Were we on camera? Two fags caught holding hands, in public?

"Dude." Casey leaned over and spoke into my ear. "Isn't that your dad?"

It was.

He was on the field level, just behind the Dodgers' dugout. He stood there singing, oblivious . . . then he saw himself on the screen, and his face drained of color, while the woman next to him, with her arm snaked around his . . .

"Holy shit," Casey said. "That's Charissa Dunbar, isn't it? The actress?"

I managed to nod. The rest of me, below the neck, was stiff as a corpse. "Yeah. She goes to our church."

"I bet they spend a lot of time in confession."

"We aren't Catholic."

Before I could babble anything else my guts seized up again. The implications were hitting me—that hand with the thousand-dollar manicure clutching Dad's elbow, the way the two of them were leaning toward each other, and worst of all, that look of caught-in-the-act panic on Dad's face . . .

My limbs went numb. My vision blurred around the edges and turned painfully sharp in the center. I stumbled sideways, into Casey. He grabbed my arm.

"Tyler?"

"I'm going to throw up. I'm *seriously* going to throw up."

"Let's get out of here."

On the way out I spent what felt like forever in the men's room, puking up beer and half-digested hot dogs. Even after emptying my stomach, I huddled there with the dry heaves, clutching the toilet bowl. Casey stood guard outside the stall, peeking in now and then to make sure I was still alive.

Finally he got me to my feet, cleaned me up, and hustled me out to the car. Some Wide Awakes stopped us in the parking lot, but Casey bluffed past them like a pro. "No problem here, Neighbors—my buddy just had a little too much to drink. Nation First!"

Back inside, the crowd erupted. The Dodgers must have just scored another run.

By the time I dropped off Casey and made it home, Dad's car was in the driveway. Before going inside I paced around the front porch, taking deep breaths and counting to a hundred.

Dad, you asshole. You fucking asshole.

He was on the couch, watching the news. His eyes were like scuffed-up glass marbles. There was a half-empty drink in his hand, and an even emptier bottle on the coffee table.

He tried to be casual with me. "Enjoy the game?"

"I had to leave early," I said. "Something made me sick."

The cutting tone in my voice made him flinch. His shoulders drooped. He looked tiny, shriveled.

"Where's Mom?" I asked.

Dad waved vaguely at the stairs. "She went to bed."

"Passed out again?"

And how much of that was because of him, anyway? Was drinking herself into a stupor every night the only way she could live with this? Live with *him?*

Dad seemed to know where my train of thought was headed. "Son . . . your mother and I . . . it's been very difficult—"

"Whatever."

I pivoted away and made for my room.

"Tyler?"

I halted on the stairs and looked back over my shoulder. "Yeah, Dad?"

"Have you told anyone about today?"

So. That was all he was worried about.

It was so tempting, just to let it all out. *No, Dad, I haven't. Oh, wait . . . except for this guy I've been having sex with for the last month and a half. Yes, a guy—your eldest son is a faggot. Put that in your pipe and smoke it, Father.*

"No, Dad. My lips are sealed."

I took the stairs three at a time and slammed my bedroom door shut behind me.

CASEY halted in front of the house and squinted to see the numbers stenciled on the mailbox. "Here it is—this is the place. Eight six—"

"Shut up. I told you—don't tell me the address."

"All right, all right, settle down. Jesus, dude. What crawled up your ass tonight?"

This was one of the Valley's older, seedier areas. The neighborhood lacked both sidewalks and streetlights, and the streets themselves were riddled with potholes—I'd nearly sprained an ankle just walking here from the car. The houses sat on huge lots with deep, weed-infested front yards, some with attached stables from the horse-and-buggy days, overhung with trees that looked like they hadn't been trimmed in decades. Maybe a third of the houses looked occupied.

This wasn't my party. Casey was the one with the password to get in. Heck, it wasn't a party at all. It was way more dangerous than that.

"Casey, let's just bail. This political stuff—it's bad news."

"I know, OK? But I told Bec I'd keep an eye on her

brother. That EML's about to do something stupid—I can smell it."

Yeah, and so what? Casey and Randall weren't exactly best buddies. For sure, Casey didn't share Randall's enthusiasm for overthrowing the government. *I'm only a rebel from the dick down*, he sometimes joked.

I was desperate to warn him, to tell him the Dentists had gotten to me. But what if he didn't believe that I'd only recently been turned? He might well conclude instead that I'd been a snitch all along. And anyway, if I did try to alert Casey, Mr. Ludlow would find out the next time he debriefed me.

I followed Casey up the walkway. The house was low-slung and flat-roofed, a style that must have seemed oh-so-modern fifty years ago but now just looked decrepit and sad. It was dark, with the curtains drawn, but I heard movement inside as Casey rang the doorbell.

The door opened, and a girl appeared. Casey murmured the password to her, and she let us in.

The place was already crowded—high-schoolers, mostly, with a scattering who looked old enough for college. They clumped in twos and threes, or stood off by themselves, with an invisible do-not-approach bubble surrounding each of them. A few were taking turns with a copy of that WE ARE THE SECRET SIX flyer—the one Billy Hanna had shown us at the Dawn Patrol meeting—reading it, folding it up, and passing it on.

Casey spotted Randall, huddled with some guy dressed all in black, and started toward them. "Wait here."

I retreated into a corner, hugging myself and sending out stay-away-from-me signals of my own. It was quieter than a library, or a morgue. Nobody mingled, nobody made eye contact, nobody spoke above the barest of whispers, and everybody looked peeing-their-pants scared of being recognized.

They ought to be scared. Scared of me.

Randall's black-garbed friend had left—now he and Casey were arguing. I couldn't hear what they were saying, but their gestures looked heated. Casey raised his hands like he was about to wring Randall's neck, but then spun around and came back over to me, fuming.

The crowd migrated deeper into the house, through the kitchen and into a family room decorated in a way-overdone Aloha from Hawaii theme—fern-green and banana-yellow tropical-print wallpaper, wooden pseudo-Polynesian carvings all over the place. There was a pool table at one end, a cluster of bamboo furniture surrounding a TV set at the other, and a matching bar along the wall between them. I swept in and claimed the last empty barstool. Casey took up position beside me, standing as far back as he could so he wouldn't block anyone's view behind him.

Next to the TV, a girl stood up. I could tell she was a girl only because of the boobs under her sweater—on her head she wore a black knit ski mask, covering everything but her eyes. The crowd simmered down, and every face in the room turned toward her. Looking around, I noticed several other people disguised the same way. One of them, I realized, was the guy I'd just seen talking to Randall.

The girl waited for the last few stragglers to settle in—on the floor, on top of the pool table, against the walls—and then spoke.

"Thank you all for coming." The girl had a strangely deep voice, or maybe that was just because of the mask. "You're all very brave, risking your freedom—even your lives—to hear about what's really happening in this country. If you're having second thoughts about being here and you wish to leave, please do so now."

Silence. I glanced over at Casey, hoping he might want to take the offer. He looked deeply unthrilled to be here, but he didn't move. Nor did anyone else.

The girl nodded. "Good. I'm proud of you. A warning—some of you may find what you're about to see very disturbing. Some of it may sadden you, even sicken you. You've been raised on nothing but Muldoonie lies—the truth won't go down easily. But no matter how you feel, keep watching. Turn your sadness into anger—turn your anger into inspiration. And when it's over, ask yourself, what can I do to make things right?" She looked at one of her masked comrades on the other side of the room. "Get the lights."

Chaffs

The video's picture was badly degraded—a copy of a copy of a copy. The sound warbled and occasionally dropped out altogether. But the original had been a professional job, no question—not expensive, but polished. One thing about having a dad in the industry—I knew high production values when I saw them.

Music swelled, and images floated across the screen—the sunrise glinting off the Washington Monument, children filing past the Liberty Bell, wheat fields rippling in the wind, the golden shimmer of the sunset playing off the Golden Gate Bridge and the Space Needle. The pictures could have come straight from the Office of Communications and Public Morale—pure from-sea-to-shining-sea stuff. They riveted me—they riveted everyone in the room. There was a narrator—a woman's voice, steady and soothing—but we didn't have to hear what she was saying. We'd grown up with these images—they pulled us in all by themselves.

Slowly, I became aware that they were taking us back, as if Casey's wished-for time machine really existed. There was a shot of a piece of parchment covered with elegant lettering—was that the Constitution? We'd learned about it in class but had never studied it—Mr. Scudder said it was obsolete. More images . . . a black man in a suit and tie, addressing an audience of thousands on the steps of the Lincoln Memorial . . . a line of people outside what must have been a voting booth, from when we still held elections . . . a newsstand filled with dozens of newspapers and magazines, not just from around this country but from all over the world . . . a group of Jews praying, with those round caps on their heads that they used to wear . . . striking workers on a picket line . . . Muslims bowing toward Mecca . . .

I suddenly knew where this was going. The music shifted into a minor key, dark and ominous, a lambs-to-the-slaughter march of doom. Images streamed by, at frantic speed, so fast they stopped registering . . . but then the torrent slowed down and finally paused, on a long aerial shot of New York City —

Smash cut to footage of a mushroom cloud.

Around me, people gasped. Somewhere in the back of the room, a girl let out a frightened squeal.

After that came scenes of horror. Figures in lead-lined suits that made them look like invading aliens, moving down streets strewn with wrecked cars and flanked by buildings that had been shattered, charred, even *melted*. Blackened skeletons off of which the last bits of flesh had been vaporized. Others of the dead who were nothing but shadows, the silhouettes of their last moments seared onto the nearby walls.

Then, deprivation—refugees from the attack clogging the highways . . . soup kitchens . . . lines at gas stations that stretched for miles. Followed by anger and fear—fights breaking out in supermarkets. . . race riots in the cities . . . armed patrols in the suburbs. Congress voting to give emergency powers to the then President, a distinguished but crushed-looking man who clearly knew already that he was going to lose the next election to . . .

"Accepting the nomination as his party's candidate for President of the United States . . . Harold Patrick Muldoon."

And there he was—a decade and a half younger than now, and not yet Our Commander-in-Chief, but still mesmerizing. I'd watched this speech a million times—I knew every word by heart. Muldoon's voice boomed, his hands carved the air. Down on the convention floor, the delegates worked themselves into a chanting frenzy. *FAITH . . . FAMILY . . . FREEDOM . . .*

Meanwhile, at the foot of the podium, there stood a line of stone-faced men in blue shirts and matching caps—armed only with baseball bats, not joltsticks and guns—not yet—but still unmistakably Wide Awakes.

Another smash cut. All over the country, piles of books were set on fire, schools and libraries ransacked, people penned up behind razor wire, others hanged and shot. The soundtrack had also changed. Instead of the narrator, we were now hearing excerpts from Muldoon's speeches and from upbeat-sounding news reports—while on the screen, ghettos burned and black people were herded onto buses at gunpoint and Hispanic children starved in the Protection Zones and bombs fell from huge, evil-looking aircraft with the eye-and-rising-sun logo painted on their bellies . . .

Chaffs

The whole onslaught—all these atrocities, committed in our name, by people we'd trusted, people whose lies we'd swallowed—had become too much for many in the room. The woman in the ski mask was right—we weren't letting the truth in without a struggle. Some of us were bawling, even screaming. Others were yelling curses at the TV and swinging their fists at anyone trying to shut them up. One guy had toppled off his perch on the edge of the pool table and was curled in a fetal position on the floor.

Next to me, Casey's hand had a vise grip on my shoulder. I was hunched over on the barstool, my arms clutching my stomach in a futile attempt to shield it from the invisible fist gut-punching me over and over.

Suddenly the soundtrack cut out, and the screen went blank. The room plunged into darkness. Nothing broke the silence but the quiet sobbing of those who'd been overwhelmed.

When the video resumed, the music had a brighter tone, still anguished but somehow more hopeful than before. The narrator had come back. She was now speaking about the resistance—about the people who'd braved the police and the Wide Awakes to fill the streets after Muldoon declared martial law, about the legislatures in those states that had attempted to secede, about the hymn-singing men and women who'd laid down in front of the buses evacuating the ghettos. To this day, she said, there were people—all races, all religions, rich and poor, even within the Party itself—making videos like this one, circulating banned books and newspapers, helping dissidents and fugitives escape over the borders into Canada and Mexico or across the ocean to Europe, where they could live to tell their stories and let the world know what was happening here . . .

And others, fighting the Muldoonies more openly.

On the screen flashed a map of Texas, with the triangular portion in the south pulsating red, like it was inflamed. Then the scene shifted to what looked like a theater or meeting hall—jittery handheld-camera footage of a young Mexican man on a stage, wearing a green army jacket and with a rifle slung over one shoulder. Obviously this was one of the guerrilla leaders. His face was hard to make out—because of the poor image quality, or maybe the filmmakers had blurred it on purpose to hide his identity—but as soon as he appeared, a girl near me gasped and blurted out, "The Junk Man!"

The Junk Man? Another one of the items on Neighbor Lenskold's list. I glanced sidelong at Casey to see if he recognized it, but if he did, he gave no sign.

The man was speaking in Spanish, with subtitles in English along the bottom of the screen.

"I have seen the face of the enemy. You think you're scared, friends? Let me tell you, your fear is nothing compared to the fear I've glimpsed in the face of our enemy—his true face. Underneath that mask of rage and hatred he wears, he is terrified."

I hardly needed to read the subtitles—the man's message went beyond language. It came through in his voice and his mannerisms, in the pure confidence that poured out of him, even filtered through this grainy piece of video. This was a man totally unafraid, unashamed.

"We all know the saying, 'It is better to die on your feet than to live on your knees.' Wise words—but they don't go far enough. To defeat the Muldoonies, we must LIVE on our feet. We must drop our own masks of fear and powerlessness. We must laugh, sing, dance, savor every breath, love each other, and show the enemy—show the world—what it really means to be alive."

Around me, the sobbing had ceased. In the darkened room, young heads basked in the glow from the screen—held up high, or nodding as the Junk Man spoke to them. It was really happening, right before my eyes.

The masks were dropping. Here, everywhere.

I parked my car the usual discreet distance from the Peach Pit, but I didn't shut off the engine or headlights.

"Aren't you coming in?" Casey asked. "You've been acting weird all night."

I gripped the steering wheel and hunted for words. Watching that video had given me hope. But now it felt more like desperation, and I was choking up with fear that Casey would just laugh.

"Let's run away. You and me. Let's join them."

Casey didn't laugh. But his deadpan face was almost as bad.

"Join who?"

"Those guerrillas in Texas. We could help them. I'm in the Dawn Patrol—I know how to fight. I can shoot, I can even field-strip a rifle. There's other stuff I know too—first aid, wilderness survival—"

"And what about me? I don't know any of that shit."

"You can learn. I can teach you." My voice was cracking. "You're smart, you're tough, you're in good shape. Come on, Casey—"

"Damn it, do you think I've never thought about this? I have, a million times. Lots of Chaffs try to run when their numbers come up. They never make it." He folded his arms and stared hard out the windshield. "There's no place *to* run, anyway. Not for us."

"But if we can make it to Texas—"

"*Texas*, dude? We'd get lynched. And even if we could find those guerrillas, what makes you think they're going to want a couple of white guys? A couple of *gay* white guys? Mexicans hate fags as much as the Muldoonies do."

My hopes were withering as quickly as they'd bloomed. Was he right? Was there really no escape for people like us, no refuge?

"Casey, I just . . . When you're gone . . . I don't know what I'm going to do. I think about what's going to happen to you, and . . . I have to *do* something."

"You want to do something? Go on with your life. Graduate. Go to college. Play baseball. Hell, marry that girl and squirt out a bunch of kids. You know you'll have to, anyway."

"Don't say that. Please." That bursting-dam sensation was building again behind my eyes. "You know how I feel about you. Why are you saying all this?"

"I'm being realistic. Once I'm gone, it'll be like I was never here. I know it, and you know it."

He sighed and ran a hand through his hair. "Look, let's not fight, OK? Let's just make the most of the time we've got—no deep conversations, no crazy escape plans. I'll see you at the reservoir tomorrow."

Before I could say anything else, he opened the door and got out. My gaze followed him as he crossed the path of the car's headlights and then winked out, swallowed up in the black night surrounding us.

After that, the dam finally broke. By the time the flood had receded, my throat was raw from screaming, and the palms of my hands were ablaze with pain from slamming them against the wheel.

S O. This *gathering*." Mr. Ludlow put an ugly emphasis on the last word. "You didn't recognize anyone there? Other than that boy, Randall?"

"No, sir." I'd already learned to stick to yes-or-no answers. Mr. Ludlow still got all the information he wanted out of me, but at least this way he had to work for it.

We were in the Ludlows' living room, me in an armchair, Mr. Ludlow on the couch with his legs crossed, sipping iced tea. He'd offered me a glass too, but I'd declined. I always did. I had no idea if truth drugs existed outside of movies, but I didn't want to find out.

"And Randall—you say he and Monahan argued?"

"Yes, sir."

"But you didn't overhear what they were arguing about."

"No, sir."

He set the glass down on the end table. His voice became terrifyingly mild. "Did you *try* to overhear? Be honest."

I swallowed and shook my head.

"In the future, Tyler, I encourage you to take more initiative."

There was the sound of a car pulling into the driveway. Then Unity's voice, at full volume and at the top of her register. "Ty! Daddy!"

Mr. Ludlow gave me a we'll-finish-this-later look, then stood up to greet his daughter. I did the same.

Unity flung open the door, streaked through the foyer into the living room, and leaped into my arms hard enough to send both of us spinning in a 360.

"The test came back! Dr. Fleming called me at school to give me the results—Ty, I'm pregnant!"

"Really?" I gaped at her. It wasn't a huge shock—Unity had missed her last period, and even I knew what that might mean.

"Dr. Fleming said I might be as much as six weeks along. It might have even happened right after we started—" She broke off, with a sheepish glance at her dad. "I'm sorry—I'm just so happy. Isn't it wonderful, Ty?"

Her smile was luminous, her cheeks rosy and shimmering with tears of joy. The noise I kept hearing—that clang of a cell door slamming shut—was only in my head.

"God, yes." I smiled back, kissed her, and wrapped my arms around her again. "Unity, that's wonderful . . . "

Mr. Ludlow just stood there, studying us both.

"Daddy, let's have dinner at the Eagle's Nest tonight." Unity detached herself from me and floated over to her dad, taking his hands in hers. "I want to celebrate."

"Of course, Pumpkin." Unity's dad was beaming. "But that place is very popular, you know—I'm not sure we can get a reservation on such short notice."

"Oh, like Investigator Ludlow of the Department of Domestic Security can't get a table at any restaurant in Los Angeles." With one hand, she reached for me, drawing me into a huddle with her and her dad. "Tonight I am going to have a nice, intimate dinner with my two favorite men in the world, if I have to have someone thrown in jail to do it."

Mr. Ludlow laughed. "I'll make the call."

Chaffs

The week after Unity broke the news, I slipped out for one of my predawn meetings with Casey. I hung out for as long as I could—over an hour. I even ran a couple of laps around the reservoir while I waited.

Casey never showed up.

I tried not to worry. But it snuck through every barrier I put up. It had finally happened—Casey had been arrested, or worse. Maybe the Evaluators had decided to knock him off early. Maybe Mr. Ludlow, now that Unity was pregnant, had ordered the execution himself—to simplify matters, and to punish me for cheating on his daughter.

Or maybe . . . maybe this was Casey's way of ending it. Things with us had gone more or less back to normal since our argument after watching that video, and when I told Casey about Unity, he'd shrugged it off—had *congratulated* me, actually—but maybe it had been too much even for him to deal with.

During the drive home I talked myself down. Casey had probably just forgotten. He might have been out partying last night and overslept, or he might have run into a police checkpoint and been forced to turn back. These things happened. This wasn't the first time one of us had missed a rendezvous.

And if Casey really was breaking up with me—well, that might be for the best.

I'd been thinking along the same lines.

Was it fair to him, keeping this up? Casey had only nineteen days left—the countdown had gone from weeks to days—and he had the right to spend them without Mr. Ludlow's gun pointed at his head.

And Unity—I needed to think of her and the baby. Impending fatherhood was an awfully loud wake-up call.

I pulled into the driveway, walked in the house—and found my whole family in the living room. Even Mom was already awake, standing behind the couch where Dad and Eric sat staring at the TV.

"What's going on?" I circled around to where Mom was. Neither she nor the others so much as glanced at me—their attention was fixed on the screen.

BOMB FACTORY IN THE VALLEY, said the words crawling

along the bottom. Above them the reporter, microphone in hand, was chattering against a backdrop of smoldering debris and billowing smoke. On a palm tree-lined street that looked familiar . . .

"I'm surprised this story made it past the censors," Mom was saying.

"Too many witnesses," Dad replied. "The story will be all over L.A. by noon, regardless—the OCPM had no choice but to greenlight it, at least locally. We'll keep a lid on it nationally, of course."

As I watched, the camera panned over to the charred wreckage . . . on a palm tree-lined street that looked familiar . . . and I caught a glimpse of peach-colored stucco.

The Peach Pit.

"Tyler, are you all right?" Mom laid a hand on my forehead, like she was checking my temperature. "You look like you're coming down with something."

My knees were about to buckle. I had to grip the back of the couch to stay on my feet. "Wh-what . . . what happened?"

"There was an explosion last night," Dad said. "Some terrorists blew themselves up making bombs. Not far from here—some abandoned apartment complex being used as a Reclaimee squat."

"Reclaimees." My little brother glared at the screen. "Dirty Chaffs. We should just kill them all."

I jerked upright, like I'd just taken a joltstick in the small of the back. "I've got to get going. I . . . I've got an early practice."

"Tyler, you're all sweaty," Mom said. "You should at least shower first."

"I'll shower at school. I've got to go."

I was out the door again before any of them could interrogate me. I'd lied to them—there was no early practice today. I just had to get out of that house. I couldn't stand there and play dumb, watching what might well have been Casey's funeral pyre.

I had to find him.

As I drove, the plume of smoke marking the Peach Pit's location grew larger, curling like an oily black question mark.

Chaffs

The traffic became stop-and-go, full of drivers slowing down to gawk, finally halting altogether a few blocks from Ground Zero. Ahead, the intersection was blocked—with black-and-white police cars, and snub-nosed blue vans with the Wide Awakes logo in glittering gold on the side panel.

Shit. I should have known that they'd already have the area cordoned off. Good luck getting anywhere near the place.

I swung onto a side street, parked, and kept going on foot until I reached a cluster of people milling around behind a line of yellow tape. On the other side, men in blue uniforms stood guard, but there were no confrontations—these were just curious onlookers. A lot of them were in pajamas, as if the blast had rousted them out of bed.

No one knew anything. I paced around the fringes of the crowd, eavesdropping, trying not to appear frantic even through I could feel myself getting more crazed by the second. But they gave me nothing, no info—on who caused the blast, on how high the death toll was—nothing to hint at whether Casey was alive or dead . . .

I turned around . . . and then nearly jumped out of my own skin.

Freya. She was standing right behind me.

"He's OK," she said, before I could open my mouth.

Casey, I love you. He must have told—or bribed—Freya to stick around and keep an eye out for me. I could have kissed her just then.

Freya must have sensed that, because she took several hasty steps back. "Meet him tonight after curfew, behind the bowling alley on DeSoto."

"Great, thanks. Did he say anything else? What happened here?"

But she was already melting back into the crowd. A couple of eye-blinks and she was gone.

I trudged back to the car. My arms and legs had gone heavy with relief. Behind me, the smoke was thinning and turning white—the fire was almost out.

Casey was still alive.

And I had to keep him that way.

☆   ☆   ☆

I'd never been to the bowling alley after closing time. Normally the front façade, with its 1960s rocket-shaped sign, was a seizure-inducing wall of neon, while on the inside the place pulsated with the beeping of video games and the clatter of bowling pins. Tonight, deserted and with the lights off, it looked like a mausoleum.

I ducked around back, searching for Casey. I heard his voice, and his friend Bec's, coming from behind a row of dumpsters. Bec sounded like she was crying.

"Why didn't you stop him?"

"I tried, Bec! He wouldn't listen to me. And I'm not your brother's keeper—don't blame me."

I crept around the dumpsters and into view, taking care not to startle them. I waved at Casey. "Hey."

He and I both moved toward each other, but then stopped short. Rushing into each other's arms, like in some sappy movie? Bad idea. Bec just stood there, glaring at us. In the dim light from the neighboring streets and buildings, I could see her eyes. If they'd been laser beams, I'd be a pile of charcoal already.

Casey pulled himself together, then let out a deep breath. "You made it."

"Yeah, Freya found me. What happened?"

"Randall. That fucking moron. That stupid piece of—" An apologetic glance at Bec. "They recruited him. Gave him a vest packed with explosives. I guess he couldn't resist playing around with it. Stupid."

"You're not making any sense. Explosives? Recruited? By who?"

"Terrorists, anarchists, pyromaniacs—who the fuck knows?" He paced in a circle, pressing the heels of his hands into his eye sockets. "It happens. Chaffs get close to the end, they've got nothing to lose—and they get recruited. To blow shit up. Malls, schools, churches, whatever. It happens all the time. Hell, maybe it's the government doing it all. To keep people scared."

I'd never heard about this. About the bombings, sure—they popped up in the news once or twice a month on average—but . . . the bombers were Chaffs? Committing suicide, and taking others with them? And the idea that the government might be behind them—not long ago I would have rejected that, called it seditious, but now . . .

That Reclaimee boy has some questionable associates.

"Casey, you've got to run."

His eyes narrowed. "What are you talking about?"

"Run! Out of L.A., out of the country! The Dentists . . . Casey, they've been watching you! They're going to think you had something to do with this!"

"Excuse me." Bec was shooting more eye-lasers at me. "What are *you* doing here, anyway?"

"He's my friend," Casey said.

Bec snorted. "Yeah. You and your *friends*. I asked around about this one. His girlfriend's dad is a Dentist. He's probably been snitching on us."

"Oh, for chrissake, Bec, he hasn't been snitching. I am so sick and tired of your jealous bullsh—" He cut himself off, then tensed up. His head swiveled in my direction. "How do you know the Dentists are watching me?"

My tongue lay paralyzed in my mouth.

"Shit, Treppenhouse. You *have* been snitching, haven't you?"

"No!" A jolt, and my power of speech came back. I stretched my hands toward Casey, palms up. "Unity's dad—he found out about us. He's been pressuring me, but I haven't told him anything. Nothing about you."

"Nothing about me." His voice was like dry ice. "But you have been telling him something."

"Nothing important. Casey . . . please . . ." I was losing him—he was walking away. I went after him. "I had to play along—if I didn't cooperate Mr. Ludlow was going to have you arrested, maybe even killed! I had to protect you—"

"Fuck you!" He spun around and advanced on me, backing me up against the wall of the bowling alley. "I told you, I *don't need your protection!*"

He loomed over me, his breath hissing. His fists were clenched, like he wanted to beat me to death, except that his eyes . . . they were pained. I'd never seen Casey look so hurt, so . . . so *betrayed*.

Bec was jabbing her finger in my face. "You fucking narc. We ought to kill you right here."

"Shut up, Bec!" Casey snapped.

"Don't you tell *me* to shut up! You're the one who keeps taking Muldoonies to bed. What was the last one's name? Kevin Something? Sanders, I think?"

Total silence. It was like every sound had been sucked out of the universe. I tried to register what Bec had said. Then I tried a hundred times harder to *un-register* it.

"Kevin?" I turned to Casey. *Please tell me I didn't hear what I just heard.* "You and . . . You and *Kevin?*"

Casey was huddled against the dumpster. His arms were folded tight, like the wings of a sick bird.

"Oh, God. You and Kevin. That was why he . . . " My mind went back to Neighbor Lenskold's office, the night we broke into it. I saw Casey at her desk, staring at her computer, his mouth hanging open and his face drained of color. "You saw it, didn't you? Kevin failed his Evaluation . . . *because of you.*"

Slowly, Casey raised his head. He lowered his arms and let them dangle at his sides. When his eyes finally met mine, they were like fossilized pieces of amber, cold and dead, containing . . . no regret, no remorse, nothing but resignation.

"Yeah," he said. "Because of me."

My vision went red. I screamed. My hands shot up, twisting themselves into claws, reaching for Casey's neck. But at the last instant, before ripping his throat out, I stopped myself. My left hand pulled back—my right hand became a fist and punched the side of the dumpster.

I shrank away from him, shaking.

"You bastard. You whore. You . . . you faggot." I wiped my eyes—I could barely see. "I'm glad your time is running out. I hope they make you suffer."

Casey was just a blur. The whole world was a blur. Another spasm of grief and rage hit me, and I turned and ran. Into the night.

Chaffs

Into darkness.
Into nothing.

MY knuckles scabbed over right away after punching that dumpster, but they still ached for days.

Casey was out of my life now. Good riddance.

The whole thing had been doomed from the start—it had simply crashed and burned a little early. Once the bastard's Evaluation day came and went, I'd never have to think about him again. I'd be free.

Heck, I already was free.

So why did it feel like I'd disemboweled myself with my bare hands?

Of course, I couldn't just walk around with my intestines spilling out. I had to stuff them back in, and hold them there—at home, at school, at church, on the ballfield, with Unity. This was Kevin all over again—worse, because at least there had been others who'd known Kevin and grieved for him, even if they couldn't show it. Nobody knew about me and Casey.

Except Mr. Ludlow.

"This is the best possible outcome for you," he told me the next day. "There was no future for you with that boy. You were going through a phase. That phase is over. Now your life can continue . . . unimpeded."

I wanted to laugh, talking about this with Unity's dad, of all people. How did a DDS investigator become the only person in the world I could confide in?

"I just don't know, sir. It's . . . painful."

"Strange as it may seem, even Dentists have human feelings. I do know what it's like to love someone, and then lose them." A quick glance at the photo of Unity's mom on his desk. "The pain will lessen with time. You're young, you're resilient, you're a Son of the Fourth Great Awakening. The Nation will give you strength."

One of the Dawn Patrol's slogans came to mind—OUR HEARTS DON'T BLEED. There was also a verse in the Bible about putting away childish things. Maybe I ought to go back to those fundamentals—what the Party taught me, what God taught me. Put away this queer stuff, this . . . phase.

Only it sure didn't *feel* like a phase.

"Unity will be home soon. We should get down to business." Mr. Ludlow folded his arms on the desk and leaned forward. "Did Monahan give you any indication that he had advance knowledge of this bomb plot?"

Mr. Ludlow wanted me to denounce him. *Oh, sweet payback.* Because of Casey, my best friend had been made to disappear, was probably dead—it was only fitting, wasn't it, that I drive the last nail into Casey's coffin? A single word to Mr. Ludlow—*Yes.* That was all it would take . . .

But I couldn't.

"No, sir. I don't think he knew anything."

"Are you *sure*, Tyler?"

"Believe me, if I thought Casey knew something, anything, I'd say so."

Or maybe not—probably not. A part of me still loved him. It had kept me from strangling him that night—what made me think it would let me harm him now?

I sat up straight and shook my head. "I'm not going to lie just to make myself feel better—I can't. I'm sorry."

Mr. Ludlow never lost his temper. But he had this way of looking at me—head tilted back, eyes peering just under the bottom edge of his glasses—that conveyed disappointment better than words.

I woke up to voices, harsh, shouting. Then boots coming up the stairs. My bedroom door banged open, and there was another voice. Mom's.

"Tyler!"

The light came on. My eyes slammed shut against it. Gloved hands grabbed me, yanked me out of bed, hauled me to my feet, hustled me downstairs. I had nothing on but briefs and a T-shirt. I felt a hand between my shoulder blades, shoving. I stumbled, stubbed a toe on the steps, and caught the handrail just barely in time to keep from falling and breaking my neck.

I forced my eyes open. Through the dazzle I saw uniforms. Blue.

This is it. It's happening.

Up in my room, I heard my closet door being opened, drawers being pulled, stuff being dumped out of them. Similar sounds came from my parents' room, and Eric's. As I reached the bottom of the stairs I heard a bone-jarring thump, shattering glass, clanging bells. Our grandfather clock was lying face down on the living-room floor.

What time is it? The middle of the night—it had to be. They always came for you in the middle of the night —

"On your knees. Hands behind your head."

I obeyed.

Did they get Casey too? I was swimming in fear, the Wide Awakes were ransacking my house and the carpet was rubbing my knees raw and I had to fight not to pee in my briefs—and yet Casey was all I could think about. If only I hadn't cursed him and run off like that. If only my last words to him hadn't been so hateful . . .

Mom was next to me, also kneeling. Her face was terrified, but clear—younger-looking, and strangely beautiful. Eric was on the other side of her. *His* face I couldn't read at all. It was like a mannequin's, as expressionless as those of the figures in blue.

Mom's gaze was fixed, aimed straight ahead like a rifle sight at . . .

At Dad.

"It's that Hollywood whore, isn't it?" Mom hissed. "Look at me, James. What in God's name have you done to this family? *Look* at me, damn you!"

Dad was in the middle of the room. His head was bowed, his hands cuffed behind his back. He was wearing even less than I was—just boxers, no shirt. Stripped down like this, he was repulsive to look at, with his doughy skin and chicken legs and soft belly sagging over his waistband.

A Dentist was standing over him, with two Wide Awakes. All three had their joltsticks turned on. Bluish-white sparks danced between the prongs, spitting and crackling.

Two more Wide Awakes came out of the den. One of them had Dad's computer. The other one was carrying some boxes—full of disks or paper printouts, probably.

The trashing of our house went on and on. Impossible to tell how much of it was actual searching for evidence and how much was gratuitous destruction. But it didn't matter. Me, Mom, Eric—we looked at each other, and we understood. We were there to watch. This was for humiliation's sake—arresting the traitor in front of his family, destroying his life before his eyes.

The Dentist nodded to his companions. The joltsticks lashed out, hitting Dad two, four, six times. Dad collapsed, screaming, every muscle twitching. He crapped himself—I could smell it from across the room. Once the spasms ceased, the Wide Awakes took him under the arms, lifted him up, and dragged him out of the house.

The Dentist followed them out. After a few more minutes of stomping around and breaking things, the other Wide Awakes left as well.

Mom was still glaring at the empty space where Dad had been. Eric was staring at the door, but then he glanced sidelong at me, his face still a total blank.

I gazed back at him and Mom, hoping to God that my expression looked right. I hoped they thought it looked like shock, or grief.

Anything but the relief I was really feeling.

Relief that they'd come for Dad instead of me.

☆   ☆   ☆

Mom kept me and Eric home from school, to clean up the mess while she disappeared into her room with the phone for several hours. When she came downstairs again, I'd just lifted the grandfather clock back into position and was trying to get it running. It was no use—the clock's whole mechanism was busted.

"Tyler, Eric, come into the dining room."

Mom took the seat at the head of the table—Dad's old seat. Eric and I sat down on either side of her.

"Your father's not coming back." From the way she said it, you'd think Mom had just won a free trip to Hawaii. "Officially, the DDS won't even say they have him. I had to call in some favors to get the full story."

"What did they arrest him for?" I asked. For having an affair? That seemed awfully extreme.

"That slut actress, Charissa Dunbar. She's been arrested too. She has a brother—some subversive type, got himself thrown in a detention center. She thought your father could use his 'influence'"—she put air-quotes around the word *influence*—"to get him out. The Dentists found evidence at James' office, at the slut's home, even here—letters, electronic mails, pictures, recordings. I knew James couldn't keep it in his pants, but I never dreamed he was *this* stupid."

"Wait, you said they found evidence *here? How*—"

While I was speaking, by chance, my eyes met Eric's. My brother looked away, down at the table. But then he raised his head, glaring defiance.

He called the Dentists. He turned Dad in.

Mom spread her hands flat on the table. "I'm making a formal statement denouncing him. Tyler, you need to do the same."

Chaffs

"What?" Denounce my own father? I'd lost all respect for him after the Dodger game, sure, but I never would have wished *this* on him.

"Be glad I wasn't arrested, too—otherwise you and your brother would be going into Reclamation." Mom paused. "Your whole future could depend on this, Tyler—your scholarship, your chance for a baseball career, everything. This kind of political baggage can follow you around for the rest of your life. You need to dump it right away." She gazed off to one side, her mouth twisting into a snarl. "That selfish bastard. It's not enough for him to humiliate us by parading around with that bitch—no, he has to drag us into some seditious plot as well. He probably won't get a trial—too bad. I would love to see the look on his face when they take him away."

Had Mom always hated Dad this much? She never talked like this unless she'd been drinking. But she hadn't touched a drop all morning. This was the most sober I'd ever seen her.

The next day, I was at my locker when I saw Freya coming down the hall toward me. My heart leaped. *Casey! Freya's got a note from him!* I angled away from her and let my hand fall open at my side, but she walked by me without stopping.

I still hated Casey for what he'd done with Kevin, but . . . God help me, I still loved him. Still needed him. Without him, I was totally alone.

Word had already gotten around school about Dad. I kept my eyes downcast so I wouldn't see people's reactions—the ones staring with accusation and self-righteousness, the others turning their backs out of pity or so I wouldn't see them snickering. I wore my Dawn Patrol uniform like a suit of armor.

Our game later in the week—against Banning, a division powerhouse—just piled on the humiliation. The Mighty TNT had gone AWOL—I committed two errors, each costing us a run, and I went down swinging in all three at-bats. We wound up losing 2-1, thanks to me.

After the game, Coach called me into his office. "Treppenhouse, I want you to sit out the next few games."

"Coach, no." My mind scraped for counterarguments. "I'll do anything. I'll put in extra practice time, I'll work on my fielding. Please don't bench me."

"This isn't a punishment. You're a million miles from the ballfield, mentally—understandably so." His voice softened—he must have seen the desperation on my face. "You're our best player—we need you at a hundred percent for the playoffs. Just relax, sit the next few out, and take the time to clear your head."

Clear my head? How was I supposed to do that, without baseball? I'd lost Casey, my family was imploding—the game was all I had left.

I clomped over to my locker, yanked it open, and flung my glove into it. Everyone else had showered and headed home—except for Brad, Danny, and Rick, who were still getting dressed. The looks they gave me were sympathetic—they must know what Coach had told me.

Brad came up and clapped a hand on my shoulder. "Dude, you know I think you're awesome, but Coach is right. You're not thinking straight. Taking time off will do you some good."

I squirmed out from under Brad's touch and pulled my jersey off over my head. "Look, I get that you're trying to help, but just leave me alone."

"How about we get in some more practice, on Friday after school? It'll help you blow off some steam. And I can get some work in on my swing."

I'd started unbuckling my belt, but then I paused. "We don't have practice this Friday. Coach is going to that Party youth athletics thing, remember?"

"So? We don't need him. Come on—we'll hit fungos for an hour, then go grab burgers at Sambo's, just the four of us. Whaddya say, TNT?"

This was the chummiest he'd been with me since that day I pulled him off Casey in the parking lot.

I looked at their faces—Brad's, Rick's, Danny's. These were my teammates, my friends—my brothers, in a way. I'd forgotten that for a while. Despite everything that had gone wrong—with Kevin, with Casey, with Dad—they were still here for me.

I took my pants off, grabbed my towel, and shut the locker door.

"OK. Friday. Now let me go shower."

With no practice scheduled on Friday, the area around the gym was deserted. Brad was waiting for me by the soda machines. As I walked up, he blinked, like I'd just woken him up from a deep sleep.

"Hey, TNT."

"Where are Rick and Danny?"

"Oh, they're already inside. I was just waiting for you."

Our footsteps echoed down the long hallway, from the gym entrance to Coach's darkened office at the other end. I tugged at the collar of my Dawn Patrol uniform. I'd been wearing it all day—I couldn't wait to get out of it and into my practice gear.

As we turned the corner into the locker room, the others straightened up—not just Rick and Danny, but the whole team. Deke O'Beirne, Jay Devereaux, Billy Hanna . . .

What's Billy Hanna doing here?

Brad turned around. I looked at his face.

Oh, shit —

A fist jabbed me from behind—first the right kidney, then the left. The pain rocketed to my fingers and toes and up into my skull, filling my brain, filling the universe. Two more, smaller pains fluttered through the larger agony as my knees and then my forehead smacked hard against the floor.

I was being dragged by the ankles. Dimly, I heard shouting and laughing. I didn't struggle. I couldn't. It was all I could do just to find my lungs and force air into them. Underneath me, the texture of the floor shifted, from gritty linoleum to cold and clammy porcelain tile. The shower room.

My feet dropped. I lay face down, not moving.

"Roll over, faggot."

The toe of a shoe slammed into my ribs when I didn't obey. It actually helped—it jump-started my diaphragm and I could breathe again.

I rolled onto my back. The others stood over me in a circle. Their faces . . . I looked away from them and turned my head to the side—I couldn't bear to see that hate, couldn't bear to know it existed, to know it was aimed at me . . .

There was someone else on the floor beside me—I could see the shape through the forest of legs. The forest parted.

It was Casey. Naked, bruised, bloody, his wrists and ankles tied with shoelaces, so tightly his hands and feet had turned purple.

"We thought we'd give you lovebirds a chance to say goodbye."

THE circle closed again. Billy Hanna came into view, along with Brad and a couple of other guys—more guys not on the team.

"Get that uniform off him," Billy said.

Brad and the others descended. I didn't resist, and I kept my mouth shut. Fighting back would only egg them on. They didn't stop until I was as naked as Casey.

"Well?" Brad nudged me with one foot and folded his arms across his chest. "You two fruits gonna say goodbye, or what?"

"Give him a kiss!" somebody said.

"Yeah, go on." Danny Magruder was smirking. "Just pretend we're not here."

"I guess I know now why you'd never let me pound this Chaff." Brad's upper lip twisted in disgust. "Geez. Being queer is bad enough. But . . . with *this?*"

Casey was conscious. While I was being stripped he'd rolled onto one side so he could see what was happening. He had a massive shiner around one eye, but the other one was clear, gazing at his tormentors with cool contempt.

I raised myself onto my elbows and searched the faces around me. I opened my mouth—to say what, I had no clue—but a tiny shake of Casey's head stopped me. I knew what he meant by it. *Don't worry about me. Protect yourself.*

Brad snorted. "Nothing to say, faggot?"

He glanced at Billy, who reached into his pocket and pulled out something black and rectangular. A tape recorder. Billy held it up where I could see it, then pressed a button on the side.

"Let's run away. You and me. Let's join them . . . those guerrillas in Texas . . . "

My elbows slipped out from under me, and I fell back. *A tape? How did they get us on tape?*

Then I remembered. That morning when Brad called me to bum a ride to practice. Leaving—*pretending* to leave—his stuff in my car, asking for my keys so he could go back and get it, insisting that I go on in and suit up, that he'd only be gone a minute . . .

Only a minute. But long enough to plant a bug.

"Casey, I just . . . When you're gone . . . I don't know what I'm going to do."

"Aw, that's so sweet," someone said.

"Ah jess don't know whut ahma gonna do!" Rick Nagy falsettoed.

"Shut up." Billy Hanna put up a hand, and the room went silent. "Let me guess, Treppenhouse. You're going to tell us that this Chaff seduced you. You're going to say that it was all his fault, that you *never* would have gone queer if it wasn't for him. Is that what you're going to tell us?"

What could I say? After finding out about him and Kevin I would have happily thrown Casey to the wolves, but now . . .

"Is it?"

The cold floor was making me shiver. I struggled to a sitting position again and stared up at Billy. He and I had never been buddy-buddy, but we'd known each other since kindergarten. Maybe if I just told him what he wanted to hear, for once . . .

"I'm not queer. I'm not."

Billy smiled. "Good. You're going to get to prove it. Stand up."

As I obeyed, Billy whispered something in Brad's ear, and Brad grinned.

Down on the floor, Casey made a movement. One of the mob kicked him, and he lay still again. I turned away so I wouldn't look him in the face, even accidentally. *I'm not queer*—why did I lie like that? No one believed it. Neither Billy nor Brad believed it, Casey sure didn't believe it—*I* didn't believe it. But I'd gone ahead and lied anyway . . .

There were murmurs of excitement. Brad had gotten something out of the locker room. A baseball bat.

My bat.

"You're on deck, TNT."

He held it out to me, handle pointing up. I recoiled. They weren't serious. They weren't really expecting me to do this, to take my own bat and —

"Just don't kill him," Billy said. "Save him for the Dentists." He jerked his head at Rick and Danny. "Nagy. Magruder. Untie the Chaff and get him on his feet."

Brad offered me the bat again. I took it—or my hands did, while I watched, unable to control them. I wanted to refuse, or take the bat and, with two swings, smash Brad's head and then Billy's like watermelons—but I couldn't. My brain seemed to have been disconnected from my body.

From somewhere in the back of the room, a chant started.

"T-N-T . . . T-N-T . . . T-N-T . . . T-N-T . . . "

Casey stood facing me—swaying a little, but otherwise calm. He looked at me, and nodded. All the awful things I'd said to him the other night, and still, he was more worried about me than about himself. He must have thought he was already a dead man.

"T-N-T . . . T-N-T . . . T-N-T . . . T-N-T . . . "

The whole mob was chanting. The porcelain walls and chrome fixtures in the shower room gave their voices a hellish ring.

My hands choked up on the bat handle. I'd regained control over them, but only to the point where I could decide when and where to swing, not whether.

Casey nodded again. Then I saw his lips move.
Do it.

I shook my head one last time. He answered me with a roll of the one eye that wasn't swollen shut.

DO IT.

My hands raised the bat . . .

I checked my swing just before impact. It caught Casey in the stomach. He doubled over with a grunt and a blast of air from his lungs.

Cheers exploded all around me.

"Harder!" someone yelled.

The next one got Casey in the ribs. I tried to check my swing again, but there was too much momentum. Casey stumbled and fell to his knees, but kept silent.

"HARDER!"

"MAKE THE FAGGOT SCREAM!"

Something was surging inside me—hate? rage? anguish? all of them mixed together?—through my veins and into my muscles, trying to push me out of my own body. I fought it, hard, but I was losing.

Then Casey looked up at me, his breathing labored, and I —

Kevin. I saw him—him and Casey, together. My hate and my rage roared to the surface. But in the midst of it, other thoughts bubbled up—everything Casey had meant to me, everything I'd meant to him—and with it, a terrible realization that his ordeal wasn't going to end in this room, not if Brad and Billy and the rest had any say in the matter. I imagined the things they'd do to him, all the creative agonies that the Dawn Patrol and the Dentists had in store . . .

Unless I put him out of their reach.

Casey understood. I saw that, too. He drew in one more heaving, painful breath and then slumped, bowing his head.

And I took my final swing.

At the base of his skull.

☆   ☆   ☆

I lay on the floor, alone. I must have blacked out. The

others were gone. Casey was gone. But my bat was still here, just a few feet away, streaked with red and brown.

When I saw it, everything came back.

I couldn't do it. I couldn't deliver that killing blow. And in that instant of hesitation, Brad had seen my intentions, had twisted the bat out of my hands.

"Sorry, dude. Too easy."

Then he and the others started in on Casey.

I squeezed my eyes shut, turned my head away. But then in my ear I heard Billy Hanna's voice. "You want to be next, Treppenhouse? No? Then you open your eyes and *watch* this, all of it."

So I did. It went on and on and on. I watched them beat on Casey until the blood was draining down the hole in the shower room floor. I watched Rick Nagy tear out clumps of his hair, jumping up and down like a howler monkey. I watched it all—I forced myself to, and not just because Billy had ordered me. Casey was being shown no mercy—what made me think I deserved any?

Casey never screamed. Not once. Not even when they stretched him out and Brad picked up the bat and stuck the handle —

When I came to again, my whole body was convulsing. I was whispering to myself, praying, begging God to make the pain in my chest blossom into a fatal heart attack.

Of course, it never did. God wasn't about to let me off that easy.

Eventually I got tired of waiting, and I stood up. I had no idea how long I'd been lying there—hours, maybe.

My clothes were missing. I hobbled over to my locker and took out a T-shirt, some briefs, and a pair of sweatpants that I hadn't gotten around to throwing in the laundry. They reeked like an abandoned cheese factory, but it was either put them on or wander around naked. The guys had made off with my shoes, too, so I grabbed my cleats out of my locker as well.

I'd just finished dressing when, down the hall, the front door of the gym opened and closed with a clatter. I dropped into a crouch. They'd come back—Brad and the others, back to pick up where they'd left off.

Footsteps—a single set, with a heavy tread—and then a voice.

"Treppenhouse! Where are you?"

Coach.

I backed up and pressed myself against the lockers. There was no place to hide, not from Coach—and anyway, he already knew I was here. He must have decided to stop here on the way home from that Party athletics event, then seen my car in the parking lot.

Coach's bearish form appeared from around the corner. He went past the lockers and into the shower room.

"Damn it, Treppenhouse, where the hell are—?"

He halted mid-stride, and stiffened. His gaze took in the smear of blood on the floor, then the soiled bat lying next to it.

"Sweet Jesus."

Finally, he spotted me. "Tyler! Are you OK? Are you injured?"

I cringed away, shielding my face with my arms. "Coach, please—it wasn't me! I didn't do anything!"

"I didn't ask if you did anything—I asked if you were OK! Who did this? The other boys on the team? Did they . . . hurt you?"

His voice had an edge that I'd never heard from him before. When I lowered my arms, I saw how wide his eyes were, saw his jaw clenching and unclenching.

"No, they didn't . . . not me."

"Then who? That other kid? The skater?"

He meant Casey.

He knows about Casey?

I shut my eyes and turned my face toward the lockers. "Please, Coach. Please . . . just go away."

"I can't do that. I'm a teacher—I have a responsibility." He blew out a deep breath. "OK, I'll can the questions for now. But I need to get you out of here. Can I give you a ride home?"

Chaffs

Home. *Mom* —

"No! Don't take me home!" I searched Coach's face, but I could barely make it out through the film of tears. My voice was a squeak. "I don't have anywhere to go."

"I'll take you to my house—you can stay there tonight." Gently, he steered me out of the locker room and toward his office. "I'll call my wife right now and let her know what's going on."

He parked me outside his office door, unlocked it, and went inside. Through the window, I watched him go to his desk and pick up the phone. To call . . .

His wife?

Another wave of panic hit me. What if he was calling the Dentists instead? He sounded sincere, but so had Brad, so had the rest of the team. My legs twitched with the need to get out of there, to bolt and run for my life before —

"Damn it, Tyler! No!"

I was already down the hall. I burst out of the gym, into the dark. The Fenris was still there, parked under a lamppost, sitting in a circle of light like it was on display in the showroom. I made a break for it . . .

But then stopped. I retreated—two, three steps. My cleats caught on a crack in the asphalt, and I stumbled.

My car's windows were all shattered, the tires punctured, the roof bashed in. On the side, along its entire length, the word FAGGOT had been painted. No, not painted—scratched, gouged right into the surface.

I went numb. It was like some kind of circuit breaker tripped, shutting me down. Distantly, I thought only that my car keys were in my other pants and that I couldn't have driven out of there anyway.

Then Coach was beside me, coaxing me to my feet. "Come on, Tyler, let's go."

Coach lived in a modest house in a less-than-fancy neighborhood. A tall, blonde woman greeted us at the door. I recognized her from the photo in Coach's office.

"Tyler, this is Elaine." He turned to his wife. "Sorry I didn't call ahead—it was an emergency. Tyler's going to be staying with us for a couple of days."

The two exchanged a look, and then Elaine smiled and shook my hand.

"Welcome to our home," she said. "So you're the Mighty TNT. I've seen you play. That's a powerful bat you have."

She'd meant it as a compliment—I knew that—but it still made me wince.

Coach's brow had deep furrows. "Elaine, have you swept the house today?"

"As soon as I got home. We're clean—no bugs, no cameras. Tyler, is there anyone you want to call? Your mom?"

Coach shook his head. "Let's hold off on that. We don't know how safe it is."

"Please don't make me go home," I said.

Elaine smiled again. "We're not going to make you go anywhere." She took me by the arm and guided me toward the rear of the house. "Let's get you freshened up. I'll find you a change of clothes—there should be something in Dale's closet that fits you."

In the bathroom, I filled the sink with cold water and dunked my head several times. *T-N-T . . . T-N-T . . .* My nickname—the once welcome, now hateful sound of it was still burning in my ears. Would I ever again be able to stand hearing it chanted from the bleachers? Would I ever be able to pick up a bat again?

I loved baseball. It was my whole life. Those bastards—they'd taken that away from me too.

The bathroom door was half-open—so Coach and his wife could rush in if I tried to kill myself, probably. They were outside, speaking in low voices. I heard snippets—*his own bat, Jesus . . . how the other boys found out . . . let me talk to him alone . . .*

I could do it—kill myself. Bash my brains out against the sink, or grab a razor from the medicine cabinet and slit my wrists. They wouldn't have time to stop me. But I didn't. It would have been cruel, not to mention ungrateful, killing myself in Coach's home, after he and his wife had been so kind to me. I'd simply be leaving a mess for other people to clean up.

There was a knock, and Elaine entered, just long enough to pass me a pair of chinos and a Cal State Northridge sweatshirt. The pants were a little loose around the waist, but they'd stay on. And it did feel good to get out of those stinky gym clothes.

I came out of the bathroom and took a seat on the living room couch, hugging myself. The room was Jock Central— mismatched furniture, a pool table in the dining room, a bigscreen TV for watching games.

"I'll be in the kitchen," Elaine said. "Tyler, can I get you anything? A glass of water? Something to eat?"

"No. Thanks." Anything I tried to put in my stomach right now would just end up on the carpet.

Coach waited for Elaine to leave the room, then pulled up an ottoman and sat down on it, facing me.

"OK—man to man. What happened at school?" When I didn't answer, he scooted closer. "Look, you can trust me. I already know about you."

My heart started hammering. "Know . . . what?"

"Tyler . . . I *know*. I've suspected for a while. You're not the first one I've seen in my years of coaching high school kids. Honest." He ran one hand over his receding hairline. "At first I thought you and Kevin Sanders might have been . . . together. Why do you think I gave you that warning after he failed his Evaluation?"

I just blinked at him.

"But it wasn't Sanders, was it? It was that other Reclaimee—Monahan? I've noticed him watching you at practice."

I nodded.

Coach's face went stony, every word ground out between clenched teeth. "Tell me. *What did those boys do to him?*"

It was like twisting open a faucet as far as it would go. The words poured out of me amid a gush of tears and snot. I was bawling like an infant. I couldn't bear to look Coach in the eye, to see the disgust I knew was there—disgust with me, this faggot that had snuck onto his team, into his house.

219

I braced myself—for him to throw me out in the street, break every bone in my body, call the Dentists, anything . . .

I was not braced for him to put his arms around me.

I nearly panicked again—I thought he was going for my throat. But all he did was hold me, for what seemed like hours. I collapsed onto him and hung on by pure instinct, sobbing into his chest until his shirt was soaked clear through.

He drew back, his hands gripping my shoulders. His wife was sitting next to him now, her face just as stricken as his.

"Listen to me." Coach's tone was familiar—the same reassuring tone he used to calm me down after striking out at the plate—but with a layer of iron underneath. "There is nothing wrong with you—*nothing*. You want to see wrong? Look at Nemechuk, Hanna, this whole country, all the way up to that guy in the White House—*they're* the ones who are wrong. You hear me?"

"But Casey . . . what I did . . . "

"What they *made you do*." Coach's grip tightened. "They would have brutalized you too, maybe even killed you, if you'd tried to resist them. You did what you had to do." He let go and rubbed the bridge of his nose with one hand. "Don't hate yourself—you can't afford it. People like us get enough hate as it is."

People like us . . . ?

My eyes went wide.

"Yes, Tyler. I'm gay."

I looked at Coach, then at his wife, then at Coach again. "But . . . you guys are *married*. How can you—?"

"I'm gay, too," Elaine said.

I slumped against the back of the couch, my jaw falling open.

"You kids have always wondered why I never made it to the Show. That's why." Coach laughed. The laughter had a dry and bitter sound. "Let's just say, none of the big-league teams wanted a queer on the roster."

"You were . . . out of . . ." What was that phrase Casey used? Out of the cupboard? I never did pick up all the lingo.

"Oh, I didn't advertise it. But I wasn't very discreet,

either, especially when I was younger. Then Muldoon came to power, and suddenly not just my career but my life was in jeopardy." He gave his . . . wife? . . . a quick glance and took her hand. "Elaine and I had been friends in college. She was in the same . . . predicament as me, and so we struck a deal. To become each other's beard."

"Beard?"

"Sorry. A term from the old days. Basically, Elaine and I got married for camouflage." A weary sigh. "We even tried having a baby. But Elaine's diabetic—the first time she got pregnant, she had a miscarriage and almost died. We won't be giving children to the Nation anytime soon."

My brain felt like it was about to explode. "Why are you telling me all this?"

"Because kids like you are why I'm still here." Coach leaned forward and locked eyes with me. "There are a lot of things I hate about my job—not the least of which, having to look at the likes of Brad Nemechuk every day and pretend they're the greatest thing since sliced bread. But then, every so often, a kid like you comes along, and I thank God I'm in a position to help him." A pause. "I do wish I'd reached out to you sooner—I feel awful about that. If I had, I could have helped your friend too."

"Helped? How?"

Coach got up. He paced slowly across the living room, over to the TV set and back again.

"Tyler, what I'm about to tell you can never leave this house—it would put us all in terrible danger if it did. Before I go on, I need your solemn promise not to repeat a word of it to anyone."

Oh, Jesus. What now?

"I promise."

He stood with his feet apart and his hands clasped behind his back—the same stance he always took when giving a pre-game pep talk.

"Have you ever heard of the Secret Six?" he asked.

I had. From Neighbor Lenskold's list, and from those flyers that had shown up in the lockers at school.

"Are you guys terrorists?"

"That depends on whose side you're on. Neither I nor Elaine has killed anyone or blown anything up, if that's what you mean." A smile. "I prefer to think of what we do as resistance, not terrorism. We circulate underground pamphlets and videos, we spread the truth about what the Muldoonies are up to—and, now and then, we help people escape."

"People . . . like us."

"All kinds of people. You don't have to be gay—or black or Hispanic or Jewish or Muslim, for that matter—to see that this country has gone off the rails. Though when you are one or more of those things, it does tend to drive the point home."

And I thought my brain was going to explode *before*. Sure, Casey and I had talked about escaping—or, I'd talk about it and Casey would shoot me down—but it was never more than talk. This was real. I could really do this.

And the thought of doing it scared the crap out of me.

"Where would I go?"

"Wherever you want." Coach sat back down, bringing himself to my eye level. "There's a whole big world outside of this nuthouse, Tyler. How many gay people have you met in your life, that you know of? You can count them on one hand, I suspect. Now imagine whole neighborhoods full of gay people. Whole cities."

"So how come you haven't left?"

Elaine broke in. "For some of us it's not easy to leave home, no matter how bad things have gotten."

Coach gave her a fond look. "And some of us believe this is our country too, and hell if we're going to let the Muldoonies just have it."

My gaze took them both in, then wandered to the far wall. For the first time, I saw it, isolated from all the awards plaques and autographed jerseys—that portrait of President Muldoon, Our Commander-in-Chief, the same portrait every household displayed to show its allegiance to the Party and the Nation for which it stood. And here it was, in the home of two queers in a marriage of total convenience.

Talk about camouflage.

A truck blew by, pelting the phone booth with gravel. I pressed the receiver against one ear and plugged the other one with my finger so I could hear Mom if and when she picked up.

I felt like an idiot, calling her from this truck stop on the Grapevine, a full hour's drive from L.A. But Coach was right—her line might have a trace on it. If so, better that it lead to the middle of nowhere—it might even fool the Dentists into thinking I was on my way out of town.

Calling Mom at all was crazy. But I owed it to her—I couldn't just disappear forever, with no explanation. She didn't deserve that.

"Hello?"

"Mom!"

"Tyler. Is it true?"

Just like that, the speech I'd rehearsed a million times crumbled and blew away. Mom already knew.

"Yes, it's true. I'm gay."

The silence was like a solid wall around me. Not even the noise from the trucks could break through it.

"Mommy?"

"Don't ever come home. If you do, I'll have to have you arrested."

She hung up.

After that, I went catatonic for a while, curled up like an armadillo on the sofa bed in Coach's den. He and Elaine sat with me, sometimes together, sometimes just one of them. Neither one tried to speak to me. They seemed to understand that I needed time to think, to digest.

It helped. Disowning me so coldly was the best thing Mom could have done. It was like getting hit by a pitch—it simply made me want to blow the cover off the ball, my next time at the plate.

That night, I slept for twelve full hours. When I woke up Sunday morning, my mind was swarming with questions.

"Sir . . . what was it really like? You know, before?"

"For people like us?" Coach sat down at the kitchen table and stirred his instant coffee. They couldn't afford the real stuff. "Believe it or not, things were getting better. It still wasn't easy to be gay, especially in sports, but more and more of us were out and people were getting used to it."

Elaine was at the stove, making pancakes. She flipped them over and then stared at the spatula in her hand, lost in what looked like some regretful memory. "There was even some talk about letting us marry."

"You mean, letting you marry another woman, and Coach marry—seriously?" My brain was still having trouble with the idea that Coach could be gay, much less married to another guy. In *this* country? Muldoon would sooner let a man marry his dog.

"So what happened?" I asked. "Why did things go so wrong?"

Coach sighed. "It was a scary time. And not just because of Nuke York, though that was a big part of it. People were losing their jobs, their homes, crime was skyrocketing . . . it really did feel like the country was coming apart." A pause. "Tyler, do you know what a scapegoat is?"

I nodded. "Someone you blame for all your problems."

"Muldoon gave people a lot of scapegoats. Can't find a job? It's because the Mexicans are taking them all. Lose your home? Blame the Jews who own the banks. Hate paying taxes? Look at all those blacks on welfare. Think the Nation's moral fiber is unraveling? Blame the homosexuals."

"And Muldoon promised to get rid of them. Of us."

Coach pursed his lips. "There was more to it than that. The people who voted for him weren't just scared and angry—they felt worthless, stepped on. Muldoon made them feel like they mattered."

Elaine came over and set down two plates stacked with pancakes. "Sure, he did. By giving them someone else to step on."

"It's the easiest way in the world to feel important."

Coach grabbed the syrup, drizzled it over his pancakes, and handed me the bottle. "Now, dig in. It's not often that you'll get the chance to enjoy honest-to-God lesbian pancakes. I'm usually the one who makes breakfast around here."

Elaine, sitting down with her own plate, rolled her eyes. "If, by making breakfast, you mean mixing powdered milk with water and pouring it over corn flakes."

She and Coach both laughed. I joined in. The way they joked around, so at ease, so free of bitterness and paranoid undercurrents—fake marriage or not, it just felt so *normal*. I wished they could adopt me.

After breakfast Coach drove me to a safe house in Pacoima, at the other end of the Valley, an old Mexican neighborhood that had been emptied years ago. It was risky, going there in broad daylight, but less so than at night, with checkpoints everywhere. From the back seat of the car, peeking out from underneath the blanket concealing me, I saw shattered storefronts, faded Spanish signs, packs of stray dogs, and streets where the asphalt had worn all the way down to the dirt.

The house was tiny, with boarded-up windows and no front porch, bracketed by a fire-gutted ruin on one side and an overgrown vacant lot on the other. The inside, though, was clean and furnished—basic, nothing fancy, but decent.

"Sorry about moving you so abruptly." Coach was combing through the place, lifting up couch cushions and peering into cracks in the drywall—looking for cameras or listening devices, I gathered. "You'd be more than welcome to keep staying with Elaine and me, but we need to remain one step ahead of the Dentists."

"I'm putting you guys in danger, aren't I?"

"An occupational hazard." He nodded, satisfied that the house wasn't bugged, and then sat down. "It's just for a day or two, or less. I'll be back tonight—by then, hopefully, we'll have arranged transportation."

"Transportation? Where?"

"Out of the country, I presume." His brow furrowed. "What's wrong?"

"I don't know." I was hugging myself—the room suddenly felt like a refrigerator. "I just hate that I'm running away, sir."

"Better than walking around with a big pink target on your back." His expression softened. "Look, Tyler, you have your whole life ahead of you. Live to fight another day— that's my advice."

"And Casey? What's he got ahead of him?" He could have run, but he chose not to. What would he think of me if I ran away now? And what difference did it make, anyway? I didn't even know if he was alive or dead.

"I'll see what I can find out about your friend," Coach said. "If there's any way I can help him, I will."

I closed my eyes and kept them closed until I felt the tears receding—I was tired of crying. "Thank you, Coach. For everything."

"Call me Dale. I'm not your coach anymore."

"Oh, yeah. I guess I'm off the team now, huh?"

"Those boys are getting the fear of God put into them

tomorrow, mark my words. I'm not at all happy about losing my best hitter right before the playoffs."

For a second his face darkened. But then he laughed and clapped me on the shoulder, just like he used to when I hit a home run or needed reassurance after a strikeout. Except that this time, it felt different—no longer coach to player, or teacher to student, but friend to friend, man to man.

Once Coach left, and I had nothing to do but think—the house had no TV or radio, no phone, and nothing to read but a stack of picked-over crossword puzzle magazines. It didn't take me long to start wallowing.

I missed Casey so much. Yet here I was, abandoning him. Those fantastic pictures Coach had painted, of whole cities filled with gay people—no more pretending, no more terror, no more hate—Casey should be the one escaping there, not me. It wasn't fair.

Fair? What world do you live in?

I desperately wanted to believe he was still alive. But did I dare even hope for that? If he was still alive, God only knew what was being done to him. Still, I couldn't just give him up for dead. It was too final.

About an hour later, there was a knock at the door. The sound made me jump, and I froze, afraid to answer it. But then it repeated, and I recognized the pattern of knocks Coach had told me to listen for.

I opened the door a crack, and then almost fell over.

"Gwen?"

"Hey, Tyler." Gwen Smith slipped inside, took a quick look back as if to make sure she hadn't been followed, and then shut the door. "I'm here to keep you company."

From the way Gwen hardly even glanced around the room, I got the sense that she'd been here before. Babysitting other fugitives, probably. And then there was that morning I saw her in Coach's office, having what looked like a very dire conversation . . .

"Those flyers they found at school," I blurted. "That was you."

"Maybe, maybe not."

She held out her hand. I shook it.

"Welcome to the Secret Six. And congratulations—on, you know, coming out of the closet. That's got to be hard."

"So are you gay too?"

"Me? No. Actually, I've had a crush on you since fourth grade. I'm just a little bit heartbroken now." She smiled, then clasped her hands like she was praying. "If you must know, I got into the Six because of my parents. They're Unitarians."

"What's that? The thing where you're not allowed to eat meat?"

Gwen laughed. "It's their religion. They're not open about it, otherwise they'd be arrested. But anyway." A gesture toward the house's back hallway. "You want to play a game? They've got a whole bunch of board games here—backgammon, Scrabble, Battleship, Monopoly . . ."

I picked the Game of Life.

For the next few hours—sitting on the bare floor of that living room, spinning the wheel in the center of the game board and moving my tiny plastic convertible from one square to the next—I was able to relax, to forget. We were just two kids hanging out on a Sunday afternoon.

And Gwen was fun to hang out with. Underneath that quiet and unremarkable exterior I'd never seen through until now, she was smart and funny, and she never stopped talking. As we kept playing, she told me about how her parents had met, years before, when they were both in something called the Peace Corps. Just the name of it rang as weirdly in my ears as Elaine's talk about gay people marrying each other. It really must have been a bizarre time to live in, pre-Muldoon.

I gave the wheel another spin, but slumped and let my hand drop before moving my car across the board. "I wish I could have gotten to know you better before now. We've been going to school together all this time—we could have been friends."

"We're friends now, aren't we?"

Gwen was smiling as she said it. I smiled back.

"Yeah. I guess we are."

"Good thing we never dated, though, huh? That would have been awkward."

When I was done laughing, I moved my game piece— one, two, three squares—to the big red stop sign labeled MARRIAGE. I reached for one of the pink pegs, to stick in the car next to the blue one in the driver's seat—but then I thought about it, a defiant chuckle came out of me, and I grabbed another blue peg instead.

Gwen raised an eyebrow. "That's against the rules."

I just sat back and looked at her. "Says who?"

Gwen had to go home for dinner, so she left around five o'clock. While putting the game away, I found a few sheets of paper and a pen, so I decided to try writing a letter to Unity.

The words refused to flow. Either there weren't enough to squeeze out onto the page, or there were too many, and they clogged my brain. Eventually, after much struggling, I got two whole sentences. *I hope you forgive me someday. But if you don't, I understand.*

I stared at the note for a long time, but then tore it up and flushed the pieces down the toilet. It was too dangerous, trying to communicate with her, even just to say goodbye. Coach and Elaine and Gwen were already risking their lives for me—asking them to stick their necks out even further by sneaking a note to Unity, past her father, just so I could feel better about my own mistakes and lies? What right did I have, to do that?

Besides, I could write a whole book and it still couldn't fix what I'd done to Unity. In that story *I* was the bad guy, and we both already knew it.

Just before sunset Coach returned, along with Elaine, bearing Chinese food. They made small talk while we ate, but their faces were thin-lipped, their postures tense.

"What's wrong?" I asked.

Elaine glowered at her husband. "Dale, I still don't like this. He's just a kid. It's too dangerous."

"And I agree." Coach's voice had a weariness to it. "But he's not a kid, not anymore. He has the right to make this decision for himself."

"The Six shouldn't even be *asking* him to make this decision!"

"Um, hello?" I raise my voice and waved a hand at them. "What decision?"

Coach smiled sheepishly. "Sorry, Tyler. We shouldn't be talking about you like you're not in the room."

"Just tell me what's going on."

He tapped his index fingers together and stared at them, like he was using the motion to compose what he was going to say. "It's all set—your escape route. You can be on your way tonight."

"Really? Great!"

Neither of them said a word. Elaine's fists were still clenched. Coach had bowed his head and was rubbing his eyes.

In an instant, my elation was swallowed up by wariness. "But . . . ?"

Coach blew out a deep breath.

"But . . . the Six would like you to consider an alternative."

"Neighbor Lenskold?"

The Morality Officer stopped and turned at the sound of my voice. "Tyler. What are you doing here so early? School doesn't start for an hour."

I remained seated, staring into my lap, my hands fidgeting with the untucked tails of my shirt. "I . . . need to talk to you, ma'am."

Chaffs

"Of course. Come on in."

I shuffled into her office and dropped like a lead weight into the chair beside the desk. Neighbor Lenskold took the seat on the other side and folded her hands, waiting.

"Ma'am, I have a confession." As I spoke, I could feel myself disconnecting from my body. These weren't my fingernails that had been bitten down to the nubs. These tears on my cheeks belonged to someone else. "I'm sick."

A single eyebrow shot up. "I see. Could you be more specific?"

"I've been having these . . . feelings. About other guys." From somewhere outside of myself, I saw Not-Me's face look up. His voice had a tremor in it. "I've been having them for a while. I've been trying to fight them. I have. But—"

"Tyler, are you saying you're a homosexual?"

"I . . . don't know, ma'am. I don't want to be, I swear. I don't want to dishonor the Nation. I don't . . . "

Not-Me broke down sobbing, burying his face in his hands.

Neighbor Lenskold pushed a box of tissues across the desk. "You realize this is very serious."

"Yes, ma'am." Not-Me took a tissue from the box and dabbed at his eyes.

"I understand there was an incident last week, in the locker room."

"That was my fault. I lost control, and I made . . . advances . . . at Rick Nagy. The other guys, Brad Nemechuk and the others—they stopped me." Not-Me's shoulders straightened up. "They did it for my own good. They're my teammates, my friends. They helped me understand what I have to do."

"Which is?"

Just like that, I was me again, back in my own body.

"I need help, ma'am. I've heard about these places, places where people like me can go and get—I don't know. Treated? Cured? Do those places really exist?"

"They do." Neighbor Lenskold fingered the cross around her neck. "Are you volunteering to be committed to one?"

"Can I do that?"

"It's not unheard of."

"Then yes. Please, Neighbor Lenskold, I can't take this anymore."

I inched forward. I was still holding the tissue. I crumpled it in my hands and rolled it into a tight, hard ball.

"You know I have a girlfriend, right? She's pregnant. We're going to get married as soon as she graduates. I have to do this, get clean, get cured—not just for myself, but for her, for the family I'm going to have." Blinking, I glanced over at the smiling face of President Muldoon. "For the Nation."

Neighbor Lenskold peered at me over her chubby, steepled fingers. I felt like I was floating in the air, right on the edge of the earth's gravity, waiting to see if I was going to drift off into space, or plummet back to the ground.

Finally, the Morality Officer's head bobbed up and down.

"Yes. I think it's worth trying." She stood up. "Thank you for your honesty, Neighbor Treppenhouse. It's very courageous of you to come forward like this."

"I'm not courageous, ma'am. I just want to serve the Nation."

"And the Nation is grateful. Wait here."

She stepped out, locking the door behind her. I waited, forcing steady breaths in and out of my lungs. My gaze wandered over to Neighbor Lenskold's closet, and for just a second I was back in there, in the dark, with Casey. Back where it had all begun.

Then there were boots outside. The door opened, and Neighbor Lenskold came back in, along with two Wide Awakes. The joltsticks in their hands were already buzzing.

"Turn those things off." She gave them an irritable look, and then smiled at me. "Go with these men, Tyler. Everything will be OK, I promise you." She stood at attention and snapped off a salute. "Nation First."

"Nation First." I saluted back.

Holy crap. She bought it.

I could have sworn I'd laid it on way too thick, all that tormented-sounding garbage about how sick I was. But Lenskold actually bought it. I had no idea I was such a good actor.

The Wide Awakes were marching me through the whole campus—past the mural of the Commander-in-Chief, across the quad, past the cafeteria, toward the gym. As we went by, just-arrived students gawked at me. This was no secret arrest—I wasn't being made to disappear in the night. This was a public shaming.

OK. If that was what they wanted, I'd play along.

I dragged my feet and stumbled as I walked. My head hung forward, my neck muscles limp, my eyes flitting from side to side, reading my classmates' reactions—smugness, anxiety, bewilderment . . . and pity.

Under my mask of humiliation, I replayed last night at Coach's house.

". . . the Six would like you to consider an alternative."

Coach kept his voice even, but the look on his face turned my blood to ice. You saw the same look in old war movies, when the commander had to give orders that he knew would send his men into certain death.

"What is it, Coach?"

He took a deep breath and met my eyes. "You've heard about the Reorientation Centers? There's one in particular—the Six wants to put someone on the inside. They think you'd be well-suited for this mission."

"Me? Mission?" What the heck did I know about clandestine operations? I couldn't even keep being gay a secret from half of L.A.

"What happens if I say no? Does that mean the deal is off?"

"Of course not. The Six will still help you get out of the country, if that's what you decide. They'll also extract you from the Reorientation Center when your mission is complete, if you choose to accept it."

Extract. It made me sound like a tooth being pulled.

"So what's the mission?"

"I don't know the specifics. I'm sorry."

Coach laid both hands on my shoulders. His grip was tight, like he was trying to keep me from jumping off a cliff. "Tyler, I can't recommend that you do this. Like Elaine said, it's too dangerous. I honestly don't know what the Six is thinking, sending you into a place like that."

I came so close to saying no. The word was right there on my tongue. I was done—with the Muldoonies, with everything. I just wanted a life of my own, outside of this nightmare.

But something stopped me. Coach hadn't told me everything. There was some leverage that this Secret Six had on me, leverage that Coach didn't want to apply.

"There's more to it, isn't there?"

Coach nodded. "They've sweetened the offer."

The faces streamed past. I knew so many of them—some since kindergarten, others only from seeing them in the bleachers at games, cheering on the Mighty TNT as he blasted yet another home run.

In their midst, I spotted Gwen. In the background as always, hidden in plain sight. Perfect cover for opposing the Muldoonies. She smiled, touched her fingers to her forehead—a furtive salute—and then faded away.

This was my whole life passing before my eyes. These people, this place—most likely, I would never see any of them again. And even if I did, far in the future, things wouldn't be the same. *I* wouldn't be the same.

Faith. Family. Freedom.

I'd lost my faith, but found love. I'd lost my family, but found myself. Now I was losing my freedom, without knowing what—if anything—I'd find in return. All I had was hope, and a thin hope at that.

"Casey's still alive?"

"That's what they tell me. If you accept the mission, the Six will arrange to have him sent to the same place as you. You can be together. And then, when the time comes, they'll extract you both."

"And if I don't accept it?"

Coach looked like he had to force himself not to gag on his own words. "The Six will still see you safely out of the country. But our resources are limited. There are millions of people in need of rescu-ing—tens of millions. We can't—"

"I get it."

Either I took this mission, or Casey rotted. So. The Dentists weren't the only ones stooping to blackmail.

"I didn't want to tell you, but that was wrong of me—this is your decision to make, not mine." Coach's voice seemed to be coming from the other side of the world. "I'm still urging you—no, I'm begging you not to do this. Just go, Tyler—get out, leave this place behind, start a new life for yourself."

For just an instant, I wished I'd never met Casey Monahan. If I hadn't, I wouldn't be here. I wouldn't have to make such terrible, evil, impossible choices.

But then, just as fast, this became the easiest choice I'd ever made.

The blue van was waiting by the gym. As we neared it, the Wide Awakes grabbed me by the arms and frog-marched me forward.

From out of the gym emerged Brad, Danny, Rick . . . the whole team, all suited up for morning practice. Coach came out next, riding herd on them. The team crossed the driveway between the gym and the baseball field just as my escort and I reached the van parked in front of it. They stopped to watch. Deke O'Beirne and Jay Devereaux were both decent—or embarrassed—enough to look away. The others just stared—except for Brad, who smirked and then blew me a kiss.

"All right, ladies!" Coach barked at them. "Move it. We haven't got all morning."

The van's side door slid open with a rumble. Against the pull of the Wide Awakes gripping my arms, I twisted around for one last glimpse of Coach. He was still there, thick arms folded over his chest, eyes blazing with compassion and anguish in a face transformed into solid granite. As I looked at him, he gave me the barest of nods—unnoticeable to anyone besides me, but enough to straighten my spine and keep my knees from buckling. The strength I drew from that nod—I would have to make it last as long as I could.

Then I got in the van, Coach vanished, the door closed, darkness fell, and my old life came to an end.

Part Three
FREEDOM

THE bus slows down. Outside, the sun has just come up. Guard towers, blue vans, and razor-wire fences creep past the window.

We're here.

I'm suddenly very thirsty. I swallow and suck on my cheeks to force some saliva into my mouth. It doesn't help. As long and hellish as this bus ride has been, I've been dreading the end of it.

"Oh, God." Next to me, Steven is patting his pink outfit with both hands. "My paperwork! Where'd it go?"

My hand touches the chest pocket where I've stashed mine—ID, personal info, arrest and transfer orders, all tucked into a cardboard folder like an airline ticket. Not something you want to lose track of.

"Maybe it's under the seat." Steven leans forward, trying to look. "God, I hope it didn't fall out when they let us off to pee—"

The bus halts with a jerk and a hiss of brakes. Steven lurches, bumping his head. Then the doors fly open. Joltsticks buzz, voices bellow, from every direction.

"Out, faggots! You've got fifteen seconds! Out, out, OUT!"

Total chaos follows—pink-clad bodies colliding and shoving, like in the pit at that show I went to with Casey. I keep my head down and muscle my way into the center, neither the first off the bus nor the last, the better to avoid the guards' wrath.

"OUT! MOVE! Line up, single file! Do it now!"

The heat blasts me in the face. It must be a hundred degrees already. I risk a quick look around, but there's nothing to see but dusty blacktop and flat-roofed cinderblock buildings under a cloudless, achingly blue sky.

We fall in line. Four Wide awakes come strolling up, a pair on either side of us. Their joltsticks are in their hands. Their gun holsters are unsnapped. They have blank expressions and sharklike eyes, but they're young, barely older than me. One has a smudge of reddish-blond peachfuzz on his upper lip.

"Uh, sir? I have a question?"

That's Steven, standing behind me. I cringe. *Damn it, dude, shut up!*

The guard with the peachfuzz glances at his partner. "She has a question."

In a movement almost too quick to see, the second guard swipes out with his joltstick. Steven spazzes and falls to the ground, kicking my ankle, making me stumble. I straighten up fast and get back in line.

Peachfuzz stands over him. "You have a question, bitch? THAT'S YOUR ANSWER!" He looks at me. "She with you, prettyboy?"

His breath smells like an old toothbrush soaked in whiskey. I shake my head at him. Don't speak without permission—that's the first lesson you learn.

"She is now," Peachfuzz says. "Get her up and keep her quiet."

I stoop and grab Steven by the arm. He's still twitching. His eyes are sunken. His kicked-puppy expression has returned.

We stand at attention. This part is easy—I've done it in Dawn Patrol a million times. We're facing what looks like the main building—two stories, with vertical slits for windows on the second floor, U.S. and Party flags on the roof, and a sign saying FRESH STARTS REORIENTATION CENTER in big and cheerful letters above the entrance. Beyond, I see another fence, more towers. This is just the outer perimeter.

Minutes go by—five, ten. The sun rises as we stand there. The heat is like nothing back home—it's sucking the moisture right out of my pores. I'm holding steady on my feet, but a few of the others are starting to sway. The Wide Awakes inch closer, hovering, waiting for the first one to fall over . . .

Another bus pulls up. A second set of pink figures tumbles out of it, amid the same greeting of barked orders and buzzing joltsticks that we received. There's another fifteen seconds of chaos, and then the second group is queued up behind us.

One of the Wide Awakes, with sergeant's insignia, struts to the head of the line.

"All right, girls—off to Intake. Follow the green line on the ground in front of you. MOVE IT!"

Forward, into the building, down one hallway, then another. The AC is going full blast. After the heat from outside, the chill is a shock to the system, like being dunked in a tub of ice water. I clench my teeth to keep them from chattering.

We file into a spacious, low-ceilinged room, wider across than it is deep, with a row of computer terminals behind scuffed-up Plexiglas windows and, in front of them, lines of waist-high posts strung together with chains. It looks like a DMV office, only drearier. More joltstick-wielding guards move in on us, pushing and prodding until we're lined up between the posts.

The line inches forward. It takes at least an hour just to move a few feet. My stomach is growling—we haven't been fed since before we were packed onto the bus in L.A.—and my feet are throbbing in the ill-fitting flip-flops the DDS issued when they confiscated our shoes.

I distract myself by checking out the surroundings. The guards don't seem to care anymore if we turn our heads or move around, so long as we don't step out of line. There's not much to look at, but I memorize it all—the cracks in the walls, the locations of the Hawkeyes, the number of doors leading out. Even the most minor detail might become a lifesaver later on.

I'm on a mission. I say that to myself over and over. Along with the words Coach gave me, the code phrase my Secret Six contact would be using—*I love watching the fog roll in over the Golden Gate Bridge.*

Steven is now ahead of me in line. I'm not sure how that happened—we must have switched positions during the confusion of the lineup. He's quaking like a Chihuahua. He creeps up to the nearest window, and I hear him trying to explain what happened to his paperwork.

"Uh, I know I had it on the bus. I think I dropped it—I was about to pick it up when . . . I mean, if you just let me go back for it, I'm sure I can—"

The sour-faced man at the computer makes a sharp gesture, and two Wide Awakes appear. Each one is at least twice as big as Steven. They grab him under the arms. Steven sags in their grip and lets out a whimper, then starts babbling. "Please, let me go look for it, I know it's there, please—"

The scream is high-pitched and seems to come all the way from the soles of Steven's feet. The Wide Awakes have yanked his arms up and back, twisting them in their sockets. He's bent double, unable to look at anything but the floor right underneath him. The Wide Awakes hold him in that position as they pull him away from the window and march him out a door at the far end of the room.

No one says a word. Once Steven is gone, the room goes dead quiet.

Then the man at the window zeroes in on me. "Next!"

From there, I'm shunted off to another room—larger, dazzlingly bright, and partitioned into a maze of open cubicles. The air is thick with ammonia and rubbing alcohol, a medical torture stink.

The guard steers me into one of the cubicles, where a man in a white coat is putting on a pair of latex gloves.

"Strip," the man says.

The guard's joltstick comes hissing to life. I take the cue and peel out of my scrubs with lightning speed before either of these guys can get impatient.

I grit my teeth as the man in white examines me. Or maybe he's just feeling me up. He turns up my eyelids, shines a light up my nostrils and in my ears and down my throat, thumps a rubber mallet against my knees and elbows, crawls over every square inch of me with those gloved fingers, jams them into every orifice. Every so often he picks up a hand-held tape recorder and mutters some medicalese into it.

Finally he waves me over to a chair with a strange device fastened to the armrest. I sit. The man swabs the back of my right hand with alcohol and closes the device over it. The thing contracts around my hand and forearm, holding it in place.

"Count of three." The man taps on a keyboard, peers into a scope, turns some knobs. "One, two—"

A sudden stabbing pain in the back of my hand. For the first time since I got here, I scream. Another sensation follows, just as intense and even more unpleasant—an injection, like the stinger of some parasitic insect, laying its eggs under my skin.

The machine releases me. I jerk my arm away and hold it against my chest, cradling my hand. It's oozing blood, and there's a lump on it now the size of a lima bean.

"It's your tracking chip." The man grabs my hand and slaps a bandage over the wound, then motions for me to stand up. The machine spits out a strip of paper with letters and numbers on it. The man tears it off and slaps it into my good hand.

TTCA1066

"What's your name?" the man asks.

"Tyler."

A quick shock from the guard's joltstick, low setting, just enough to make me gasp and jump.

Douglas P. Lathrop

"Wrong." The man points at the piece of paper. "That's your name now. Remember it. Welcome to Fresh Starts."

I stare at my new name, long and hard. Then, with spastic movements, I put the pink scrubs on and shamble out of the cubicle, on to the next stop. The guard follows me, the joltstick still buzzing. With each step, a little bit more of my old name—my old self—evaporates in the dry air of this desert prison.

I T'S almost lights-out by the time I get my cabin assignment. The cots are bolted to the floor, spaced barely far enough apart to thread between.

As I squeeze by, eyes look up at me. A few light up with a pained, pitiful lust, quickly snuffed out. The rest just give me a dull, apathetic glance before going back to their prayers, or their whispered conversations, or their traumatized staring into space. Half of the guys in the cabin—they're called cabins instead of barracks, like we're at summer camp—are already lying down, hands in plain view on top of the blankets.

Lying down is a great idea. Once I reach my cot, my legs give out and I collapse onto the thin, musty-smelling mattress. I roll over, and the rough weave of the blanket scrapes like sandpaper against my shaved head. Between the day and a half without food, the grueling bus ride, the hours I've spent being processed, and the three-hour orientation video I had to sit through, I already feel like I've been through a sausage machine. And I haven't even been here a full day yet.

This is real. This isn't just a nightmare.

Of all things, it was the head-shaving that finally did me in. I've never paid much attention to my hair, beyond getting it cut once a month. Watching it fall in clumps to the floor, feeling the dry and artificially chilled air rasping my naked scalp—that accomplished what all those weeks of DDS interrogations couldn't. It wrecked me. I couldn't just go into my own skull anymore and pretend I was watching a video of someone else. This was really happening. To me.

But it's OK. I survived the Dentists—I can survive this. And I'm on a mission—I need to stay focused on that, keep my wits intact until the Six gets in touch with me. My contact could be anyone—a fellow prisoner, even a guard.

I repeat the code phrase for what must be the billionth time. *I love watching the fog roll in over the Golden Gate Bridge . . .*

"Hey," someone whispers. "You're new, ain't you?"

It's the guy in the next cot over. He's on his side, looking at me. About my age, slim but not emaciated—thank the Lord, they don't seem to be starving anyone here, like I've heard they do at other camps—with a constellation of freckles on both cheeks and across the bridge of his nose. He has a Southern accent.

"RJTN5981," he says. "What's your number?"

"TTCA1066."

I've already cracked part of the code. The first pair of letters are your initials—the second pair is the state you came from. So, this guy is R.J., and he's from . . . Tennessee?

Maybe this is my contact. *I love watching the fog —*

"Want to get off?"

"What?"

"I need to get off so bad. I ain't even played with myself in two weeks." He whines like a dog begging for table scraps. "Suck me off, please? I'll suck you off, too."

"Suck . . . ? No!" I keep my voice down and do a head-jerk up at the Hawkeyes in the ceiling. "Are you crazy?"

"They won't know. They don't really use them things. And I don't care anyhow. I'm gonna explode if I don't get off."

"Forget it." I can't even imagine getting wood in this place. And besides, anything sexual is absolutely forbidden. Even Jack Palm and his five brothers are banned here.

R.J.'s face goes hard and menacing. "I can make you. If you don't get me off, I'll tell them you went after me. You'll get whupped."

"If you do, I'll kill you. Or I'll tell everyone you're a snitch, and *they'll* kill you."

Never cave in to a threat—I learned that early on, in the DDS holding tank. If you do, even once, you're everyone's bitch forever.

My own threat has the desired effect. R.J. crumples and sinks back down on the cot, pulling up the covers and laying his hands on top of them. "You didn't have to say that. I'm just aching to get off, that's all."

Now I'm feeling guilty for intimidating the poor guy. Who knows what I'll be like, after enough time in this place? I might end up just as pathetic as him. But I don't dare apologize either—that would only make me look soft.

The cabin goes dark—it's lights out. I close my eyes and fold my hands on my chest. I haven't prayed in months, but I do so now, silently. Even though I have no idea if God is listening here.

During the night I lie awake—*Wide Awake*, ha!—and replay my time in DDS custody. Every second of it, over and over.

The Dentists tried to make me say that my . . . perversions . . . were Dad's doing. Obviously they wanted to hang a few molestation and incest charges on him along with all his other crimes. That was ridiculous—Dad had never touched me like that, and I refused to say that he had. After a while they gave up that line of questioning.

But my own story, about wanting to be cured? Neighbor Lenskold might have bought it, but the Dentists sure didn't.

Boy, did I ever misuse the word *torture* back in my former life. *"That trig test sure was torture, huh?" "I thought Coach was going to torture us to death at practice today.*" I will never throw that word around so casually again.

It's not like the Middle Ages or anything—they don't tie you to a rack and keep turning the wheel until you confess to being a witch. The Dentists are way more subtle. First, the torture happens—the beatings, the joltsticks, and that thing where they handcuff you to a chair and put a plastic bag over your head until your whole body is thrashing and you're peeing your pants and you'll do anything for them if only they let you breathe—and *then* come the questions. The questioners are all like Mr. Ludlow—polite, but with an undertone of pure menace in their quiet voices. Any backtalk from you, any answers they don't like, and they'll send you back to the torture chamber in a heartbeat. And the interrogations go on forever—hours, days—no sleep, no food, no bathroom breaks, nothing but one question after another.

I'm not sure how I withstood it. Maybe I'm tougher than I thought. Maybe dealing with Mr. Ludlow—who I never saw even once, making me wonder if his own actions had gotten him in trouble with his superiors—taught me how to manipulate them. Or maybe it's because I kept thinking of Casey, how he never screamed when the guys were waling on him. Of course, I'm not Casey—I screamed my head off.

But I survived. That's all that matters.

At four a.m. the lights snap back on and a growling alarm, like a machine stripping its gears, blasts through the cabin. Instantly we're all on our feet, and there's another scramble as we make our beds—they have to be perfect, hospital corners, blankets absolutely smooth—and jockey for position at the cabin's four toilets.

We have thirty minutes to do our business before roll call. Thirty minutes, four toilets, about a hundred guys. The math is brutal.

There are no stalls around the toilets—that's the worst part. I learned in the Dawn Patrol how to make a bed military-style, but taking a dump in under a minute, in the open, surrounded by guys badgering you to hurry up and yelling at you not to use all the toilet paper? There was nothing in the handbook about that.

Once the half-hour is up, the cabin's Housemother—*Resident Supervisor* is the official term—a baboon-faced man in the same pink getup as the rest of us, but carrying a joltstick and with a blue armband showing his superior status—starts barking orders. "Fall out, faggots! Outside! Move, move, MOVE!"

We double-time it into the floodlit assembly yard. Even at four-thirty in the morning, it feels like I'm stepping into an oven.

The cabins are arranged in a semicircle around the yard, across from the two-story building where we were processed. Near the center sits a shoulder-high platform on which two Wide Awakes are standing, holding oversized clubs and flanking a T-shaped structure, like a gallows, with a slotted metal cylinder hanging from each arm. The cylinder on the left is moving. One of the Wide Awakes notices, and hits it with his club, making it swing and producing a sort-of-human moan from the inside.

Beyond the glare of the floodlights I can see the outlines of more structures and the glint of razor wire surrounding them, but past that, it's just darkness. I'll have to wait until daylight to see how big this place really is.

We form ranks. Directly behind me, a couple of guys are muttering to each other in some weird jargon.

"You get the dish on M.K.? Went to the Cactus Garden yesterday."

"Really? Shit. I thought she'd never snap."

"Me neither. Set your betties on this noob in front of us—think she'll be next?"

"She does have Conover's trade written all over her."

"Yeah. Poor bitch."

I recognize *noob*—Casey used to call me that—but before I can puzzle out the rest, the Housemother bellows for silence, and we snap to attention.

The roll call goes just as the orientation video said it would. There's another shouted order, through a loudspeaker this time, and the inmates—close to a thousand total, it looks like—raise their right arms, fingers extended, palms facing the ground. With a slowness that seems calculated, guards with scanning devices stroll up and down the ranks, pressing the scanners against the back of each inmate's hand. Only then, after our tracking chips are read and our presences recorded, are we allowed to lower our arms.

I'm feeling lightheaded. The heat, the lack of food, the lack of sleep—it's all catching up with me. My arm is trembling from the strain of holding it up. I pour every last bit of energy into staying on my feet and holding my position. If I let my arm drop, the Housemother will give me a jab with the joltstick—if I fall down, I'll get a beating from the guards and God only knows what other kind of punishment . . .

The guard scans my hand. The scanner chirps, and he moves on. I can lower my arm now.

By the time they're done, over an hour has gone by, and the sky is brightening. A sigh ripples across the yard—a sound of both relief and weariness. That's the whole point of this exercise, I'm guessing—to leave us terrified and worn-out before the day has even started. Me, I just want it to be over with so I can get some breakfast—they *have* to feed me eventually—and find out where I'm going next. To Aversion Therapy? To Self-Criticism? Or maybe they'll assign me to a work detail. That might not be too bad—I could make myself useful . . .

"RJTN5981! Step forward!"

The command nearly blows out the speaker, it's so loud. We all jump, then murmur among ourselves, looking around until our eyes settle on who was just called . . .

R.J., the kid who propositioned me last night.

He stands there, blinking, paralyzed, until two guards march him, with an occasional shove, to the front of the yard and up a ladder onto the platform.

The voice speaks again. Filtered through the loudspeaker, it sounds metallic, not human. "This one made lewd advances to another inmate. How does she plead?"

R.J. licks his lips and stammers, "N-not guilty."

One of the Wide Awakes swings his club. It meets R.J.'s kneecap with a crunch that resonates across the yard. R.J. screams and collapses.

"HOW DOES SHE PLEAD?"

"Guilty! Guilty!"

The loudspeaker drops to a distortion-free volume. "As this is her third offense, this one has forfeited her place at Fresh Starts. After punishment is administered, she will be transferred to a general detention center, effective immediately."

I cringe. Everyone around me does. *Her third offense.* They operate on a three-strikes system here. You break the rules twice—and there are a lot of rules to break—you get punished. A third time, you get transferred out as well, and that means —

Another crunch. This time the club has smashed one of R.J.'s hands. His scream shoots up the scale and turns into an operatic trill before descending into a jerky, sporadic whimper. He rolls onto his side, cradling his shattered hand, and he hardly notices when the guards drag him off the platform, his useless leg trailing behind.

"TTCA1066! Step forward!"

Silence. More anxious glances. Eventually the eyes all focus on me.

I'm as paralyzed as R.J. was. I can't believe it's my number that was just called. I must have heard it wrong. It's only my first day—I haven't had *time* to break any rules . . .

A guard approaches, reaching for his joltstick. The sight of him shocks me out of my stupor and sends me scrambling out of the ranks. The long walk to the platform seems to stretch for miles.

"This one failed to report a rule violation by another inmate," the voice says. "How does she plead?"

"Guilty!" My response is instant. I'm not about to repeat R.J.'s mistake.

"Stand facing the others. Put your hands behind your head. Spread your feet farther apart."

One of the Wide Awakes is circling me. He's holding that club with both hands. The thing is as big around as my arm, with an even bigger ball of hardened rubber at the business end. I stare out across the yard and try not to think about where he's going to hit me. It's not just my kneecaps or hands I need to worry about—that club could easily pulverize a shoulder, burst my guts open, drive splintered ribs into my lungs.

What I did, to get summoned up here—I should have figured it out on my own. The video was very clear. It doesn't matter that I refused R.J.'s advances—what matters is that I didn't report it to the Housemother. If you see a rule being broken and don't report it, it's as bad as if you broke the rule yourself . . .

Without warning, the guard spins around, gives the club an underhanded swing, and hammers it with all his strength between my legs.

I double over, clutching my groin with both hands. I can't even scream—the pain has blasted all the breath out of me. A huge collective gasp rises from the yard—or maybe that's just the agony exploding in my skull. I've taken hits to the nuts before, but never like this. I could swear the pulped remains of them have been launched halfway up my body cavity.

As the pain ebbs, a sickening dread creeps in to replace it. I'm lucky to be here, the video said. Our Commander-in-Chief is giving me the opportunity to redeem myself, to prove my worth. All I have to do in return is follow the program and obey the rules. But I get only three chances. If I blow them . . .

I get transferred.

It's the ultimate threat. General detention, where queers are as hated as the Muldoonies—by the politicals, by the Mexicans, by the crooks and murderers, by everyone. Out there, wearing pink amounts to a death sentence. And the execution isn't nearly as clean and quick as a bullet in the head.

Three strikes and I'm out.

And this was Strike One.

FOR the next several days I pee blood, walk bowlegged, and can't sit down without grimacing. But then it all tapers off, and I don't seem to have suffered any permanent damage. My punishment could have been much worse.

I'm assigned to do road work outside the camp—*Hardship Therapy*, it's called. Our natural male urges have been dormant—some good physical labor will awaken them. That's the theory.

We aren't issued work gloves, of course, or hats to keep off the sun. If you complain about this, the guards make you wear a girl's bonnet and frilly lace gloves. Complain again, and you're practically begging to get clubbed in the nuts at roll call.

By the end of the first day, my hands are covered with blisters and my shaved head looks like a ripe tomato. On the way back to camp, one of the other guys passes me a tube of sunscreen. He doesn't say where he got it. He just leers at me. "You can pay me back later."

For a place designed to cure my gayness, I sure do get propositioned a lot.

The roads are nothing like L.A.'s—no lights or signals, no on- or off-ramps, just thin ribbons of gray criss-crossing the bleak, rust-hued landscape. From the signs, I pick out the names of towns—Deming, Silver City, a few others with Spanish names. The nearest is over twenty miles away. I also see a sign for El Paso. That's in Texas. I think.

Each day I throw myself into the job, blisters, sunburn, and all. The asphalt fumes sear my throat and lungs, and by noon my joints and vertebrae are grinding together like an old man's from all the bending, stooping, lifting—but I don't complain. I can't let anyone—not the guards, and especially not the other workers—think I'm some delicate little pansy from a Party family who can't carry his own weight.

Besides, this isn't so bad. *I could do worse* has become my personal motto. At least we're not being purposely worked to death, like what I've heard happens to politicals and Mexicans. Our day ends like clockwork an hour before sunset, the food is gross but adequate—grits for breakfast, green-tinged bologna sandwiches for lunch, and some mysterious stew you don't want to look at too closely for dinner—and no one gets beaten or joltsticked so long as the work gets done.

Even our guard detail seems light, just two Wide Awakes for close to fifty guys. Aren't they worried we'll try to escape?

"Escape? To where?" LBWA5773—the guy who gave me the sunscreen—just laughs. "Look around you—nothing but desert. You wouldn't make it halfway to the Interstate. Besides, that chip in your hand tracks your location—you'd be picked up and stuck in the Birdcage before nightfall." He laughs again, and his voice goes all nasal. *"Whut we've got heah is a failure to communicate."*

L.B. likes to toss out random quotes from old movies. "I worked at a video store when I was in high school in Seattle. When the Muldoonies started banning movies, we hid the banned ones in the basement—my co-workers and I would watch them on our breaks. We thought we were being so *rebellious*." He smiles at me. "You look a little like a young Paul Newman. Has anyone ever told you that?"

Chaffs

Despite L.B.'s not-at-all-hidden agenda for sleeping with me, he seems OK. Not bad-looking either—he has a wicked smile, and the road work has bulked him up. I could do worse.

But no. I'm not going to risk breaking any more rules. I need to find people I can trust, way more than I need sex.

The days blur. Morning roll call—and punishment of rule breakers—work, lunch, work, back to camp, dinner, evening roll call, more punishments, a half-hour for toilets and bed checks, then lights-out. Six days a week, with church on Sundays.

Except for the days—I never know which days—when I'm sent to the Clinic. It's some distance away from the assembly yard, a dazzlingly white building that looks exactly like its name. Everyone gets summoned there at least twice a week.

The Clinic is where I undergo Aversion Therapy.

I'm strapped into a chair, naked, in a small, soundproof booth. The chair is padded and comfortable, or it would be if I weren't restrained at every joint. Even my head is clamped and immobile, facing forward.

On the screen in front of me, men are fucking. Men and boys, of every age and skin tone and body type—fucking and sucking and doing other things that even Casey and I at our horniest couldn't have imagined. A lot of the scenes are disgusting, not arousing at all, but others . . . I find myself watching them, heating up . . .

And as soon as I do, I'm in pain, instantly.

Behind me, there's a machine, with a technician at a control panel, and with wires connecting to clips on my earlobes, nipples, fingers, toes. More wires run between my legs to this rubber tube that the technician calls a phallometer.

The machine knows before I do—it knows when I'm about to sprout wood. The shocks don't last long, but each one is like a thousand joltsticks cranked up to full power. The pain is like being castrated and dismembered and skinned alive, simultaneously.

On the screen, the grunting and grinding goes on and on, oblivious to my agony. In each corner of the booth, a video camera records my reactions.

Each session lasts an hour. By the end, I can't move without spazzing. And for the rest of the day, whenever I think about the things I saw on that screen—about anything sexual at all—I get a metallic taste in the back of my mouth and my whole body goes tense, waiting for the next jolt.

As much as I dread Aversion Therapy, I'd spend twenty-four hours a day in that chair if it meant never again going to Self-Criticism.

If you're the one being critiqued, they make you stand at attention in the center of the group. During some sessions you're forced to bend over and grab your ankles, or hold your arms high in the air, like wings. Like the fairy you are.

"FLAP YOUR WINGS, TINKERBELL!"

"FAGGOT!"

"COCKSUCKER!"

The words attack you from every direction—the words and the laughter and the gagging noises. The others aren't allowed to touch you, but they can scream in your ear, spit in your face. Occasionally the facilitator—an older man, with a blue armband and an intellectual air, like he might have been a professor in his former life—will break in to berate you more surgically, his words cutting out chunks of your soul and tossing them out for the others to chew on.

Each session has a different victim. If you're new, you're chosen automatically—otherwise someone in the group is picked at random. I don't know which is worse—being the one in the middle of the circle, or being part of the feeding frenzy.

Usually, whether from work or from the Clinic, I come back to the cabin so exhausted that I drop like a sack of cement as soon as I reach my cot. But there are still moments, in the desolate hours between lights-out and the morning alarm, when I lie there, unable to sleep, just me and my fears.

I fear that Casey is already dead. I fear that the Secret Six will never get in touch with me—that they screwed up, that I got sent to the wrong place and they don't know where I am. I fear that I'll end up rotting here.

I'm totally alone, with no one who'd notice or care if I died here tomorrow. I'm not even Tyler Treppenhouse anymore. I'm TTCA1066.

And it's all Tyler's doing. He put himself here because he couldn't pretend anymore—because, once Casey showed him who he really was, he just had to live it. Was that really worth losing everything? What difference does it make, being your true self, if no one even knows you exist?

Tomorrow is Sunday. No one in the work detail will shut up about it—Sunday is our day off. We'll be spending most of it in church, but it's a relief from pouring asphalt and dodging scorpions.

At around noon a blocky, military-type vehicle with official markings pulls up at the work site. Three men get out—two chimpanzees in blue, and a willowy figure in pink with a blue armband. The one in pink shows some papers to the foreman, who points in our direction.

"Aw shit," L.B. mutters next to me. "He's coming this way. Look at him, all *I'm ready for my close-up, Mr. DeMille.*"

"Who is he?" I ask.

"One of Conover's stableboys. Thinks he's the queen of the whole camp."

"I *am* the queen, my dear Lawrence. Can I help it that my tiara has been confiscated?" The man swans up—yeah, *swans* is the right word—and plants one hand on his hip while the other hand gestures with the paperwork. He has wide lips, and eyes spaced too far apart on his face. "You're TTCA1066? Be honest. Has this *prole* been poisoning your mind against me, before we've even met? Do I look like some chickenhawk to you?"

I blink at him. "Uh . . . "

"Rest assured, I mean you no harm. My intentions are completely honorable." He gives me a long and luxurious once-over, and sighs. "Being honorable is *such* a burden."

L.B. snorts. "You're on a one-way trip to the Cactus Garden, you know that, Duncan?"

"Perhaps, but I'm enjoying the ride." Duncan— DTCA7318, according to the tag on his scrubs—pauses, clears his throat, and waves the paperwork at me. "Actually, I'm here on business. My orders are to bring *this* fine specimen back to camp immediately. Neighbor Conover has a job opening."

The name makes warning sirens go off. Conover? That's the man those two guys behind me mentioned during roll call my first day here. *This noob does have Conover's trade written all over her. Poor bitch . . .*

I shoot a look at L.B., but he just shrugs.

Duncan pivots, beckoning me to come along. I obey. My feet cling to the roadbed, like they know better than my brain does that I'd better not go. Getting yanked off what everyone says is one of the cushiest work details in the whole camp— this can't be good.

I climb into the back seat. As usual, I'm drenched with sweat the instant the AC hits me. Duncan slides into the back as well, angling slightly toward me and crossing his legs above the knee. The chimplike guards get in the front.

"So what's your story, Tyler?" Duncan sees me flinch at the use of my name instead of my number, and he pats me on the arm. "Relax, sweetie—we're all sisters here. Save the alphabet soup for the guards." A quick tip of the head toward the front. "You're a volunteer, I understand. We don't see many of those. By now you're probably wondering what the hell you were thinking."

I shrug. "It seems OK."

"Ah, a man of few words. I *like* that." He winks at me. "So you're from Los Angeles? What's *that* like? I visited the place a few times, in my former life. Has it fallen into the ocean yet?"

I hunch down in the seat. What is he doing? Is he flirting with me, or trying to provoke me into breaking some rule so these Wide Awakes have a reason to abuse me? He's not cowed by them himself, that's for sure.

"Me, I'm from San Francisco. Beautiful city, absolutely *gorgeous*. Far more fabulous in the old days, of course, but there's still no place like it." Another sigh. "It's the little things that I miss the most. Like the way it looks in the evening. I just love watching the fog roll in over the Golden Gate Bridge."

Dead silence, broken only by the hum of the car's engine. I manage not to react, beyond a couple of eye-blinks, but . . . *this* guy? He's my *contact?*

Duncan is waiting for my response to the code phrase. It takes my brain several seconds to come up with it.

"I . . . I'd rather watch the sunset from the Santa Monica Pier."

A scant flutter of his eyelashes says everything. *We'll talk later.*

Another pat on the arm, and then he settles back, whistling a peppy-sounding tune. I recognize the melody, but I can't recall the title, no matter how hard I dig for it.

Back at camp, Duncan takes me up to the second floor of the main building, to a cubicle maze like the one in which I was examined and chipped. Except this one smells like new carpet, not ammonia and alcohol, and instead of screams and barked orders, the air is filled with ringing phones and murmuring voices and the clicking of computer keyboards. Every so often I see a flash of pink going from one cubicle to another.

Duncan threads through the maze and stops at an office door with a brass plaque on it—ORVID CONOVER, CHIEF ADMINISTRATOR. He knocks, I hear a grunt of, "Come in," and he ushers me inside.

Conover is eating lunch. On his desk he's got a bucket of fried chicken from a fast-food place in town. Around it are scattered a bunch of side dishes—a couple of corn cobs, some biscuits, a big tub of coleslaw. He ignores me and

Duncan and keeps tearing into the chicken. We wait silently.

Finally, he looks up. "Has that shipment for the guard barracks arrived yet?"

"This morning," Duncan says. "Six cases. Nothing but the best for the Shock Troops of Liberty."

"Hm." He glares at me, then at Duncan. "Go wait outside. I'll have you show this one around after I'm done with her."

With a nod at Conover and a quick, not-at-all-reassuring glance at me, Duncan leaves and shuts the door.

Conover drops the gnawed remains of a chicken breast onto a paper towel, then reaches into the bucket and grabs a drumstick. The sight of it, so crispy and delicious, makes my stomach growl, and I have to swallow so I don't drool all over my scrubs. Already it seems like I've had nothing to eat but grits and rancid bologna my entire life.

"So you're a volunteer, huh?" Conover's voice is thin, with a sucking-on-helium pitch that clashes with his doughy but powerful-looking form. "What drove you to Fresh Starts? You get caught blowing the gym teacher?"

I was already nervous when I walked in here—now I'm blushing on top of it. "Uh, no, sir. I—"

"Spit it out, faggot. Or are you the type that swallows?"

He laughs at his own joke. He's not wearing any uniform to speak of—just a short-sleeved white button-down shirt with grease dribbles on the front and more ancient, indelible stains under the arms and around the collar. His skin is pale and shiny, like it was grown in a vat and then stapled on, and it just sort of hangs off his bones, forming flaps and creases. Even his hair is off-putting. It's . . . flesh-colored.

I give him the same story I manufactured for Neighbor Lenskold, the one where I attacked Rick Nagy in the shower room. As I talk, his moist gaze slides all over me, and from between his grease-smeared lips the tip of his tongue protrudes, like a slug.

"Typical athlete. Cocky bitch, think you own the world. We'll squeeze that attitude out of you here, you can count on it."

He picks the drumstick clean, spits out a piece of gristle, and belches. "Fine. You'll do. Now be a good little queer and clear this crap off my desk. D.T. will show you where the garbage chute is. You'll report here after roll call Monday morning."

I nod and obey, scooping the bones into the bucket and piling the untouched side dishes on top. It's so tempting to pocket a biscuit or two, even the coleslaw, but you get punished at roll call for stealing food.

I meet Duncan, follow him down the hall, and throw out all the leftovers. As I listen to them tumbling down the chute, my stomach growls again.

Duncan makes a sweeping gesture toward the elevator. "Shall we?"

Once we're outside, he falls into an easy stride along the edge of the assembly yard. The cabins are mostly empty, the doors open, the inmates either off working or in therapy. Just a few scurry in and out on cleaning detail, carrying mops and buckets and spray bottles of disinfectant under the glaring eyes of each cabin's Housemother.

I quicken my pace to keep up with Duncan's. "So . . . this Conover guy. I'm going to be working for him?"

Duncan chuckles. "Don't sound so enthused, now. And Conover isn't just a guy, he's *the* guy, the Supreme Diva of everything around here—except personal hygiene and table manners, obviously." Another look of attempted reassurance. "You'll do fine. This is the perfect job for you."

I get it. The Six wants me working for Conover. I make eye contact with Duncan, and he brushes one fingertip casually across his lips. *Not yet.*

Beyond the assembly yard, the camp is a rat's maze of narrow passages flanked by razor-wire fences, monitored by Hawkeyes mounted on posts at regular intervals. Duncan avoids looking straight at them. I do likewise.

"So have you been here a long time?" I ask.

"Long enough. I've gone through every kind of treatment they've got here. Well, almost every—they stopped doing the hormone shots not long after I arrived. Too many odd side effects. Consider yourself lucky."

Clearly, the treatments didn't take. I don't need Casey's gay radar to see that. How does someone so swishy survive in a place like this? Heck, how did he live so long on the outside without being discovered?

As we walk, Duncan does a verbal sketch of the camp's layout. Past the chapel—a cinderblock pile like the other buildings, only decorated with the rifle-scope cross of the Nation's Covenant Church—he points out an exercise yard, a baseball diamond . . .

"You play baseball, don't you, Tyler? We have a team here. A softball team, actually, and they only play each other, but I personally can't tell the difference—it's all cute boys swinging big sticks and running around on the grass, to me. You should join."

After the way Brad and the others defiled the game for me? "I don't know. I'm surprised it's even allowed."

"So long as we're not diddling ourselves or each other, they don't much care how we blow off steam." Duncan goes left, down a long, straight passage. "There were riots a few years ago, before I got here—men were killed, both inmates and guards. It may seem like we're here to be disposed of, but remember, we're still part of the blessed white race—they'd much rather cure us than exterminate us. *'Every white man who dies without a son and a daughter—'*"

"'*— is a nail in the Nation's coffin.*'" Even here, the Muldoon quotations come out automatically.

Duncan's voice seems to be dropping in register, becoming more solemn—or maybe I'm just hallucinating it. "Even if softball isn't for you, you ought to do *something* to stay in shape. It will come in handy later."

I'm not hallucinating—Duncan's whole demeanor is changing. His strides are lengthening, becoming firmer—he even seems to have grown taller. His Queen of the Camp routine is dropping away right before my eyes.

"Over there"—a wave down another razor-wire-lined passage—"are the armory and the guard barracks. We have a whole platoon of Wide Awakes stationed here. No admittance to inmates except by invitation."

"Uh, invitation?"

"It's not for tea and cupcakes, honey."

He turns another corner. "You'll be over at the Clinic fairly often, running files and progress reports back and forth.

It's all supposed to be in the computer system, but Conover is one of those types who doesn't trust computers, so he keeps almost everything on hard copy. Far, far too much of it."

From here, looking at the Clinic, I can just barely make out a smaller, even more nondescript building attached to it. "What's that?"

"The Annex." Duncan doesn't elaborate.

He swings right, goes halfway down another passage, and then slows down. Every step is an effort of will for him now, it seems like. His voice has a new, strained edge in it. "Plus, there's the . . . well, there's no good way to prepare you for this. You're just going to have to see it."

We reach an unlocked gate. Duncan opens it, we go through —

And I'm staring right into the face of a corpse.

I lurch back, and stumble into the fence. *"What the fuck?"*

The dead man stares back at me. Or he would, if he still had eyes. His eyeballs have dried up—the empty sockets yawn at me like bottomless pits. The remains of his uniform hang in faded pink strips over his leathery skin. Except for that, he looks like one of those gory paintings of Jesus from the Middle Ages, only he hasn't been crucified, just tied to a metal post with cables under the armpits and around the waist. His arms are free, but stiff and twisted, like the arms of . . .

Of a cactus.

"The Cactus Garden?"

Duncan just nods.

I inch forward. I've never seen a dead body before—and there are dozens of them here, maybe hundreds, a whole morbid orchard of them stretching as far as I can see. They're not rotting, not in this desert—the parched air and blazing sun have mummified them. Some look like stone fossils, they've been here so long. Others are more recent. From a distance, you'd think they were just at roll call.

"What are. . . how did they get here?"

"Suicide, mostly. A few work-related accidents, too, and a few more who had heart attacks during Aversion Therapy. Then there are the cases where the guards got carried away with the discipline." He stares hard into the forest of staked-out bodies. "But the majority put themselves here. Hanging is the most popular method."

"But what are they doing *here?* Why not just bury them?"

"Bury them? Where's the educational value in that?" A bitter amusement creeps into Duncan's voice. "A grave is just a hole in the ground. Putting them on display like this—it's the Muldoonies' way of showing us exactly what our corruption leads to. *The wages of sin is death.*"

The corpses are dancing now, gyrating like they're at some macabre gay prom. No, I'm the one who's swaying—I'm on the verge of passing out. I close my eyes and take several deep breaths. The smell here isn't what I would have expected. It just smells dusty and abandoned, an odor of hopelessness.

I can barely speak above a whisper. "Can we get out of here, please?"

"Not yet. We have business to discuss."

"Here?"

"It's the safest place. Nobody wanders over here casually, not even the guards. And I've arranged for the Hawkeyes to be disabled. We have a few minutes."

He uncrosses his arms and beckons me closer. "You've figured out why we brought you here, I take it?"

By *we*, he means the Secret Six. "Yeah. You want me working for Conover."

"More than that. We need you to get close to him." His gaze goes flat and detached. "Don't be coy. You know what I'm talking about."

I do, and it's making me want to slither out of my own skin. "You want me to . . . Conover is *gay?*"

"Gay? Good lord, no. More like a diabetic who can't resist an occasional jelly donut." A shrug. "He must have friends in high places—otherwise he'd be dead, or an inmate here, rather than the one running the place. Still, they probably shipped him here to keep him from embarrassing them."

"And I'm . . . a jelly donut."

"His favorite flavor." Another eyelash flutter. "Can you do it?"

Chaffs

I look again at the dried-up human husks around us. "Can you tell me why?"

"Not until you're securely positioned. If you know too much too soon, and your cover is blown, the whole op will be compromised." His expression softens, but only a little. He knows this isn't what I signed up for. "If you can't do this, speak up now."

Do I have a choice? If I bail, will the Six still keep their end of the bargain? And what about Casey? Helping him is the whole reason I'm here. If I don't see this through, the Six *might* still help me get out, to start a new life somewhere else—but if I leave Casey at the Muldoonies' mercy for the sake of my own freedom, how much would that freedom be worth? Zero. Or even less.

"Yes. I can do it."

For Casey. I'm doing this for Casey.

That's the only way I can get the words out, and not throw up.

28

A ND *when Jesus had come into the countryside, there he met two men possessed by demons, exceedingly fierce. And they called out, saying, 'Art thou come hither to cast us out?'"*

The chaplain has none of the bombastic rage of Reverend Blanchard back home. He's wearing pink like the rest of us, with a cross on his blue armband—a soft and blotchy little man who reads the gospel verse in a quivering, please-don't-zap-me-with-that-joltstick-again type of voice.

"Now a good way off from them there was a herd of many swine feeding. And Jesus said unto the demons, 'Go.' And when they came out, they went into the herd of swine—and behold, the whole herd of swine ran down the slope into the sea, and perished in the waters."

Something's missing. Didn't the demons *ask* Jesus to cast them out? Reverend Blanchard would have grabbed that and run with it. The possessed men are homosexuals, he'd say, and the demons are the unclean thoughts inside them, begging to be purged. Isn't that why we're at Fresh Starts in the first place?

Or maybe he'd say we were the swine, drowning ourselves in the sea.

I miss my old church. I miss Reverend Blanchard's tirades, I miss the hymns—all music is banned here—I miss seeing Unity up in the choir, singing her heart out. I wonder how she's doing. Has she had . . . ? No, the baby isn't due until January, and I know I haven't been here that long. Is she still planning to give it to the Dare Institute? Or did they reject her application once they found out the father is queer?

The sermon doesn't hold my interest, so I bow my head and pray—for Unity, for Casey, and especially for myself.

My mission begins tomorrow.

I get why Duncan can't tell me yet what the mission is—I do. I know exactly what I need to know, and no more—it's safer that way. But what I do know is already making me want to back out, before I've even started.

I'll be working for Neighbor Conover. Not just working for him—letting him touch me. Letting him do things.

Being his whore.

Though I suppose, technically, I'm the Six's whore. After all, they're the ones paying me.

At lunchtime I suck down my green bologna sandwich and go over to the exercise yard. On Sundays, after church, we get the afternoon to ourselves—the only long stretch of waking hours where we aren't being yelled at, worked to exhaustion, or wired up to electrodes. Only a handful use the free time to exercise—for most it's too hot out.

Out on the field, I spot the softball team Duncan told me about. Part of me longs to join them, but I just can't do it—even looking at a bat puts me right back in that shower room at school. Instead, I make for a bench press in a far corner of the yard.

God, I'm *so* out of shape. Back home I could bench almost three hundred pounds—but now, after just a few weeks in this place, I can lift barely a third that weight, and only six reps at that.

"Hey. I thought I'd seen the last of you."

It's L.B., the guy who befriended me on the work detail. I'm looking at his face upside-down, so I can't tell if he's smiling at me, or leering.

"Want me to spot you?" he asks.

"Yeah, sure."

I try another couple of reps, then set down the weight and sit up. "So . . . Lawrence?"

"Larry. Only that nelly Duncan calls me Lawrence."

"OK, Larry. How did you end up here?"

"I was stupid. I cruised the wrong guy—turned out that the Dentists were using him as bait." For a second his face takes on that distant look everyone gets when talking about the Dentists. He blinks and shakes it off. "We're the lucky ones, you know, getting sent here and not off to the meat grinder. Prettier scenery here, too." He chuckles and shakes his head when I start fidgeting. "Don't worry. You're one of Conover's boys now—I wouldn't dare try anything."

He knows all about Conover, apparently. I suspect everyone in the camp does.

I go back to the weights. With Larry spotting, I manage to complete a full set of reps, then another, before calling it quits.

Just then, I notice a frail figure lurking on the fringes of the yard—Steven. I haven't seen him since the Wide Awakes frog-marched him out of the intake room.

"Is he the one?" Larry asks.

"The one what?"

"You've shot down all *my* passes—I figure there must be someone special for you. Is it him?"

"Steven? We just rode up on the bus together."

"Well, that's a relief." His eyebrows shoot up. "You haven't heard?"

I shake my head.

"Some of the guards signed him out over the weekend, took him back to the barracks for some playtime. *'Squeal like a pig. Squeal!'*" Another one of Larry's obscure movie quotes, I'm guessing. The joking look on his face evaporates as he glances at me. "Sorry. I guess some of us aren't so lucky after all."

Steven's skin is pale, his eyes are squinting, and he cringes when anyone comes close. He's . . . how old? Fourteen? As I recall from what he told me on the bus, his own sister turned him in. Does she, or the rest of his family, have any idea what they've condemned him to?

And what's Larry's deal, anyway? He definitely knows the ins and outs of this place—I could learn a few things from him.

But can I really trust him? *Trust* is such a life-and-death word here.

"Have you ever watched the fog roll in over the Golden Gate Bridge?" I ask.

"No, I've never been to San Fran." Another distant look. "Probably never will."

With my new assignment, I also get new quarters, one of the cells for administrative staff on the second floor of the main building. It's only eight feet by ten, but it has a window, and an honest-to-God enclosed bathroom—no more taking a dump out in the open. It's like a five-star hotel, compared to the cabins.

I smile hello at my cellmate, a quiet, dark-featured kid with Clark Kent glasses who's sitting cross-legged on his cot, with a Bible open in his lap. On his side of the cell he's taped up a picture of President Muldoon torn from a magazine, and on the shelf underneath there's a copy of *Rise and Shine*. That and the Bible are the only two books allowed in this place, and his look like they've been read a million times, with cracked bindings and lots of dog-eared pages.

"So what's your name?" I ask.

"ZMNV0473." He gives me a quick, wary look before burrowing back into Holy Scripture.

"Yeah, I can read your tag. What's your *name?*" I'm bending the rules, if not breaking them, but I'm feeling bold right now—probably from the jump up in status. "Zachary? Zeke? Zebediah?"

"ZMNV0473."

So. He's bought into the program. Either that, or he's worried that I'm a snitch out to entrap him.

Just before lights-out, he puts the Bible away and asks me to pray with him. I turn him down as politely as I can. I'm all prayed out.

I've never tried to seduce anyone. I've never had to. At school, girls were constantly angling for a date with me—if I hadn't been so shy, or so gay, I could have just taken my pick. Unity fell for me the instant we met. And Casey—well, *I* was the one being seduced there. Not that Casey had to work very hard.

So no, a master of seduction I'm not. Especially not when the target physically repulses me the way Conover does.

On my first day it doesn't look like I'll even get a chance to try.

Just after sunrise, three busloads of new inmates come in. Through the slitlike windows on the second floor, I can hear the commotion of scrambling feet and buzzing joltsticks and bellowed verbal abuse below. Some of the admin staff stand and watch. I can't. The memory of my own arrival is still too raw.

Conover watches too. But then he goes in his office and shuts the door, and the rest of us plunge into our duties. As the new arrivals are processed, their paperwork is brought up, and I spend the morning creating files for them, pulling out staples and punching holes and sticking labels on folders. When I'm done, I bring each file to Conover, who calls up more records from the computer on his desk, talks it over with a couple of white-coated assistants—discussing what kinds of treatment will be inflicted on the new inmate, I suppose—then gives it back for me to stash in the file room.

By the time I get through one pile of paperwork, another one has been dropped onto my workstation.

Yet even amid all this nonstop activity, I can't stop thinking about what's happening to those new guys downstairs.

Chaffs

From here, this place feels like a machine. And I'm one of the buttons being pushed.

After lunch, it's time to do cabin assignments. This involves dividing up the arrivals, putting them on lists, and delivering the lists to each cabin's Housemother. Making room for them is the Housemother's job—if the cabin is full, he decides which of his current charges gets transferred out, to free up space. This is his opportunity to get rid of trouble-makers, or guys he simply doesn't like.

The doomed ones—the ones getting shipped off to certain death in general detention—learn their fate at the evening roll call. A couple of them fall to their knees, weeping and pleading. Two or three others become violent and have to be pummeled into submission before they're dragged off. And then there's one who just seizes up and topples to the ground. The guards' joltsticks make his limbs twitch, but he doesn't get up.

One more for the Cactus Garden.

With that last bit of drama, the day comes to an end. By the time I trudge out of my cubicle, I'm a million kinds of wrung out. Even the roadwork never left me this exhausted—physically, mentally, every way I can think of.

"TTCA1066."

It's Conover. He's drunk—his voice has the same slur my mom gets when she drinks. His eyes are like two raw and unshelled oysters lying on beds of crushed ice.

"Come with me," he says.

Now? He wants me right now?

I plaster on what I hope looks like an enticing smile. Conover turns and waddles up the empty corridor. I follow him.

Just get it over with, I tell myself. I'm on a mission—I already agreed to do this. It's just sex, anyway. I'll just close my eyes and pretend I'm with Casey . . .

We enter Conover's office. He crosses halfway to his desk and stands facing me. "Close the door."

I turn to obey —

And something hammers me in the back of the head.

The impact is like a joltstick on full power. Every nerve short-circuits, and I fall forward, smacking my face on the door. Before I can slide to the ground a hand grips me by the collar, drags me up until my feet are dangling, then slams me into the door again. I ricochet off of it. A billion flashbulbs go off in my head, blinding me. Then another hand, huge and clammy, with fingers like uncooked sausages, reaches around, undoes the drawstring of my pants, and yanks them down around my thighs. My underwear is next.

"Sir, please." I'm babbling, scraping for some control. "You're . . . you don't have to . . . I'll do—"

"Shut up!"

The alcohol on his breath makes my eyes water.

I'm spinning, my legs tangled in the pink fabric. I slam face down onto Conover's desk. His hand pins my neck, grinding my face into the cold metal surface. I'm tasting blood in my mouth, gagging on it.

"Please, I . . . you're hurting—"

"SHUT THE FUCK UP FAGGOT!"

He presses down. My neck feels like it's about to snap. My body struggles, but a couple of kidney punches make it go limp again. My breath is hissing through my teeth. I zero in on the sound and try to follow it into my skull where I can hide till this is over . . .

I feel Conover's gelatinous weight on top of me. Folding me over. Prying my knees apart.

Then the pain starts. And doesn't stop.

'M hunched over on the toilet seat, my head between my knees. My pants lie in a pink wad around my ankles. I have no idea how I got back to my cell. Conover must have had the guards drag me here.

At least the bleeding has stopped. I think. To make sure, I grab a few sheets of the wood-pulpy stuff that passes here for toilet paper, make a pad, and carefully wipe myself. Even that light touch is agony, but when I look at the pad, it's clean.

With my other hand, I feel my nose. It's not bleeding anymore either. I don't think it's broken, though it's doubled in size from being smashed into Conover's desk. A blessing in disguise—it means I won't have to spend the night smelling his stink all over me. I won't have a chance to shower until morning.

There's a soft knock at the door, and I flinch. But it's only Z, asking if I'm OK, for about the millionth time.

"I'm fine," I grind out. "Leave me alone."

"I'm sorry." Z sounds sincere. "It's lights-out in five minutes. I just thought you should know. I . . . I'm sorry."

One spasm after another wracks my whole body. It's like my soul can't stand to be inside it.

Like it isn't *my* body anymore—it's his. Conover's.

He didn't have to *use* me the way he did. I would have done anything he wanted. That's why the Secret Six wanted me here in the first place. To get close to him.

But it didn't matter. Using me, hurting me, tearing me open—that *was* what Conover wanted.

Another tremor hits. I curl up even tighter, until my forehead is brushing the floor. I'm seeing Conover's eyes again, the way they looked when he was done with me. Gray and dead, but also delighted.

Then the wave passes, and I no longer feel anything.

I sit up. I can't stay in here forever. With a shudder, I reach down for my pants, hitch them up, and start to rise. Halfway, I double over again and bite back a scream, but then I push through the pain and force myself onto my feet.

Before hobbling out of the bathroom, I lift up my shirt and run one fingertip along the fresh incision just to the left of my belly button—about two inches long, perfectly straight, just deep enough to draw blood and leave a scar.

Z is sitting on his cot, his legs under the covers and his Bible in his lap. His gaze connects with mine, but he doesn't raise his head or speak. That's fine—I don't want to hear what he has to say. If he opened his mouth right now, I'd probably punch him.

I lie on my side, facing the wall. The coarse fabric of my shirt rubs against the wound on my abdomen, and it all comes back. The look in Conover's eyes. The gleam of the scalpel in his hand. And the rumble of his voice as the blade parted my flesh.

"One."

Then it's lights out, and the blackness swallows me.

There's no formal roll call for the admin staff. As we file into our separate mess hall—brightly lit and immaculately clean, with the same grinning portrait of President Muldoon on the wall as in the cafeteria at school—each of us simply presents his chipped hand to the guard for a quick scan.

We're fed way better than the other inmates, too—eggs, bacon, real coffee, even orange juice. Mom used to complain about how expensive orange juice was, and that was in California—it must cost a fortune out here in the armpit of nowhere.

We admins are the elite at Fresh Starts. All these tiny privileges—from our semiprivate cells to the food on our plates to our relative freedom of movement around the camp—remind us of that. But as with everything in this place, they come with a threat attached—an awareness that any and all of these luxuries could vanish in a heartbeat. Muldoon giveth, Muldoon taketh away.

I choke down my breakfast. My taste buds are as numb as the rest of me—I might as well be eating Styrofoam. Nobody says a word to me, of course—I'm new, *and* I'm Conover's fuck-toy. If I were them, I wouldn't talk to me either.

Duncan is here, floating around like a butterfly. He makes some witty remark that I can't hear, and even a couple of the guards laugh. As he does so, he slips a plastic bottle of clear liquid to another guard, who hands him an unmarked but fully stuffed envelope in return.

"Good morning, Tyler." He rubs the fuzz of new hair growth on my head, and sits down. "How's the newest addition to the sewing circle? Are you settled in yet?"

I grit my teeth and keep silent. I don't dare yell *Conover fucking raped me last night, you son of a bitch!* Even if I weren't surrounded by Hawkeyes and potential snitches, telling Duncan would only make matters worse. Either he already knows what Conover did to me, and doesn't care, or he'd pull me off the op, thinking I don't have what it takes for the mission. I can't let that happen. I'm not putting myself through this for my own sake, and certainly not for this goddamn Secret Six—I'm doing it for Casey. I can't let it be for nothing.

"Don't worry about the others—they always give the new girl a hard time. They'll warm up eventually." He leans in.

"I've got a project for you. Interested?"

I inch away. "What is it?" *Who do you want me to bend over for now?*

"We're hosting a mixer next month with Second Chances—that's the women's Reorientation Center up north. I've been appointed chairman of the planning committee." He preens a bit, and then goes on. "You, my dear, would be perfect for it."

"Mixer? Like a dance, or something?"

"Oh, it's quite the event. A chance for all of us to mingle with the opposite sex and show the Nation how rehabilitated we are. There's a crew coming in from the Office of Communications and Public Morale, so we really need to shine. Are you on board? Please say yes—I'll be your best friend forever."

His smile has an edge. This is an order, not a request.

"Sure. I guess."

"Fabulous!" He gives me a wave as he walks off. "We'll talk later. Ciao."

I'm starting to see how Duncan survives here. For one thing, he keeps everyone entertained, like some kind of court jester. He also seems to have connections outside the camp, giving him access to things even the guards can't get hold of. Did the Six recruit him after he arrived here, or did they send him in as an infiltrator, like me?

Or is all that stuff about the Secret Six just another lie? Maybe Duncan is simply Conover's pimp.

I hate thinking of this as rape. It's not like Conover jumped me in some dark alley. It isn't really rape if it's something you signed up for, is it?

But I can't come up with a better word.

Conover . . . rapes me . . . every third night on average. I don't think he has the stamina to go more often. Each time, when he's done, he's red-faced and wheezing, with hardly even enough energy to pick up the scalpel and carve another mark on my stomach.

Chaffs

Between times, he ignores me. I see him only when I'm bringing him paperwork. His eyes avoid me, like I'm a temptation he's resisting. Then, on the third day, he starts drinking before lunchtime, his gaze fixes on me and goes glassy, and I know how the day is going to end.

The longer he goes without, the worse I get it. After four nights he becomes psychotically violent—those are the nights he wales on me with his fists, or loops his belt around my neck and yanks on it until I pass out. He also gets that way when it's been a rough day—when busloads of new inmates come in, or when people from the DDS or the Party come to visit.

Those are the nights I'm afraid I won't live through.

The notches now number half a dozen. I try not to count them, but I can't help it.

Steven is dead.

His Housemother found him behind his cabin in the predawn hours. The body was whisked off before roll call. Speculation is rife. Did he hang himself—the most common way of committing suicide here—or slit his wrists, or do something more gruesome?

The news hits me a lot harder than it should. I didn't really know Steven—I'd never met him before being packed onto that bus—but I'd talked to him, heard a little about his life. Now that life is over. I've never known anyone taken by death that abruptly. Disappearing, sure—like Kevin, like Casey—but never flat-out dying.

Or, being killed—say, during another one of those . . . parties . . . in the guard barracks. That's the possibility no one will voice out loud. At Fresh Starts, nobody dies except by his own hand.

It guts me. So naturally, I'm the one Conover assigns to plant Steven in the Cactus Garden.

At the morgue I hand over some papers and wait, until an orderly appears with a gurney holding Steven's body. At least I assume it's Steven. Without thinking, I go over and raise the sheet covering him.

So much for suicide. Steven couldn't possibly have done *that* to himself.

It takes a minute for the heaves to quiet down. Once I'm steady, I take one end of the gurney and start wheeling it outside.

"Hey, what are you doing?" The orderly steps out and blocks the gurney's path. "No taking equipment out of the building."

"What am I supposed to do, carry him?"

The orderly shrugs. "Ain't like she's gonna give a damn."

I give up. Shaking my head, I lift Steven and sling him over my shoulder, using the fireman's carry I learned in Dawn Patrol. He's a lot lighter than I expected.

The wind is gusting. One of those violent desert storms is brewing—already, a line of thunderheads is spreading across the horizon. Among the staked-out bodies in the Cactus Garden, wisps of dust and grit spiral up from the ground and attack me—I have to put a hand over my eyes to shield them. The corpses themselves undulate in the wind, the pink shreds of their uniforms flapping.

Not far from the gate, a new post has already been stuck in the ground, with metal and leather straps attached, waiting to embrace the garden's newest flower.

I ought to be doing what I can to give Steven back some dignity—treat his remains gently, maybe say a prayer or two—but now all I can think about is getting out of there before the storm hits.

Quickly, I prop him against the post. The body has some leftover stiffness, making it hard to manipulate. Steven's arms are locked in place, tucked in over his chest, his fingers curled like he died clutching something close to his heart. The straps aren't tight enough, and he sags against them—he'll probably slip out of them completely after I leave him here—but it's the best I can do.

There's a rumbling in my ears. At first it sounds like a flutter in my heartbeat, but it goes on and on until I realize it's coming from outside. Thunder. In the last few minutes the clouds have gotten much larger and darker.

I listen until the thunderclap fades to nothing.

Then I fall to my knees.

I think about Casey, to give myself strength, but his image is faint and blurry. From above, more sharply, Steven's mangled countenance, and the boiling tar-black clouds framing it, fill my vision. The sight robs me of everything I had left, every last morsel of hope that hadn't been beaten or raped out of me. All that's left are these mutilated remains of a human face, ground to pulp under the heel of a boot.

The clouds swallow the sun, and the skies blacken. A fat raindrop splashes against my forehead. A gust of wind, and then another blast of thunder, much louder than the last one, knock me out of my stupor.

As I rise, something catches my eye.

One of the other bodies, behind Steven and to the left. His shirt is ripped down the front. In the wind, it snaps open and shut, open and shut. My eyes are at his waist level, and I see them, marching across the taut and desiccated skin of his abdomen.

A row of straight vertical scars, beginning right next to his belly button.

Another clap of thunder—or no. This time it really is my heart skipping a beat.

I come closer. My hand is rubbing the wounds on my own stomach. The other guy's scars are faint, fading as his corpse mummifies, but also numerous. Enough of them to disappear under the jumpsuit and then reappear on the other side. They must run all the way around his torso.

One for each time Conover violated him.

Who was he?

His face is too shriveled to make out what he looked like when alive. I lift one of the torn edges of his shirt instead— and yes, the tag with his number is still there on the chest. I don't have anything to write with, so I commit the number to memory. I may have sucked at math in school, but I always had a knack for remembering numbers—all those batting averages and pitchers' ERAs I had to store in my head . . .

MKCO6295.

"You get the dish on MKCO6295? Went to the Cactus Garden yesterday."

"Shit. Really? I thought she'd never snap."

The rain intensifies. But I can't leave, not yet. I check more bodies, looking for others Conover might have marked. I find two more—one with the same number of marks as I have, and another with just four. I memorize their tags too.

By the time I get back to the main building, the rain is turning to hail, and the lightning is flickering like flashbulbs on the red carpet at a movie premiere. Conover is gone—he lives in town, and probably ducked out early to get home before the storm.

All but one of the other admins have gone back to their quarters as well. The remaining one gets up, hooking a couple of file folders under his arm.

"I'll take those for you. I have to file that, anyway." I point to Steven's folder, sitting on the desk in my own cubicle.

The admin shrugs and hands his folders off to me.

The file room is down a long hallway. There's a guard posted at the door, but I show him the folders I'm carrying and let him scan the chip in my hand, and he buzzes me through.

I need to move fast. There's a Hawkeye overhead, of course, but I'll have to take my chances. I'm more worried the guard will get suspicious if I'm in here too long.

I put the other folders away first. Carefully, and I double-check to make sure I haven't misfiled them. Once I'm done, I take Steven's across the room, to the tall cabinet in the corner labeled INACTIVE.

The drawer makes a hair-raising squeak as I open it. Behind me, it feels like the Hawkeye is burning a hole between my shoulder blades. I replace Steven's file and then, trying my best to act casual, I run my finger along the row of tabs until I find the one I'm looking for. MKCO6295.

I flip to the first page, with the mugshot that was taken the day he was arrested . . .

He's me.

Or, he looks an awful lot like me. Same hair color, same general appearance.

I read. *Matthew Louis Kampfer*, from Fort Collins, Colorado. Brought to Fresh Starts in February, committed suicide by hanging about four months later—around the same time I arrived.

I keep going. Part of me is screaming to hurry up—just put the folder away, look up the other two numbers, and get the hell out of there—but now that I know a little about this one, I need to learn more. The file contains all the basics— vital statistics, arrest orders, family history, racial background, Dawn Patrol and school information . . .

He played baseball.

The screaming in my head stops. The thumping of my heart fills the file room.

In a frenzy, I look up the others. *Jonathan David McKenzie*, from Dubuque. Iowa. *Alan Keith Whitehead*, from La Jolla, California. Again, the same physical likeness. Both suicides by hanging. One was a quarterback, the other one captain of the lacrosse team.

Jocks, all four of us. No, not just jocks—star athletes. This isn't just about what we look like. It's about who we are—or were.

"Cocky bitch, think you own the world. We'll squeeze that attitude out of you here, you can count on it."

He's got some sort of grudge against athletes. He gets off on breaking them, using them up. And once he's finished, they go to the Cactus Garden.

But does he really drive his victims to suicide, or does he kill them himself?

Does it even matter? Whether he murders them outright, or simply destroys them so thoroughly that they see no other way out—what difference does it make?

Either way, I'm next.

Knowing what Conover has in store . . . There was a time, not long ago at all, when I would have gone catatonic from that knowledge. But not now—this time there's no fear, no despair. Nothing but a sudden, icy strength. I feel like I could tear the whole camp apart with my bare hands.

I return the files to the drawer, close the cabinet, and leave, pausing only long enough for the guard in the hallway to scan my chip again.

Conover is not going to kill me.

Because I'm going to kill him first.

I've become very adept at begging. Conover likes to hear me beg. If he thinks I'm being too uppity he'll hurt me until I adjust my attitude. But I can't be too abject with the groveling either—that only gets him worked up.

Now that I know his true agenda, I need to be calculating. If he does his own killing, what sets him off? Does he get bored with his victims once he's broken them? Or does he kill them out of frustration if they fight too hard? Submission or defiance—which will keep me alive longer?

One night, just to see how Conover reacts, I give in totally—I become Mr. Eager-to-Please. It's a mistake—all it does is enrage him. *"Are you enjoying this now, faggot? Who else are you getting it on with, you little pussy?"* He chokes me out with his belt, revives me, then hands me over to some Wide Awakes and has them beat me while he watches. The next morning, I can hardly walk—I need Z to help me out of bed and down to breakfast.

From then on, my lingering doubts about Conover's intentions number exactly zero. This isn't going to end until one of us is dead.

In a way, understanding that makes everything more bearable. I have another mission now, besides the one the Secret Six has yet to disclose.

Now, I need a weapon.

A gun would be ideal, but also well-nigh impossible to get hold of. Even if I could snake one from the guards, I'd go down in a hail of bullets from the others before firing a shot. A joltstick might do—each of the Housemothers carries one, as do some of the other admins whose jobs involve enforcing rules. Crank the thing up to full power, give Conover a good jolt, and bash his brains in while his flabby carcass is still spazzing. But there's still the problem of stealing one, never mind avoiding discovery until I have the chance to use it.

I'm only going to get one swing at the ball here.

Chaffs

As I think about it, though, I realize I already have a weapon at hand. I've always had access to it. It just needs sharpening.

Time to turn my own body into a weapon.

I start off slow—just a set of push-ups in my cell before lights-out. Back in Dawn Patrol, when I was in peak condition, I once did a hundred in under two minutes—now my arms are on fire before I reach twenty. Months of confinement and abuse have taken a lot out of me. But by the end of the second week I can do fifty, no problem, and I'm adding sit-ups to the routine. On Sundays I hit the exercise yard like a madman.

Z doesn't say a word during these nightly workouts. My cellmate just sits with his nose in that Bible. Then, when the lights go out, his whispered prayers fill the darkness.

He's thinking the same thing as all the others—the admins, the Housemothers, even the guards. I see it in their eyes, whether they're looking at me with sympathy or contempt. I see it in Larry's as we work out together. They're all wondering when I'm going to snap. Some of them probably have bets going.

They couldn't be any farther off base. As my body gets stronger, an unbreakable serenity grows in my mind. The ground under me feels more solid than at any time since before Kevin disappeared and Casey entered my life.

That whole world from before—it's gone. And soon enough, I'll be gone as well. I'm not stupid—I know I won't survive this. If I do succeed in killing Conover, my own execution will soon follow. But my last moments won't be of Conover defiling me. I'll be dying as myself, as a man who knows who he is.

They can plant my remains in the Cactus Garden afterward, for all I care.

The day has just started, and I can already tell it's going to end with me bent over Conover's desk. It's been several days, and he has the look.

That's OK. I drop my own gaze and shuffle my feet as I move, putting on a show of meekness that I no longer feel. *You'll get yours. But not today. I can wait.*

I'm standing in his office, waiting for orders. A new batch of inmates came in this morning—a small one, just odds and ends from various places. A few, I gather, are special cases requiring unique attention.

Conover takes a set of paperwork from the stack on his desk. He scowls, and a hiss of annoyance escapes from him.

"A *Disposal Unit?* That can't be right. Looks like the Labor Department's screwed up again. Why didn't they just shoot the little fairy?"

He slides the paperwork across the desk toward me.

"Have D.T. get on the phone with Labor and confirm this. If they're going to send us their bottom scrapings, they'd better have a damn good reason. Assuming this isn't just some bureaucratic mixup." A pause. "You hear me, boy?"

"Y-yes, sir."

My response is just a reflex. I'm staring at the mugshot on the first page. I don't dare move, or breathe.

Jason Lee Crandall, from Provo, Utah.

The name is fake. The face attached to it has changed—it's narrower than before, and starved-looking—but I still recognize the soul behind it.

I've kissed those lips and gazed into those honey-colored eyes too many times not to know him on sight.

C ASEY.

"Something wrong, boy?"

The bark in Conover's voice startles me out of my trance.

"No, sir. I'm sorry, sir."

"He a friend of yours?"

"No, sir. I . . . He looked familiar for a second, but I was wrong."

Conover's gaze zeros in on me. But then he breaks off and turns his attention back to Casey's—Jason's—file.

"I guess we'll park him in the Clinic for a while. Maybe they'll need another guinea pig over in the Annex." He's talking to himself. The roll of fat under his chin wobbles as he does. Then he shoots another glance at me. "Why are you still here? Go find D.T."

He means Duncan.

I slink out of Conover's office like a whipped dog. There's no need for fakery here—my fear and cringing are real.

How much does he know?

Does he know about me and Casey? Maybe Conover has been searching for him. Maybe he found him. Maybe he had Casey brought here, to torture me further. To kill him, or worse, and make me watch . . .

No. Conover wouldn't falsify Casey's name—he'd throw the real one in my face. It was the Six—it had to be. They did promise to reunite me with Casey, after all.

Duncan isn't in his cubicle. I make a full circuit of the admin floor—he's nowhere to be found, and no one knows where he went. People are staring at me, and I pass one hand over my face to try and relax it. I'd better not let myself look too agitated.

In each cubicle there are two pads of sticky notes, blue and yellow. We normally use blue—yellow is for urgent matters only. I lay Casey's bogus paperwork on Duncan's desk and slap a yellow note on it. SEE ME—T.

From there, I go ask a guard for permission to use the bathroom. The stalls have no doors, and someone else could walk in at any time. Nevertheless, once I'm inside I lean on one of the partitions and rest my forehead against the cool stainless steel, taking deep breaths, forcing calm and relief into my system.

He's alive. I say it to myself over and over. *He's alive.* That's more than I was hoping for when I woke up this morning.

To my surprise, Conover doesn't summon me into his office at the end of the day. He stays behind closed doors, alone, and then leaves without a word.

On the way back to my cell, I pass Duncan. He gives me a fleeting moment of eye contact—*message received*—but then cuts me off with a headshake. The hallway is too busy—not to mention the Hawkeyes in the ceiling—and Duncan is probably also afraid I might demand to see Casey. He's right—I would.

My relief at Casey's reappearance doesn't last long. He's here, and he's alive, but in what condition? One haggard-looking mugshot isn't much to go on.

Chaffs

I do know one thing—this Secret Six is more powerful than I thought. This was no simple task, tweaking the Muldoonie bureaucracy to get Casey sent here, much less giving him a fake name. The Six must have people on the inside—in the Party, in the Wide Awakes, maybe even in the DDS.

Still, the ruse won't hold for long. And when it fails, the game will be over—for Casey, for me, for Duncan, for all of us.

The following afternoon, I go to Self-Criticism. Today, I'm the one selected to stand in the circle and be yelled at.

Normally, all the verbal abuse just slides off me. I've gotten so used to it—and what are a few insults, anyway, compared to the things Conover does to me on a regular basis? Like a love poem, that's what.

But today I'm a raw nerve. And the facilitator sees it. As soon as there's a lull in the shouting, he moves in, armed with nothing but that droll voice of his.

"How do you feel about what they're saying, TTCA1066?"

I don't argue. "They're right, sir."

"They're saying these things to you for your own good. You don't want to end up in the Cactus Garden, like that pretty friend of yours. Do you?"

He's talking about Steven. But his words conjure an image not of Steven, but of Casey. Staked out under the sun, mummifying in the heat and then crumbling into dust—

It takes everyone in the room to wrestle me to the ground. My knuckles are coated with the facilitator's blood. I'm screaming, just one long wordless scream after another, until the guards with joltsticks come in to subdue me.

My punishment is meted out at morning roll call—ten lashes, followed by twenty-four hours in the Birdcage.

I hardly even feel the whip on my back. I'm too twisted up inside to feel anything. The whipping soon stops, my back is sprayed with something—an antiseptic, probably—and then I'm bundled into one of the metal cylinders in the center of the assembly yard, and hoisted aloft.

Strike Two.

Between today's punishment, and the one I received on my first day, I've maxed out the count. One more strike, and I'm off to general detention, where no one in pink survives for long.

The Birdcage turns into an oven as the sun rises. But being cooked alive isn't the worst part. Confined like this, I have too much time to think. To think, to worry. To hate.

I don't know who I hate more—myself, Conover, or the Secret Six.

They've played me for an idiot *again*. I was all set to kill Conover—but now, in one stroke, the Six has taken that off the table. They recruited me by promising to help Casey—and now they're keeping me in line by dangling him in front of me, like a carrot. They know I'd never abandon him, or do anything to put him in more danger.

This has to be Duncan's doing. He must have figured that I'd given Casey up for dead, that the Six was losing its leverage on me.

Fine. I'll play their game a little longer. But Duncan is going to tell me what this mission involves. I'm done being strung along, by him or anyone else.

I keep thinking. And as I do, a plan evolves.

When they open the Birdcage again, I spill out of it, barely conscious. But I revive fast, and after a few hours in the infirmary, I'm cleared to go back to work. I've seen admins punished for rule-breaking by being demoted back to the cabins, but I know that won't happen to me. Conover wants to keep me close at hand.

Sure enough, he unloads on me that very night. It's been a whole week, and whatever the demons driving him, they're practically clawing through his skin in their frenzy to get at me. There are moments when I truly believe that this is the end, that I'm going to die right here, with Conover tearing me apart like a rabid dog and me too weakened from the Birdcage to put up even token resistance. So much for my plan.

But Conover has also been getting careless. The drinking is starting earlier and earlier—sometimes he's already drunk when he shows up in the morning. Tonight he almost passes out while he's still on top of me—I have to squirm out from underneath his sweaty bulk on my own when he's finished.

The scalpel wavers in his hand. He can hardly hold onto it. I realize that this is my chance—to wrest the scalpel away and spray the walls with his arterial blood before anyone can stop me . . .

But I don't. I let Conover cut me again.

"Thirteen."

He sets the scalpel on the desk, puts his pants back on, and staggers out of the office, leaving me alone and naked on the floor.

I sit up and get dressed. After more than a dozen times, being raped isn't as painful as it used to be.

Then I see the scalpel.

Normally, Conover locks it in a drawer. This time, in his drunkenness, he must have forgotten. He'll be gone for several days next week—plenty of time to borrow the scalpel and put it back before he misses it.

With as casual a motion as I can manage, I slip the scalpel into my pocket. I turn my back to the Hawkeye in the ceiling as I do so—I'm pretty sure Conover has the thing deactivated on the nights he abuses me, but best not to assume it.

Now, time to set up a meeting with Duncan.

The Six aren't the only ones who can apply leverage.

It takes a few more tries, but I finally make it clear to Duncan that he can't put me off any longer, and he agrees to meet me Sunday afternoon.

I kill an hour in the exercise yard beforehand. Even after the Birdcage, I'm now close to bench-pressing the same weight I could back home. An encouraging thing to know, going into this meeting.

When I arrive at the Cactus Garden, Duncan is already there, standing at ease among the dried-out bodies. I keep my hand in my pocket, fingering the scalpel I stole from Conover's office.

I get straight to the point. "Casey's here. But you already know that, don't you?"

"Yes." Duncan doesn't even bother denying it. "I knew he was being sent here, but I didn't know when. You found out before I did."

"I want to see him. And I want to know about this mission of ours."

"No." He puts his hands on his hips and sets his jaw. "Like I said before, it's too dangerous to know too much too soon. Likewise if Conover catches wind that you and your friend have a prior relationship. Be patient."

"Patient?"

I pull out the scalpel. My original plan was to threaten Duncan with it, but in the instant it takes my hand to leave my pocket, I realize that plan won't work.

I hold the blade against my throat instead.

Duncan makes a move toward me, but then stops short. "What are you doing?"

"I'm done." I can feel my hot pulse under the cold metal. Just a little pressure will sever my carotid and bleed me out in seconds. "If you don't let me see Casey, and tell me what's going on, I'm *done.*"

"Committing suicide won't help your friend."

"It won't help him if Conover kills me either." With my free hand, I lift my shirt to show the marks on my abdomen. "How many others has he done this to? I know I'm not the first. There are others right here with these same scars. Look around you."

Duncan keeps his eyes on me—not even a glance to search for marks on the corpses around him.

I cover myself back up. "You knew about this, didn't you?"

"Tyler, believe me, we're not going to let—"

"You knew! You bastard!" Down the front of my neck I feel a warm trickle—I must be pressing down with the scalpel hard enough to draw blood. "You guys are no better than the Muldoonies. You use people, you play with them, like this is just some game to you. I'm not going to be one of your pawns."

That strikes a nerve. Duncan looks away, and a shadow passes over him—cold, but also deeply sad.

"Oh, honey. We're *all* pawns."

He stares off into space, pondering. But then his shoulders slump, and he blows out a deep breath. "Put the knife down."

I hold off for a second, looking for signs of surrender on his face. Once I'm convinced he's not trying to trick me, I lower my hand.

Duncan clasps his hands behind his back, suddenly all businesslike again. "Your friend is in the Clinic building."

"In the infirmary?"

"No, an isolation ward. Go there after dinner—I'll make sure the Hawkeyes are out of commission. I can get you five minutes with him—ten, tops."

"Won't there be other people around?"

"Just a single orderly on Sundays. I know him—I've rewarded him in the past for looking the other way." An unpleasant smile. "Would you like to know *how* I rewarded him? We all have to sacrifice our virtue for the cause on occasion, child."

He sounds like Mr. Ludlow right now. *We do what Our Nation requires.*

"And are you going to tell me about the mission?"

"After you've seen your friend."

With that, Duncan makes his exit. I stay behind for a minute or two—there's no one else around, but it's still unwise to leave together.

The scalpel is still in my hand. I put it back in my pocket, then reach up and dab at the rivulet of blood on my neck. In the desert air, it's already become dry and flaky.

Was I *really* going to slit my own throat just now? If Duncan had called my bluff, I just might have. Killing myself wouldn't help Casey, but when I think about dying with Conover on top of me, inside me . . .

I look around the Cactus Garden, and a shudder ripples through me. I'm even closer to becoming a permanent fixture here than I was before.

The isolation ward is a double row of cells in a musty-smelling part of the building. The orderly looks me over with the usual despairing, barely-suppressed lust. I glare back—*I'm Conover's meat, not yours*—until he breaks eye contact and ushers me to the last door on the left. He makes a five-finger gesture, then leaves.

The cell has two hospital beds. A plastic curtain separates them. The bed near me is empty, but I hear breathing sounds coming from the one behind the curtain.

I pause to steady myself. I've been aching to see Casey again for so long, but now that he's here, I'm terrified of what I'm going to see. Finally I'm on the other side of the curtain. I stand at his bedside, grip the rail, and let my gaze take him in.

He's asleep—either that or doped up. Jesus, he's so *thin*. His skin looks like tissue paper—I can make out the outline of the bones underneath. I used to know Casey's body better than my own, and right now I don't even recognize it.

"Casey?" I can't raise my voice above a whisper.

The lower half of Casey's body is covered by a sheet. I trace his form with my eyes, working my way down—but then I stop. My breath catches.

Below the knee, both his legs are gone.

I jam my knuckles into my mouth to keep from crying out. My own legs feel like they're being sawed right out from under me.

Casey stirs. Either he heard me whispering his name, or he's feeling a tremor from my grip on the bed rail. His head lolls toward me. There are deep pain-lines carved into his face, but his eyes—they turn me inside-out, just like they used to.

"Tyler?"

"Uh, hi."

"Is that you?" Casey's voice sounds thick. "Or is this the drugs again?"

"It's really me. God, Casey, I am *so* glad to see you."

"What's left of me."

His gaze drops to where his legs used to be.

I reach for him with my hand—it's shaking as it settles in his palm.

"Listen, I can't stay long." My fingers lace through his and squeeze, gently. "Just hang in there, OK? I'm going to get us out of here."

A hoarse chuckle. "Yeah. It's the drugs again."

The way he says that—it's just so Casey. I can't help it—I start laughing.

"I missed you so much, you have no idea." Tightening my grip, I bring his hand to my lips, linger there with it, and then press it against my cheek. "I love you."

For a heartbeat or two, Casey doesn't move. But then he turns his hand over in mine and cups it against me, his fingertips stroking my face. In the midst of this hell, that touch is like a lifeline from heaven, and I hold onto it for as long as I can, until the time comes when I have to go.

RUMORS about "Jason" tear up the camp's grapevine. Nobody but me knows his real name, or anything else, but that just generates all kinds of garbled theories.

"Is it true he's a cripple?" Larry sets down the free weight he's been using and picks up the next heaviest one on the rack. "I heard he blew himself up trying to bomb a Dawn Patrol meeting."

I drop down from the chin-up bar and let my arms fall to my sides. "Really? I wouldn't know."

"Oh, come on. I know you've seen him."

Shit. Larry is way too perceptive. I'd better think fast.

"Conover just sent me to check up on him. There are some special orders, I guess—the guy's hands-off. Conover wants to make sure nobody messes with him."

"Yeah, I can imagine—some of those orderlies are real perverts. You wouldn't want them playing with DDS property." He looks off in the direction of the Clinic building. "I hope he enjoys it here while it lasts. I hate to think about what the Dentists have planned for him."

Chaffs

Just what I wanted to spend the rest of the day thinking about. Thanks, Larry.

At least, for now, Casey is safe—or, as safe as anyone can be, in this place.

Safer than me, that's for sure.

I snag as much time with Casey as I can—a few minutes every few days, only when Conover is away from the camp. Duncan doesn't even try to forbid it. Either this is his way of making nice, or he's assuming I'd sneak off to see Casey anyway. This way, at least, he can disable the Hawkeyes and take other steps to minimize the risk.

The first couple of meetings, Casey hardly speaks. He seems to think I'm a hallucination. I don't try to force him—I just hold his hand and whisper to him, hoping he'll eventually know that I'm real, that I'm still me, that the Muldoonies haven't destroyed us and they never will.

But on the inside, my heart is breaking. Where is the Casey I knew? This one is so . . . *wrecked.* So little remains of the guy who came crashing into my life on his skateboard. What happened to that force of nature?

At last, he talks. In these furtive, five-minute snatches, Casey tells me everything that's happened to him since that day in the shower room at school. Once he starts, I have to fight the urge to beg him to stop. But I don't—I make myself listen.

"I don't remember much about that day. I was skating down the street, a car pulled up, Nemechuk and the other troglodytes jumped me, and then . . . everything's a blank. That's probably for the best. I do wonder what happened to my board, though—I hope it didn't just end up in a landfill somewhere. Not that I'll ever be able to skate again.

"Now, the interrogation—that, I remember every second of. Those Dawn Patrol fucks are rank amateurs compared to the Dentists. They grilled me about you, about the explosion at the Peach Pit . . . and about your dad, for some reason. What's that about?"

"Long story," I say. "I'll tell you another time."

Casey's voice is thick, like he has to push the words out through a drugged haze. "I didn't know shit about shit, of course, and I didn't scream loud enough to get them off, so after a while they just dumped me in a cell and left me there. In a way, that was worse than being tortured nonstop—being abandoned like that. I started to think I was going to waste away in there." A deep breath. "But hey, the trash has to go out eventually, huh?"

"Where did they send you from there?"

He's staring into space, avoiding my eyes. "A Comfort House."

"A what?" Comfort House? I'm picturing a place with down-filled pillows on the beds and waffles and bacon for breakfast. I don't have to look Casey in the eye to know that picture is wrong.

"A lot of failed Reclaimees end up there—the girls, especially, and a few of the guys. Only the best-looking ones—the men who come there to get . . . comforted . . . have high standards, you know. Party bigwigs, businessmen, preachers . . ." He shakes his head. "I'm not sure why they picked me—I'm nowhere near pretty enough. Maybe they figure gay guys have special skills."

"You mean . . . ?"

"They had me doing five or six men a day. More, if there was a Party conference or some other circus in town. I was the only white guy working there—most of the others were Mexican or black, and all but a couple of us were girls—so I was in demand. Hell, even some of the girl-only customers took me for a test drive once in a while."

His mouth twists up in what I think is supposed to me a smile.

"Some people would say I'd lucked out. All that dick, around the clock? Like winning the lottery, right?" The gruesome smile peels away. "Not so much."

I haven't told Casey yet about me and Conover—now I

don't know if I ever will. And here I thought *I'd* been turned into a thing to be used and thrown away.

"I was only there for a few weeks, though," he goes on. "I have no clue why they chucked me. Maybe they thought I'd make trouble, dirty Chaff that I am. Or maybe my novelty had worn off and I was shipped out to make room for fresh meat. All I know is, one day, no warning, no explanation, I was packed off. To a Disposal Unit."

He wraps his spindly arms around himself.

"Tyler, have you ever wondered where all the black people went? Before the Comfort House I'd never even seen one, except on TV. Where did they go? Have you ever asked yourself that?"

Now that he mentions it, I never have. Sure, I know what I was taught, that the blacks were resettled—moved to Liberia at government expense, like we started to do after the Civil War, or relocated to the new Afro-American Homelands, in North Dakota and Alaska and a few other relatively unpopulated states—but I never had any reason to think about whether that's what really happened.

"They fought back, the blacks did. I heard about it from this black woman at the Comfort House—she saw it go down. Muldoon had to send in the army." He wrenches his gaze back to meet mine. "There are burial sites outside of every big city—every place where a ghetto was liquidated. I got sent to one near Philadelphia. The land was being developed—a new mall, or something—the bodies had to be dug back up. You'd think that after so many years it wouldn't be too bad, but oh God, Tyler, the *smell* . . ."

He hugs himself tighter and squeezes his eyes shut, burrowing his chin into his chest like he's trying to make himself disappear. Out of his throat comes one low, soul-ripping sob after another. His shoulders are still convulsing when my five minutes come to an end and I have to leave.

The next time, he's calmed down, and he picks up the story where he left off. "That's where I fucked up my legs. I slipped in the mud and a truck ran over them. I thought I was a dead man—usually, if you get injured or sick, or just too weak to keep working, they put a bullet in your head and

add you to the pile. That's why it's called a Disposal Unit—
we're the ones being disposed of. I'm not going to lie—I was
relieved.

"But no. They put me under the knife instead and then
kept me all doped up until they decided what to do with me.
Hell if I know why. Someone thought I'd make a good door-
stop, I guess." A harsh, grinding chuckle comes out of him.
"And then I wind up here. A fucking Reorientation Center,
you say? How perfect is that?"

The rest of our time together passes in silence. I'm too
overwhelmed to speak. What Casey just told me—it's so
gigantic, I have trouble comprehending it well enough even
to be horrified.

But I'm also glad I heard it. I bet this is why Duncan let
me visit Casey in the first place. Now that I've heard his story,
I no longer have any doubts who the real enemy is.

"What the hell is that?" Conover growls at me.

"I don't know, sir." I put the tall, narrow box on
Conover's desk. A sloshing sound comes from inside it. "It
came by courier this afternoon. From your friends in the state
capital—those were the courier's exact words."

"Has it been screened?"

"Yes, sir. It's clean."

"Hm."

His fingers are dancing across his computer keyboard—
deactivating the Hawkeye in his office. He has a program
connected to the security system—illegally, I'm told. Duncan
has access to a similar program, hidden on another terminal
somewhere in the camp. I knew Conover had a way of turning off the Hawkeye so he wouldn't be caught on video with
me, but this is the first time I've ever witnessed him using it.

He opens the box, and his eyebrows twitch at the ornate-
ly labeled smoked-glass bottle he pulls out of it. "Glenfiddich

1937, huh? All the way from Scotland—those jokers upstate must really think they need to kiss my ass. I wonder who Neighbor Hightower had to suck off getting *this* through the embargo."

He opens the bottle and chugs from it like it's moonshine from a jug. A trickle of brown liquid spills down his chin and onto his shirt.

"You want some, don't you?"

I shake my head and look at the floor. "Inmates aren't allowed alcohol, sir."

"Don't bullshit me. I know what you faggots do—drinking that homemade battery acid while you fuck each other in the ass between the cabins every night. I know."

He rocks forward and out of the chair. "Get on your knees. I've got something else for you to drink."

I obey. *Easy, easy.* I just need to stall him. Soon, whatever he just unknowingly drank will kick in . . .

I pretend my hands are shaking too hard to work the zipper. What's taking so long? Duncan said Conover would be out cold in thirty seconds, tops.

Two of Conover's clammy fingers are playing with my ear.

"You thought you were such a hotshot, didn't you?" His voice oozes contempt—though it also has a strange echo, like he's not really talking to me but rather to someone far away in both time and space. "Big Man on Campus, pretty girlfriend—you could do anything you wanted, to anyone you wanted. How does it feel, being nothing? Nothing but a worthless piece of faggot trash?"

His hand seizes my ear, and twists. I cry out before I can stop myself.

"Say it." He twists harder. "Nice and loud. I AM A WORTHLESS PIECE OF FAGGOT TRASH."

Through the pain, I grind the words out. "I AM A WORTHLESS PIECE OF FAGGOT TRASH."

He lets me go with a hard shove that leaves me sprawled on the floor.

"You think I want your filthy mouth anywhere near my cock? Go take your clothes off and bend over."

He intends to kill me tonight—I'm certain of it. It's in his eyes, his voice, the way his fists are clenched, everything. With those eight words I just spoke, I've signed my own death warrant. Those are the words he's been waiting to hear me say.

I do as I'm told. My mind is racing as fast as my pulse. My ear is still burning from where Conover twisted it. Behind me, I hear the clinking of his belt buckle, the snapping of the leather in his hands . . .

And everything goes red.

This isn't like the other times my rage has overcome me. I haven't *lost* control. I'm more *in* control now than I've ever been in my life.

I shoot to my feet and spin around. Conover has the bottle in one hand, his belt looped into a noose in the other. He's swaying, off balance. I grab the belt, raise it, swing it. The buckle catches him just above the left eye, lacerating him across his eye and down one side of his nose. He rears back and falls. The bottle hits the floor with a thump and spews pungent amber liquid across the carpet.

Silence. Conover's uninjured eye is bleary and filled with murder—but also terror. He's afraid. Of me. The rush of seeing that is almost orgasmic. *WHO'S THE WORTHLESS PIECE OF TRASH NOW?*

He tries to get up. He fails, and starts shaking. I move toward him, to finish this —

Then his head tilts back. A weird, gurgling groan comes out of him. The trembling stops, and his jaw flops open. His breathing is slow, loud, and wet.

The spiked Scotch has done its job.

As the fury drains out of me, a wave of nausea rushes in. I grope for the edge of the desk and lean on it while I choke down the vomit bubbling in the back of my throat.

Then I realize I'm still naked, and I reach for my scrubs.

Time to get to work.

Conover is still signed on to his computer. That simplifies things—I don't have to spend precious minutes digging around in his desk for his password, or trying to guess it. The machine is more advanced than my dad's, but it's similar enough that I can find my way around.

I check to make sure the Hawkeye is still disabled, then close that program and open up Conover's electronic mailbox.

There are other computers in the camp, but according to Duncan this is the only one linked to an outside network. And that's what I need to do, the reason—or one of the reasons—the Secret Six brought me here and dangled me in front of Conover like bait on a hook. To get a message outside . . .

2 Timothy 4:7

That's all—just a Bible verse. I have no clue what it's supposed to mean, or even who I'm sending it to—the address is a sort of blind drop, anonymous at both ends.

Conover's unconscious form makes retching sounds. I close the mailbox and then freeze in place. But the gagging stops and he settles back down. He's snoring.

I could kill him right now. Just put my hands over his nose and mouth for a minute or two—that's all it would take.

A quick twitch of my shoulders, and the urge is gone. It isn't intense enough to act on, anyway—not this time. Murdering Conover for revenge won't help Casey.

Turning back to the computer, I reach into my pocket, take out the disk Duncan passed to me at dinner, and insert it into the drive. I don't have to do anything else—the file on the disk copies itself into Conover's system, and after two or three seconds the disk ejects.

I slip it into my pocket, make to shut down the computer—then stop. Duncan said the drugged Scotch would leave Conover with short-term memory loss, but best to keep everything here as I found it.

Or . . . almost everything.

I make sure the last drop of Scotch has soaked into the carpet. Then I unlock the desk drawer, take out the scalpel, and cut another notch in my abdomen. This way, Conover will think he blacked out after raping me again, rather than before. There's still the cut on his face, but I'll just have to hope he assumes he cut himself when he fell.

As I'm leaving, I pause for one more look at his snoring bulk on the floor. I wish he'd swallow his own tongue and choke to death. Still, the desire to kill him myself is no longer there. If this plan succeeds, the payback will be sweeter than anything I could do to him with my hands.

And I'll still be alive to enjoy it. Along with Casey.

When I get back to my cell, I ask to borrow Z's Bible. He hands it to me with a surprised smile. I sit down on my cot and flip through the tissue-thin pages. It's an edited version, like the one we used in church back home, with the more problematic stories like the Moneychangers and the Good Samaritan replaced by single-paragraph summaries—but I still find the verse I just sent to the outside world.

"I have fought the good fight, I have finished the race, I have kept the faith."

"Hey, Z?" I close the Bible and hand it back. "Do you really think God is watching over us here?"

"I do."

He looks away, cradling the Bible against his chest.

"Z?"

"But . . . sometimes . . . I do wonder if the God I know is the same God I was taught to believe in."

"Yeah. Me too."

I'm back in the Cactus Garden. The bodies hardly faze me anymore. I feel almost like I know them now, and that I ought to apologize for disturbing them.

"You've uploaded the file?" Duncan asks.

I look him in the eye, and nod. "I also mailed the message you told me to. The Bible verse."

His wide mouth stretches into an ear-to-ear grin, his hands clasp together, and he does a little hop on the balls of his feet. "Fantabuloso, my dear! I could kiss you for a whole month!"

"Uh, no, thanks."

He's breaking character. Normally, during these meetings in the Cactus Garden, he leaves all that flamboyance on the other side of the gate. But lately, these personas of his have been blurring together. Which one is the real Duncan, I wonder?

I cross my arms over my chest. "OK, so what now?"

"Yes, I do believe it's time you learned about the mission." He clears his throat, suddenly all business again. "Thank you for your patience. You've certainly proven that you don't wilt under pressure."

"Whatever. Just tell me what's next."

"A word of caution first. Since talking to your friend, you undoubtedly believe you know what the Muldoonies are capable of. You don't. You haven't even scratched the surface."

Duncan's face, so lit up just a few seconds ago, now looks like a blank mask.

"We're breaking into the Annex. That's our mission—to find out what's going on there. The Six has its suspicions, but we need hard evidence."

The Annex—that small, nondescript building attached to the rear of the Clinic. No windows, no doors, no one going in or out—at least not during the fleeting and distant glimpses I've gotten of the place. You'd think a place as mysterious as the Annex would have spawned a billion rumors—but no one in the camp seems eager to acknowledge that it even exists. Even Conover has only mentioned it once or twice in the time I've spent around him.

"Evidence of what?" My blood is already starting to curdle, and he hasn't even given me the details yet.

"Weapons research. Specifically, biological." Duncan peers at me as if he's not really convinced I'm ready to hear this. "You're not old enough to remember, but I'm sure you've heard about it—the disease that attacked our people back in the old days? The one that the Muldoonies claim to have eradicated?"

"They haven't, have they?" I know Casey never bought that line—that's why he always insisted we use condoms.

"Just the opposite. They've been studying it. Altering it. Trying to make it into a weapon. That disease, and others."

He pauses. The silence is like a living thing. Even the mummified forms around us seem to be hanging on his next word.

"They need to be stopped. If they perfect this weapon, they'll use it. I'm older than I look—I remember what it was like back then, watching friends die slowly, wondering if you were next. If the Muldoonies can make it into something even quicker and deadlier, something they can drop from the air, onto whole populations . . ."

He's wringing his hands. His usual glib detachment is gone—this is something real for him. And he's right. Casey told me some of the stories he heard about that disease—about men wasting away, covered with sores, coughing their guts out, delirious and screaming. The stuff of nightmares, except that nightmares aren't so vivid.

And exactly the sort of thing Muldoon would love to have as a weapon. Like one of those God-sent plagues in the Bible, with him playing God.

So this is it. I'm in all the way now. The ladder has been pulled up. Not that climbing back out was ever really an option—I gave that up a long time ago, when I agreed to come here, or maybe even in Neighbor Lenskold's closet when my lips first touched Casey's. Still, until now I've always kept one eye on the world above, never going any deeper than I need to go.

That's over. I can't get in any deeper than this.

"The program you uploaded to Conover's computer is what we call a Trojan Horse," Duncan goes on. "Once installed, it camouflages itself and then opens a hole in the computer's security, which our people outside can exploit. The Bible verse you mailed was a code, telling them when the balloon goes up."

"And when is that?"

He smiles and flutters his eyelashes. "Take a guess, Tyler. A night when hope is in the air, and everyone is distracted."

Guessing takes less than a single heartbeat.

"The mixer."

I still don't think it's straight." Larry frowns at the hand-let-tered WELCOME SECOND CHANCES banner hanging on the wall. "What do you think?"

Before I can reply, Duncan materializes. "Of course it's straight, my dear Lawrence! Everything here is straight. You just need to adjust your perspective." He lets out a high-pitched laugh at his own cleverness. "But seriously, it looks fabulous—you boys have done a great job decorating. I'm so glad you volunteered to help out."

Larry shrugs. "One less day I'm pouring asphalt. And hey, I'm looking forward to this—maybe I'll meet the bull-dyke of my dreams." He tosses me the roll of crepe paper he's been holding. "I have to take a piss. See you later, Tyler."

We've commandeered the chapel for the mixer. The pews have all been removed, the floor scattered with glitter and confetti, the walls and ceiling decked with streamers, crepe paper, tinfoil stars and crescent moons—like the Senior Prom I didn't get to attend, having been arrested and all. The welcoming banner—which *is* a bit lopsided, actually—hangs opposite the rifle-scope cross of the Nation's Covenant Church, while from the wall between them, the square-jawed face of President Muldoon grins down upon us all.

Another admin comes up and whispers something to Duncan. He listens, and then his hands start flapping. "It's arrived? Wonderful!" He turns back to me. "Some libations for the Housemothers and the guards, to keep them festive. We don't want any joltstickings in front of the cameras—all that unpleasant footage the OCPM will have to edit, you know. It pays to keep everyone well-lubricated."

His hands settle on his hips, and he heaves a big, breathy sigh. "It's sad. So few people appreciate the hard work that goes into planning an event—all they see is the glamour. Well, this is going to be the most memorable event Fresh Starts has ever seen! I don't care if I kill myself and everyone else making it happen."

Before walking off, Duncan leans close to my ear. "Whatever you do, don't drink the punch."

The video crew shows up at around two o'clock—a half-dozen cameramen, a hair and make-up girl, an interviewer, and a producer, all in tailored wool blazers with the same OCPM lapel badge that Dad used to wear. They must be melting in the heat, dressed like that. The interviewer and producer both do passable jobs of hiding their disgust at being surrounded by faggots. The others don't bother.

I watch, serving coffee, while they interview Conover. He's wearing a patch over his left eye, and he's stuffed himself into . . . a *Dawn Patrol* uniform? He's outgrown it by at least three sizes, but—Jesus, it's got *Patrolmaster's* insignia! They let *him* be a Patrolmaster?

He sweats, stammers, and mutters through the interview—he obviously has no experience in front of a camera. I doubt he'll end up in the finished video—interviewing him was just a courtesy.

This event is putting him under a huge amount of stress—and I can tell he's planning to take it out on me, the first chance he gets. He's fighting to keep from looking at me, and when he gives in, his eyes have that dead-oyster look I've come to recognize.

I stare back, without cringing. He looks baffled by the lack of fear in my eyes. As Duncan promised, the knockout drugs have left him with no memory of what happened the other night.

He's not staying for the festivities, anyway. Not that it matters. If tonight goes off as planned, I will be far away from here. And if it crashes and burns instead . . .

Either way, Conover is never touching me again.

At around four-thirty, the lesbians from Second Chances arrive. In spite of everything else that's going on, I can't help gawking as each busload marches into the camp, with an escort of Wide Awakes. They're dressed alike, in powder blue pleated skirts and loose-fitting blouses buttoned up to the neck.

Except for Coach's wife, I've never met a real live lesbian. All the images in my head come from videos or TV shows or Dawn Patrol lectures—ugly, musclebound creatures with hairy legs and twisted, man-hating faces. These girls look like cheerleaders. Except for the cropped hair, and the pale skin. They must not spend a lot of time outdoors.

They're scared, too, though some conceal it well—with fake cheer, with resignation, with anger. One, a pretty brunette, is incinerating the camp and everyone in it with her eyes. And then there are others, whose faces show a spark of actual hope—hope that some guy here will connect with her, maybe even marry her, prove that she's been cured of her repulsive urges and is ready to serve the Nation.

A lot of the guys have that same hope—I can tell just looking at them. They truly want tonight to be their ticket out of this place.

Just for the heck of it, as each girl walks by, I give her a once-over, checking myself for any signs of attraction, of lust. I feel nothing—not even for the brunette, who looks a little like Unity. I'm even gayer now than I was before I arrived here.

The girls disappear inside the chapel. A half-hour or so later, the guys are herded in as well. We line up awkwardly on opposite sides—skirts on the left, pink scrubs on the right. In the space between, some ancient big-band tune fills the air—the ban on music has been lifted for this occasion. The video crew has finished its interviews and is now drifting around shooting extra footage. Nobody looks at the cameras.

Apart from the music, the room is silent except for the shuffling of feet and a few nervous coughs. Then, slowly, people start to mingle. The cameramen prowl around for some close-ups—it takes a while, because when you see them coming your first instinct is to hide your face—round up some couples for a few minutes of awkward and halfhearted dancing, and then clear out.

The mixer goes on. Now that the film crew is gone, things loosen up a bit. Some of the dancers show actual enthusiasm. In the corners, I notice a few inmates and guards swaying and staggering—they must have overdone it on the punch already.

I hang back, propping up the wall and trying to be invisible. At one end of the room, under the WELCOME SECOND CHANCES banner, Duncan is lording over the punchbowl, being the perfect social butterfly . . .

"Hey, handsome."

I look down. It's the brunette I spotted earlier. Her eyes are still blazing, but her mouth is split open in a big, toothy grin, like a man-eating shark's.

"Uh, hi." I glance at her nametag. "Hi . . . Jessica. Can I get you some punch?"

"No, thanks. I saw you staring at me on the way in. Do you like what you see?"

Any resemblance to Unity is gone—Unity was never this aggressive.

Jessica presses up against me. Her arms encircle my neck, and then that toothy mouth is engulfing me, biting my lower lip, her tongue attacking mine.

"Let's go someplace private," she whispers, pulling me

down so my ear is brushing her lips. "I want to watch the fog roll in over the Golden Gate Bridge."

Jesus Christ, another one? This time, though, my surprise is gone in an instant, and my response is perfectly smooth.

"I'd rather watch the sunset from the Santa Monica Pier."

"Lead the way, stud."

I take her back to my cell. Z won't be there, with the mixer going on. No one tries to keep us from leaving—pairing off is the whole point of this show, after all. Even the guards seem weirdly aloof—that *lubrication* Duncan talked about must be working.

To my alarm, Z is there—only he's fast asleep. His Bible is lying open on the floor, pages down.

Jessica starts to speak, but I shake my head and point first at Z, then at the Hawkeye in the ceiling. She shrugs, smiles, and jumps me again.

We spend the next . . . minutes, I have no clue how many . . . making out. Or, whatever you'd call it when two people have zero attraction to each other. We're just marking time, playacting for the Hawkeye's benefit.

You'd think that kissing anyone—even a girl—would make me explode after months of no erotic contact at all. But no, I'm as limp as overcooked spaghetti—and after all of Conover's abuse, simply being touched sets off twinges of panic. I push through and do my best to look passionate.

We're still at it when the lights go out.

The emergency lights come on, throwing everything into harsh, black-and-white contrast. Jessica disengages from me and smooths down her skirt.

"Whew. Glad that's over." She strides over to the cell door and peers through the window slit. "No offense. You're a very good kisser."

"So what do we do now?"

"Go find our leader and report in."

She clearly means Duncan. But . . . report in? How, with even more inmates and guards roaming the camp than usual? I am so sick of this need-to-know crap . . .

Z. He's still asleep. Hasn't moved a muscle this whole time, in fact.

Before the thought even registers I start toward him. Is he dead? All the commotion should have woken him up. And his Bible—he'd never leave it lying on the floor like that. Before retiring he always lays it, reverently, on the shelf above his cot, right next to his copy of *Rise and Shine* . . .

Not dead. Drugged. But still . . . drugged with—?

Whatever you do, don't drink the punch.

"The coast is clear," Jessica says. "Let's move."

Just around the corner, we run into a pair of guards crumpled in the hallway. One is out cold. The other one is still awake, but unable to do anything but moan in protest as we step over them. At his feet, an open bottle is dribbling its contents onto the tile floor.

Jessica is moving fast. I trail along like I'm on a leash, trying to keep up. There's no chance to stop and check on any of the incapacitated forms littering the camp, to see if any are dead and not just unconscious. If I do, she'll just go on without me.

We make it back to the chapel. The big-band music has stopped. The interior is an obstacle course of inert lumps, male and female.

Duncan is waiting by the empty punchbowl. "We don't have much time. We can't count on everyone having drunk the Kool-Aid—even with power and communications disabled, an alert is bound to get out." He glides around the punchbowl and plucks two pistols and an automatic rifle off a pair of blue-uniformed heaps on the floor. He hands the rifle to Jessica and one of the pistols to me. "You learned to shoot in Dawn Patrol, didn't you?"

I nod.

"The extraction team will be in position for exactly thirty minutes, starting about an hour from now. If we don't make it to the pickup point within that window, we're fucked."

The gun won't stay in my waistband, so I slip it into my pocket as I follow the others out of the chapel.

We move carefully, torn between speed and stealth— Duncan up front, then Jessica, and then me bringing up the rear. Except for them, I can't see a thing. Since I got here there hasn't been a night when the whole camp wasn't floodlit to retina-scarring levels—now, with the power out, the darkness is so thick I feel like I'm swimming through it.

Duncan pauses at the entrance to the Clinic building. The light above the door handle, which normally flashes red when locked, is dark, as is the keypad display. Duncan grabs the handle, takes a breath, and yanks. The door opens.

"Those computer crashers know their shit, I'll give them that." He turns to me. "Go and collect your friend. Meet us at—" He rattles off some directions—left turn, right turn, down a long passage to a set of double doors, wait there. Then he's gone, taking Jessica with him.

I'm running now. No more creeping around. At the isolation unit the orderly is passed out at his desk, with a coffee cup in front of him still half full of booze. Farther down, I spot a wheelchair in the hallway. I unlock the brakes and push it to the room where they've stashed Casey.

He's in some kind of distress. He's curled up on his side, sweating, panting, and clutching the stumps of his legs.

"What's wrong?" I rush over to him. "Casey?"

He takes two or three shallow breaths and rolls onto his back. "It's like I can still feel my legs—like they're being twisted or crushed or something. But then I look down and . . . nope, they're still gone. It's fucking with my head." He grimaces and tenses up. "Where is everybody? I should have gotten another shot by now."

I park the wheelchair next to the bed and hunt around for the switch to lower the bedrail. "Listen, Casey, we're getting—"

Several loud pops, somewhere in the building. Gunshots. I spin around. The gun Duncan gave me is out of my pocket and in my hand, aimed at the door.

Casey has bolted upright. "What the *fuck* was that?"

I wait, listening—for more gunshots, footsteps, voices, anything. But all I hear is the rasp of my own breathing.

"It's OK." I find the switch, and lower the bed rail. "We're getting out of here."

"Jesus. This is *real?*"

"Yes." I lock eyes with him. "This is real. *I'm* real. Do you trust me?"

Casey hesitates for a second, but then nods.

311

I half-lift, half-scoot him into the wheelchair. There's no seatbelt—I wrap one arm around him to keep him from falling out as I wheel him into the hall. The stumps of his legs stick out over the edge of the seat.

I follow Duncan's directions. The chair's wheel bearings are worse than a shopping cart's—I have to throw my whole weight behind it to steer around corners. But eventually we reach the double doors at the end of the passage, with a sign on them saying AUTHORIZED PERSONNEL ONLY . . .

And two dead Wide Awakes on either side. I know they're dead, not drugged, because of the dual splatters of blood and tissue on the wall. These two, clearly, had been too smart to drink the punch.

On the doors, and the sign above them, there's a circular symbol, like a propeller made out of crescent-shaped knives. A biological hazard warning, I think.

I poke my head through the doors. There's a vestibule, then another pair of doors with windows, then a long, straight corridor. No telling how far it goes—even with the emergency lights on, the corridor fades into blackness after just a few yards.

I listen for voices or more gunshots, but it's as tomb-silent as the rest of this place.

I return to Casey's side. "How are you doing?"

"Hanging in there." He's sliding forward in the seat. With his arms he pushes up and manages to scoot back an inch or two. "Tyler, what the hell are you mixed up in?"

I can't help it—I start laughing. I need to recover before I can get any words out. "Dude, I don't even know where to start."

Casey is looking at me like I've lost my mind.

Once my hysterical laughter passes, my fight-flight instincts come surging back. The reek of blood and gunshot residue fills my head. Duncan said to wait for him and Jessica—but for how long? A minute, an hour? And what if they never show up at all?

Another noise. I jump, and again draw the pistol. Not a gunshot this time—a thump, like a door slamming. We're not alone.

Chaffs

I steal another glance at the doors, and at the symbols decorating them. *Shit. Shit shit shit shit shit.*

"We're sitting ducks here." I put the gun away and grab the handles of Casey's wheelchair. "We need to keep moving."

I punch through both sets of doors and start down the corridor. It's narrow—the wheelchair almost scrapes the walls. The wheels squeak on the linoleum floor. There's a right turn at the end, with a brighter light around the corner—a harsh fluorescent light, sterile and blue and cold.

We turn the corner, go through yet another pair of doors, and then I have to wrangle Casey and the chair down a short set of steps . . . but once we reach the bottom we're in what looks like the main complex. The ceiling is low and covered with acoustic tile. The air is stale and thick. On each side, ahead of us and behind, closed and locked cell doors march off in either direction.

I creep up to one of the cells and peer through the tiny square window —

And I leap back.

The shape lying on the cot is human—the right size, anyway, and with head and arms and legs in the right places. The spastic rising and falling of the chest tells me it's still alive. But that's all I can tell about him—or her. Everything else— the sex, the age, even the race—has dissolved into a riot of open, weeping sores and mottled purple and black skin with nothing but naked bone underneath.

It moves. It must sense me staring at it. The head lolls toward the window —

I turn away, but then I squeeze my eyes shut at the sight of another . . . I can picture them now, one in each of these cells—dozens of them. People—what used to be people— reduced to these . . . things . . .

Casey is craning his neck. "What is it? I can't see."

"You don't want to."

I hear voices. One of them sounds like Duncan's.

I tear off toward the voices. More cell doors flash by. I have to force myself not to look through the windows.

A left turn, a right turn, and then we're in a lab—a bright but grimly functional room cluttered with computer terminals, waist-high counters, strange and unfamiliar pieces of equipment covered with dials and gauges and buttons.

Duncan and Jessica are at the far end. As I burst in with Casey, they jump and spin around. Suddenly I'm staring down two gun barrels.

"Whoa!" I throw up my hands. "It's just me!"

"What are you doing here?" Duncan barks. "You were supposed to wait for us."

"You were taking too long," I lower my hands. "Duncan, there are people in those cells. What are we—?"

"Nothing. Not part of the mission, and they're beyond our help anyway. Since you're here, give us a hand."

On my way across the room I step over two white-coated men on the floor, hogtied and gagged but alive. Duncan is opening a glass-doored cabinet, its racks filled with an assortment of vials, test tubes, and Petri dishes. The keypad on the door has been removed and is dangling by loose wires—Duncan must have had to hack into it by hand.

He scans the contents, one finger gliding back and forth along the racks. Then, gingerly, he picks up one vial, then another. He hands one to me.

"What's this?"

"Just don't open it."

I'm not sure I could, even if I wanted to. It's about as big as a size-C battery, clear glass, heavy, and welded shut, with an opalescent white powder inside.

I tuck the vial into a pocket. Duncan hands another vial to Jessica, who's been at a computer, copying files onto disks and stuffing them into a leatherette pouch with some unfamiliar but official-looking logo on the front.

"We're done," Duncan says. "Let's go."

We head back the way we came in. Again, I avert my gaze from the cell windows flashing by. That vial in my pocket thumps against my leg, like a fresh-picked and juicy orange injected with poison. I just know the stuff inside is what rotted and mutilated the damned souls down here, turned them into those—

Never mind. No time to think. Just a little farther to go now . . .

The stairs take less time going up, with two other people to help carry Casey. We reach the top, push open the doors —

And someone is blocking our way. It takes me a second to recognize him.

"Larry? What are you—?"

"The punch was too sweet." Larry's voice is robotic, like it's taking him inhuman effort to keep it level. "I didn't drink it. Then I saw people dropping like flies. Tyler, what are you doing? You're trying to break out, aren't you?"

He has a gun. He must have grabbed it off one of the unconscious guards. As my gaze falls on it, Larry raises the gun and takes aim. At Casey's head.

"Is this your boyfriend? You tell me what's going on or I'll blow his brains out."

I don't dare move. Duncan and Jessica are on either side of me. Out of the corner of my eye, I see Jessica raise her rifle. In the same instant, Duncan shakes his head at her and makes a sharp downward gesture.

"Don't do this, Tyler." Larry is goggle-eyed, switching from threats to pleading without even pausing for breath. "You don't want to go back out there. Why would you? We're safe here. Protected."

"Safe? *Protected?*" I'm yelling at the top of my lungs. "You *asshole!* You're not the one who Conover's been—"

"Why don't you come with us, Lawrence?" That's Duncan. He takes one smooth step toward Larry, then another one. He raises a hand, beckoning him. "Plenty of room on the escape train. Hop on board."

He's lying. I know it. Larry knows it too.

"You selfish prick," he spits. "You don't give a shit what happens to any of us. You know what they do after escape attempts—we'll all get punished. We'll get beaten, transferred out—that's as good as death, you know—sent to the Cactus Garden, sent *here.*" The tears are spilling down his cheeks. His gun hand is shaking. "I saw what happened the last time—not again. I swear, if you do this, I'll—"

"Come with us, Lawrence."

"Fuck you!"

Duncan leaps past me in a pink blur. I'm moving too, on

315

reflex, jumping over the wheelchair, putting myself between Larry and Casey. There's an eardrum-stunning bang, and a Hawkeye in the ceiling explodes. By the time I can focus, Larry's gun is on the floor and Duncan has him in a sleeper hold, one arm around his neck, the other one braced behind him, shoving his head forward into the V formed by his elbow. Larry struggles, but his face is already turning purple, and his prying at Duncan's arm is weakening into a newborn kitten's batting of paws. He goes out, limbs dropping, feet sliding out from under him.

I take a breath and turn toward Casey . . .

Then Duncan makes a quick twisting motion, tiny, barely visible, but sharp and violent. There's a crunching sound, and Larry's body falls in a heap, his neck snapped.

I gape at him. Even Jessica looks horrified.

"Duncan! What—?"

"I had no choice." Every trace of the old Duncan is gone—even the hardened agent he seemed to be under his Queen of the Camp mask. This man is no one I've ever met before. "He would have betrayed us once he came to. I had no choice."

"Bullshit! You didn't have to kill him! You didn't—"

I'm flying backwards, slamming against the wall. Duncan's forearm is pressing under my chin and against my voice box, just hard enough to keep me from speaking.

Duncan is hissing like a rattlesnake. "Are you going to shut up and do what I say, or do I have to kill you and your friend too? I've spent over a year in this godforsaken place just to carry out this mission—I'll kill you, I'll kill everyone here—hell, I'll kill myself if I have to. This mission means *everything*."

He's insane. Completely insane.

I manage a nod. Duncan releases me. I stagger for a second, coughing and rubbing my throat.

"Let's go," Duncan says.

I take the handlebars of Casey's wheelchair and start pushing. Again, I'm holding him in the seat with one arm so he doesn't fall out.

We go through the Cactus Garden. I actually nod and say

silent goodbyes to some of the dried-up cadavers on display—I've been here so many times, I feel like I've gotten to know them. Especially the ones who preceded me bent over Conover's desk. Casey just looks around at them and blinks, with none of the shock and horror I felt the first time. He seems . . . beyond it.

Twists and turns along razor-wire-lined passages . . . and then, finally, we're back at the loading area, where I stumbled off the bus my first night here. No buses now, just a single Wide Awakes van, dark, deserted, its side door sitting open. The power is still out.

We make our way toward the van, with nothing but the moon and stars illuminating our road to freedom . . .

"FREEZE!" says a voice from above.

F LOODLIGHTS snap on. I wrench my eyelids open against the glare, and see about a dozen Wide Awakes, guns drawn. They're standing inhumanly still, like giant blue chess pieces. Someone else is in their midst, a bulky civilian.

Conover.

Behind me, beyond the open van, another group of Wide Awakes blocks our escape. I know they're there even before I turn my head to look.

Voices. Conover's and Duncan's—they're having words. I can't make out what they're saying. Through the torrent of blood making my every vein and artery vibrate and hum, it's all just muffled sneering.

Then Duncan moves.

At first it looks like he's drawing his own gun. But his grip is all wrong. Then I see it—one of the vials we stole from the Annex. Duncan holds it up like he's about to throw it.

Conover stiffens. His face, already washed out by the floodlights, turns ghost-pale. Around him, the Wide Awakes brace themselves to shoot, but Conover yaps at them like a panicked little dog. "Hold your fire! *Hold your fire!*"

At the edge of my vision, Jessica takes her vial out and

holds it up the same way as Duncan. My own hand closes around the one I'm carrying. For a heartbeat or two, I hesitate, but then I do likewise.

"You know we're not letting you go." Conover's voice is even, but I can tell it's a strain for him to keep it that way.

"Then we all die, sweetie," Duncan says coolly. "Which of us here has the most to lose? Not me, certainly." He takes a step forward, gesturing behind him with his other hand. "Tyler. Jessica. Go to the van."

Jessica walks backwards with a steady caution, still holding her vial aloft. I put mine away, take the handles of Casey's wheelchair, and follow her.

Duncan continues to advance. Conover retreats, waving his entourage back with a frantic pinwheeling of his flabby arms. The Wide Awakes spread out, the spaces between them widening—they're at least a dozen yards now from me and Casey. Meanwhile, we ease toward the van behind us—just a few more feet . . . almost inside . . .

Someone's gun goes off.

"Get down!"

I'm diving for cover before the command even registers. As I do, I grab Casey under the arms and yank him out of the wheelchair, flipping it over.

Everything is in slo-mo. As I hit the ground, I see Duncan's vial leave his hand in the same instant that a blood-red fountain explodes from his spine. Two more erupt right after. Then I'm watching the vial fly end-over-end and shatter at Conover's feet, watching the death-white cloud envelope him and the two nearest Wide Awakes.

Conover screams. The other Wide Awakes scatter. More gunshots ring out. I flatten myself against Casey, shielding him with my body.

"The van! Get in the van!"

It's Jessica. She's inside. I wait for a lull in the gunfire, but none is forthcoming. With a burst of adrenaline, I pick up Casey, fling him into the van, and leap in after him.

I barely get the door closed when there's a lurch, a screeching of tires, and an acceleration that sends both me and Casey rolling to a stop against the rear door of the van.

Jessica is at the wheel and is flooring it toward the gate amid a *pop pop pop pop pop* of gunshots punching against the van's armor plating like a hailstorm of pure evil . . .

I wrap myself around Casey, close my eyes, and hold on.

The hailstorm worsens. The van swerves and bucks. Lights spear through the cracks in my eyelids. Metal crunches and groans. And then the lights go out.

I hold on tighter, and pray.

"Tyler . . . you're crushing me."

The sound of Casey's voice slaps me back to awareness.

We're still moving. Fast. I can tell from the hum of the van's engine. The gunfire has stopped. Impossible to tell how long it's been since we crashed the gate—five minutes, ten, fifteen, more? Time itself feels all stretched and twisted.

Behind the wheel, Jessica is glaring out the windshield. I don't dare ask her anything—she looks like she'll pull my head off with one hand if I do.

"Sorry." I loosen my grip on Casey. "Are you OK? Did you get shot?"

"No. Did you?"

"I don't think so."

I pat myself down, just to make sure I really am unscathed. In my head I keep seeing those geysers of red spew out of Duncan's back. And my nose smells it all—the blood, and the gunpowder.

Or—I get a good look at the van's interior—maybe that's how it always smells in this thing.

This isn't my first time in one of these vehicles, but before I was too busy getting the crap beaten out of me to notice the decor. It's *medieval* in here. In racks lining the walls, implements rattle and sway—joltsticks, handcuffs, shackles, pliers and knives and crowbars, other ugly and odd-shaped tools whose use I don't even want to imagine.

"Tyler, what the fuck are we doing here? Where are we going?"

"I don't know. Maybe Jessica does." I steel myself and

turn toward the front seat. "Jessica?"

No answer.

"Jessica, come on. Where—?"

The van lurches forward. We're decelerating. I get my balance back and clamber to the front. The smell of blood has thickened.

Jessica is slumped against the steering wheel and half-slipping out of the driver's seat. We're still slowing down, and drifting off the road. The van's wheels go *thunkthunkthunk* against the raised lane markers, then start buzzing as they hit the ridge along the road shoulder.

I grab for the steering wheel, pushing Jessica's limp form back into the seat. Her blouse and skirt, and the cushion underneath her, are soaked with blood. In the glow from the dashboard, and the almost-nonexistent light outside, it glistens like tar.

I can't reach the brake with Jessica in the way—it's all I can do just to stretch across her bloody lap and steer the van off the road. One tire, then another, slips off the roadbed, flinging me sideways and almost wrenching the steering wheel out of my hands.

Once it's done rocking, the van is resting at an angle. The instruments on the walls are clattering like the percussion section of Hell.

I lay Jessica out on the floor and search for a pulse. Nothing.

"Is she dead?" Casey asks.

"Yeah." I gape at her. "I don't understand. She was fine . . ."

She must have been shot in the melee. A wound that appeared minor, but had nicked an artery, just enough for it to worsen with every heartbeat—Jessica might not even have noticed it until it tore open and she started bleeding out. She was too focused on driving to notice, too focused on getting away at top speed from —

From the Wide Awakes.

They'll be right behind us.

I scramble back behind the wheel. I'm sitting in a pool of Jessica's blood, and the stink of it is making me gag, but that doesn't matter. We need to keep moving.

Then I look out the window, at the road shooting into the darkness.

Keep moving *where?*

To the nearest town? There's bound to be an alert out—we'll be recaptured the minute we hit civilization. Maybe sooner—the roads must be swarming with search parties by now. And even if . . .

I rub the back of my right hand. Even if we do make it to town and find a place to hide, these chips in our hands will lead our pursuers straight to us.

But what other choice do we have?

My gaze slides off to the side, past the edge of the road. Into the desert. Endless miles of it, flat and sun-baked and waterless. Deadly to anyone stupid enough to try crossing it on foot.

It goes against everything I learned in the Dawn Patrol about surviving in the wilderness. Leaving your vehicle, leaving the road, wandering off where no one can find you—it's slow suicide.

But if we *are* found, we'll end up just as dead. Or worse. Better to die out here than to be sent back to the camp. Back to Conover. Back to . . .

I climb out of the driver's seat, step again over Jessica's body, and rejoin Casey in the rear of the van. "Listen, I think we'd better—"

"Ditch the Torturemobile, yeah."

"We'll have to take our chances in the desert. Are you with me?"

"Yeah. But . . . " Casey glances down at the stumps of his legs.

"I'll carry you."

He laughs. "Who do you think you are, the Hulk?"

"If I have to be." First things first, though. I tap the back of my right hand with one finger—this is going to be unpleasant. "We need to get these tracking chips out."

I search through the racks of torture implements until I find one suitable for the task—a tool with a short, retractable blade, like a box cutter. I test the edge against the pink fabric of my uniform. Nice and sharp.

In one corner of the van there's something that looks like a medicine cabinet. I open it, and hit the jackpot—a bottle of rubbing alcohol, gauze bandages, surgical tape. I guess these people need the means to patch their victims up, if they get carried away.

I wipe down the blade with the alcohol, then kneel next to Casey, take his hand, and pour more alcohol over the back of it.

"Wait," Casey says.

"What's wrong?"

"My blood. Don't get my blood on you." At my puzzled look, he adds, "They never tested me, at the Comfort House—I wasn't there long enough."

Oh. Right. Now that Casey mentions it, *I* was never tested either. God only knows what Conover might have exposed me to. I push the thought aside for now. I'll worry about it if Casey and I survive the desert.

More rooting around in the cabinet produces some latex gloves. I snap on a pair and pick up the cutting tool again.

"Are you ready?"

Casey nods, closes his eyes, and lets his head fall back.

His skin is like tissue paper—I hardly have to press down with the knife. I make an inch-long cut and then, gently, ease the chip through the incision with my thumbs. Casey grimaces, but doesn't try to pull away, or even cry out—either his pain threshold is way higher than mine, or he's already been through so much agony that slicing open his hand hardly registers.

Once the chip is out, I make a pad out of some gauze and press it against the wound until the bleeding stops, then wrap more gauze around it and tape it securely.

Now, my turn. I'm nowhere near as quiet about it as Casey—it feels like I'm sawing my own hand in half—though I manage to keep the noise down to a few grunts and hisses. Overall, the job I do on myself is sloppier and bloodier, but I get it done.

I grab a joltstick from the rack, lay both chips on the floor of the van, and pound on them with the joltstick's handle until they're both in a million pieces.

Casey, rubbing his bandaged hand, flicks up his eye-brows. "You enjoy that?"

"Oh, *fuck*, yes."

And then I do it—I bend down and kiss him. It's long and tender, and it's the first time we've kissed since before I found out about him and Kevin, before I said all those evil things to him, before my whole world imploded.

None of that matters anymore. We're on the run, in this mobile dungeon, with a dead body on the floor, God only knows how many Wide Awakes in pursuit, only one pair of legs between us, and no conceivable means of surviving in the desert—but right now, in this instant, everything is OK.

Live or die—either way, we're in it together.

And I'm not planning to die.

I cut out Jessica's chip too, just for good measure. I feel like I ought to bury her. But even if I had the time, there's nothing handy I can use to dig a grave.

Using a flashlight I find in the van's glove compartment, I scope out the area until I come across a shallow depression in the ground a few yards off the road. I carry Jessica there, lay her out with as much dignity as I can—legs straight, hands on her chest, eyes closed—and cover her with any rocks and bits of foliage I can scrape together without wandering too far afield.

It's not ideal, but it's better than just leaving her like a discarded fast-food wrapper. If nothing else, the elements might reclaim her before the Wide Awakes do.

It's as quiet as death out here—as quiet, as lonely, and as infinite. If our pursuers are closing in, I ought to be able to hear them, or see their headlights on the road. So why isn't their absence reassuring?

I've been putting up an optimistic front, for my own sake as well as Casey's, but as I gaze out across the desert, only just now being illuminated by the sliver of moon rising above the jagged mountains to the east, my fears begin nibbling away at that happy façade. The landscape just gets more desolate and threatening the longer I look at it.

And this is the middle of the night. What are we going to do in a few hours, with the sun beating us down?

The Secret Six. I need to get in touch with them.

Which I'm going to do . . . how? My only contacts with the Six—except for Coach, who's back in L.A., out of reach—were Duncan and Jessica. Who are both dead. The Six may not even know Casey and I are out here. Assuming they care . . .

Focus, TNT.

It's like what Coach always said—*Don't swing at every piece of crap.* It's a long way around the bases. Right now, focus on making it to first.

Focus on staying alive. Shelter, water, food. In that order. Attain those things, *then* worry about contacting the Six.

I can do it. I've got plenty of tools. I've still got my physical strength—if Casey's too injured and weak to make it on his own, I can be strong enough for both of us. I've got the skills I learned in the Dawn Patrol—I *earned* those merit badges. I just wish I had a copy of the handbook with me.

Then there's my spirit—mine *and* Casey's. Conover tried to break me. He failed. Casey hasn't broken either—whatever he's gone through, he still has some fight left.

What was that quote of Muldoon's, from *Rise and Shine?* *"The things that don't kill us, make us stronger."* That might be the only time that bastard ever told the truth.

When I get back to the van, Casey is curled up in pain again, like he was when I came to pick him up tonight.

"Is there anything I can do?"

He's forcing the words out between gasps. "Any drugs in that cabinet?"

All I see are a few tiny bottles with long and unfamiliar names on the labels. "I don't know what any of this stuff does."

"Just give me something. Anything."

"Dude, I'm not a doctor. I could *kill* you."

"So what's your point?"

I take a closer look at the stumps of his legs. The bandages are crusty with dried blood and yellowish fluid. But the skin underneath doesn't look too bad—no redness or sores or swelling. The stump ends are soft to the touch, nothing like I expected they'd feel, each one closed off with a line of tight, regular stitches, very clean, surgical.

Casey is breathing more easily now. Whatever these attacks are, this latest one seems to be tapering off.

I grab another roll of gauze and get to work applying new dressings to the stumps. "You don't look like you've got an infection, anyway. When we're someplace safe, I'll have you checked out."

"You're really going to carry me across the desert."

"All the way to Canada, if I have to."

I finish the dressings, then scavenge the van for anything useful. More first-aid supplies. The flashlight. The cutting tool I used to remove our tracking chips. One of those ball-cap-style Wide Awakes helmets, which I put on Casey's head.

That pistol from the camp already has a full magazine, so I pass on the boxes of ammunition I find—too much extra weight. I don't bother with the joltsticks, either. The pistol might come in handy for hunting food or fending off predators, but a joltstick? Hitting a mountain lion with one would only piss it off.

I pat the pocket where I stashed one of the vials we stole from the Annex, and I remember—Jessica had one, too. A quick search turns up the pouch she was carrying, lying on the floor between the seats, tacky with drying blood. The vial and the disks she stole are still inside. I zip it up and start to pocket it with the vial Duncan gave me, but then I change my mind and put the pouch in Casey's pocket instead. When we find the Six, we might need these as bargaining chips—best not to put them all in one basket.

Off we go.

I hoist Casey onto my back. With all the weight he's lost, both from being starved and from his legs being amputated, he's easy to lift—I've carried packs on Dawn Patrol hikes that were heavier. But for all that, he's also stronger than I expected. His thighs still have enough muscle to grip me around the waist, and he locks his arms over my shoulders like he's hanging onto the wing of a jet aircraft.

Our progress is slow but steady. I train the flashlight beam on the scrubby, rock-strewn terrain at my feet, scrutinizing every flip-flop-clad step before I take it, watching out for anything sharp, slippery, or venomous.

"Don't worry," Casey says. "If a rattlesnake bites you on the dick, I'll suck out the poison."

"Shut up." I come to a halt until I can get my laughter under control. "You're going to make me trip and drop you on your head."

Most of the time we move quietly, mindful of danger. But then there are moments when we're talking and joking around just like we were back at the Peach Pit or the reservoir. Simply feeling Casey against me, hearing his voice, feeling his breath on my neck—it's keeping my spirits afloat.

We have to stop every few hundred yards, to rest, or to let Casey ride out another wave of those hideous pains. During these pauses I scan the area, listening for cars or voices behind us and looking up for signs of pursuit from the air.

That's when I see the lights.

I can't tell how far we've traveled. The road, and the van we abandoned on the side of it, are no longer visible, and against the featureless landscape and glittering velvet sky there are no points of reference with which to judge distances. But still, I can tell these aren't just stars—they're moving, coming up from the south.

"Looks like the hunt is on," I say out loud.

Or is it? The lights aren't getting any nearer. Nor are they fanning out, the way I imagine they would if they were combing the desert for two escaped prisoners—they're clumping together, descending.

Soon, they're so tightly clustered that they've become just a blur, dropping into the shimmer of heat that rises from the desert floor even in the dead of night. Then, they wink out, as if someone simply flipped a switch and shut them off.

I can't be certain, but I suspect the spot where the lights landed marks the location of the camp.

I don't get it. Shouldn't our pursuers be . . . pursuing?

Then again, maybe they're just waiting until the sun comes up. Casey and I need to find cover before it does. Not just for shelter from the heat, but for protection against unfriendly eyes.

☆   ☆   ☆

Just before dawn, we happen across an old bridge crossing a dry streambed. I set Casey down and explore. Whatever the bridge used to carry—a dirt road, maybe train tracks—is long gone, but the bridge itself still looks in decent shape. Underneath, on the embankment lifting it over the streambed, there's a ledge wide enough to lie on.

This will do as a rest stop, I decide. The streambed is filled with brush, providing decent cover. We'll have to watch for flash floods, but the ledge looks high enough to keep us from drowning.

Besides, if the stream does flood, that means water. We're not going to make it far, unless I find us some.

We huddle under the bridge, lying still and trying not to sweat while the rising sun scorches the earth around us. Neither Casey nor I can sleep, even though we're both exhausted. At around noon Casey has another spasm, a bad one. I draw him closer and hold him until the tremors stop.

Afterwards, we talk some more. I fill him in on everything—*almost* everything—that's happened in the last few months.

"You're shitting me. *Coach Ferguson?* I totally did not see that one coming."

"Me neither. I guess that gay radar doesn't always work, huh?"

"I guess not." He lies back, gazing at the underside of the bridge. "So do you think he's telling the truth? About those all-gay cities?"

"I think *he* believes it. But does that mean it's true? Honestly, I don't know."

Whatever games the Six may have played to recruit me, I refuse to believe that Coach had a direct hand in them. He was the one who'd urged me to get out, who'd warned me against what I was signing up for. To him, at least, I wasn't simply a pawn.

"Anyway, there's this whole big world that the Muldoonies have been keeping from us. Who knows what's really out there? I want to find out."

Casey blinks once, twice, and then raises an emaciated hand to wipe his eyes.

"You ought to be out there right now," he says. "Not hauling my crippled ass from nowhere to nowhere."

"And leave you behind? I could never do that. If anyone deserves to live free and gay, it's you."

Casey doesn't look at all convinced.

I prop myself up on one elbow and smile at him. "Happy birthday."

"What?"

"I know it's a few months late, but happy birthday. You're eighteen. You're not a Chaff anymore."

He answers with a combined laugh and headshake. "I'll always be a Chaff. But thanks, anyway."

We finally take turns dozing, one of us catching an hour or two of shuteye while the other one keeps watch. My own sleep is spotty and filled with nightmares—I dream that Conover is raping me on a mountain of black people's corpses. I wake up just before the stench asphyxiates me.

It's raining, hard—one of those late-afternoon storms. A clap of thunder jars me, and I get an idea. I reach for the box-cutter that I took from the van and grab the Wide Awakes helmet off Casey's head. Plugging the helmet's vent holes with pieces of leftover first aid tape, I set it on top of the bridge, upside down, until the rain stops.

Once it does, I poke my head out and take a quick survey of the area. We've made more progress than I thought. The mountains are a lot closer than they looked by night, just a few hours' walking distance. Reach them, and we'll be in better shape—cooler temperatures, less exposure, better chances of finding water and food.

The helmet leaks—the plugged holes aren't watertight—but I've managed to collect a few ounces. I take a single swallow for myself, then let Casey have the rest.

His spasms are getting more frequent and more intense. I'm afraid even to touch him now—when I do, it's like I'm only making the pain worse. Each time, after the wave passes, he seems a little bit weaker.

He's dying.

No. I eject the thought from my skull. I can't afford to start thinking that. I can't.

Eventually the sun sets, and it's time to move. Every muscle in my body screams in protest at the idea. If anything, I'm even more tired than I was before.

Casey climbs again onto my back. "So when do we start eating bugs and drinking our own piss?"

He laughs as he says it, but I can tell he's half-serious.

"When we get into the hills I'll find us some food," I say. "I've still got this gun—maybe I can shoot a jackrabbit, or something."

"Or maybe we'll both get eaten by a bear."

"Nah. I don't think there are any bears around here."

There are mountain lions, though. Coyotes, too—them, I can hear. Their yips and howls fill the balmy night air, in every direction, like they're communicating with each other across the miles. I wonder if they're talking about me and Casey. They definitely know we're here. At one point I actually see some—five or six of them, marching across a twilit hillside like a column of soldiers. The leader stops, looks straight at us, and dips its tail over and over. The rest of the pack does the same. Some kind of signal—*This is our territory, get the hell out*, I'm guessing.

Our pace is slower than last night's. The terrain is getting treacherous, with thickets of sharp-leafed bushes and toe-stubbing rocks everywhere on the uneven ground. Within an hour my toenails are all split and bleeding. I would gladly trade my left nut for a pair of boots. The intervals between our rest stops are shrinking, from a few hundred yards last night to barely a dozen. Sometimes, just as I'm picking up some speed, I feel Casey's grip on me weakening and I have to grab his arms so he doesn't fall.

His next spasm is the worst so far. He screams—piercing, trilling screams that reverberate in the hills on one side of us and across the desert floor on the other. Each time one leaves Casey's lungs, it sounds like it's taking chunks of his soul with it.

"I don't want to die." He looks up at me once the spasm is over. His eyes are pits of anguish and fear. "Please don't let me die."

"I won't. I promise."

He must really be in bad shape, if he's not even trying to play the tough guy anymore. Though at least now he wants to live. That's new.

The rest of the night passes in silence. There's no energy left for conversation. Although Casey's screams appear to have scared the coyotes away, I'm worried he might have attracted other kinds of attention, human or otherwise.

We've come to the base of a rock formation—thirty, forty feet high, made up of slabs heaped together like toy blocks. I'm scanning the bottom, looking for the easiest path around it, when I spot a gap between two of the slabs.

A cave.

Thank you, Lord. The prayer is sincere. It's still hours until sunrise, but we aren't going to make it much farther tonight.

I shine the flashlight inside, to make sure it's empty. The only resident is a black tarantula, which does a startled hop away from the flashlight beam and then skitters out of sight between two boulders.

The entrance is no more than a foot and a half high—I have to crawl through on my stomach, then turn around and drag Casey in after me. But the inside is spacious, and toward the rear there's enough headroom to stand up. The soil on the floor is sandy, much softer than the concrete ledge we slept on yesterday. I find the softest patch of ground, lay Casey on it, and then stretch out beside him.

As soon as I shut my eyes, Conover comes back. This time he has a pack of coyotes with him, and they slowly chew my arms and legs off while he violates me.

I wake up with a jolt and rocket to a sitting position—not from the nightmares, but because I thought I heard some-thing. I grab the flashlight, switch it back on, and shine it around the inside of the cave.

Nothing. Casey and I are still the only ones here.

Maybe I'm hallucinating. My head sure is spinning fast enough.

The dizziness worsens when I try to stand. I have to dig my fingertips into the wall of the cave and pull myself to my feet. Once I'm upright, I feel a pressure in my abdomen, like a lead weight resting on my bladder, so I try to pee. It burns, and the stuff dribbling out of me looks like the sludge at the bottom of a coffee pot.

I hear it again—that . . . *something*. A rushing sound, from outside—muffled and vague, and gone by the time my thirst-addled brain registers it. But it's real—I wasn't halluci-nating this time.

I go back over to where Casey is. He's awake and staring, his body shaking, but otherwise lying still. I think those pains have become continuous now—he's just gotten too weak to scream or thrash around.

"Casey?" I hunch down beside him, again using the wall of the cave to steady myself. "I think I heard something. I'm going to check it out."

"You're leaving me here."

"I'm not leaving you. I won't go far, and I'll be right back."

"I love you."

His words are matter-of-fact, but there's also a strain behind them, like he's finding them hard to say but also fears he won't get another chance.

I reach down and squeeze his hand. "I love you too."

Before crawling out of the cave, I reach into my pocket, take out the pistol, and turn off the safety.

It's almost dawn, and the wind is up. Those are the first two things I notice. The wind isn't gale-force, but it's gusty, stirring the razor-edged leaves of the bushes and kicking up ghostly swirls of dust. I step carefully around one side of the rock formation and notice, for the first time, that we're at the mouth of a ravine—a wedge-shaped gash extending into the hills until the far end disappears in a jumble of boulders and brush. The wind is coming from that direction, blowing down the length of the ravine like notes from a trumpet. And as I listen to it, I hear the rushing sound again, more distinctly. Not a rushing—more of a gurgling.

A stream.

Water.

I move forward, toward the source of the sound, like it's pulling me. Every few feet I glance over my shoulder to make sure I haven't lost sight of the cave—I told Casey I wouldn't wander off—but I can't stop. We *need* this. My head is spinning again, lost in desperation and hope. First the cave, now this? Maybe God is looking out for us two queers after all. Maybe —

I slam to a halt.

The muzzle of the double-barreled shotgun pointed at me is black and cold. The voice of the man holding it is even colder.

"Don't move."

I LET the pistol fall from my hand. I know better than to raise it. This man has the drop on me. His finger is already on the trigger. Any threatening moves from me, and the next sound Casey hears back in the cave will be the shotgun blast ending my life.

The cave. *Casey* —

I wheel around the way I came. Two more men, also armed, block my path. I stop. My arms jerk into the air.

"*Güero*, are you *deaf?*" the first man barks. "I said, don't move!"

"I won't!" I stretch my arms higher, opening my hands as wide as I can so these men can see I'm not holding any other weapons. "I won't resist you! Please don't shoot!"

The other two are younger than the first, black-haired and dark-skinned, with fuzzy adolescent beards. One of them comes toward me. He eyes my pink uniform, then smiles at his companion and makes a fluttering hand gesture. *"Mira. Es un maricón."*

Their laughter is cruel, chilling. Is that Spanish they're speaking? Did I stumble into Mexico, somehow? That's impossible. The border is a no-man's land, with mines and twenty-foot walls and guards with shoot-to-kill orders—no one gets across it.

Unless . . . has the war started? In the Dawn Patrol they always said war with Red Mexico was coming someday.

"Look, I don't want any trouble." I keep my voice calm—maybe I can talk my way out of this. "If I'm trespassing, I apologize. Please, just let me go back—"

"*¡Cállate, puto!*"

One of the younger men half-shoves-half-punches me in the shoulder, with enough force to make me stagger and fall. He stands over me, chuckling.

"What are you looking for, huh? This?" He makes a fist-pumping motion in front of his crotch. "You like it up the ass, white boy?"

"Leave him alone."

It's the older man. He has weary eyes, and his hair and full beard are speckled with gray.

A burst of heated-sounding Spanish follows. The younger men are arguing with the leader, jabbing their fingers at me. I hear *maricón* a few more times. I may not know the language, but it doesn't take a genius to figure out what a *maricón* is.

I stay down on the ground. All I can think about is Casey, alone in that cave. I need to get back to him. That means not giving these men any reason to shoot me.

The older man comes over. His gaze falls on the bandage wrapped around my right hand, and he stoops and grabs it. I grit my teeth as he pokes at the wound through the bandage.

He scowls at me, then rejoins the other two and switches back to English. "The sun is coming up. We better take him back with us. Maybe the Junk Man will want him."

"*Simón.*"

The Junk Man? Suddenly I'm in Neighbor Lenskold's office again. The Junk Man was on that list of hers. Also . . . wasn't he the man in that underground video we saw . . . ?

I'm yanked to my feet. My arms are pulled behind my back. Metal cuffs snap tight around one wrist, then the other. I twist my head for a glimpse of the path back to the cave.

Casey . . .

"Wait a minute . . . please . . . "

No one is listening. Hands grip my shoulders, spin me around, and release me with a hard shove toward the mouth of the ravine.

"Come on, faggot, let's go!"

OK, so these aren't Red-Mex invaders. They've clearly been settled for a long time. As we reach the fringes of their encampment, I see old men, women, even children.

Most of the men are armed, though. A fair number of the women are too.

The trail snakes into the hills, around randomly strewn boulders and through narrow passages so sharp and straight, they could have been cut into the rock with a saw. It's a struggle to stay on my feet—the ground is uneven, having my hands cuffed behind my back is throwing me off balance, and if I slow down, one of my captors jabs me between the shoulder blades with the butt of his rifle, making me stumble. I try to keep my bearings, to remain aware of where I am in relation to the cave—to Casey—but between the winding of the trail and the speed of this forced march, I soon lose track of how far I've gone or even which direction I'm going.

The older man walks ahead of me. He doesn't say much. He just wants to hand me off to this Junk Man as soon as possible—that's clear. But at least he's not being abusive. The other two openly hate me—because I'm a *maricón*, because I'm white, probably both. They would have kicked me to death if the older man hadn't been holding them in check.

The camp is bustling. The sun is rapidly heating up the desert, and everyone is in a hurry to get under cover—putting out cooking fires, taking down clotheslines, cleaning up after various work details. There must be two hundred people here, maybe even more, living in caves, or in shelters dug into the earth and camouflaged with soil and brush. Most of them take no notice of me—when they do, their eyes flash with suspicion but quickly simmer down to some mixture of contempt and disinterest. A few of the kids catch sight of my pink outfit, and snicker.

I don't react. They already think I'm just some frightened little faggot—I won't confirm it by acting like one.

We stop at one of the dugout shelters. It's simple, just a hole in the ground, with an improvised trap door made from a scrap of chain-link fencing and a heavy lock.

It's a cell.

My heart starts pounding. I fight to hold myself together. The older man removes my handcuffs while one of the others opens the cell door and uncoils a rope ladder. They make me climb down, the door slams shut, and I hear the lock click.

I wait until the men's footsteps fade into silence.

Then, and only then, do I let myself go to pieces.

Some time later—two or three hours, based on how bright it is up top—the door opens, and a woman comes down. One of the bullying younger guys from before stands at the opening, watching, his gun drawn.

I take the two tortillas and strip of dried meat the woman offers me, and inhale them like . . . like someone who hasn't eaten in two days. When I'm done, my body suddenly remembers that it's dying of thirst. The woman unhooks a Sierra cup from her belt, fills it with water from a plastic jug, and watches me drain it in two gulps. She hesitates when I hold the cup out for seconds, but then gives in and refills it.

"Thank you," I whisper.

"De nada."

I'm determined to be the most cooperative prisoner these people have ever had. *They* aren't the enemy—the Muldoonies are. And when—if—they bring me to plead my case before this Junk Man, I'll do just that. Plead. Beg. Grovel. Suck him off, if I have to. I've done worse.

It's too late. Casey is already dead.

Fighting off despair only makes it stronger. I keep picturing Casey in that cave, parched and in pain, all the life draining out of him while he lies there, helpless.

Wondering why I abandoned him. After promising him I wouldn't.

No. He's alive. Maybe I can even get him some help here. Screw what they taught me in Dawn Patrol—these aren't bad people. They could have killed me, shot me down and left my body for the coyotes—but they didn't.

They aren't the enemy. And I'm not theirs.

The trap door opens again. It must be close to noon. Up top, I see the Bully Brothers again. One of them flings the ladder into the cell.

"Vámonos."

I climb out. The pair fall in on either side of me. They seem less cranked-up—they aren't manhandling me so much. Maybe they got chewed out for being too rough with me before.

Except for a scattering of armed men, patrolling in pairs or perched on rock formations with binoculars, everyone is out of sight.

Who *are* these people, anyway? How long have they been living out here, outside of the Hispanic Protection Zones, off the Muldoonies' radar? I hate to imagine what it must be like, huddling in the mountains, scavenging or stealing what they need, in constant fear of discovery . . .

I'd better get used to imagining it. This might well be how Casey and I will have to live from now on.

I'm led to a tent—U.S. Army issue, it looks like, pitched between two boulders, so well camouflaged that it's nearly invisible until I'm right in front of it. One of my guards stops at the flap and clears his throat.

"Estamos aquí."

"Yeah, come in."

The flap is pulled aside. I step through. Three figures rise to greet me.

The Mexican in the middle is clearly the leader. He's shorter than me, but also stockier, with a physique like a pro boxer's. Good-looking in a blunt and pugnacious sort of way.

Clean-shaven—unusual here, where all the men I've seen have mustaches or beards, and even the boys grow peach fuzz—with short, glossy black hair framing intelligent chocolate-brown eyes.

Those eyes give me a long sizing-up, then glance past me at my guards. "Get this man something to sit on."

They scramble to obey. In the same instant, the word he used hits me. He said *man*, not *boy* or *faggot* or even *maricón* . . .

I steal a look at the other two, a man and a woman. They're both white, the only white people I've seen here. If their leader didn't have such a magnetic presence I'd be gawking at the big guy next to him. Tall and built, dark brown hair, eyes a serene blue—total all-American quarterback material. If Casey were here, he'd be drooling. The woman is a pretty but dangerous-looking redhead, with a cool facial expression and don't-even-try-to-mess-with-me body language.

All three have pistols holstered on their belts. In one corner of the tent, next to a folding table littered with random items—a map, a couple of coffee mugs, a crumb-dusted aluminum plate—a trio of automatic rifles lie in plain view and easy reach.

A folding stool is set up behind me, and the Mexican gestures for me to sit. As I do, he takes his own seat and shoots the Bully Brothers a get-out-of-here look. Again, they nearly trip over themselves in their rush to comply.

The other two remain standing. None of them speak. My own voice rushes in to fill the silence.

"So, um . . . are you the Junk Man?"

He fidgets a little. He doesn't seem to like his nickname. "Yeah, that's me. Who are you?"

"My name's Tyler."

The Junk Man grimaces slightly. My guts tighten. Did I say something wrong already?

He clasps his hands and leans forward, his elbows on his knees. His dark eyes nail me to my seat. "You're gonna have to learn fast, Tyler, so listen up. There are only two times that you're safe giving out your real name to people—if you trust them with your life, or if you're gonna kill them. Are you gonna kill us?"

I shake my head.

"Good. My real name is Al. This is my wife, Sally, and this *vato* that you can't stop making eyes at is Jackson. Do you understand?"

His meaning sinks in, and I feel like I'm dissolving. I force my eyes to stay locked onto his. "Do you trust me, or are you . . . ?"

"I don't know yet. Why are you here, Tyler?"

"I . . . I escaped. Two nights ago. From—" I stop before I say where from. I haven't seen any warmth toward people of the queer persuasion so far. Then again, the pink outfit is a dead giveaway. "From the Fresh Starts Reorientation Center."

"Show me your hand."

Either that older man didn't tell him I was no longer chipped, or he wants to see for himself. My right hand shakes as I hold it out for inspection. The Junk Man takes it, and I see that he has a scar on his hand as well—jagged and ugly, as though his own tracking chip had been not simply removed, but gouged out with a chisel.

He motions to the big white guy, Jackson, who crouches down and probes the back of my hand with his fingers—more gently than the other man did before—unwrapping the bandage just long enough to look underneath it before taping it back into place. He nods to the Junk Man, and releases me.

While this has been going on, Sally, the redheaded woman, has been at the table in the corner, poring over the map. She returns and whispers something to the Junk Man, who keeps his gaze on me as he listens. His brow furrows.

"Fresh Starts is over fifty miles from here. You didn't get that far in just two nights. Not on foot."

"No, sir. We stole a van. But we ditched it."

All three of them tense up. The Junk Man's voice sharpens. "Where did you ditch it? How far from here?"

"I'm . . . not sure." Crap. They must be worried that the van will lead the Wide Awakes here. I rack my brain for a more specific answer. "Five miles, maybe ten? You're the only people we've seen since we went off the road."

The Junk Man settles back. The other two do the same.

"So how did you manage to escape?" he asks. "That's not easy to do."

"We, uh . . . we had help."

"Outside help, you mean. You been watching the fog roll in over the Golden Gate Bridge?" He takes in my reaction to the code phrase, then looks up at Sally. "You heard about any breakout ops lately? I haven't."

Sally shrugs and crosses her arms. "Wouldn't be the first time they kept us out of the loop."

"Heh." He stares down at his own feet, looking annoyed. Then he shakes it off and again gives me his undivided attention. "You keep saying *we*. Where are the others?"

I hesitate. How much should I tell them? They seem to have mixed feelings about the Six—not that I'd hold *that* against them—and there must be some reason they've been kept in the dark about us.

Us.

Screw the Six, screw these people. This is about Casey.

"My friend is still out there." I sit up straight and look the Junk Man in the eye. "He's hurt. I left him in a cave while I went looking for water. That's what I was doing when your people grabbed me."

The Junk Man raises an eyebrow, and the corners of his mouth twitch. "Your . . . *friend*, huh?"

Something about his tone, and the faint smile on his face—it pushes a button. I half-suspect he's pushing it on purpose, but that doesn't matter. My own face heats up, and a bubble of anger rises out of my chest cavity.

"My boyfriend." My voice drops so low, it hits the ground. "Is that a problem?"

The silence that follows is stifling. But then the Junk Man's smile gets wider. He flicks a glance over at Jackson, who wiggles his eyebrows at me . . .

Wait. *Jackson?* First Coach, now him? I really do need to work on that radar.

"No, it's not a problem," the Junk Man says.

He and Sally look at each other. Did I hear him say just now that she was his *wife?* Yes, those are matching wedding rings on their fingers. That's a death-penalty offense—Race

Pollution, it's called—an even worse crime than being gay.

I see an opening. "You have no reason to trust me—I get that. But I think you're good people, and I trust you. My name is Tyler Treppenhouse, I'm gay, and the only person I care about in the whole world is in that cave." My imploring gaze bounces among the three of them. "He's going to die out there. Can't you help him? If you can't, at least let me go back so I can die with him."

The Junk Man studies me some more, then stands up and draws his companions into a huddle.

As I watch them talk, I remember—the vial! I still have it in my pocket. Could I still use it? Threaten my way out of here, if all else fails?

And would I really stoop to that, even as a last resort? Infect these three people—not to mention all the men, women, and children in this encampment—with some sort of unspeakable, invisible death, just to save myself and Casey?

The huddle breaks up. The Junk Man comes back over and sits down.

"We can't just let you go." He cuts me off with a gesture before I can say anything. "You've seen too much—we can't risk letting you get recaptured and interrogated. We'll be long gone by then, but these people"—a tip of the head toward the flap leading outside—"will still be here."

"I thought you were in charge of this place."

"No, we're just passing through. They'll be wiped out all the same, though, if the Muldoonies find them."

He runs a hand—the scarred one—through his hair. "But I'm not gonna let some poor kid die in the desert either. Do you know where this cave is?"

"Yes, sir, I do." My head bobs up and down as I talk. "Just take me back to where I was picked up. It's not far from there."

"All right. I'll send Jackson with you." Another sizing-up with his eyes. "Don't worry. Jackson's a medic—he's saved my life more than once. If anybody can help your friend, he can."

Chaffs

Before we go, I'm given a change of clothes—a pair of desert-camo pants, a threadbare T-shirt with a faded image of the Alamo on the front, and a pair of boots. The pants have a bewildering number of pockets, with zippers to keep each of them closed. I transfer my vial of death to one of them.

The boots are insanely comfortable. If my feet had tear ducts, they'd be weeping with joy. The rest of me breaks down sobbing, anyway, as I shed that pink abomination—it's like I'm finally getting my human skin back.

I'm still pulling myself together when Jackson comes to get me. He takes one look at the pink rags, and curls his lip.

"We'll burn them later," he says. "You can light the match."

We take the truck belonging to the Junk Man's crew—a well-used Thorhammer, huge and hulking, with oversized tires and a four-wheel drive that carries it over the rough terrain like it's Sunday morning on the Ventura Freeway. It's seen action—the paint job is half sandblasted away, the chassis is pockmarked, there are stains of various colors on the upholstery, and the interior has a soaked-in odor of gunpowder, dried blood, and unwashed bodies cooped up together for days on end.

Jackson puts the truck into a lower gear to heave it out of an especially deep gully. For such a big jock type, he has a surprisingly gentle demeanor, and his Texas drawl that melts on my eardrums.

"So, Jackson . . . " I hesitate, but then plunge in. "You're gay?"

"Queer as a thirty-dollar bill. You a spy?"

"Do you guys really think that?"

"If we did, you'd be dead, so no. But the other folks here?" A backward nod at the Bully Brothers, sitting behind us, and looking like they'd rather be just about anyplace else. "Your gayness aside, they aren't too fond of Anglos hereabouts."

"Yeah, I get that." I can't say I blame them, either.

"Hell, spies?" Jackson goes on. "You and your boyfriend are more dangerous than that. Y'all are Smurf bait."

"Smurf bait?"

343

"The Wide Awakes—that's what we call them, Smurfs." He takes in my baffled look. "On account of the blue uniforms? These people here are very good at not attracting attention—that's how they've survived so long. But then you drop in—far as they know, you've got a whole horde of Muldoon's finest right on your heels. They're terrified."

"But we haven't even seen any . . . Smurfs . . . since we broke out."

"Yeah, and that's another thing. They ought to be turning this whole area upside down, hunting for you. Where are they?" He pauses to ease the truck between two rock formations. Then he shrugs. "Ah, well—no use fretting about it. Tell me everything you can about your friend's symptoms."

Jackson listens to me as he drives, occasionally asking a question or two. My fear for Casey starts rising again. It's only been eight hours or so since I left him, but what am I going to find when I return to that cave?

"Are you really a doctor?"

"Second-year med student, actually." Jackson's smile turns sheepish. "I had to quit UT Medical when I was, you know, found out."

He's maybe ten years older than me—at the time Muldoon came to power, Jackson would have been in middle school. Did he already know he was gay even then? If so, why is he still here? He could have left the country—gone to Canada or Europe, to one of those fantastic gay cities Coach told me about—but here he is, fighting.

Being armed probably helps. That gun on his hip isn't a fashion accessory.

"There!" I shoot up straight in my seat and jab one finger against the window. "There it is!"

We haven't even stopped yet and already I'm bolting from the truck and scrambling up the hillside. I'm out of breath before I'm halfway to the cave—the last two days have taken their toll on me as well. Jackson parks the truck and follows easily behind me, a black medical bag in his hand. The Bully Brothers bring up the rear, carrying a stretcher.

Casey is right where I left him. He doesn't look up. I cradle his head, whispering nonstop apologies for leaving him here for so long. I can feel his breath on my cheek—*he's alive!*—but his eyes are half-closed and glazed over.

Jackson squeezes in on Casey's other side, then takes his wrist and feels around until he finds a pulse. "Here, let's get him out of this confined space. I'll have more elbow room in the truck."

He waves the Bully Brothers into the cave with the stretcher. Within minutes Casey is laid out on the truck's back seat, with an IV drip in his arm. I watch, feeling totally helpless, while Jackson examines him—heartbeat, breathing, blood pressure, shining lights in his eyes to check for a concussion, the usual. He moves down to Casey's legs and unwraps the bandages to look at the stumps.

Casey stirs. He looks down to see who's prodding him. His voice is slurred and dreamlike. "You're cute. Who are you?"

"Howdy." If Jackson had on a cowboy hat, he'd be tipping it.

"Hey, Casey." I can't decide whether to laugh or cry, so I'm doing both. "I brought you a handsome gay doctor."

"How thoughtful. Can I keep him?"

A few minutes later, Casey has fresh dressings on his legs, and Jackson is making one last check of the IV before we head back to the encampment in the hills.

"Is he going to be OK?" I ask.

"His vitals look decent." Jackson turns a valve at the base of the IV bag to adjust the rate of the drip. "He's dehydrated—that's what the IV is for, to get his fluid levels back up. We ought to try getting some food into him, too, assuming he can keep it down. From those cramps you described, I'm guessing he's in withdrawal from whatever drugs they were pumping him with. I gave him just the tiniest shot of morphine, to take some of the stress off his system while he's rehydrating—beyond that, ain't much anyone can do for withdrawal except ride it out."

As Jackson gets behind the wheel, I scoot closer to Casey and lay his head in my lap. In the rear-facing seat opposite, the Bully Brothers eyeball us. They seem vaguely repulsed by the sight of two guys together like this, but I also glimpse pain and sympathy on their faces when they take in Casey's missing legs. One of them does that drawing-a-cross-on-the-chest thing that Catholics do.

Casey is fast asleep, and he stays that way throughout the ride back. As Jackson drives, I lean sideways, rest my head against the inside of the truck, and close my eyes. I can hardly believe that the ordeal of the last three days is almost over. I swear, I could sleep for a month.

It's close to sunset by the time we reach the encampment. Among the rocks, the tents and dugout shelters are draped in deep shadow. We take Casey on the stretcher to what looks like a hospital tent, ruled over by a brawny and craggy-faced old woman even the Bully Brothers seem afraid of. Jackson confers with her in Spanish, and she responds with gestures and knowing nods.

While we're getting Casey settled, Jackson's radio starts squawking. Jackson frowns as he listens and shoots me a look. "We need to report in."

"What about Casey?"

"He'll be fine here for a few minutes."

We're a less-than-thirty-second walk from the Junk Man's tent.

As soon as I step inside, a chill stabs through me—the temperature seems to drop instantly. It's dead quiet but for the hissing of the gas lantern in one corner. The harsh light deepens the Junk Man's eye sockets, but within them I can still see his eyes glaring straight at me, like obsidian orbs. His wife looks equally pissed off. Even Jackson flinches at the looks on their faces.

The Junk Man's voice is slow and deadly.

"What . . . the hell . . . have you *done*?"

T HE Junk Man takes a couple of steps toward me, but then snaps around to face Jackson. "The other kid, this one's friend—is he sick?"

"The ill kind of sick?" Jackson shakes his head. "Injured, dehydrated, and in drug withdrawal, but if he's sick, it's no illness I've ever—" His voice cuts off, and the puzzlement on his face dissolves into a milky look of fear. "Lord have mercy."

The vial. The Junk Man knows about it.

His icy gaze turns back to me. "We got on the radio while you were gone, to check out your story. Fresh Starts isn't just on lockdown—it's under *quarantine*. They've been flying in biohazard containment teams. Do you know what those are?"

I remember those lights I saw two nights ago, in the distance, descending on the camp. *Oh, Jesus* . . .

"Whatever you did there, it's got the Muldoonies shitting their pants." The Junk Man looks away, and swallows—he's terrified too. His mask of anger can't conceal it. "Last night they extended the quarantine area to a five-mile radius around the camp. Tonight, who knows how big it'll be? Ten miles, a hundred miles, the whole goddamn state? What kind of fucking *plague* did you release into the world?"

No wonder the Wide Awakes haven't been combing the area for escapees. They're too busy trying to keep their out-of-control bioweapon from escaping instead.

Both the Junk Man and his wife have unsnapped their gun holsters. A quick look at Jackson confirms that he's done the same.

"Have you heard from the Six yet?" Jackson asks.

"We got a message out, but if they didn't tell us about this op before, they aren't gonna tell us shit about it now." Another glare at me. "If there even *was* an op."

"Come on, Al, you don't think—"

"I don't know *what* to think!" The Junk Man wheels around and off to the table at the rear of the tent. He walks with a limp—I hadn't noticed that about him before. "You remember that hospital full of dying kids we found in Rio Grande City? The Smurfs will do anything. Sending a couple of innocent-looking escapees out to infect the first bunch of Mexicans they stumble across—you don't think they're capable of that?"

He plants both hands on the table and leans heavily, his back to me. Jackson and Sally have turned away from me as well.

Run. The thought flashes in my mind, but then winks out just as fast. I wouldn't make it ten yards.

My life is hanging by a thread—my life *and* Casey's. Would they really do it—kill us both, if necessary, to thwart the spread of some humanity-destroying epidemic? They'd feel terrible about it—they aren't Muldoonies, after all—but yes, they would.

Still . . . they don't *want* to.

"I know it was the Six behind this." My voice is shaky, but clear. "I know."

The Junk Man looks at me over his shoulder. "You do, huh?"

"They contacted me, after it got out that I was gay. Casey—my friend—had already been arrested. The Six promised to get us both out, if I went to Fresh Starts and helped them."

Jackson's eyes widen. "You *volunteered* to get sent to that place?"

"Yes, sir. I didn't know what they wanted me to do. And I sure didn't know what would happen to me . . . "

My throat is seizing up. This is hitting a raw nerve. How much should I tell them? How much will I be able to tell them?

I hear the stool being set up behind me. Jackson lays a hand on my shoulder, and I sit down. The Junk Man comes back over, takes a seat, and pulls up close.

"Remember—no names." He searches my face to make sure I understand. "Don't give up your contacts. Just start from the top."

I keep Coach and his wife out of it, but beyond that I spill everything. When I get to the part about me and Conover I have to take a lot of deep breaths, but I get it out without falling apart. I even lift up the front of my shirt to show the scars.

Once I'm past that, everything else comes out with ease—stealing the vials, seeing Duncan shatter his at Conover's feet just before being gunned down, carrying Casey across the desert for two nights, and finally being captured and brought here.

When I'm finished, it's the others who seem robbed of speech. Jackson is staring hard at the ground, one huge hand covering the bottom half of his face. Sally's face is tinged with green, her no-nonsense attitude gone. Of the three, the Junk Man is holding it together the best, but even he is sitting with his jaw hanging open. His eyes have gone from angry to haunted.

He blinks, then clears his throat. "These vials—you've still got them?"

"One of them. Casey's got the other one."

"May I see it?"

I fish the vial out of my pocket and hold it at shoulder level, clamped in my fist so I won't drop it. There's a long pause, and then the Junk Man puts his hand out. I unclench my fist and lay the vial in his upturned palm. A dry, anxious tongue runs over his lips.

He coughs out a single hoarse laugh, then looks at Jackson. "I guess I'd better not open this to find out what's in it, huh?"

"Not for all the oil in Texas," Jackson says.

The Junk Man handles the vial with absolute caution, eyeing the harmless-looking white substance inside, like he's trying to convince himself that it's just talcum powder or something. Then he passes it back to me with a shudder.

"You've got *huevos*, carrying that shit around." He raises his hand to his face, about to rub his eyes, but then he jerks it away and wipes it on his pants instead. "And this other guy, the one who was killed—you say he broke open the one he was carrying? What for?"

"I don't know. To give the rest of us time to get away, maybe? He did say he'd die for the mission if he had to. He was . . . kind of crazy by then."

"Or a fanatic. And you don't think you were close enough to get infected?"

"I don't—I *hope* not." I raise the fist holding the vial. "Anyway, this is what the Six wanted. So I guess it belongs to you now."

The Junk Man looks like he'd rather cover himself with spiders than take it. But before he can say so, Sally speaks up. "Do we *want* it? More on point, do we want the Six to have it?"

The Junk Man furrows his brow. "What do you mean?"

"This . . . man, Conover? He's a rapist. No, not just a rapist—a serial killer. And the Six knew it. They purposely set up a teenage boy to be a serial killer's next victim!" The anger is making her whole body vibrate like a guitar string. "And we say the *Muldoonies* will stoop to anything."

The Junk Man stares at her, frowning, then blows out a deep breath and hangs his head, rubbing the back of his neck with one hand.

I feel Jackson touch my shoulder again.

"The three of us need to talk this over." He coaxes me to my feet and steers me toward the flap in the tent. "Go sit with your friend for a while—he ought to be lucid by now."

"Wait." The Junk Man stands up and puts his hand out again. "The vial—give it to me. Jackson, go with him and get the other one from his friend. And put a guard on them both."

Jackson doesn't say a word—he just nods sadly.

The other two watch me as Jackson escorts me up the path in the dark. They're no doubt waiting until I'm out of earshot before they start deciding my fate.

I remember something from Mr. Scudder's history class, about Christopher Columbus—how, when whites first arrived in the New World, they brought smallpox with them, and over ninety percent of the Indians died because they, unlike us, had no immunity to the disease. Mr. Scudder held that up as evidence of our racial superiority—we'd won the battle for survival of the fittest, the Indians hadn't.

Are the Muldoonies trying to make it happen all over again? On a worldwide scale this time, in an act of mass murder that will make Nuke York look like a day at the beach? I think about all the people in this encampment, unaware of the death I've brought into their midst. Have I doomed them all, just by being here?

Jackson sticks around only long enough to take the second vial, in the pouch with the stolen computer disks. Then he's gone, and one of the Bully Brothers has been posted outside the tent, to keep me from escaping.

Like I'd even try. I'm not going anywhere without Casey. Never again.

He, at least, looks like he's getting better. He's half-sitting, propped up on some pillows, and his face is less pain-wracked than I've seen it in the last two days.

"Hey." I squeeze his hand, careful not to jostle the IV needle in his arm. "How are you feeling?"

"Tired. I can't even sit up on my own. I had to get her to help me." He gives a weak nod to the brawny old woman, who's doing something with her hands—repairing a torn sheet, it looks like. "At least I'm not spazzing and shitting myself anymore—I thought I was going to die in that cave. I've got to be honest—I didn't think you were coming back."

"Hey, a million Smurfs couldn't have kept me away."

"A million what?"

"Wide Awakes. That's what these people call them. I don't get it either."

I start to sit down on the neatly made-up cot next to his, but the old woman scowls at me, so I switch to the floor, getting as close to Casey's eye level as I can.

"Tyler . . . " Casey bites his lip, like he's afraid to go on. But then he puts a tentative hand on my knee. "I need to tell you something. About me and Kevin."

"Kevin? That's like a hundred years ago. You don't need to tell me anything." I lay my own hand on top of his. "Look, it happened. Yeah, sure, I wish you'd told me about it, but it happened before we got together. If your friend Bec hadn't said anything, I wouldn't have known."

"Except that it never happened."

"What?"

"I never did it with Kevin. I just told Bec to say I did."

I'm too startled to do anything but blink at him. It takes me several breaths to get my voice back. "You told Bec to . . . Casey, why?"

He squeezes his eyes shut. Now that he's being rehydrated, the tears can flow. "I wanted you to hate me."

His hand is still resting on my knee. I haven't moved mine either. I'm scared that if I let go of him now, I'll never touch him again.

I try to keep my tone light. "OK, you're going to have to explain, because I'm not getting it. Why did you want me to hate you?"

He opens his eyes and stares off into space, his throat working. "That night we broke into Lenskold's office? I saw something on her computer. About my Evaluation."

"Yeah, I remember. It freaked you out."

"It did, but not for any reason you're thinking." The hand on my knee is trembling. "They were going to *pass* me."

OK, I'm even more confused. "Pass you? But . . . that's a *good* thing, isn't it?"

"You don't understand. They were going to pass me because . . . the Dentists. They wanted to use me, to trap other guys. Guys like you."

Now it makes sense. Casey had been with a lot of guys—not just guys our age, but older men, Party officials, men with a lot to lose. Men to whom Casey was just some Chaff they could play with and discard without putting themselves at risk. The DDS would have jumped at the chance to use him as bait.

And I would have been the first fish they caught.

"There was no way in hell I'd ever work for them—not willingly. But if I passed my Evaluation I'd have no choice—they'd put the screws to me until I gave in. So I talked to Randall's . . . friends, the ones he got his bomb-vest from, convinced them I wanted to go out with a bang, too. Only I wasn't going to take out a mall or anything—just go to the park the night before my Evaluation, and . . . kablooey." A sniff. "Then Randall had to blow himself up first, the stupid fuck."

He still hasn't moved his hand away, not even to wipe the tears from his cheeks.

"I thought I had it all figured out when we got together, Tyler. I only had a few months left until my number came up—I thought, what the hell, I'll have some fun. Bagging the hottest jock in the school? That's every teenage fagboy's number-one fantasy." He laughs through his tears. "I had it all planned. Falling for you was *not* part of the plan.

"Things were a whole lot simpler when no one gave a shit about me. That meant I didn't have to give a shit about them." His grip on my knee tightens. "Then you and I got together, and out of nowhere I found myself . . . giving a shit. I couldn't handle it. I kept thinking about how destroyed you'd be when I got snuffed, and I was so scared that you'd flush your own life down the toilet trying to save me." He looks away. "I figured you'd be safer hating my guts. It would hurt you, but then you'd go on with your life, find someone better."

"Better?"

"Better than me."

Now *I'm* about to cry. *Better* than him? He's worth more

than a thousand Muldoonies—doesn't he know that? All that toughness and self-confidence I've always admired in him— was it all just a mask, a game face, hiding what a waste of oxygen he believed he was?

But then again, maybe we all believe that about ourselves, on some level. If the whole Nation hates us, tells us we're worthless or even evil—because of our skin tone, or what our parents did, or who we love—we can fight it, but deep down, a tiny piece of that hatred will forever be lurking, waiting to trip us up.

We're all Chaffs, that way.

I get up, kneel beside the cot, and cup Casey's face in one hand, turning it toward me and locking my eyes onto his.

"You wanted to make me hate you, huh?" I smile at him. "It didn't work."

Casey tries to turn away, but I cup his face again and coax him back.

"I need to tell you something, too." My voice goes up in volume, enough to make the old woman look up, but I don't care if she hears this. "I'm gay."

A long silence, and then Casey laughs. "Yeah? We've kind of established that."

"But I can say it out loud now without cringing." Out of the blue, I recall what Coach told me, about how we can't afford to hate ourselves. "The Muldoonies are out to destroy us. Maybe they'll succeed. But they'll have to work at it— we're not going to do the job for them."

Casey is still letting that soak in when the tent flap opens. I turn, thinking it's Jackson again, but it isn't.

It's the scary redhead, Sally.

She says something to the old woman, who gathers up her work and leaves.

Without thinking, I've taken up a fighting stance and positioned myself between Sally and Casey. Casey shoots me a look. *Who the hell is this?*

Sally crosses over to the adjacent cot and sits down. "Relax, Tyler—the interrogation is over. I'm just here to meet your friend. Hello, by the way—my name's Sally." She smiles and touches Casey's hand. "So you two went to North Topanga High School? We have something in common."

My jaw drops open. "You went there too?"

"Go Conquerors."

Geez. How did she wind up out here? I'm dying to find out. But before I can ask, Sally's tone shifts to something more businesslike. "We'll have to save the small talk for later, I'm afraid. Al and Jackson will be here shortly. We're bugging out—things are about to start moving very fast very soon."

"You're taking us with you?" I don't know whether I should be happy or alarmed. "Aren't you still worried we might be contagious?"

Sally spreads her hands. "Well, as our friend from Texas pointed out, that bull is out of the pen. At least, by taking the two of you with us, we can keep an eye on you, watch out for any symptoms."

And put us down like rabid dogs, if necessary. Got it.

"Besides, it will give you some time to think things over," Sally says. "You're both going to have some choices to make."

I can't help snorting at that. "Choices? We do what you want, or we do what the Secret Six wants?"

"You're forgetting someone." She rolls her eyes at my puzzled look, but then counteracts it with another smile. "Tyler, what do *you* want?"

"Does that matter?"

"It's the only thing that does." A pause. "Sure, you can stay and fight the Muldoonies—or you can start a new life on the outside. But those are just the two basic options—the choices become much more complicated from there, and they're different for everyone."

What *do* I want? I haven't given it much thought—I never have. I wanted to play baseball, once, but even then, the rest of my life was all laid out for me. That life is gone forever, and I don't want it back.

So what now? I want out of this loony bin. I want to go to one of those gay cities, settle down with Casey, and never have to think about Muldoon or the Secret Six or the Wide Awakes or the Dare Institute—any of it—again. The full-on happily-ever-after ending. I want that.

But . . . that ending can never happen. Both Casey and I have scars that will never heal, and nightmares that will haunt our sleep no matter where we go. And then there are these vials of death we brought here, and whatever else the Muldoonies are cooking. If they have their way, there won't be anyplace safe in the world *to* go.

"I want to be with Casey," I finally say. "That's all I know right now."

"Ah, the things we do for love. I can relate." Sally's gaze drops and briefly touches the ring on her finger. "And what do you want, Casey?"

"Jesus. Where do I even start?" Casey ponders. "I've always lived like there was no tomorrow—and now, all of a sudden, I have all these tomorrows I don't know what to do with. Do I even deserve them? Everything I've seen . . . So many people never had their tomorrows. Why do I get to have mine?"

"We all deserve to have our tomorrows. That's why we fight those who would take them away."

Casey tilts his head pointedly at his leg stumps. "Me, march around with a gun?"

"There *are* other ways of fighting." A sly, humorless grin. "Al and I have some ideas about that, actually. Those . . . gifts . . . the two of you brought—we're not convinced delivering them to the Six is a good idea. But *we* don't want to keep them, either. We're currently considering . . . other options."

I feel a chill of suspicion creeping along my skin. "Options?"

Sally's grin widens. "We'll talk later."

Outside, there's a commotion—running feet, voices shouting in two languages. The tent flap flies open again, and Jackson and the Junk Man burst through. Both of them have rifles slung over their shoulders. The Junk Man is carrying a second one.

"We gotta move." There's urgency in his voice, but no panic, just matter-of-factness. "Now."

"Smurfs?" Sally asks.

The Junk Man nods and hands her the rifle he's carrying. "Air patrols, coming up from El Paso. ETA less than a half hour."

I feel my own panic starting to rise. "Have they found us?"

Neither one answers. They're both gone before the question is out of my mouth.

Jackson is packing up medical supplies and stuffing them in a duffel bag. He looks at Casey, then at me. "Can you carry him to the truck? It's about a hundred yards."

I straighten up and nod. My panic is receding as fast as it rose, now that I've been given something to do.

We've got it down to a science by now. I hunch down, Casey climbs onto my back, and we're off. Jackson follows alongside, hauling the duffel bag in one hand and holding Casey's IV bag overhead with the other.

Around us the whole encampment has sprung to life. People hurry back and forth, carrying cooking gear, bedding, bags of food. None of them are panicking either. I get the sense they've had to bug out like this a million times before. By the time the Wide Awakes—the Smurfs—arrive, no sign will remain that these people were ever here.

We reach the truck. The Junk Man and Sally are already there, loading up the rear compartment. I lay Casey on the back seat. Jackson hangs the IV bag from a hook next to it and then goes to help the other two. Once he's gone, I lie down and cover Casey with my own body the way I did back at the camp, like I'm shielding him from bullets.

Scant seconds go by. Then the others are climbing in, the truck's engine is running, and we're heading off into the unknown. Again.

36

THE parade is about to start, and the Statue of Liberty needs to fix her makeup. "Tyler? Be a sweetie and carry my torch for a second, would you?"

I take the papier-mâché torch and hold it while the robed and crowned figure—actually our next-door neighbor Ricardo, a guy from Florida who came to Toronto with his parents as a toddler, in the first wave of refugees, and now does drag shows under the name Priscilla Happiness—takes out a compact and touches up his eye shadow.

"Great job on the float," Ricardo says. "My *God*, you should have seen last year's! It looked like a funeral procession."

I didn't see last year's Pride parade, except on TV. Casey and I were still going through what the Canadians euphemistically call Acclimation. A creepy-sounding word, way too much like *Reclamation*, but the idea does make some sense—better than simply turning us loose to fend for ourselves. If they'd done that, we would have both gone nuts.

Still, I was afraid they'd never let us out. Of course, not many refugees from down south show up with vials of lethal, weaponized viruses in their pockets, so you couldn't blame the Canadians for being jumpy. Not to mention every other country in the world—I lost count of how many of their spooks debriefed us. The ones from Britain and Israel were the scariest—the Brit clearly just wanted to shoot us, while the Israeli, if she'd had her way, would have locked us in a windowless cell for the rest of our lives.

But hey, here we are. And Ricardo is right about last year's float. I wasn't the only one who wanted something more festive. That doesn't sit well with some of the other expats, but what did that Russian woman say a hundred years ago? *If I can't dance, it's not my revolution.* True words, those.

"Thanks, *querido*." With a flutter of false eyelashes, Ricardo—Priscilla—puts the compact away. "And how are you doing? I couldn't help overhearing last night."

"Oh, Casey and I just had a fight." I hand the torch back to him. "Sorry if we kept you awake."

"Honey, please. You two are *much* noisier when you're making up. I just may have to come over and investigate, one of these evenings."

He flashes me a grin, and oh-so-casually lets one manicured hand trail down my shirtless torso, stopping just short of the scars on my abs. They're still visible, but fading.

"Hey, Miss Liberty!" a voice shouts from street level. "You molesting my boyfriend again?"

Casey? I thought he wasn't coming. But sure enough, there he is, slaloming through the crowd in his wheelchair. Ricardo blows him a kiss, then does a twirl and returns to his position on the top tier of the float.

I climb down to intercept Casey as he rolls up. He's carrying something on his lap. As he stops, he spins it around on one finger and then flings it at me.

"Think fast, TNT."

It's my cap for the Wellesley Street Wallbangers, the gay men's baseball team I joined in the spring. When I'm done laughing, I sink down onto Casey's lap.

"I'm glad you decided to come," I say. "Thanks."

A wry smile. "Hey, someone's got to keep Ricardo's hands off you."

"Oh, come on. He gropes you just as much. And you're the one who's just across the hall from him all day. If anyone should be jealous, it's me."

I'm not, though. Neither is Casey. Ricardo was the first real friend we made here, and he's been an awesome one—he practically adopted us the day we met. He helped us fix up our apartment for Casey's wheelchair, introduced us to tons of people, served as shark repellent on our first naive forays into the gay scene, and saved my sanity by sharing post-op caregiver duties during Casey's round of surgeries last year. If he wants to get a little handsy with either or both of us now and then, the tradeoff is more than fair.

I give Casey a kiss, then stand up, put the cap on my head, and do a slow 360. "So how do I look?"

"Overdressed. That jockstrap's got to go."

"You can tear it off with your teeth when we get home." I waggle my eyebrows at him. "Seriously, I'm really glad you came. It means a lot to me."

Casey shrugs. "You were right last night—I've been a total recluse lately. And I know how hard you've been working on this." A pause. "I think I'm going to sign up for those computer classes, too. Hell, if I get good enough, maybe I can take out the Muldoonies without even leaving my desk."

His mood has definitely lifted—last night's blowup seems nearly forgotten. Thank God. I hate it when we fight.

We have such different ways of dealing, the two of us. For me, it's in the middle of the night that everything comes flooding back—I still wake up soaked in sweat or sobbing in a fetal position at least four times a week. But then I get up and throw myself into my day—into the construction jobs I've been doing, into planning for this parade, into baseball. Once again, I'm the Mighty TNT—only a little older, a lot buffer, and a hundred times gayer.

Casey sleeps like a rock. But when he's awake . . . Jesus. Some days, I leave for work terrified that I'll come home to find him hanging from the shower rod. Other days, I'm glad I'm leaving, because I feel like throttling him myself.

Still, we've made it this far—we must be doing something right. And since last night I've resolved not to bug him about the prosthetics anymore. He'll start wearing them in public when he feels like it—for now, he says he moves around easier *and* looks cooler and sexier in the chair. He always did carry himself like a sex god on wheels.

There's a whistle, then a voice booming through a loudspeaker. "Five minutes! Step off in five minutes!"

An idea hits me. "You want to ride with?"

"What, on the float?"

"Sure, why not?" I turn and holler at one of a pair of topless lesbians taking their places. "Hey, Janet—do we have room for Casey?"

"Yeah, I think so."

"Cool. Come on, Casey—it's Pride. Be proud."

He hesitates a second longer, but from the look in his eyes, I can tell he's just screwing with me. "Ah, what the fuck."

I wave over this other guy, Derek—a bearded older man from Wisconsin who's twice my size—and together we hoist Casey, wheelchair and all, onto the float.

"I'd better not roll off the edge," he says.

"Dude, it's a parade, not the Indy 500. Just put your brakes on and you'll be fine."

"And how am I supposed to dance with my brakes on?"

Up ahead, a roaring of motorcycles rips through the hot July air. Some group called Dykes on Bikes—they lead off every Pride parade. It's a tradition, I'm told.

I take my place on the float. About a dozen of us—the best-looking, the biggest exhibitionists, or both—are on the middle tier, wearing as little as we can get away with. In the center stands Ricardo as Lady Liberty, holding her torch aloft. Around us on the float, and marching alongside, are exactly fifty more of us, of all ages and races and genders, each carrying a state flag and wearing a T-shirt with the name of his or her hometown. Chicago . . . Dallas . . . Boston . . . Casper, Wyoming . . .

Me, I've got LOS ANGELES painted right on my bare chest. To my right, Derek has MILWAUKEE on the back of the leather vest he's wearing—his chest is too hairy to paint on. And behind me, Janet and her girlfriend Penny have split their hometown between them, one CHATTA and the other NOOGA.

Will I ever go back? I honestly don't know. Sometimes, when I read about the latest Muldoonie atrocity, or I see the Junk Man on the news and hear about how the rebellion is spreading, I have an urge to go and join the fight. But beyond that, I don't feel a thing, not even homesickness. Even if I were willing to go anywhere without Casey, Toronto is my home now. It's not exactly one of those all-gay paradises Coach promised, but there are so many of us here, along with so many others grateful to have made their way out from under the Muldoonies' shadow, that even the steel and concrete seem to shimmer with the sheer joy of being alive. Colors shine brighter, food tastes better, sex is hotter.

And yet I have a child back in L.A. The kid is already two years old. Don't I have a fatherly duty to fight for my child's tomorrows, even if he—or she—will never know who I am?

Yes, I do . . . but not today.

The motorcycles roar again. The crowd roars back. The parade starts to move, the music throbs, I shoot a lustful glance and hip-grind at Casey, and everything else drops away. Until tomorrow.

Today, we dance.

DOUGLAS P. LATHROP
August 8, 1964 – August 15, 2014

The day after Doug's birth, it was discovered his legs were broken and he was diagnosed with Osteogenesis Imperfecta. By the time he was twelve, he had been hospitalized at least twenty-five times for fractures or surgeries. Not letting these challenges get the best of him, he graduated from California State University, Northridge with a Bachelor of Arts Degree, majoring in Journalism with a minor in Political Science. After graduation he got an editing job with Windsor Publications. In 1996, he began work with the Access Center and moved to San Diego. In 1998, he joined *New Mobility Magazine* as a Senior Editor and Contributor. From 2005-09, he edited *Kids on Wheels*, New Mobility's sister publication. Most recently, he wrote a novel, *Reconquista*, which won Best Unpublished Fiction in the 2011 San Diego Book Awards. His short fiction has appeared in *The Belletrist Review*, *Kaleidoscope*, *Mindscapes Literary Magazine*, and *Palace Corbie*. He was a skilled and passionate writer.

His varied interests included *Star Wars*, *Game of Thrones*, social media, Comic-Con, *MST3K (Mystery Science Theatre 3000)*, and collecting tikis. He was also well known in the San Diego music scene. He volunteered at the San Diego LGBT center and was a valued member of the First Unitarian Universalist Church in San Diego, serving on the Board of Trustees.

He loved to travel, journeying to Europe and Australia. He attended numerous conventions for LPA (Little People of America), OIF (Osteogenesis Imperfecta Foundation) and of course, Comic-Con. Complications from a fall and resulting respiratory distress took him on August 15, 2014.

www.ingramcontent.com/pod-product-compliance
Lightning Source LLC
Chambersburg PA
CBHW032229010726
47494CB00002B/412